Stephen Coonts is a former naval aviator who flew combat missions during the Vietnam War. He is the author of thirteen published novels. A former attorney, he resides with his wife and son in Las Vegas. He maintains a website at www.coonts.com.

By Stephen Coonts

NON-FICTION
The Cannibal Queen

NOVELS
Liars and Thieves
Deep Black (with Jim DeFelice)
Liberty
Saucer
America
Hong Kong
Cuba
Fortunes of War
Flight of the Intruder
Final Flight
The Minotaur
Under Siege
The Red Horseman
The Intruders

AS EDITOR
Victory
Combat (short novels)
War in the Air

THE INTRUDERS

STEPHEN COONTS

ORION

An Orion paperback

This paperback edition first published in
the United States in 1995
by Pocket Books,
a division of Simon & Schuster, Inc.
First published in Great Britain in 2003
by Orion Books Ltd,
Orion House, 5 Upper St Martin's Lane,
London WC2H 9EA

A CIP catalogue record for this book is
available from the British Library.

ISBN 0 75284 908 5

Typeset at The Spartan Press Ltd,
Lymington, Hants
Printed and bound in Great Britain by
Clays Ltd, St Ives plc

AUTHOR'S NOTE

For their kindness in assisting with the technical aspects of this novel, the author wishes to thank Captain Sam Sayers, USN Ret., and Captain Bruce Wood, USN.

The in-flight emergencies featured in this novel are based on actual incidents. Where necessary I have simplified the complexities of cockpit switchology, emergency and air traffic control procedures in the interest of readability and pacing. I have also altered the outcome of some of the incidents. It was not my intent to write an aviation safety treatise or a manual on how to do it, but to entertain.

I also hope that you, the reader, develop a better understanding of the pride, skill, professionalism and dedication of the men and women of US Navy and Marine Corps Aviation. As you read these words, they are out there on the oceans of the earth working for all of us. This book is dedicated to them.

Eternal Father, strong to save,
Whose arm does bind the restless wave,
Who biddest the mighty ocean deep,
Its own appointed limits keep;
O hear us when we cry to thee
For those in peril on the sea.

— *The Navy Hymn*,
William Whiting

CHAPTER ONE

The huge ship towered above the pier that projected into the bay. The rain falling from a low, slate-colored sky made everything look dark and wet – the ship, the pier, the trucks, even the sailors hurrying to and fro.

At the gate at the head of the pier stood a portable guard shack where a sailor huddled with the collar of his pea coat turned up, his hands thrust deep into his pockets. There was no heater in the wooden shack so the air here was no warmer than it was outside, but at least he was out of the wind. Raw and wet, the swirling air lashed at unprotected flesh and cut like a knife through thin trousers.

The sailor looked yet again up at the projecting flight deck of the great ship, at the tails and wing butts of the aircraft sticking over the edge. Then his eyes wandered back along the ship's length, over a thousand feet. The gray steel behemoth looked so permanent, so solid, one almost had to accept on faith the notion that it was indeed a ship that could move at will upon the oceans. It looked, the sailor decided, like a cliff of blue-black granite.

Streams of water trickled from scuppers high on the edge of the flight deck. When the wind gusted these dribbles scattered and became an indistinguishable part of the rain. In the lulls the streams splattered randomly against the pier, the camels that wedged the hull away from the pilings, and the restless black water of the bay.

The sailor watched the continuous march of small swells as they surged against the oil containment booms, swirled trash against the pilings, and lapped nervously against the hull of the ship. Of course the ship didn't move. She lay as motionless as if she were resting on bedrock.

Yet she was floating upon that oily black wet stuff, the sailor mused. This 95,000 tons of steel would get under way tomorrow morning, steam across the bay and through the Golden Gate. All of her eighty aircraft were already aboard, all except the last one that was just now being lifted by a crane onto the forward starboard elevator, Elevator One. This past week had been spent loading bombs, bullets, beans, toilet paper – supplies by the tractor-trailer load; an endless stream of trucks and railroad cars, which were pushed down tracks in the middle of the pier.

Tomorrow.

Carrying her planes and five thousand men, the ship would leave the land behind and move freely in a universe of sea and sky – that was a fact amazing and marvelous and somewhat daunting. The carrier would be a man-made planet voyaging in a universe of water, storms, darkness, maybe occasionally even sunlight. And on this planet would be the ants – the men – working and eating, working and sleeping, working and sweating, working and praying that somehow, someday the ship would once again return to the land.

And he would be aboard her. This would be his first cruise, at the age of nineteen years. The prospect was a little strange and a little frightening.

The sailor shivered involuntarily – was it the cold? – and looked again at the tails of the planes projecting over the edge of the flight deck. What would it be like to ride one of those planes down the catapult into the sky, or to come across the fantail and catch one of the arresting gear wires? The sailor didn't know, nor was it likely he would ever find out, a fact that gave him a faint sense of disappointment. He was a storekeeper, a clerk. The aviators who would fly the planes were officers, all older and presumably vastly more knowledgeable than he – certainly they lived in a world far different than his. But maybe someday. When you are nineteen the future stretches away like a highway until it disappears into the haze. Who knows what lies ahead on that infinite, misty road?

The sailor wasn't very interested in that mystical future: his thoughts turned glumly to the here and now. He was homesick. There was a girl at home whom he hadn't been all that serious about when he joined the Navy after high school, but the separation had worked its insidious magic. Now he was writing her three long letters per week, plus a letter to his folks and one to his brother. The girl . . . well, she was dating another guy. That fact ate at his insides something fierce.

He was thinking about the girl, going over what he would say in his next letter – her last letter to him had arrived three weeks ago – when a taxi pulled up on the other side of the gate. An officer stepped out and stood looking at the ship, a lieutenant, wearing a leather flight jacket and a khaki fore-and-aft cap.

After the cab driver opened the trunk, the officer paid him and hoisted two heavy parachute bags. One he swung onto his right shoulder. The other he picked up with his left hand. He strode toward the gate and the guard shack.

The sailor came out into the rain with his clipboard. He saluted the officer and said, 'I'm sorry, sir, but I need to see your ID card.'

The officer made eye contact with the sailor for the first time. He was about six feet tall, with gray eyes and a nose that was a trifle too large for his face. He lowered the bags to the wet concrete, dug in his pocket for his wallet, extracted an ID card and handed it to the sailor.

The sailor carefully copied the information from the ID card to the paper on his clipboard as he tried to shield the paper from the rain. LT JACOB L. GRAFTON, USN. Then he passed the credit-card-size piece of plastic back to the officer.

'Thank you, sir.'

'Okay, sailor,' the lieutenant said. After he stowed the card he stood silently for several seconds looking at the ship. He ignored the falling rain.

Finally he looked again at the sailor. 'Your first cruise?'

'Yessir.'

'Where you from?'

'Iowa, sir.'

'Umm.'

After a last glance at the airplanes on the flight deck above, the officer reached for his bags. He again hoisted one of the parachute bags to his right shoulder, then lifted the other in his left hand. From the way the bags sagged the sailor guessed they weighed at least fifty pounds each. The officer didn't seem to have any trouble handling them, though.

'Iowa's a long way behind you,' the lieutenant said softly.

'Yessir.'

'Good luck,' the lieutenant said, and walked away down the pier.

The sailor stood oblivious to the rain and watched him go.

Not just Iowa . . . everything was behind. The ship, the great ocean, Hawaii, Hong Kong, Singapore, Australia – all that was ahead. They would sail in the morning. Only one more night.

The sailor retreated to the shack and closed the door. He began to whistle to himself.

An hour later Lieutenant Jack Grafton finally found his new two-man stateroom and dumped his bags. His room-mate, a Navy pilot, wasn't around, but apparently he had moved into the bottom bunk.

Jake climbed into the top bunk and stretched out.

Just five months into his first shore tour – after three years in a fleet squadron with two combat cruises – his tour was cut short. Now he was going to sea again, this time with a Marine squadron.

Amateur hour! Jarheads!

How had he gotten himself into this fix anyway?

Well, the world started coming unglued about three weeks ago, when he went to Chicago to see Callie. He closed his eyes and half-listened to the sounds of the ship as it all came flooding back.

'Do you know Chicago?' Callie McKenzie asked.

It was 11 A.M. on a Thursday morning and they were on the freeway from O'Hare into the city. Callie was at the wheel.

Jake Grafton leaned back in the passenger's seat and grinned. 'No.'

Her eyes darted across his face. She was still glowing from the long, passionate kiss she had received at the gate in front of an appreciative audience of travelers and gate attendants. Then they had walked down the concourse arm in arm. Now Jake's green nylon folding clothes bag was in the trunk and they had left the worst of O'Hare's traffic behind.

'Thank you for the letters,' she said. 'You're quite a correspondent.'

'Well, thank you for all the ones you wrote to me.'

She drove in silence, her cheeks still flushed. After a bit she said, 'So your knee is okay and you're flying again?'

'Oh, sure.' Unconsciously Jake rubbed the knee that had been injured in an ejection over Laos six months ago. When he realized that he was doing it, he laughed, then said, 'But that's history. The war's over, the POWs are home, it's June, you're beautiful, I'm here – all in all, life is damn good.'

In spite of herself Callie McKenzie flushed again. Here

5

he was, in the flesh, the man she had met in Hong Kong last fall and spent a bittersweet weekend with in the Philippines. What was that, seven days total? And she was in love with him.

She had avidly read and reread his letters and written long, chatty replies. She had told him she loved him in every line. And she had called him the first evening she arrived back in the States after finishing her two-year tour in Hong Kong with the State Department. That was ten days ago. Now, here he was.

They had so much to talk about, a relationship to renew. She was worried about that. Love was so tricky. What if the magic didn't happen?

'My folks are anxious to meet you,' she said, a trifle nervously Jake Grafton thought. He was nervous too, so nervous that he couldn't eat the breakfast they had served on the plane from Seattle. Yet here with her now, he could feel the tension leaving him. It was going to be all right.

When he didn't reply, she glanced at him. He was looking at the skyline of the city, wearing a half-smile. The car seemed crowded with his presence. That was one of the things she had remembered – he seemed a much larger man than he was. He hadn't changed. Somehow she found that reassuring. After another glance at his face, she concentrated on driving.

In a moment she asked, 'Are you hungry?'

'Oh, getting there.'

'I thought we'd go downtown, get some lunch, do some sightseeing, then go home this evening after my folks get home from the university.'

'Sounds like a plan.'

'You'll like Chicago,' she said.

'I like all American towns,' he said softly. 'I've never yet been in one I didn't like.'

'You men! So hard to please.'

He laughed, and she joined in.

He's here! She felt delicious.

She found a parking garage within the Loop and they went walking hand in hand, looking, laughing, getting re-acquainted. After lunch with a bubbling crowd in a pub, they walked and walked.

Of course Callie wanted to hear an account from Jake's own lips about his shootdown and rescue from Laos, and they talked about Tiger Cole, the bombardier who had broken his back and was now undergoing intensive phys-ical therapy in Pensacola.

When they had each brought the other up-to-date on all the things that had happened to them since they last saw each other, Callie asked, 'Are you going to stay in the Navy?'

'I don't know. I can get out after a year in this shore tour.' He was a flight instructor at Attack Squadron 128 at NAS Whidbey Island, Washington, transitioning new pilots and bombardier-navigators (BNs) to the A-6 Intruder. 'The flying is fun,' he continued. 'It's good to get back to it. But I don't know. It depends.'

'Oh what?'

'Oh, this and that.' He grinned at her.

She liked how he looked when he grinned. His gray eyes danced.

She thought she knew what the decision depended on, but she wanted to hear him say it. 'Not finances?'

'No. Got a few bucks saved.'

'On a civilian flying job?'

'Haven't applied for any.'

'On what then, Jake?'

They were on a sidewalk on Lake Shore Drive, with Lake Michigan spreading out before them. Jake had his elbows on the railing. Now he turned and enveloped Callie in his arms and gave her a long, probing kiss. When they finally parted for air, he said, 'Depends on this and that.'

'On us?'

'You and me.'

The admission satisfied her. She wrapped her hands around one of his arms and rested her head on his shoulder. The gulls were crying and wheeling above the beach.

The McKenzies lived in a brick two-story in an old neighborhood. Two giant oaks stood in the tiny front yard between the porch and the sidewalk. After apparently struggling for years to get enough sunlight, most of the grass had surrendered to fate. Only a few blades poked through last autumn's leaf collection. Professor McKenzie appeared to be as enthusiastic about raking leaves as he was about mowing grass.

Callie introduced Jake to her parents and he agreed that he could drink a beer, if they had any. The professor mixed himself a highball and poured a glass of wine for each of the ladies. Then the four of them sat a few minutes in the study with their drinks in hand exchanging pleasantries.

He had been in the Navy for five years, liked it so far. He and Callie had met in Hong Kong. Wasn't this June pleasant?

Callie and her mother finally excused themselves and headed for the kitchen. Jake surveyed the room for ashtrays and saw that there weren't any. As he debated whether he should cross his legs or keep both feet firmly on the floor, Callie's father told him that he and his wife taught at the University of Chicago, had done so for thirty years, had lived in this house for twenty. They hoped to retire in eight years. Might even move to Florida.

'I was raised in southwestern Virginia,' Jake informed his host. 'My dad has a pretty good-size farm.'

'Have you any farming ambitions?'

No, Jake thought not. He had seen his share of farming while growing up. He was a pilot now and thought he might just stick with it, although he hadn't decided for certain.

'What kind of planes do you fly in the Navy?' Professor McKenzie asked.

So Callie hadn't mentioned that? Or the professor forgot. 'I fly A-6s, sir.'

Not a glimmer showed on the professor's face. He had a weathered, lined face, was balding and wore trifocals. Still, he wasn't bad looking. And Mrs McKenzie was a striking lady. Jake could see where Callie got her looks and figure.

'What kind of planes are those?' the professor asked, apparently just to make conversation.

'Attack planes. All-weather attack.'

'Attack?'

'Any time, anywhere, any weather, day or night, high, low or in the middle.'

'You . . . drop . . . *bombs?*' His face was blank, incredulous.

'And shoot missiles,' Jake said firmly.

Professor McKenzie took a deep breath and stared at this young man who had been invited into his house by his daughter. His only daughter. Life is amazing – getting into bed with a woman is the ultimate act of faith: truly, you are rolling cosmic dice. Who would have believed that twenty-five years later the child of that union would bring home this . . . this . . .

'Doesn't it bother you? Dropping bombs?'

'Only when the bad guys are trying to kill me,' Jake Grafton replied coolly. 'Now if you'll excuse me, sir, maybe I should take my bags upstairs and wash my face.'

'Of course.' The professor gestured vaguely toward the hallway where the stairs were and took a healthy swig of his highball.

Jake found the spare bedroom and put his bags on a chair. Then he sat on the bed staring out the window.

He was in trouble. You didn't have to be a genius to see that. Callie hadn't told her parents *anything* about him. And that look on the old man's face! 'You drop *bombs?*'

He could have just said, '*Oh, Mr Grafton, you're a hit man for the Mafia? What an unusual career choice! And you look like you enjoy your work.*'

Jesus!

He dug in his pocket and got out the ring. He had purchased this engagement ring last December on the *Shiloh* and carried it with him ever since, on the ground, in the air, all the time. He had fully intended to give it to Callie when the time was right. But this visit . . . her parents . . . it made him wonder. Was he right for this woman? Would he fit into her family? Oh, love is wonderful and grand and will conquer all the problems – isn't that the way the songs go? Yet under the passion there needs to be something else . . . a *rightness*. He wanted a woman to go the distance with. If Callie was the woman, now was not the time. She wasn't ready.

And he wasn't if she wasn't.

He looked disgustedly at the ring, then put it back into his pocket.

The evening sun shone through the branches of the old oak. The window was open, a breeze wafted through the screen. That limb – he could take out the screen, toss down the bags, get onto that limb and climb down to the ground. He could be in a taxi on the way to the airport before they even knew he was gone.

He was still sitting there staring glumly out the window when Callie came for him thirty minutes later.

'What's wrong?' she asked.

'Nothing,' he said, rising from the bed and stretching. 'Dinner ready?'

'Yes.'

'Something is wrong, isn't it?'

There was no way to avoid it. 'You didn't tell me your Dad was Mr Liberal.'

'Liberal? He's about a mile left of Lenin.'

'He looked really thrilled when I told him I was an attack pilot.'

'Dad is Dad. I thought it was me you were interested in?'

Jake Grafton cocked his head. 'Well, you *are* better looking than he is. Probably a better kisser, too.' He took her arm and led her toward the stairs. 'Wait till you meet my older brother,' he told her. 'He can't wait for the next revolution. He says the next time we won't screw it up like Bobby Lee and Jeff Davis did.'

'How would you rate me as a kisser?' she asked softly.

They paused on the top stair and she wrapped her arms around him. 'This is for score,' he whispered. 'Pucker up.'

That night when they were in bed Professor McKenzie told his wife, 'That boy's a killer.'

'Don't be ridiculous, Wallace.'

'He kills people. He kills them from the air. He's an executioner.'

'That's war, dear. They try to kill him, he tries to kill them.'

'It's murder.'

Mary McKenzie had heard it all before. 'Callie is in love with him, Wallace. I suggest you keep your opinions and your loaded labels to yourself. She must make her own decision.'

'Decision? What decision?'

'Whether or not to marry him.'

'*Marriage?*'

'Don't tell me you didn't know what was going on?' his wife said crossly. 'I swear, you're blind as a bat! Didn't you see her at dinner tonight? She loves him.'

'She won't marry him,' Professor McKenzie stated positively. 'I know *Callie!*'

'Yes, dear,' Mrs McKenzie muttered, just to pacify the man. What her husband knew about young women in love wouldn't fill a thimble. She herself was appalled by Callie's choice, believing the girl could do a whale of a lot better if she just looked around a little.

Callie was inexperienced. She didn't dare until college and then couldn't seem to find any young men who interested her. Mrs McKenzie had hoped she would find a proper man while working for the State Department – apparently a futile hope. This Grafton boy was physically a good specimen, yet he was wrong for Callie. He was so . . . blue-collar. The girl needed a man who was at least in the same room with her intellectually.

But she wasn't going to say that to Callie – not a chance. Pointed comments would probably be resented, perhaps even resisted. In this new age of liberated womanhood, covert pressure was the proper way, the only way. One had to pretend strict neutrality – 'This is *your* decision, dear' – while radiating bad vibes. She owed her daughter maternal guidance – choosing a mate is much too important to be left to young women with raging hormones.

Secure in the knowledge that she was up to the task that duty had set before her, Mrs McKenzie went peacefully to sleep while her husband stewed.

At breakfast Professor McKenzie held forth on the Vietnam War. The night before at dinner he had said little, preferring to let the ladies steer the conversation. This morning he told Jake Grafton in no uncertain terms what he thought of the politicians who started the war and the politicians who kept the nation in it.

If he was expecting an argument, he didn't get it. In fact, several times Jake nodded in agreement with the professor's points, and twice Callie distinctly heard him say, 'You're right.'

After the senior McKenzies left the house for the university, Jake and Callie headed for the kitchen to finish cleaning up.

'You sure handled Dad,' Callie told her boyfriend.

'Huh?'

'You took the wind right out of Dad's sails. He thought you were going to give him a bang-up fight.'

She was looking straight into his gray eyes when he said, 'The war's over. It's history. What is there to fight about?'

'Well . . . ,' Callie said dubiously.

Jake just shrugged. His knee was fairly well healed and the dead were buried. That chapter of his life was over.

He gathered her into his arms and smiled. 'What are we going to do today?'

He had good eyes, Callie thought. You could almost look in and see the inner man, and that inner man was simple and good. He wasn't complicated or self-absorbed like her father, nor was he warped with secret doubts and phobias like so many of the young men she knew. Amazingly, after Vietnam his scars were merely physical, like that slash on his temple where a bullet gouged him.

Acutely aware of the warmth and pressure of his body against hers, she gave him a fierce hug and whispered, 'What would you like to do?'

The feel and smell and warmth of her seemed more than Jake could take in. 'Anything you want, Miss McKenzie,' he said hoarsely, mildly surprised at his reaction to her presence, 'as long as we do it together.' That didn't come out quite the way he intended, and he felt slightly flustered. You can't just invite a woman to bed at eight-thirty in the morning!

His hand massaged the small of her back and she felt her knees get weak. She took a deep breath to steady herself, then said, 'I'd like to take you to meet my brother, Theron. He lives in Milwaukee. But first let's clean up these dishes. Then, since you so coyly suggested it, let's slip upstairs in a Freudian way and get seriously naked.'

When Jake's cheeks reddened, Callie laughed, a deep, throaty woman's laugh. 'Don't pretend you weren't thinking about that!'

Jake dearly enjoyed seeing her laugh. She had a way of throwing her head back and unashamedly displaying a mouthful of beautiful teeth that he found captivating. When she did it her hair swayed and her eyes crinkled. The effect was mesmerizing. You wanted her to do it again, and again, and again.

'The thought did flit across my little mind,' he admitted, grinning, watching her eyes.

'Ooh, I want you, Jake Grafton,' she said, and kissed him.

A shaft of sunlight streamed through the open window and fell squarely across them in the bed. After all those months of living aboard ship, in a steel cubicle in the bowels of the beast where the sun never reached, Jake thought the sunlight magical. He gently turned her so their heads were in the sun. The zephyr from the window played with strands of her brown hair and the sun flecked them with gold. She was woman, all warm taut sleek smoothness and supple, sensuous wetness.

Somehow she ended up on top and set the rhythm of their lovemaking. As her hair caressed his cheeks and her hands kneaded his body, the urgency became overwhelming. He guided her onto him.

When she lay spent across him, her lashes stroking his cheek, her breath hot on his shoulder, he whispered, 'I love you.'

'I know,' she replied.

Theron McKenzie had been drafted into the Army in 1967. On October 7, 1968, he stepped on a land mine. He lost one leg below the knee and one above. Today he walked on artificial legs. Jake thought he was pretty good at it, although he had to sway his body from side to side to keep his balance when he threw the legs forward.

'It was in II Corps,' he told Jake Grafton, 'at the base camp. And the worst of it was that the mine was one of

ours. I just forgot for a moment and walked the wrong way.'
He shrugged and grinned.

He had a good grin. Jake liked him immediately. Yet he was slightly taken aback when Theron asked, 'So are you going to marry her?' This while his sister walked between them holding on to Jake's arm.

Grafton recovered swiftly. 'Aaah, I dunno. She's so pushy, mighty smart, might be more than a country boy like me could handle. If you were me, knowing what you know about her, what would you do?'

Both men stared at Callie's composed features. She didn't let a muscle twitch. Theron sighed, then spoke: 'If I were you and a woman loved me as much as this one loves you, I'd drag her barefoot to the altar. If I were you.'

'I'll think about it.'

'And what about you, Sis? You gonna marry him?'

'Theron, how would you like to have you throat cut?'

They ate lunch at a sports bar around the corner from the office where Theron worked as a tax accountant. After a half hour of small talk, Theron asked Jake, 'So are you going to stay in or try life on the outside?'

'Haven't decided. All I've got is a history degree. I'd have to go back to school.'

'Maybe you could get a flying job.'

'Maybe.'

Theron changed the subject. Before Callie could get an oar in, Theron was asking questions about carrier aviation – how the catapults worked, the arresting gear, how the pilots knew if they were on the glide slope. Jake drew diagrams on napkins and Theron asked more questions while Callie sat and watched.

'God, that must be terrific,' Theron said to Jake, 'landing and taking off from an aircraft carrier. That's something I'd love to do someday.' He slapped his artificial legs. 'Of course, I can't now, but I can just imagine!'

Callie glowed with a feeling of approaching euphoria.

She had known that these two would get along well: it was almost as if they were brothers. Having a brother like Theron was hard on a girl – he was all man. When you have a real man only a year and a half older than you are to compare the boys against, finding one that measures up isn't easy.

Jake Grafton did. Her cup was full to overflowing.

'Is he going to stay in the Navy?' Mrs McKenzie asked her daughter. They were in the kitchen cutting the cherry pie.

'He hasn't made up his mind.'

Grafton's indecision didn't set well with Mrs McKenzie. 'He probably will,' she said.

'He might,' Callie admitted.

'The military is a nice comfortable place for some people. The government feeds and clothes and houses them, provides medical care, a living wage. All they have to do is follow orders. Some people like that. They don't have to take any responsibility. The military is safe.'

Callie concentrated on getting the pie wedges from the pan to the plates without making a mess.

'Would he continue to fly?' Mrs McKenzie asked. 'If he stayed in?'

'I suspect so,' her daughter allowed.

Mrs McKenzie let the silence build until it shrieked.

When Callie could stand it no longer, she said, 'He hasn't asked me to marry him, Mom.'

'Oh, he will, he will. That's a man working himself up to a proposal if ever I saw one.'

Callie told her mother the truth. 'If he asks, I haven't decided what the answer will be.'

Which was, Callie McKenzie suspected, precisely why he hadn't asked. Jake Grafton was nobody's fool. Yet why she hadn't yet made up her mind, she didn't know.

I love him, why am I uncertain?

Mrs McKenzie didn't know much about Jake Grafton,

but she knew a man in love when she saw one. 'He's an idiot if he throws his life away by staying in the Navy,' she said perfunctorily.

'He's a pilot, Mom. That's what he does. He's good at it.'

'The airlines hire pilots.'

'He's probably considering that,' Callie said distractedly, still trying to pin down her emotional doubt. Had she been looking for a man like Theron all this time? Was that wise? Was she seeking a substitute for her brother?

Her mother was saying something. After a moment Callie began to pay attention. '. . . so he'll stay in the Navy, and some night they'll come tell you he's crashed and you're a widow. What then?'

'Mother, you just announced that some people stay in the military because it's safe, yet now you argue it's too dangerous. You can't have it both ways. Do you want whipped cream on your pie?'

'Callie, I'm thinking of you. You well know something can be physically dangerous yet on another level appeal to people without ambition.'

Callie opened the refrigerator and stared in. Then she closed it. 'We're out of whipped cream. Will you bring the other two plates, please?' She picked up two of the plates and headed for the dining room.

She put one plate in front of Jake and one in front of her father. Then she seated herself. Jake winked at her. She tried to smile at him.

Lord, if her mother only knew how close to the edge Jake lived she wouldn't be appalled – she would be horrified. Jake had made light of the dangers of flying onto and off of carriers this afternoon, but Callie knew the truth. Staying alive was the challenge.

She examined his face again. He didn't look like Theron, but he had the same self-assurance, the same intelligence and good sense, the same intellectual curiosity, the same easy way with everyone. She had seen that in him the first

17

time they met. And like Theron, Jake Grafton had nothing to prove to anyone. Perhaps naval aviation had given Jake that quality – or combat had – but wherever he acquired it, he now had it in spades. He owned the space he occupied.

He *was* like Theron! She was going to have to come to grips with that fact.

'The most serious problem our society faces,' Professor McKenzie intoned, 'is the complete absence of moral fiber in so many of our young people.'

They had finished the pie and were sipping coffee. Jake Grafton let that pronouncement go by without bothering to glance at his host. He was observing Callie, trying to read her mood.

'If they had any sense of right and wrong,' the professor continued, 'young men would have never fought in that war. Until people understand that they have the right, nay, the duty, the obligation, to resist the illegal demands of a morally bankrupt government, we will continue to have war. Murder, slaughter, rapine, grotesque human suffering, for what? Just to line the pockets of greedy men.'

After the prologue, the professor got down to cases. Jake had a sick feeling this was coming. 'What about you, Jake? Were you drafted?'

Jake eyed the professor without turning his head. 'No.'

Something in his voice drew Callie's gaze. She glanced at him, but his attention was directed at her father.

'Wallace,' said Mrs McKenzie, 'perhaps we should—'

'You volunteered?'

'Yes.'

'You volunteered to kill people?' the professor asked with naked sarcasm.

'I volunteered to fight for my country.'

The professor was on firm ground here. He lunged with his rapier. 'Your country wasn't under attack by the Vietnamese. You can't wrap the holy flag around yourself now, Mister, or use it to cover up what you people did over there.'

Now the professor slashed. 'You and your airborne colleagues murdered defenseless men, women and children. Burned them alive with napalm. Bombed them in the most contemptible, cowardly manner that—'

'You don't know what the hell you're talking about.'

'Gentlemen, let's change the subject.' Mrs McKenzie's tone was flinty.

'No, Mary,' the professor said, leaning forward with his eyes on Jake. 'This young man – I'm being charitable here – is courting our daughter. I think I have a right to know what kind of man he is.'

'The war's over, Mr McKenzie,' Jake said.

'The shooting has stopped, no thanks to you. But you can't turn your back on all those murdered people and just walk away. I won't allow it! The American people won't—'

But he was orating to Jake Grafton's back. The pilot walked through the doorway into the hall and his feet sounded on the stairs.

Mrs McKenzie got up abruptly and went to the kitchen, leaving Callie alone with her father.

'You didn't have to do that, Dad.'

'He's not the man for you, Callie. You couldn't live with what he did, he and those other criminal swine in uniform.'

Callie McKenzie tapped nervously on the table with a spoon. Finally she put it down and scooted her chair back.

'I want to say this just right, Father. I've been wanting to say this for a long time, but I've never known just how. On this occasion I want to try. You think in black and white although we live in a gray world. It's been my experience that people who think the dividing line between right and wrong is a brick wall are crackpots.'

She rose and left the room with her father sitting open-mouthed behind her.

In the guest room upstairs Jake was rolling up his clothes

19

and stuffing them into his folding bag. The nylon bag, Callie noticed listlessly, was heavily stained. That was the bag he had with him in Olongapo last autumn.

'I've called a cab,' he told her.

She sagged into a chair. 'My father . . . I'm sorry . . . why do you have to go?'

Grafton finished stuffing the bag, looked around to make sure he hadn't forgotten anything, then zipped the bag closed. He lifted it from the bed and tossed it toward the door. Only then did he turn to face her.

'The people I knew in the service were some of the finest men I ever met. Some of those men are dead. Some are crippled for life, like your brother. I'm proud that I served with them. We made mistakes, but we did the best we could. I won't listen to vicious slander.'

'Dad and his opinions.'

'Opinions are like assholes – everybody has one. At his age your father should know that not everyone wants to see his butt or hear his opinion.'

'Jake, you and I . . . what we have might grow into something wonderful if we give it a chance. Shouldn't we take time to talk about this?'

'Talk about what? The Vietnam War? It's *over*. All those dead men! For *what*? For fucking nothing at all, that's for what!' His voice was rising but he didn't notice. 'Oh, I killed my share of Vietnamese – your father got *that* right. They are dead for nothing. Now I've got to live with it . . . every day of my life. Don't you understand?'

He slammed his hand down on the dresser and the photo on top fell over. 'I'm not God. I don't know if we should have gone to Vietnam or if we should have left sooner or if the war was right or wrong. The self-righteous assholes who stayed at home can argue about all that until hell freezes. And it looks like they're going to.

'I took an oath. I swore to uphold the Constitution of the United States. So I obeyed orders. I did what I was told to the absolute best of my ability. Just like your brother. And what did it get us? Me and your brother? You and me? Jake and Callie – what did it get *us*?'

He took a ragged breath. He was perspiring and he felt sick. Slightly nauseated. 'It isn't your father. It's *me*. I can't just *forget*.'

'Jake, we must all live with the past. And walk on into the future.'

'Maybe you and I aren't ready for the future yet.'

She didn't reply.

'Well, maybe I'm not,' he admitted.

She was biting her lip.

'You aren't either,' he added.

When she didn't answer he picked up the folding bag and carry-on. 'Tell your mom thanks.' He went out the door.

She heard him descend the stairs. She heard the front door open. She heard it close.

Then her tears came.

Almost an hour later she descended the stairs. She was at the bottom when she heard her mother's voice coming from the study. 'You blathering fool! I'm *sick* of hearing you sermonize about the war. I'm *sick* of your righteousness. I'm *sick* of you damning the world from the safety of your alabaster pedestal.'

'Mary, that war was an obscenity. That war was wrong, a great wrong, and the blind stupidity of boys like Grafton made it possible. If Grafton and boys like him had refused to go, there wouldn't have been a war.'

'Boys? Jake Grafton is no boy. He's a *man!*'

'He doesn't *think*,' Professor McKenzie said, his voice dripping contempt. 'He *can't* think. I don't call him much of a man.'

Callie sank to the steps. She had never heard her parents address each other in such a manner. She felt drained, empty, but their voices held her mesmerized.

'Oh, he's a man all right,' her mother said. 'He just doesn't think like you do. He's got the brains and talent to fly jet aircraft in combat. He's got the character to be a naval officer, and I suspect he's a pretty good one. I know that doesn't impress you much, but Callie knows what he is. He's got the maturity and character to impress *her*.'

'Then she's too easily impressed. That girl doesn't know—'

'Enough, you *fool!*' said Mary McKenzie bitterly. 'We've got a son who did his duty as he saw it and you've never let him forget that you think he's a stupid, contemptible fascist. Your *only* son. So he doesn't come here anymore. He *won't* come here. Your opinion is just *your* opinion, Wallace – you can't seem to get it through your thick head that other people can honorably hold different opinions. And a great many people do.'

'I—'

His wife raised her voice and steamed on. 'I'm going to say this just once, Wallace, so you had better listen. Callie may marry Jake Grafton, regardless of our wishes. In her way she's almost as pigheaded as you are. Jake Grafton's every inch the man that Theron is, and he won't put up with your bombast and supercilious foolishness any more than Theron does. Grafton proved that here tonight. I don't blame him.'

'Callie won't marry that—'

'You damned old windbag, *shut up!* What you know about your daughter could be printed in foot-high letters on the head of a pin.'

She shouted that last sentence, then fell silent. When she spoke again her voice was cold, every word enunciated clearly:

'It will be a miracle if Jake Grafton ever walks through that door again. So I'm serving notice on you, Wallace, here and now. Your arrogance almost cost me my son. If it costs me my daughter, I'm divorcing you.'

Before Callie could move from her seat on the steps, Mrs McKenzie came striding through the study door. She saw Callie and stopped dead.

Callie rose, turned, and forced herself to climb the stairs.

CHAPTER TWO

After a miserable night in a motel near O'Hare, Jake got a seat the next day on the first flight to Seattle. Unfortunately, the next Harbor Airlines flight to Oak Harbor was full, so he had two hours to kill at Sea-Tac. He headed for the bar and sat nursing a beer.

The war was over, yet it wasn't. That was the crazy thing.

He had tried to keep his cool in Chicago and had done a fair job until the professor goaded him beyond endurance. Now he sat going over the mess again, for the fifteenth time, wondering what Callie was thinking, wondering what she felt.

The ring was burning a hole in his pocket. He pulled it out and looked at it from time to time, trying to shield it in his hand so that casual observers wouldn't think him weird.

Maybe he ought to throw the damned thing away. It didn't look like he was ever going to get to give it to Callie, not in this lifetime, anyway, and he certainly wasn't going to hang on to it for future presentation to whomever. He was going to have to do *something* with it.

He had been stupid to the ring in the first place. He should have waited until she said yes, then taken her to a jewelry store and let her pick out the ring. Normal guys got the woman first, the ring second. A fellow could avoid a lot of pitfalls if he did it the tried-and-true traditional way.

Water under the bridge.

But, God! he felt miserable. So empty, as if he had absolutely nothing to live for.

He was glumly staring into his beer mug when he heard a man's voice ask, 'Did you get that in Vietnam?'

Jake looked. Two stools down sat a young man, no more than twenty-two or -three. His left hand was a hook sticking out of his sleeve. His interrogator was older, pushing thirty, bigger, and stood waiting for the bartender to draw him a beer.

'Yeah,' the kid said. 'Near Chu Lai.'

'Serves you right,' the older man said as he tossed his money on the bar and picked up his beer. He turned away.

Jake Grafton was off his stool and moving without conscious thought. He laid a heavy hand on the man's shoulder and spun him around. Beer slopped from the man's mug.

'You *sonuvabitch!*' the man roared. 'What do you think you're doing?'

'You owe this guy an apology.'

'My *ass!*' Then the look on Grafton's face sank in. 'Now hold on, you bastard! I've got a black belt in—'

That was all he managed to get out, because Jake seized a beer bottle sitting on the bar and smashed it against the man's head with a sweeping backhand. The big man went to the floor, stunned.

Grafton grabbed wet, bloody hair with his right hand and lifted. He grabbed a handful of balls with his left and brought the man to his feet, then started him sideways. With a heave he threw him through the plate-glass window onto the concourse.

As the glass tinkled down Jake walked out the door of the bar and approached the man. He lay stunned, surrounded by glass fragments. The glass grated under Jake's shoes.

Jake squatted.

The man was semiconscious, bleeding from numerous small cuts. His eyes swam, then focused on Grafton.

25

'You got off lucky this time. I personally know a dozen men who would have killed you for that crack you made in there. There's probably thousands of them.'

Slivers of glass stuck out of the man's face in several places.

'If I were you I'd give up karate. You aren't anywhere near tough enough. Maybe you oughta try ballet.'

He stood and walked back into the bar, ignoring the gaping onlookers. The ex-soldier was still sitting on the stool.

'How much for the beers?' Jake asked the bartender.

'Yours?'

'Mine and this gentleman's. I'm buying his too.'

'Four bucks.'

Jake tossed a five-spot on the bar. Through the now-empty frame of the window he saw a policeman bending over the man lying on the concourse.

Jake held out his hand to the former soldier, who shook it.

'You didn't have to do that.'

'Yeah I did,' Jake said. 'I owed it to myself.'

The bartender held out his hand. 'I was in the Army for a couple years. I'd like to shake your hand too.'

Jake shook it.

'Well,' he said to the one-handed veteran, who was looking at his hook, 'don't let the assholes grind you down.'

'He isn't the only one,' the man murmured, nodding toward the concourse.

'I know. We got a fucking Eden here, don't we?'

He left the bar and introduced himself to the first cop he saw.

It was about four o'clock on Monday afternoon when a police officer opened the cell door.

'You're leaving, Grafton. Come on.'

The officer walked behind Jake, who was decked out in a

blue jumpsuit and shuffled along in rubber shower sandals that were several sizes too big. He had been in the can all weekend. He had used his one telephone call when he was arrested on Saturday to call the squadron duty officer at NAS Whidbey.

'You're *where?*' that worthy had demanded, apparently unable to believe his own ears.

'The King County Jail,' Jake repeated.

'I'll be damned! What'd you do, kill somebody?'

'Naw. Threw a guy out of a bar.'

'That's all?'

'He went out through a plate glass window.'

'Oh.'

'Better put it in the logbook and call the skipper at home.'

'Okay, Jake. Don't bend over to pick up the soap.'

This afternoon he got into his civilian clothes in the same room in which he had undressed, the same room, incidentally, in which he had been fingerprinted and photographed. When he was dressed an officer passed him an envelope that contained the items from his pockets.

Jake examined the contents of the envelope. His airline tickets were still there, his wallet, change, and the ring. He pocketed the ring and counted the money in the wallet.

'Don't see many white guys in here carrying diamond rings,' the cop said chattily.

Grafton wasn't in the mood.

'Dopers seem to have pockets full of them,' the cop continued. 'And burglars. You haven't been crawling through any windows, have you?'

'Not lately.' Jake snapped his wallet shut and pocketed it.

'Bet it helps you get laid a lot.'

'Melts their panties. Poked your daughter last week.'

'Sign this receipt, butthole.'

Jake did so.

They led him out to a desk. His commanding officer,

Commander Dick Donovan, was sitting in a straight-backed chair. He didn't bother watching as Jake signed two more pieces of paper thrust at him by the desk sergeant. One was a promise to appear in three weeks for a preliminary hearing before a magistrate. Jake pocketed his copy.

'You're free to go,' the sergeant said.

Donovan came out of his chair and headed for the door. Jake trailed along behind him.

In the parking lot Jake got into the passenger seat of Donovan's car. Donovan still hadn't said a word. He was a big man, easily six foot three, with wide shoulders and huge feet. He was the first bombardier-navigator (BN) to ever command the replacement squadron, VA-128.

'Thanks for bailing me out, Skipper.'

'I have a lot better things to do with my time than driving all the way to Seattle to bail an officer out of jail. An *officer!* A bar brawl! I almost didn't come. I shouldn't have. I wish I hadn't.'

'I'm sorry.'

'Don't shit me, Mister. You aren't *sorry!* You weren't even drunk when you threw that guy through that window. You'd had exactly half of one beer. I read the police report and the witnesses' statements. You aren't sorry and you've got no excuse.'

'I'm sorry you had to drive down here, sir. I'm not sorry for what I did to that guy. He had it coming.'

'Just who do you think you are, Grafton? Some comic book superhero? Who gave you the right to punish every jerk out there that deserves it? That's what cops and courts are for.'

'Okay, I shouldn't have done it.'

'You're breaking my heart.'

'Thanks for bailing me out. You didn't have to do it. I know that.'

'Not that you give a good goddamn.'

'It really doesn't matter.'

28

'What should I do with you now?'

'Whatever you feel you gotta do, Skipper. Write a bad fittie, letter of reprimand, court-martial, whatever. It's your call. If you want, I'll give you a letter of resignation tomorrow.'

'Just like that,' Donovan muttered.

'Just like that.'

'Is that what you want? Out of the Navy?'

'I haven't thought about it.'

'*Sir!*' Donovan snarled.

'Sir.'

Donovan fell silent. He got on I-5 and headed north. He didn't take the exit for the Mukilteo ferry, but stayed on the freeway. He was in no mood for the ferry. He was going the long way around, across the bridge at Deception Pass to Whidbey Island.

Jake merely sat and watched the traffic. None of it mattered anymore. The guys who died in Vietnam, the ones who were maimed . . . all that carnage and suffering . . . just so assholes could insult them in airports? So college professors could sneer? So the lieutenants who survived could fret about their fitness reports while they climbed the career ladder rung by slippery rung?

June . . . in the year of our Lord 1973.

In Virginia his dad would be working from dawn to dark. His father knew the price that had to be paid, so he paid it, and he reaped the reward. The calves were born and thrived, the cattle gained weight, the crops grew and matured and were harvested.

Perhaps he should go back to Virginia, get some sort of job. He was tired of the uniform, tired of the paperwork, even . . . even tired of the flying. It was all so absolutely meaningless.

Donovan was guiding the car through Mount Vernon when he spoke again. 'It took eighty-seven stitches to sew that guy up.'

Jake wasn't paying attention. He made a polite noise.

'His balls were swollen up the size of oranges.' The skipper sighed. 'Eighty-seven stitches is a lot, but there shouldn't be any permanent injuries. Just some scars. So I talked to the prosecutor. There won't be a trial.'

Jake grunted. He was half listening to Donovan now, but the commander's words were just that, words.

'The prosecutor walked out from the Chosin Reservoir with the Fifth Marines,' Donovan continued. 'He read the police report and the statements by the bartender and that crippled soldier. The police file and complaint are going to be lost.'

'Humpf,' Jake said.

'So you owe me five hundred bucks. Two hundred which I posted as bail and three hundred to replace that window you broke. You can write me a personal check.'

'Thanks, Skipper.'

'Of course, that jerk could try to cash in on his eighty-seven stitches if he can find a lawyer stupid enough to bring a civil suit. A jury might make you pay the hospital and doctor bill, but I doubt if they would give the guy a dime more than that. Never can tell about juries, though.'

'Eighty-seven,' Jake murmured.

'So you can pack your bags,' Donovan continued. 'I'm sending you to the Marines. Process servers can't get you if you're in the middle of the Pacific.'

With a growing sense of horror Jake realized the import of Commander Donovan's words. 'The *Marines?*'

'Yeah. Marine A-6 outfit is going to sea on *Columbia*. They don't have any pilots with carrier experience. BUPERS' – the Bureau of Naval Personnel – 'is looking for some Navy volunteers to go to sea with them. Consider yourself volunteered.'

'*Jesus H. Christ*, Skipper!' he spluttered. 'I just completed two 'Nam cruises five months ago.' He fell silent, tongue-tied as the full implications of this disaster pressed in upon him.

Shore duty was the payback, the flying vacation from two combat cruises, the night cat shots, the night traps, getting shot at, shot up and shot down. Those night rides down the catapults . . . sweet Jesus how he had hated those. And the night approaches, in terrible weather, sometimes in a shot-up airplane, with never enough gas – it made him want to puke just thinking about that shit. And here was Tiny Dick Donovan proposing to send him right back to do eight or nine more months of it!

Aww, fuck! It just wasn't fair!

'The gooks damn near killed me over North Vietnam a dozen times! It's a miracle I'm still alive. And now you feed me a shit sandwich.'

That just popped out. Dick Donovan didn't seem to hear. It dawned on Jake that the commander probably couldn't be swayed with sour grapes.

In desperation, Jake attacked in the only direction remaining. 'The jarheads maintain their planes with ball peen hammers and pipe wrenches,' he roared, his voice beyond its owner's control. 'Their planes are flying death-traps.'

When Donovan didn't reply to this indisputable truth, Jake lost the bubble completely. 'You can't *do* this to me! I—'

'Wanna bet?'

There were three staff instructors seated at stools at the bar nursing beers when Jake walked into the O Club. The afternoon sun streamed through the tall windows. If you squinted against the glare you could see the long lazy reach of Puget Sound, placid in the calm evening, more like a pond than an arm of the sea. If you looked closely though, you could see the rise and fall of gentle swells.

Jake broke the news that he was on his way to the

Marine squadron going aboard *Columbia*. He could see by the looks on their faces that they already knew. Bad news rides a fast horse.

Heads bobbed solemnly.

'Well, shore duty gets old quick.'

'Yeah. Whidbey ain't bad, but it ain't Po City.'

Their well-meaning remarks gave Jake no comfort, although he tried to maintain a straight face. Not being a liberty hound, the whores and whiskey of Olongapo City in the Philippines had never been much of an attraction for him. He felt close to tears. *This* was what he wanted more of – the flying without combat, an eight-thousand-foot runway waiting for his return, relaxed evenings on dry land with mountains on the horizon, the cool breeze coming in off the sound, delicious weekends to loaf through.

The injustice of Donovan's decision was like a knife in his gut. It was his turn, yet he was leaving all the good stuff and going back to sea!

'Lucky you aren't married,' one of the barflies said. 'A little cruise in the middle of a shore tour would drive a lot of wives straight to the divorce court.'

That remark got them talking. They knew four men who were in the process of getting divorces. The long separations the Navy required of families were hell on marriages. While his companions gossiped Jake's thoughts turned morosely to Callie. She was a good woman, and he loved her. He could see her face, feel her touch, hear her voice even now.

But her father! That jerk! A flash of heat went through him, then flickered out as he surveyed the cold ashes of his life.

'Things happen to Marines,' Tricky Nixon was saying when Jake once again began paying attention to the conversation.

Tricky was a wiry, dark, compact man. Now his brows

knitted. 'Knew a Marine fighter pilot once. Flew an F-4. He diverted from the ship into Cecil Field one night. Black night. You guys know Cecil, big as half of Texas, with those parallel runways?'

His listeners nodded. Tricky took another swig of beer. After he swallowed and cleared his throat, he continued: 'For reasons known only to God, he plunked his mighty Phantom down *between* those parallel runways. In the grass. Hit the radar shack head-on, smacked it into a million splinters.'

Tricky sighed, then continued: 'The next day the squadron maintenance officer went into Cecil on the COD, looked the plane over pretty good, had it towed outta the dirt onto a taxiway, then filled it with gas and flew it back to the ship. It was a little scratched up but nothing serious. Things happen to Marines.'

They talked about that – about the odds of putting a tactical jet with a landing weight of 45,000 pounds down on grass and not ripping one or more of the gear off the plane.

'I knew a Marine once,' Billy Doyle said when the conversation lagged, 'who forgot to pull the power back when he landed. He was flying an F-4D.'

His listeners nodded.

'He went screeching down the runway with the tires smoking, went off the end and drove out across about a half mile of dirt. Went through the base perimeter fence and across a ditch that wiped off the landing gear. Skidded on across a road, and came to rest with the plane straddling a railroad track. He sat there awhile thinking it over, then finally shut 'er down and climbed out. He was standing there looking 'er over when a train came along and plowed into the wreck. Smashed it to bits.'

They sipped beer while they thought about forgetting to pull the throttle to idle on touchdown, about how it would feel sitting dazed in the cockpit of a crashed airplane with the engine still running as the realization sank in that you had really screwed the pooch this time. *Really* screwed the pooch.

'Things happen to Marines,' Billy Doyle added.

'Their bad days can be spectacular,' Bob Landow agreed in his bass growl. He was a bear of a man, with biceps that rippled the material of his shirt. 'Marine F-8 pilot was trans-Pacing one time, flying the pond.'

He paused and lubricated his throat while his listeners thought about flying a single-seat fighter across the Pacific, about spending ten or twelve hours strapped to an ejection seat in the tiny cockpit.

Landow's growl broke the silence. 'The first time he hit the tanker for gas, the fuel cells overpressurized and ruptured. Fuel squirted out of every orifice. It squirted into the engine bay and in seconds the plane caught fire.

'At this point our Marine decides to eject. He pulls the face curtain. Nothing happens. But not yet to sweat, because he has the secondary handle between his legs. He gives that a hell of a jerk. Nothing. He just sits there in this unejectable seat in this burning aircraft with fuel running out of every pore over the vast Pacific.

'This is turning into a major-league bad day. He yanks on the handle a couple more times like King Kong with a hard on. Nothing happens. Gawdalmighty, he's getting excited now. He tried jettisoning the canopy. Damn thing won't go off. It's stuck. This is getting seriouser and seriouser.

'The plane is burning like a blowtorch by this time and he's getting *really* excited. He pounds and pounds at the canopy while the plane does smoky whifferdills. Finally the canopy departs. Our Marine is greatly relieved. He unstraps and prepares to climb out. This is an F-8, you understand, and if he makes it past that tail in one piece he will be the very first. But he's going to give it a try. He starts to straighten up and the wind just grabs him and whoom – he's out – free-falling toward the ocean deep and blue. *Out*, thank God, *out!*

'He falls for a while toward the Pacific thinking about Marine maintenance, then decides it's time to see if the parachute works. It wasn't that kind of a day. Damn thing streams.'

'No!' several of his listeners groaned in unison.

'I shit you not,' Bob Landow replied. He helped himself to more beer as his Marine fell from an indifferent sky toward an indifferent sea with an unopened parachute streaming behind him.

'What's the rest of it?' Tricky demanded.

Landow frowned. There is a certain pace to a good sea story, and Tricky had a bad habit of rushing it. Not willing to be hurried, Landow took another sip of beer, then made a show of wiping his lips with a napkin. When he had the glass back on the bar and his weight lifter's arms crossed just so, he said, 'He had some Marine luck there at the end. Pulled strings like a puppeteer and got a few panels of the rag to blossom. Just enough. Just enough.'

He shook his head wearily and settled a baleful gaze on Jake Grafton. 'Things happen to Marines. You be careful out there, Jake.'

'Yeah,' Jake told them as he glanced out the window at the reflection of small puffy clouds on the limpid blue water. 'I will.'

CHAPTER THREE

Jake Grafton was dressed in khakis and wearing his leather flight jacket when he stepped onto the catwalk around the flight deck. The sun was out, yet to the west a layer of fog obscured the higher buildings of San Francisco and all of the Golden Gate Bridge except the tops of the towers. The gentle breeze had that moist, foggy feeling. Jake shivered and tugged his ball cap more firmly onto his head.

The pier below was covered with people. The pilot rested his elbows on the railing of the catwalk and stood taking it all in. listening to the cacophony of voices.

Sailors, Marines, officers and chiefs stood surrounded by their families. Children were everywhere, some clinging to their mothers, others running through the crowd chasing one another, the smaller ones being passed from hand to hand by the adults.

A band was tuning up on Elevator Two, which was in the down position and stuck out over the pier like a porch roof. Even as Jake watched, the conductor got the attention of his charges and whipped them into a Sousa march.

On the pier near the stern another band was assembling. No doubt that was the Naval Air Station band, which tooted for every ship's departure. Well and good, but *Columbia* had a band too and apparently the ship's XO thought there couldn't be too much music.

Above Jake's head the tails of aircraft stuck out precariously over the edge of the flight deck and cast weird shadows on the crowded pier. Occasionally he could see people lift their gaze to take in the vast bulk of the ship and the dozens of aircraft. Then the people turned their attention back to their loved one.

Last night he had stood in line at one of the dozen phone booths on the head of the pier. The rain had subsided to occasional drips. When his turn for the booth came, he had called his folks in Virginia, then Callie. It was after midnight in Chicago when she answered.

'Callie, this is Jake.'

'Where are you?'

'On the pier at Alameda. Did you get my letters?'

'I received three.'

He had written the letters and mailed them from Oceana, where he had been sent to do field carrier qualifications with a group of students from VA-42. He had completed his field quals, of course, but didn't go to the ship. There hadn't been time. He would have to qual aboard *Columbia* after she sailed. He needed ten day and six night traps because it had been over six months since his last carrier landing.

'Another letter is on the way,' he told Callie, probably a superfluous comment. 'You'll get it in a day or two.'

'So how is the ship?'

'It's a ship. What can I say?'

'When do you sail?'

'Seven-thirty in the morning.'

'So when I wake up you'll be at sea.'

'Uh-huh.'

They talked desultorily for several minutes, the operator came on the line and Jake fed in more quarters, then he got down to it. 'Callie, I love you.'

'I know you do. Oh, Jake, I'm so sorry your visit was such a disaster.'

'I am too. I guess these things just happen sometimes. I wish . . .' And he ran out of steam. A phone booth on a pier with dozens of sailors awaiting their turn didn't seem the place to say what he wished.

'You be careful,' she said.

'You know me, Callie. I'm always careful.'

'Don't take any unnecessary chances.'

'I won't.'

'I want you to come back to me.'

Now Jake stood watching the crowd and thinking about that. She wanted him to come back *to her*.

He took a deep breath and sighed. Ah me, life is so strange. Just when everything looks bleakest a ray of sunshine comes through the clouds. Hope. He had hope. She wouldn't have said something like that unless she meant it, not Callie, not to a guy going on an eight-month cruise.

He was standing there listening to the two bands playing different tunes at the same time, watching the crowd, watching sailors and women engage in passionate kisses, when he saw the Cadillac. A pink Cadillac convertible with the top down was slowly making its way down the pier. People flowed out of its way, then closed in behind it, like water parting for a boat.

Cars were not allowed on the pier. Yet there it was. A man in a white uniform was driving, yet all of his passengers were women, young women, and not wearing a lot of clothing either. Lots of brown thighs and bare shoulders were on display, several truly awesome bosoms.

In complete disregard of the regulations, the car made its way to the foot of the officers' gangway and stopped. The driver got out and stretched lazily as he surveyed the giant gray ship looming beside the pier. The women bounded out and surrounded him.

It's Bosun Muldowski! Who else could it be? No sailor could get a car past the guards at the head of the pier and few officers under flag rank. But a warrant officer four? Yep. Muldowski.

He had been the flight deck bosun on *Shiloh*, Jake's last

ship. Apparently he was coming to *Columbia*. Now Jake remembered – Muldowski never did shore duty tours. He had been going from ship to ship for over twenty-five years.

Look at those women in hot pants and short short skirts!

Sailors to the right and left of Jake in the catwalk shouted and shrieked wolf whistles. Muldowski took no notice but the women waved prettily, which drew lusty cheers from the onlooking white hats.

With the bosun's bags out of the trunk of the car, he took his time hugging each of the women, all five of them, as the bands blared mightily and spectator sailors watched in awe.

'The bosun must own a whorehouse,' one sailor down the catwalk told his friends loud enough for Jake to hear.

'He sure knows how to live,' his buddy said approvingly. 'Style. He's got *style*.'

Jake Grafton grinned. Muldowski's spectacular arrival had just catapulted him to superstardom with the white hats, which was precisely the effect, Jake suspected, that the bosun intended. The deck apes would work like slaves for him until they dropped in their tracks.

All too soon the ship's whistle sounded, bullhorns blared and sailors rushed to single up the lines holding the great ship to the land. The men on the pier gave their women one last passionate hug, then dashed for the gangways. As seven bells sounded over the ship's PA system, cranes lifted the gangways clear and deposited them on the pier.

The last of the lines were released and the ship began to move, very slowly at first, almost imperceptibly. Slowly the gap between the pier and the men crowding the rails widened.

Sailors tossed their Dixie cups at the pier and children scurried like rats to retrieve them. The strains of 'Anchors Aweigh' filled the air.

When the pier was several hundred feet away and aft of the beam, Jake felt a rumble reach him through the steel on which he stood. The screws were biting. The effect was noticeable. The pier slid astern slowly at first, then with increasing speed.

Now the pilot climbed to the flight deck and threaded his way past tie-down chains toward the bow, where he joined a loose knot of men leaning into the increasing wind. Ahead was the Bay Bridge, then the Golden Gate. And the fog beyond the Golden Gate was dissipating.

The ship had cleared the Bay Bridge and was steaming at eight or ten knots past Alcatraz when the loudspeaker sounded. 'Flight Quarters, flight quarters. All hands man your flight quarters station.'

The cruise had begun.

Jake was in the locker room donning his flight gear when a black Marine in a flight suit came in. He had railroad tracks pinned to the shoulders of his flight suit, so he was a captain, the Marine equivalent of Jake's Navy rank of lieutenant. He looked Jake over, nodded to a couple of Marines who were also suiting up to get some traps, then strolled over to Jake.

'They call me Flap. I guess we're flying together.'

The BN had his hair cut in the Marine Corps' version of an Afro – that is, it stuck out from his head about half an inch and was meticulously tapered on the sides and back. He was slightly above medium height, with the well-developed chest and bulging muscles that can only be acquired by thousands of hours of pumping iron. He looked to be in his late twenties, maybe thirty at the most.

'Jake Grafton. You're Le Beau?'

'Yep.'

'How come you weren't at the brief?'

'Hey, man. This is CQ!' CQ meant carrier qualification. 'All we're gonna do is fly around this bird farm with the wheels down, dangling our little hook thingy. Where is *your* bag. You can hack it, can't ya?'

Jake decided to change the subject. 'Where you from?'

'Parris Island. Get it? Le Beau? French name? Parris Island?'

'Ha ha.'

'Don't let this fine chocolate complexion fool you, my man. It's French chocolate.'

'French shit,' said one of Le Beau's fellow Marines.

'Eat it, butt breath,' Flap shot back. 'I'm black with a seasoning of Creole.'

'Sorta like coffee with cream,' Jake Grafton remarked as he zipped up his torso harness.

'Yeah man. That's exactly right. There was a planter in Louisiana, Le Beau, with a slobbering craving for black poontang. After the Civil War he took personal offense when his former slaves adopted his last name. They did it 'cause most of them was his sons and daughters. But Le Beau didn't like the thought of being recognized in history as a patriarch, didn't want to admit his generous genetic contributions to improving a downtrodden race. Hung a couple of his nigger kids, he did. So all the blacks in the parish adopted the name. More damn black Le Beaus in that section of Louisiana than you could shake a stiff dick at. Now that redneck Cajun planter bigot was one of my many great-great-grandpappys, of whom I am so very proud.'

'Terrific,' said Jake Grafton, who checked to see that the laces of his new G-suit were properly adjusted.

'We heard you were coming. The Nav just didn't think us gyrenes could handle all this high tailhook tech. So we heard they were sending an ace Navy type to indoctrinate us ignorant jarheads, instruct us, lead the way into a better, brighter day.'

Grafton didn't think that comment worth a reply.

'It'll be a real pleasure,' said Flap Le Beau warmly as he grabbed his torso harness from his locker, 'flying with a master hookster. Just think of me as a student at the fount of all wisdom, an apprentice seeking to acquire insights into the nuances of the arcane art, appreciate the—'

'Are you always this full of shit or are you making a special effort on my behalf?' Jake asked.

Le Beau prattled on unperturbed. 'It's tragic that so many Navy persons are dangerously thin-skinned in a world full of sharp objects! One can infer from your crude comment that you share that lamentable trait with your colleagues. It's sad, very sad, but there are probably gonna be tensions between us. None of that male-bonding horse pucky for you and me, huh? Tensions. Stress. Mis-understandings. Heartburns. Hard feelings. Ass kickings.' He sighed plaintively. 'Well, I try to get along by going along. That's the Cajun in me coming out. I am so very lucky I got this white blood in me, ya know? Lets me see everything in a better perspective.'

The Marine bent slightly at the waist and addressed his next comment to the deck: 'Thank you, thank you, Jules Le Beau, rotting down there in hell.'

Back to his locker and flight gear – 'Lots of the bros ain't as lucky as I am – they can't tell trees from manure piles, and—'

'Oh, for Christ's sake, Flap,' someone in the next row said. 'Turn off the tap, will ya?'

'Yeoww,' Flap howled, 'I feel *great*! Gonna get out there and fly with a Navy ace and see how it's *done* by the best of the best!'

'How did I wind up with this asshole?' Jake asked the major two lockers down.

'No other pilot wanted him,' was the reply.

'Hey, watch your mouth over there,' Flap called. 'This is my rep you're pissin' on.'

'Pisson' on, *sir!*'

'Sir,' Flap echoed dutifully.

The sun shone down softly through a high thin cirrus layer. The wind out of the northwest was heaping the sea into long windrows and ripping occasional whitecaps from the crests as gulls wheeled and turned around the great ship.

Two frigates and four destroyers were visible several miles away, scattered in a haphazard circle around the carrier. These were the carrier's escorts, an antisubmarine screen, faithful retainers that would attend the queen wherever she led.

On the eastern horizon land was still visible. It would soon drop over the earth's rim since the carrier would have to spend the next several hours running into the northwest wind, then the universe would consist of only the ships, the sea and the sky. The land would become a memory of the past and a vision of a hazy future, but the solid reality of the present would be just the ships and the men who rode them. Six small moons orbiting one wandering planet . . .

Jake's vision lingered on that distant dark line of earth, then he turned away.

The ship rode easily this morning, with just the gentlest of rolls, which Jake noticed only because he didn't have his sea legs yet. This roll would become a pitching motion when the ship turned into the wind.

Sensing these things and knowing them without really thinking about them, Jake Grafton walked slowly aft looking for his aircraft. There – by Elevator Four.

She was no beauty, this A-6E Intruder decked out in dull, low viz paint splotched here and there with puke green zinc dichromate primer. An external power cord was already plugged into the plane. Jake lowered the boarding ladder and opened the canopy, then climbed up and placed his helmet bag on the seat. He ensured the safety pins were properly installed in the ejection seat, let his eye rove over the cockpit switches, the gear handle, the wing position lever and the fuel dump switches, then checked the fuel quantity. Ten thousand pounds. As advertised. He toggled the seat position adjustment switches, noted the whine and felt the seat move, then released them. Jake climbed down the ladder to the deck and began his preflight inspection.

In Vietnam he had flown A-6As, the first version of the Intruder. This plane was an A-6E, the second-generation bomber, the state-of-the-art in American military technology. Most of the updates were not visible to the naked eye. The search and track radars of the A-6A had been replaced with one radar that combined both search and track functions. The A's rotary-drum computer had been replaced with a solid-state, digital, state-of-the-art version. The third major component in the electronics system, the inertial navigation system, or INS, had not yet been updated, so it was now the weak point in the navigation/attack system. The new computer and radar were not only more accurate than the old gear, they were also proving to be extraordinarily reliable, which erased the major operational disadvantage of the A-6A.

The E had been in the fleet for several years now, yet it had not been used in Vietnam, by Pentagon fiat. Had the updated E been used there, the targets could have been hit with greater accuracy, with fewer missions, thereby saving lives and perhaps helping shorten the war, but inevitably some of these planes would have been lost and the technology compromised, i.e., seen by the Soviets.

So lives had been traded to keep the technology secret. How many lives? Who could say.

As Jake Grafton walked around this A-6E looking and touching this and that, the raw, twisted Vietnam emotions came flooding back. Once again he felt the fear, saw the blood, saw the night sky filled with streaks of tracer and the fiery plumes of SAMs. The faces of the dead men floated before him as he felt the smooth, cool skin of the airplane.

It seemed as if he had never left the ship. Any second Tiger Cole would come strolling across the deck with his helmet bag and charts, ready to fly into the mouth of hell.

Jake felt his stomach churn, as if he were going to vomit. He paused and leaned against a main-gear strut.

No!

Six months had passed. His knee had healed, he had visited his folks, done a little flight instruction at Whidbey Island, visited Callie in Chicago ... thrown that asshole through the window at Sea-Tac ... why was he sweating, nauseated?

This is *car quals*, for Christ's sake! It's a beautiful day, a cake hop, a walk in the park!

He stood straight and, looking out to sea, took several deep breaths. He should have popped the question to Callie – should have asked her to marry him. And he should have resigned from the Navy.

He shouldn't even be here! On the boat again! He had done his share, dropped his share of bombs, killed his share of gomers.

For God's sake – another cruise – with a bunch of jack-off jarheads!

He took his hand off the strut and stood staring at the plane, his face twisted into a frown. Primer splotches everywhere, dirt, stains from hydraulic leaks ... And it was a fairly new plane, less than a year old!

Camparelli would have come screaming unglued if they had sent a plane like this to *his* squadron. Screaming-meemy fucking *unglued!*

Somehow the thought of Commander Camparelli, Jake's last skipper in Vietnam, storming and ranting amused Jake Grafton.

'Looks like a piece of shit, don't it?'

Bosun Muldowski was standing there staring at the plane with his arms crossed.

'Yeah, Bosun, but I ain't looking to buy it. I'm just flying it this morning.'

'Sure didn't expect to find you aviatin' for the jugheads, Mr Grafton.'

45

'Life's pretty weird sometimes.'

The bosun nodded sagely. 'Heard about that shithead that went through the window at Sea-Tac.'

Jake nodded and rubbed his hand through his hair. 'Well, I guess I lost it for a little bit. I'm not the smartest guy you ever met.'

'Smart enough. Thanks.'

With that, the bosun walked forward, up the deck, leaving the pilot staring at his back.

'Hey, my man! Is this mean green killing machine safe to fly?' Flap. He came around the nose of the plane and lowered the BN's boarding ladder.

'We'll find out, won't we?'

'It's an embarrassing question to have to ask, I know, yet the dynamics of the moment and the precarious state of my existence here in space and time impel me to ponder my karma and your competence. No offense, but I am growing attached to my ass and don't want to part with it. What I'm getting at, Ace, is, are you man enough to handle the program?'

The pilot slapped the fuselage. 'This relic from the Mongolian Air Force is going off the pointy end of this boat in about fifteen minutes with your manly physique in it. That's the only fact I have access to. Will your ass stay attached? Will sweet, innocent Suzy Kiss-me succumb to the blandishments of the evil pervert, Mortimer Fuck-butt? Stay tuned to this channel and find out right after these words from our sponsors.' He turned his back on Flap Le Beau.

'I have no doubt this thing will go *off* this scow, but can *you* get it back aboard all in one piece?'

Jake Grafton shouted back over his shoulder: 'We'll fly together or die together, Le Beau. None of that macho male bonding crap for hairy studs like us.'

The bosun – he didn't have to say that. And it was a beautiful day, the sun glinting on the swells, the high, open sky, the gentle motion of the ship . . .

The plane would feel good in his hands, would do just as he willed it. She would respond so sweetly to the throttles and stick, would come down the groove into the wires so slick and honest . . .

As the sea wind played with his hair the pilot found himself feeling better.

CHAPTER FOUR

Wings spread and locked, flaps and slats to takeoff, Roger the weight-board – it all came back without conscious thought as Jake followed the taxi director's hand signals and moved the warplane toward the port bow catapult, Cat Two. Flap didn't help – he didn't say or do anything after getting the inertial aligned and flipping the radar switch to standby. He merely sat and watched Jake.

'Takeoff checklist,' Jake prompted.

'I thought you said you could fly this thing, Ace.'

Jake ran through the items on his own as he eased the plane the last few feet into the catapult shuttle and the hold-back bar dropped into place.

The yellow-shirt taxi director gave him the 'release brakes' signal with one hand and with the other made a sweeping motion below his waist. This was the signal to the catapult operator to ease the shuttle forward with a hydraulic piston, taking all the slack out of the nose-wheel tow-launching mechanism. Jake felt the thunk as he released the brakes and pushed both throttles forward to the stops.

The engines came up nicely. RPM, exhaust gas temperatures, fuel flow – the tapes ran up the dials as the engines wound up.

The Intruder vibrated like a living thing as the engines sucked in rivers of air and slammed it out the exhausts.

'You ready?' Jake asked the bombardier as he wrapped the fingers of his left hand around the catapult grip while he braced the heel of the hand against the throttles.

'Onward and upward, Ace.'

The taxi director was pointing to the catapult officer, who was ten feet farther up the deck. The shooter was twirling his fingers and looking at Jake, waiting.

Oil pressure both engines – fine. Hydraulics – okay. Jake waggled the stick and checked the movement of the stabilator in his left-side rearview mirror on the canopy rail. Then he saluted the cat officer with his right hand. The shooter returned it and glanced up the cat track toward the bow as Jake put his head back into the headrest and placed his right hand behind the stick.

Now the cat officer lunged forward and touched the deck with his right hand.

One heartbeat, two, then the catapult fired. The acceleration was vicious.

Yeeeaaaah! and it was over, in about two and a half seconds. The edge of the bow swept under the nose and the plane was over the glittering sea.

Jake let the trim rotate the nose to eight degrees nose up as he reached for the gear handle. He slapped it up and swept his eyes across the instrument panel, taking in the attitude reference on the vertical display indicator – the VDI, the altimeter – eighty feet and going up, the rate of climb – positive, the airspeed – 150 knots and accelerating, all warning lights out. He took in all these bits of information without conscious thought, just noted them somewhere in his subconscious, and put it all together as the airplane accelerated and climbed away from the ship.

With the gear up and locked, he raised the flaps and slats. Here they came. Still accelerating, he stopped the climb at five hundred feet and ran the nose trim down. Two hundred and fifty knots, 300, 350 . . . still accelerating . . .

To his amusement he saw that Flap Le Beau was sitting upright in his ejection seat with his hands folded on his lap, just inches from the alternate ejection handle between his legs.

At 400 knots Jake eased the throttles back. Five miles coming up on the DME . . . and the pilot pulled the nose up steeply and dropped the left wing as he eased the throttles forward again. The plane leaped away from the ocean in a climbing turn. Jake scanned the sky looking for the plane that had preceded him on the cat by two minutes.

He had four thousand pounds of fuel – no, only three thousand now – to burn off before they called him down for his first landing, in about fifteen minutes.

Better make it last, Jake. Don't squander it. He pulled the throttles back and coasted up to five thousand feet, where he leveled indicating 250 knots in a gentle turn that would allow him to orbit the ship on the five-mile circle.

Flap sighed audibly over the intercom, the ICS, then said, 'Acceptable launch, Jake. Acceptable. You obviously have done this once or twice and haven't forgotten how. This pleases me. I get a warm fuzzy.'

There the major was, almost on the other side of the ship, level at this altitude and turning on the five-mile arc. Jake steepened his turn to cut across above the ship and rendezvous.

'I almost joined the Navy,' Flap confided, 'but I came to my senses just in time and joined the Corps. It's a real fighting outfit, the best in the world. The Navy . . . well, the best that can be said is that you guys try. Most of the time, anyway.'

He talked on as Jake got on the major's bearing line and eased in some left rudder to lower the nose so he could see the major out the right-side quarter panel. Rendezvousing an A-6 with its side-by-side seating took some finesse when coming in on the lead's left because the pilot of the joining aircraft could easily lose sight of the lead plane. If he let himself go just a little high, or if he let his plane fall a little behind the bearing line – going sucked, they called it – and

50

attempted to pull back to the bearing, the lead would disappear under the wingman's nose and he would be closing blindly. This was not good, a situation fraught with hazard for all concerned.

This morning Jake stayed glued to the bearing. If Flap noticed he gave no indication. He was saying, '. . . the closest I ever came to being in the Navy was the wife of some surface warrior I met at MCRD' – Marine Corps Recruit Depot – 'O Club on a Friday night. She rubbed her tits all over my back and I told her she was going to give me zipper rash. She was all hot and randy so I thought, Why not. We went over to her place . . .'

When he was fifty feet away from the major's plane Jake lowered the nose and crossed behind and under. He surfaced into parade position on the right side, the outside of the turn. The BN gave him a thumbs-up.

Jake's BN talked on. '. . . I just put the ol' cock to her . . .'

After a frequency shift that the major's BN signaled and Jake had to dial in because Flap wasn't helping at all, they made two more turns in the circle, then started down.

'She had those nipples that are like strawberries, you know what I mean? All puffed up so nice and sweet and red and they're just made for sucking on? I like them the very best. Can't understand why God didn't equip more women with 'em. Only about one broad in ten has 'em. It's a mystery.'

They were descending through patches of sunlight interspersed with shadow. The occasional golden shafts played on the planes and made the sea below glisten, when Jake could steal a second from holding position on the lead plane and glance down.

His plane handled well. Slick and tight and responsive. He contented himself with moving his plane a few inches forward on the lead, then a few inches back, staying in absolute control. When he felt comfortable he moved in on the bearing line so that the wing tips overlapped. He stopped when he could feel the downdraft off the lead's wing and the tip was just two feet from his canopy. He held it there for a moment or two to prove to himself that he could still do it, then eased back out to where he belonged.

Flying is the best that life offers, Jake Grafton thought. *And carrier flying is the best of the flying. These day traps and cat shots are going to be terrific.* He fought back the sense of euphoria that suffused him.

'. . . as close as I ever came to being in the Navy, I'll tell you that.'

If Flap would just shut up!

But he won't. So no sense making a scene.

The two warplanes came up the ship's wake at eight hundred feet glued together. There were already two other planes in the pattern with their gear and hooks down, two A-7 Corsairs, so the major delayed his break. Then the BN kissed him off and the major dumped his left wing and pulled. Jake watched the lead plane turn away as he counted to himself. At the count of seven he slammed the stick sideways and pulled as he reached for the gear handle with his left hand and slapped it down. Then the flaps.

Turning level, three G's . . . gear coming, flaps and slats coming . . . seven thousand pounds of fuel.

Stable on the downwind he toggled the main dump and let seven hundred pounds squirt out into the atmosphere. He wanted to cross the ramp of the ship with precisely six grand.

Precision. That's what carrier flying is all about. That's the challenge. And the thrill.

'. . . just don't see why anybody would want to float around in the middle of the ocean on these bird farms. Eight months of this fun. The Navy is full of happy masturbators . . .'

Hook up for the first pass, a touch-and-go. Let the LSO get his look and learn that I'm not suicidal.

Coming through the ninety, on speed, exactly 118 knots

with a three-o'clock angle-of-attack . . . there's the meat-ball on the Fresnel lens. Cross the wake, roll out, coming in to the angled deck, watch the lineup! There's the burble from the island . . . power on then off fast. Keep that ball in the center . . .

The wheels smacked into the deck and the nose came down hard as Jake Grafton shoved the throttles to the stop and closed the wing-tip speed brakes with the throttle-mounted switch. The Intruder shot up the angled deck and ran off into the air. He brought the stick back and got her climbing.

'The amazing thing is that the Navy finds so many of you masturbators to ride these floating aviaries. You wouldn't think there were this many jack-off artists in the whole world. Not if you just looked at the world casually. I mean, most people like their sex with *somebody else*, y'know? No doubt a lot of you guys are queer. Gotta be.'

On the downwind Jake lowered the hook and checked that his harness was locked. Normally he flew with it unlocked so that he could lean forward if he wished or wiggle in the ejection seat.

He toggled the seat up a smidgen and adjusted the rheostat that brightened the angle-of-attack indicator.

The interval between Jake and the major was good, and the major trapped on his first pass as Jake was reducing power at the 180-degree position. Down and turning, on speed, looking for the ball crossing the wake, wings level and reducing power, now power on for the burble, watching the lineup and flying that ball . . .

The Intruder swept across the ramp and slammed into the deck As the throttles went forward the tailhook caught a wire and dragged the plane to a dead stop.

Then the plane began to roll backward. Jake jabbed the hook-up button and added power to taxi out of the gear. The director was giving him the come ahead as Flap said, 'The whole concept of having five thousand guys crammed together without women is unnatural. Everybody horny, jacking off in the shower, into their sheets – this boat is a floating semen factory! In nineteen seventy three! My God, haven't we humans made any progress in understanding man's sexual needs in all these years of . . .'

Queued up waiting for Cat Two, checking the gear and flap settings, the fuel, then following the yellow shirt's signals as he brought the plane into the shuttle – Jake was doing the things he knew how to do, the things that made the hassles worthwhile.

Throttles up . . . the salute – and wham, they were off to do it again. This time Jake left the gear and flaps down. He flew straight ahead upwind until the major passed him on the left going downwind.

Jake banked for the crosswind turn. The plane entered a shaft of sunlight and the warmth played on his arms and legs. Inside his oxygen mask Jake grinned broadly.

After four traps Jake was directed to fold his wings and stop near the carrier's island with the engines running while the plane was refueled, a 'hot' turnaround. He opened the canopy and took off his oxygen mask. His face was wet with sweat. He swabbed away the moisture and watched the planes making their approaches.

Flap Le Beau also sat watching, silent at last.

Heavenly silence. Except for the howl of jet engines at full power and the slam of the catapult and an occasional terse radio message. The flight deck of an aircraft carrier was the loudest place on earth, yet oh so pleasant without Flap's drivel.

In a few minutes Jake had 6,500 pounds of fuel and gave the purple-shirted fuel crew the cut sign, a slice of the hand across his throat. Mask on, canopy closed, parking brake off, engage nose-wheel steering and goose the throttles a smidgen to follow the director's signals. Now into the queue waiting for the cat . . .

*

All too soon it was over. Jake had the ten day traps the law required and was once more day qualified as a carrier pilot. He shut the plane down on the porch near Elevator Four and climbed down to the deck still wearing his helmet. After a few words with the plane captain, he descended a ladder to the catwalk, then went down into the first passageway leading into the 0-3 level, the deck under the flight deck.

Flap Le Beau was behind him.

'You did okay out there this morning, Ace,' Flap commented.

'You didn't.' Jake stopped and faced the bombardier-navigator.

'Say again?'

'I got an eighty-year-old grandmother who could have done a better job in the right seat than you did today.'

'Kiss my chocolate ass, Ace. I didn't ask for your opinion.'

'You're going to get it. You flew with me. I expect a BN to help me fly the plane, to act as a safety observer at all times, to read the checklists.'

'I just wanted to see if you could—'

'I *can!* While you were sitting there with your thumb up your butt and boring me to tears with the story of your miserable life, you could have been checking out the computer and radar for the debrief. You never even brought the radar out of standby! Don't *ever* pull that stunt again.'

Flap put his face just inches from Grafton's. 'I ain't taking any shit from the Navy, swabbie. We'd better get that straightened out here and now.'

'Le Beau, I don't know if you're senior to me or I'm senior to you and I really don't give a rat's ass which way it is. But in that cockpit I'm the aircraft commander. You're going to do a solid, professional job – there ain't no two

55

ways about it. If you *don't*, your career in the grunts is gonna go down the crapper real damn quick. You won't be able to catch it with a swan dive.'

Flap opened his mouth to reply, but Jake Grafton snarled, 'Don't push it.' With that he turned and stalked away, leaving Flap Le Beau staring at his back.

When Jake was out of sight Flap grinned He nodded several times and rubbed his hand through his hair, fluffing his Afro.

'Flap, my man, this one's gonna do,' he said. 'He's gonna do *fine*.' And he laughed softly to himself.

Jake was seated in the back of the ready room filling out the maintenance forms on the airplane when the air wing landing signal officer, the LSO, and the A-6 squadron LSO came in. The A-6 guy Jake knew. He was an East Coast Navy pilot who had been shanghaied like Jake to provide the Marines with 'experience.' His name was McCoy and by some miracle, he was Jake's new roommate. If he had a first name Jake didn't learn it last night, when the LSO came in drunk, proclaimed himself to be the Real McCoy, and collapsed into his bunk facedown.

'Grafton,' the senior air wing LSO said, consulting his notes, 'you did okay.' His name was Hugh Skidmore. 'Touch-and-go was an OK, then nine OKs and one fair. All three wires. You're gonna wear out that third wire, fella.'

Jake was astonished. OKs were perfect passes, and he thought he had five or six good ones, but nine? To cover his astonishment and pleasure, he said gruffly, 'A *fair?* You gave me a *fair?* Which pass was that?'

Skidmore examined his book again, then snapped it shut. 'Seventh one. While you were turning through the ninety the captain put the helm over chasing the wind and you went low. You were a little lined up left, too.' He shrugged, then grinned. 'Try a bit harder next time, huh?'

Skidmore went off to debrief the major but McCoy lingered. 'Geez, Real, you guys sure are tough graders.'

'Better get your act together, Roomie.'

'What did you do to rate a tour with the Marines? Piss in a punch bowl?'

'Something like that,' the Real McCoy said distractedly, then wandered off.

After lunch Jake went to his stateroom to unpack. He had gotten the bulk of his gear on hangers or folded when McCoy came in, tossed his Mickey Mouse ears on his desk, and collapsed onto his bunk.

'I threw a civilian through a plate glass window,' Jake told the LSO. 'Just what did *you* do?'

McCoy sighed and opened his eyes. He focused on Grafton. 'I suppose you'll tell this all over the boat.'

'Try me.'

'Well, I made too much money. I got to talking about it with the guys. Then I had the Admin guys draft up a letter of resignation. Before I could get it submitted the skipper called me in. He said a rich bastard like me could just count his money out on the big gray boat.'

'Too much money? I never heard of such a thing. Did you loot the coffee mess?'

'Naw. Nothing like that.' McCoy sat up. He rubbed his face. 'Naw. I just got to playing the market.'

'What market?'

'*The* market.' When he saw the expression on Jake's face, he exclaimed, 'Jesus H Christ! The *stock* market.'

'I never knew anybody who owned stock.'

'Oh, for the love of . . .' McCoy stretched out and sighed.

'Well, how much money did you make, anyway?'

'You're going to tell every greasy asshole on this ship, Grafton. It's written all over your simple face.'

'No, I won't. Honest. How much?'

McCoy regarded his new roommate dolefully. Finally he

said, 'Well, I managed to save about sixteen thousand in the last five years, and I've parlayed that into a hundred twenty-two thousand three hundred and thirty nine dollars. As of the close of business in New York yesterday, anyway. No way of knowing what the market did today, of course.'

'Of course,' Jake agreed, suitably impressed. He whistled as he thought about $122,000, then said, 'Say, I got a couple grand saved up. Maybe you could help me invest it.'

'*That's* what got me shipped out here with these jarheads! All the guys in the ready room wanted investment advice. Everybody was reading the *Wall Street Journal* and talking about interest rates and P/E ratios and how many cars Chrysler was gonna sell. The skipper blew a gasket.'

McCoy shook his head sadly. 'Ah well, it's all water under the keel. Can't do nothing about it now, I guess.' He looked again at Jake. 'Tell me about this guy you threw through the window.'

When they had exhausted that subject, Jake wanted to know about the officers in the squadron.

'Typical Marines' was the Real's verdict, spoken with an air of resigned authority since he had been with this crowd for three whole weeks. 'Seems like three months. This is going to be the longest tour of my life.'

'So how many are combat vets?'

'Everyone in the squadron, except for the three or four nuggets, did at least one tour in 'Nam. Maybe half of them did two or more. And six or eight of them did tours as platoon leaders in Vietnam before they went to flight school. Your BN, Le Beau? He was in Marine Recon.'

Grafton was stunned. Le Beau? The San Diego cocks-man? 'You're pulling my leg.'

'I shit you not. Recon. Running around behind enemy lines eating snake meat, doing ambushes and assassinations. Yeah. That's Le Beau, all right. He's a legend in the Corps. Got more chest cabbage than Audie Murphy. He ain't playing with a full deck.'

Jake Grafton's face grew dark as he recalled Flap's rambling cockpit monologue. And that aura of bumbling incompetence that he exuded all morning!

Seeing the look, McCoy continued, 'God only knows why the Marines made him a BN. HE went back to Vietnam in A-6s. Punched out twice, the first time on final to DaNang. Walked through the main gate carrying his parachute and seat pan. The second time, though, was something else. His pilot got his head blown off and Le Beau ejected somewhere near the Laotian border. Maybe in Laos or Cambodia – I don't know. Anyway, nobody heard anything. Just nothing, although they looked and looked hard. Then seventeen days or so later a patrol stumbled onto him out in the jungle in the middle of nowhere. He was running around buck naked, covered with mud and leaves, carrying nothing but a knife. Was busy ambushing the gomers and gutting them. They brought him back with a whole collection of gomer weapons that he had stashed.'

From the look on Grafton's face, McCoy could see that he was not a happy man.

'That ain't the amazing part, Jake,' the Real McCoy continued. 'The amazing part is that Le Beau didn't *want* to get rescued. Two guys have told me this, so I'm assuming that there's something to it. He didn't want to come back because he was having too much *fun*. The grunts on that patrol almost had to tie him up.'

'Why me, Lord?'

'His last pilot didn't cut the mustard,' McCoy continued, 'not to Le Beau's way of thinking. Was having his troubles getting aboard. Oh, he wasn't dangerous, but he was rough, couldn't seem to get a feel for the plane in the groove at night. He might have come around, then again he might not have. He didn't get the chance. Le Beau went to the skipper and the skipper went to CAG and before you could whisper "Semper Fi" the guy was transferred.'

'*Le Beau* did that?'

'Whatever it takes to make it in the Corps, that dickhead has it. He just got selected for promotion to major. Everyone treats him with deference and respect. Makes my stomach turn. Wait till you see these tough old gunnies – they talk to him like they were disciples talking to Jesus. If he lives he's going to be the commandant someday, mark my words.'

'Strangers in a strange land,' Jake murmured, referring to himself and McCoy.

'Something like that,' the Real agreed. He pulled off his steel-toed flight boots and tossed them carelessly on the floor. 'This tour is going to be an adventure,' he added sourly.

'Uh-huh.'

'We've got an all-officers meeting in the ready room in about an hour. I'm going to get fourteen winks. Wake me up, huh?'

'Okay.'

McCoy turned over in his bunk and was soon breathing deeply.

Jake snapped off the overhead light, leaving only his desk lamp lit, the little ten-watt glow worm. He tilted his chair back against McCoy's steel foot locker and put his feet up on his desk.

Thinking about Le Beau, he snorted once, but his thoughts soon drifted on to Callie. The gentle motion of the ship had a tranquilizing effect. After a few moments his head tilted forward and sleep overcame him.

The skipper of the squadron was Lieutenant Colonel Richard Haldane. He was a short, barrel-chested, ramrod-straight man with close-cropped black hair that showed flecks of gray. In this closed community of military professionals his bearing and his demeanor marked him as an officer entitled to respect. He took Jake aside after the all-officers meeting – boring administrative details in a crowded, stuffy room filled with strangers – and asked him to sit in the chair beside him.

Haldane had Jake's service record on his lap. 'We didn't get much of a chance to talk last night, Mr Grafton, but welcome aboard. We're glad to have someone with your carrier experience.'

'Thank you, sir.'

'We're going to assign you to the Operations Department. I think your experience will be the most help to us there.'

'Yessir.'

'During this transit to Hawaii, I want you to put together a series of lectures from CV NATOPS.' CV NATOPS was the bible on carrier operations. The acronym stood for fixed-wing carrier naval air training and operation procedures. 'We've been through it several times while working up for this deployment,' Colonel Haldane continued, 'but I'd like for you to lead us through the book again in detail. I want you to share with us everything you know about A-6 carrier operations. Do you think you can do that?'

'Yes, sir.'

Richard Haldane nodded his head a millimeter. Even sitting down he exuded a command presence. Jake sat a little straighter in his chair.

'I see from your record that you have plenty of combat experience, but it's experience of the same type that most of the officers in this room have had – bombing targets ashore.'

'Single-plane day and night raids, some section stuff, and Alpha strikes, sir, plus a whole hell of a lot of tanker flights.'

'Unfortunately our combat experience won't do us much good if we go to war with the Soviets, who are our most likely opponent.'

This remark caught Jake by surprise. He tried to keep his face deadpan as Haldane continued: 'Our part in a war with the Russians will probably involve a fleet action, our ships against their ships. Mr Grafton, how would you attack a Soviet guided-missile frigate?'

Jake opened his mouth, then closed it again. He scratched his head. 'I don't know, sir,' he said at last. The truth was, he had never once even thought about it. The Vietnam War was in full swing when he was going through flight training, when he transitioned into A-6s, and during his three years in a fleet squadron. The targets were all onshore.

'Any ideas?'

Jake bit his lip. *He* was the naval officer and he was being asked a question about naval air warfare that in truth he should know something about. But he didn't. He decided to admit it. 'Sir, I think the answer to that question would depend on a careful analysis of a Soviet frigate's missile and flak envelope, and to be frank, I have never done that or seen the results of anybody else's look. I suspect the Air Intelligence guys have that stuff under lock and key.'

'So what weapons does a Soviet frigate carry?'

Jake squirmed. 'Colonel, I don't know.'

Haldane nodded once, slowly, and looked away. 'I would like for you to study this matter, Mr Grafton. When you think you have an answer to the question, come see me.'

'Aye aye, sir.'

'That's all. Good luck tonight.'

'Thank you, sir.' Jake rose and walked away, mortified. Well, hell, the stuff he had spent his career attacking was all mud-based. Of course he *should* know about ships, *but* . . .

What Haldane must think – a *naval* officer who doesn't know diddly-squat about *naval* warfare!

Congratulations, Jake. You just got your tour with the Marines off to a great start.

CHAPTER FIVE

There was still a little splotch of light in the western sky and a clearly discernible horizon when Jake Grafton taxied toward the catapult that evening. This first shot would be a 'pinky,' without severe sweat. He needed six landings to attain his night qualification, which meant after this twilight shot there would be five more . . . in stygian darkness. A pinky first one was just dandy with him.

He carefully scanned the evening sky. The cloud cover was almost total, with the only holes toward the west, and low, maybe seven or eight thousand feet. Wind still out of the northwest, but stiffer than this morning. That was good. Tonight the ship could steam slower into the wind and yet still have the optimum thirty knots of wind over the deck. Since every mile upwind took her farther from the coast and the airfields ashore, the fewer of those miles the better.

Car quals are always goat-ropes, Jake thought, something going wrong sooner or later, so there is at least a fifty-fifty chance I'll have to divert ashore once tonight. And if my luck is in, maybe spend the night in the Alameda BOQ, call Callie . . .

No matter how long you've been ashore, after a half hour back aboard one of these gray tubs you're tired, hungry and horny. No way to cure the horniness, but a night ashore in a real bed would work wonders on the other syndromes, with real food and a long, hot shower and Callie's voice on the phone—

His reverie was interrupted by Flap Le Beau's voice on

the intercom system, the ICS. 'Don't do nothin' cute tonight, huh? My internal table ain't so stable when we're out here flyin' through black goo.'

'You and Muhammad Ali. How about laying off the monologue. When I want comedy I watch TV.'

'Golden silence to practice your pilot gig. You got it. Just fly like an angel flitting toward paradise.'

'You do the radio frequency changes and I'll do the transmissions, okay?'

'Fine.'

'Takeoff checklist,' Jake said, and Flap began reading off the items. Jake checked each item and gave the appropriate response.

And soon they were taxiing toward the cat. Automatically Jake leaned forward and tugged hard on the VDI, the televisionlike display in the center of the instrument panel that functioned as the primary attitude reference. It was tight, just as it should be.

'Flashlight on the backup gyro, please,' Jake said to Flap, who already had it in his hand. If both generators dropped off the line, the little gyro would continue to provide good attitude information for about thirty seconds, long enough for Jake to deploy the ram-air turbine, called the RAT, an emergency wind-driven generator.

Of course a double generator failure was rare, and if it happened on a launch with a discernible horizon there wouldn't be a problem. Yet on a coal black night . . . and all nights at sea were coal black. Jake Grafton well knew that emergencies were quirky – they only happened at the worst possible time, the time when you least expected one and could least afford it. Then you would have to entertain two or three.

The A-7 on the cat in front of Jake was having a problem with the nose-tow apparatus. A small conference was convening around the nose wheel, but nothing obvious seemed to be happening.

Jake looked again at the sky. Darkening fast.

Automatically he reviewed what he would do if he got a cold cat shot – if the catapult failed to give him sufficient end speed to fly. From there he moved into engine failure. He fingered the emergency jettison button, caressed the throttles and felt behind him for the RAT handle. Every motion would have to be quick and sure – no fumbling, no trying to remember exactly what he had to do – he must just do it instinctively and correctly.

They were still screwing with the A-7. *Come on, guys!*

He felt frustrated, entitled to a pinky. These guys had better get with the program or this shot will be like being blasted blindfolded into a coal bin at midnight.

'Gettin' pretty dark,' Flap commented, to Jake's disgust. The pilot squirmed in his seat as he eyed the meeting of the board under the Corsair's nose.

'Why did you stay in the Navy anyway?'

What a cracker this Le Beau is! 'I eat this shit with a spoon,' Grafton replied testily.

'Yeah, I can see you're loving this. Me, I'm too stupid to make it on the outside. It's the Marines or starve. But you seem smarter than me, so I wondered.'

'Put a cork in it, will ya?'

Jake smacked the instrument panel with his fist and addressed the dozen men milling around the Corsair: 'For Christ's sake, let's shoot it or get it off the cat. We gonna dick around till the dawn's early light?'

And here came Bosun Muldowski, striding down the deck, gesturing angrily. 'Off the cat. Get it off.'

And it happened. The Corsair came off the cat and Jake eased the Intruder on. Into the hold-back, the thump as the shuttle was moved forward hydraulically, off the brakes and full power, cat grip up, cycle the controls, check the flaps and slats, now the engine gauges . . .

Time to go.

Jake flipped on the external lights, the nighttime

equivalent of the salute to the cat officer. He placed his head back into the rest, just in time to catch Flap giving Muldowski the bird.

Wham!

As the G's slammed them back into their seats Jake roared into the ICS: '*Yeeeeoooow*,' and then they were airborne. A pinky! *All right!* Not very pink, but pink enough.

Engines pulling, all warning lights out, eight degrees nose up – his eyes took it all in automatically as he reached for the gear handle and slapped it up.

With the gear coming, the bird accelerating nicely, the pilot keyed the radio transmitter: 'War Ace Five One One airborne.'

'Roger, Five One One,' the departure controller said from his seat in front of a large radar screen in Air Ops, deep in the bowels of the ship. 'Climb straight ahead to six thousand, then hold on the One Three Five radial at sixteen miles. Your push at One Seven after the hour.'

'Five Eleven, straight up to Six, then hold on the One Three Five at Sixteen.' Jake moved his left thumb from the radio transmit button to the ICS key and opened his mouth. He wanted to say something snotty to Flap about the gesture to the bosun, but the bombardier beat him to the switch.

'Hey, I damn near ejected on the cat stroke. What in hell was that squall you gave back there?'

'I—'

'You damn fool! I came within a gnat's eyelash of punching out. I coulda *drowned!* If I got run over by the boat you wouldn't be so damn happy. Yelling on the ICS like a wildcat with a hot poker up your ass – that's the stupidest thing I ever . . .'

Jake Grafton waited until the flaps and slats were safely in, then he reached over and jerked the plug on Flap's mask.

Silence. Blessed silence.

Damn you, Tiny Dick Donovan. Damn you all to hell.

The night quickly enveloped them. The world ended at the canopy glass. Oh, the wing-tip lights gave a faint illumination, but Jake would have had to turn his head to see them on the tips of the swept wings, and he wasn't doing much head turning just now. Now he was flying instruments, making the TACAN needle go where it was supposed to, holding the rate-of-climb needle motionless, making the compass behave, keeping his wings level. All this required intense concentration. After five minutes of it he decided enough was enough and reached for the auto-pilot switch. It refused to engage.

Maybe the circuit breaker's popped. He felt the panel between him and the bombardier. Nope. All breakers in.

He punched the altitude-hold button three more times and swore softly to himself.

Okay, so I hand fly this monument to Marine maintenance, this miraculous Marine Corps flying pig.

He hit the holding fix, sixteen miles on the One Three Five radial, and did a teardrop entry. Established inbound he pulled the throttles back until he was showing only two thousand pounds of fuel flow per hour on each engine. This fuel flow would soon give him 220 knots indicated, he knew from experience, the plane's maximum conserve airspeed. Would as soon as the speed bled off.

Hit the fix, start the clock, turn left. Go around and around with the tailhook up, because this first one is a touch-and-go, a practice bolter.

The second time he approached the fix the symbology on the VDI came alive and gave him heading commands from the plane's onboard computer. Flap. He glanced over. The BN had his head against the black hood that shielded the radar scope and was twiddling knobs. Sure enough, the mileage readout corresponded with the TACAN DME, or distance measuring equipment.

'You plugged in?' Jake asked.

'Yep.'

'Thanks for the help.'

'No sweat.'

'Autopilot's packed it in.'

'I noticed.'

Just like an old married couple, here in the intimacy of a night cockpit. There are worse places, Jake thought, than this world of dials and gauges and glowing little red lights. Worse places . . .

At exactly seventeen minutes after the hour he hit the fix for the third time, popped the speed brakes and lowered the nose. This was the pushover. The A-7 that had been holding at five thousand feet was inbound in front of them a minute earlier.

Jake keyed the mike: 'Five One One is inbound at One Seven, state Seven Point Six.'

'Roger, War Ace Five One One. Continue.'

At five thousand feet Jake shallowed his descent as Flap called on the radio: 'Five One One, Platform.'

'Roger, Five One One. Switch button One Seven.'

Flap changed the radio frequency. Jake watched the TACAN needle carefully and made heading corrections as necessary to stay on the final bearing inbound. Soon he was level at 1,200 feet, inbound. At ten miles he dropped the gear and flaps. This slowed the plane still more. He checked the gear and flap indications and soon was stabilized at 120 knots. Flap read the landing checklist and Jake rogered each item.

Seventy-five hundred pounds of fuel. He toggled the main dump and let a thousand pounds bleed overboard into the atmosphere. If this worked out, he should cross the ramp with exactly six thousand pounds remaining, the maximum fuel load for an arrested landing.

Jake adjusted the rheostat on the angle-of-attack indexer, a small arrangement of lights on the left canopy bow in front of him. These lights indicated his airspeed, now a smidgen fast. One hundred eighteen knots was the speed he wanted, so he eased off a touch of throttle, then eased it back on. The indexer came to an on-speed indication. He checked his airspeed indicator. Exactly 118. Okay.

There – way out there – the ship! It appeared in the dark universe as a small collection of white and red lights, not yet distinguishable as to shape. Oh, *now* he could see the outline of the landing area, and the red drop lights down the stern that gave him his lineup cues. The ball on the left side of the landing area that would give him his glide slope was not yet visible.

The final approach controller was talking: 'Five One One, approaching the glide slope, call your needles.'

The needles the controller was referring to were cross-hairs in a cockpit instrument that was driven by a computer aboard the ship. The computer contrasted the radar-derived position of the aircraft with the known location of the glide slope and centerline. It then sent a radio signal to a box in the aircraft, which positioned the needles to depict the glide slope and centerline. The system was called ACLS, automatic carrier landing system, and someday it would indeed be automatic. Right now it was just the needles. Jake had to fly the plane.

'Down and right.'

'Disregard. You're low and slightly left . . . Five One One, slightly below glide slope, lined up slightly left. Come a little right for lineup, on glide path . . . on glide path . . .'

At the on-glide path call Jake squeezed out the speed brakes and concentrated intently on his instruments. He had to set and hold a six-hundred-foot rate of descent, hold heading, hold airspeed, keep the wings level and this plane coming down just so delicately so.

'I've got a ball,' Flap told him at two miles.

The controller: 'Left of course. Come right.'

The pilot made the correction, then glanced ahead. Yes,

he could tell from the drop lights he was left. When he was properly lined up again he took out most of the correction. Still his nose was pointed slightly right of the landing area. This correction was necessary since the wind was not precisely down the angled deck, which was pointed ten degrees left of the ship's keel. Except for an occasional glance ahead, he stayed on the gauges.

'Five One One, three-quarter mile, call the ball.'

Now Jake glanced out the windshield. There's the meatball, centered between the green datum lights. Lineup looks good too. Jake keyed the mike and said, 'Five One One, Intruder ball, Six Point Oh.'

'Roger, ball. Looking good.' That was the LSO on the fantail, Skidmore.

The ball moved in relation to the green reference or datum lights that were arranged in a horizontal line. When the yellow 'meatball' in the center moved up, you were above glide path. When it appeared below the reference line, you were low. If you were too low, the ball turned red, blood red, a stark prophecy of your impending doom if you didn't immediately climb higher on the glide slope. The back end of the ship, the ramp, lurked in red ball country, waiting to smash a plane to bits.

Yet as critical as proper glide slope control was, lineup was even more so. The landing area was 115 feet wide, the wing span of the A-6, 52. The edges of the landing area were defined by foul lines, and aircraft were parked with their noses abutting the foul lines on *both* sides of the deck. Landing aircraft were literally sinking into a canyon between parked airplanes.

And Jake had to monitor his airspeed carefully. The angle-of-attack indexer helped enormously here, arranged as it was where he could see it as he flew the lineup and glide slope cues. Any deviation from an on-speed indication required his immediate attention because it would quickly affect his descent rate, thereby screwing up his control of the ball. Running out of airspeed at the ramp was a sin that had killed many a naval aviator.

Meatball, lineup, angle-of-attack – as he closed the ship Jake's eyes were in constant motion checking these three items. Nearing the ship he dropped the angle-of-attack from his scan and concentrated on keeping properly lined up, with a centered ball. As he crossed the ramp he zeroed in on the meatball, flying it to touchdown.

The wheels hit and the nose slammed down. Jake Grafton thumbed the speed brakes in as he smoothly and quickly shoved the throttles forward to the stops. The LSO was on the radio shouting, 'Bolter, bolter, bolter,' just in case he forgot to advance the throttles or to positively rotate to a flying attitude as he shot off the edge of the angled deck.

Jake didn't forget. The engines were at full song as the Intruder left the deck behind and leaped back into the blackness of the night. Jake eased the stick back until he had ten degrees nose up and checked for a positive rate of climb. Going up. Gear up. Accelerating through 185 knots, flaps and slats up.

Now to get those six traps.

The radar controller leveled him at 1,200 feet and turned him to the downwind heading, the reciprocal of the ship's course. He was stable at 220 knots. Jake reached for the hook handle and pulled it. Hook down.

The controller turned him so that he had an eight-mile groove, which was nice. As soon as the wings were level he dropped the gear and flaps. Once again he concentrated intently on airspeed and altitude control, nailing the final bearing on the TACAN, retrimming until the plane flew itself with only the tiniest of inputs to the stick to counter the natural swirls and currents of the air. This was precision flying, where any sloppiness could prove instantly fatal.

'Five One One, approaching glide slope . . . Five One

One, up and on glide slope . . . three-quarters of a mile, call the ball.'

'Five One One, Intruder ball, Five Point Six.'

Deep in the heart of the ship in Air Ops, a sailor wearing headphones wrote '5.6' in yellow grease pencil on the Plexiglas board in front of him and the time beside the notation that said 'Grafton, 511.' He wrote backward, so the letters and numbers read properly to the air officer, the air wing commander, and the other observers who were sitting silently on the other side of the board watching the television monitors and occasionally glancing at the board.

Just now the picture on the monitors was from a camera buried on the landing centerline of the flight deck, which pointed aft up the glide slope. As they watched the officers saw the lights of Jake's A-6 appear on the center of the screen, in the center of the crosshairs that indicated the proper glide slope and lineup. As the plane closed the ship the lights assumed more definition.

Up in the top of the carrier's island superstructure was Pri-Fly, the domain of the air boss. His little empire was pretty quiet just now since all the air traffic was being controlled via radar and radio from Air Ops, but two enlisted men behind the boss's chair were busy. One held a pair of binoculars focused up the glide slope. He saw the approaching Intruder, identified it, and chanted, 'Set Three Six Zero, A-6.' Regardless of a plane's fuel state, the arresting gear was always set at the maximum trap weight, in the case of the A-6, 36,000 pounds.

To his left, the other sailor made a note in his log and repeated into a sound-powered phone that hung from his chest, 'Set Three Six Zero, A-6.'

The air boss, a senior commander, sat in a raised easy chair surrounded by large bullet-proof glass windows. He could hear the radio transmissions and the litany of the sailors behind him, and noted subconsciously that they agreed with what his eyes, and the approach controller, were telling him, that there was an A-6 on the ball, an A-6 with a maximum trap weight of 36,000 pounds.

Under the after end of the flight deck in the arresting gear engine rooms, all four of them, sat sailors on the Pri-Fly sound-powered circuit. Each individually spun a wheel to mechanically set the metering orifice of his arresting gear engine to 36,000 pounds, then they sang out in turn, 'One set Three Six Zero A-6,' 'Two set Three Six Zero A-6,' and so on.

When the fourth and last engine operator had reported his engine set, the talker in Pri-Fly sang out, 'All engines set, Three Six Zero A-6,' and the air boss rogered.

On the fantail of the ship directly aft of the island, on the starboard side of the landing area in a catwalk on the edge of the deck, stood the sailor who retracted the arresting gear engines once they had been engaged. He too was on the Pri-Fly sound-powered circuit, and when the fourth engine reported set, he shouted to the arresting gear officer who stood above him on the deck, right on the starboard foul line, 'All engines set, Three Six Zero A-6.'

The gear officer looked up the glide slope. Yep, it was an A-6. He glanced forward up the deck. The landing area was clear. No aircraft protruded over the foul lines, there were no people in the landing area, so he squeezed a trigger switch on the pistol grip he held in his right hand.

This switch operated a stop-light affair arranged twenty feet or so aft of the landing signal officer's platform on the port side of the landing area. The LSO waving tonight, Hugh Skidmore, saw the red light go out and a green light appear.

'Clear deck,' he called, and the other LSOs on the platform echoed the call.

'Clear deck!'

This entire evolution had taken about fifteen seconds.

The ship was ready to recover the inbound A-6. Now if Jake Grafton could just fly his plane into that little sliver of sky that would give him a three wire

He was trying. He was working the stick and throttles, playing them delicately, when he slammed into the burble of air disturbed by the ship's island. The plane jolted and he jammed on some power, then as quickly pulled it off as he cut through the turbulence into the calm air over the ramp. On he came, aiming for that eighteen-inches-thick window where the third wire waited, coming in at 118 knots in an eighteen-ton plane, the hook dangling down behind the main gear, coming in . . .

Hugh Skidmore strode about five feet into the landing area, inboard of the LSO's platform. Against his ear he held a telephonelike radio headset connected with the ship's radios by a long cord. Forward of the LSO's platform was a television monitor, the PLAT – pilot landing assistance television – which he checked occasionally to ensure the plane in the groove was properly lined up. He could hear the approach controller and he could hear and talk to Jake Grafton. Yet there was nothing to say. The A-6 was coming in like it was riding rails.

Then it was there, crossing the ramp.

Jake still had a steady centered yellow ball as the wheels smashed home. The ball shot off the top of the lens as he slammed the throttles to the stops and the hook caught, seemingly all at the same time. The deceleration threw the pilot and bombardier forward into their harnesses.

The A-6 Intruder was jerked to a halt in a mere two hundred and sixty feet.

It hung quivering on the end of the arresting gear wire, then Jake got the engines back to idle and the rebound of the wire pulled the plane backward.

The gear runner was already twenty feet out into the landing area signaling the pilot with his wands: hook up. When he saw the aircraft's tailhook being retracted, the runner waved one of his wands in a huge circle, the signal to the arresting gear operator in the fantail catwalk to retract the engine.

Obediently the operator selected the lever for number-three engine and pulled it down. Since the lever was connected by a wire over three hundred feet long to a hydraulic actuating valve on the engine, this pull took some muscle. When he had the yard-long lever well away from the bulkhead, the sailor leaped on it with his feet and used the entire weight of his body to force the lever down to a ninety-degree angle.

By now the A-6 that had just landed was folding its wings as it taxied out of the landing area. By the time the tail crossed the foul line, the third engine operator said 'battery,' and the retract man got off the lever and let it come back to its rest position. As he did he heard the Pri-Fly talker sing out, 'Set Two Seven Zero A-7.'

On the LSO platform Hugh Skidmore leaned over to his writer, tonight the Real McCoy. 'Give him an OK three. Little lined up left at the start.'

McCoy scribbled the notation in his pocket logbook like this: 511 OK3 (LLATS).

Then both men turned their full attention to the A-7 in the groove as they waited for the clear-deck light to illuminate.

The second cat shot, into a sky as black as the ace of spades, went well. Jake leveled at 1,200 feet and turned downwind, as directed by the controller. He held 250 knots until the controller told him to dirty up, which he did at the same time he told Jake to turn base. So Grafton was turning as he changed configuration – slowing, retrimming and trying to maintain a precise altitude, all at the same time. He lost a hundred feet, a fact that Flap instantly commented upon.

Jake said nothing, merely kept flying his plane. *This is the big leagues. Gotta do it all here and do it well. Flap has a right to comment.*

A short, tight pattern left him still searching for a good steady start when he hit the glide slope. The secret to a good pass is a good start, and Jake didn't have it. He wasn't carrying enough power and that caused a settle. By the time he was back up to a centered ball he was fast, which he was working off when he hit the burble. He added power. Not quite enough. The ball was a tad low when the wheels hit the deck.

'A fair two-wire,' he told Flap as they rolled out.

Aviation Boatswain's Mate (Equipment) Third Class Johnny Arbogast enjoyed his work. He operated the number-three arresting gear engine, the one that got the most traps and therefore required the most maintenance. Still, Johnny Arbogast loved that engine.

During a slow, rainy day in port this past spring, the gear chief had worked out how much energy an engine absorbed while trapping an F-4 Phantom. The figure was nine million foot-pounds, as Johnny recalled. Nine million of anything is a lot, but *man!* Those planes make this engine sing.

Any way you cut it, an arresting gear engine was one hell of a fine piece of machinery. And Johnny Arbogast was the guy who ran *Columbia*'s number three, which was pretty darn good, he thought, for a plumber's kid from Cotulla, Texas, who had had to struggle for everything he ever got.

The engine consisted of a giant hydraulic piston inside a steel cylinder about thirty inches in diameter that was arranged parallel with the ship's beam. Almost fifty feet in length, the cylinder containing the piston sat inside a large steel frame. Around the piston were reeved two twelve-hundred-foot strands of arresting gear cable, one-and-five-eighths-inch-thick wire rope made of woven steel threads. These two cables ran repeatedly around sheaves at the head and foot of the main piston and squeezed it as the aircraft pulled out the flight deck pennant above Johnny's head. It was the metering of the fluid squeezed by the piston from the cylinder – pure ethylene glycol, or anti-freeze – through an adjustable orifice that controlled the rate at which the aircraft was arrested. Johnny set the size of this orifice for each arrestment as ordered by the talker in Pri-Fly.

To maintain proper tension on the engine cable as the aircraft on the flight deck was pulling it out, two anchor dampeners that held the bitter ends of each cable stroked simultaneously. These fifty-foot-long pistons inside cylinders about twelve inches in diameter pulled slack cable off the back, or idle, side of the engine, thereby keeping the wire taut throughout the system.

When he first reported aboard *Columbia*, the arresting gear chief had impressed Johnny with a story about an anchor dampener that sheared its restraining nut during an arrestment. The suddenly free dampener, as big as a tele-phone pole, was forcibly whipped through the aluminum bulkhead of the engine room into the 0-3-level passageway, where it cut a sailor on his way to chow sloppily in half. The running cable whipped the dampener like a scythe. It sliced through a dozen officers' stateroom bulkheads as if they were so much tissue paper. When the dampener had accomplished a 180-degree turn, it reentered the engine room and skewered the engine like a mighty spear, explod-ing sheaves and showering the room, and the operator, with sharp, molten-hot metal fragments. All this took place in about a second and a half. Fortunately the plane on the flight deck was successfully arrested before the now-unanchored cable could run completely off the engine, but the engine room was a shambles and the operator went to the hospital with critical injuries.

As a result of this little story, Johnny Arbogast developed a habit of running his eyes over the anchor dampeners after each arrestment. Tonight, after setting the engine to receive an A-6, he saw something that he had never before seen. As the anchor dampeners stroked back into battery after the last engagement, the steel cable on one of them had kinked about six inches out from the connecting socket that held the bitter end of the cable to the dampener piston.

A kink, like a kink in a garden hose.

Johnny Arbogast stared, not quite sure his eyes could be believed.

Yep, a kink.

If this engine takes a hit, that cable could *break*, right there at the kink!

Johnny fumbled with the mouthpiece of the sound-powered phone unit hanging on his chest. He pushed the talk button and blurted, 'Three's foul. Three's not ready.'

'*What?*' This from the deck-edge operator, who had already told the arresting gear officer that all the engines were set. And he had delivered this message over a half minute ago, maybe even a minute.

'*Three's not ready,*' Johnny Arbogast howled into his mouthpiece. '*Foul deck!*'

And then Johnny did what any sensible man would have done: he tore off the sound-powered headset and ran for his life.

Up on the fantail catwalk the deck-edge operator shouted at the arresting gear officer, 'Three's not ready.'

The gear officer was still standing on the starboard foul line on the flight deck and he didn't hear what the operator said. He eyed the A-6 in the groove and bent toward the sailor, who was also looking over his shoulder at the approaching plane, now almost at the ramp.

'Foul deck,' the sailor roared above the swelling whine of the engines of the approaching plane.

The gear officer's reaction was automatic. He released the trigger on the pistol grip he held in his hand and shouted, 'What the hell is wrong?'

Across the landing area on the LSO's platform the green 'ready deck' light went out and the red 'foul deck' light came on.

Hugh Skidmore was looking intently at the A-6 Intruder almost at the ramp when he saw the red light on the edge of his peripheral vision. He was faced with an instant decision. He had no way of knowing why the deck was foul – he only knew that it was. A plane may have rolled into the landing area, a man may have wandered into the unsafe zone . . . any one of a hundred things could have gone wrong and all one hundred were bad.

So Hugh Skidmore squeezed the red button on the pistol grip he held in his hand, triggering a bank of flashing red lights mounted above the meatball. At the same time he roared into his radio-telephone, 'Wave-off, wave-off.'

The flashing wave-off lights and the radio message imprinted themselves on Jake Grafton's brain at the same time. His reaction was automatic. The throttles went full forward as he thumbed in the speed brakes and the control stick came aft.

Unfortunately jet engines do not provide instantaneous power as piston engines do: the revs can build only as fast as the burners can handle the increasing fuel flow, which is metered through a fuel control unit to prevent flooding the engine and flaming it out. The power builds with revs. Tonight the back stick and the gradually increasing engine power flattened the A-6's descent, then stopped it . . . four feet above the deck.

The howling warplane crossed the third wire with its nose well up, boards in, engines winding to full screech, but with its tailhook dangling.

From his vantage point near the fantail the arresting gear officer watched in horror as the tailhook kissed the top of the third wire, then snagged the fourth. The plane continued forward for a heartbeat, then seemed to stop in midair.

It was a lopsided contest. An 18-ton airplane was trying to pull a 95,000-ton ship. The ship won. The airplane fell straight down.

As he took the wave-off, Jake Grafton instinctively knew that it had come too late. The ship was *right there*, filling the windscreen. He kept the angle-of-attack on the optimum indication – a centered doughnut – by feeding in back stick while he tried to bend the throttles over the stops.

Somehow he found the ICS switch with his left thumb and shouted to Flap, 'Hook up!' but the aircraft was already decelerating. The angle-of-attack indexer showed slow and his eye flicked to the AOA gauge on the panel, just in time to see the needle sweep counterclockwise to the peg as the G threw him forward into his harness straps.

Then they fell the four feet to the deck.

The impact snapped his head forward viciously and slammed him downward into the seat, stunning him.

He got his head up and tried to focus his eyes as cold fear enveloped him. Are we stopped? Or going off the angled deck? Dazed, scared clear through and unable to see his instruments, he instinctively placed the stick in the eight-degree-nose-up position and kept the engines at full power.

The air boss exploded over the radio: 'Jesus Christ, Paddles, why'd you wave him off in close?'

On the LSO platform Hugh Skidmore was having trouble finding the transmit button on his radio. He fumbled for it as he stared forward at the A-6 straining futilely against the fourth wire with its engines still at full power. Miraculously the airplane seemed to be all in one piece. Here a hundred yards behind those two jet exhausts without the protection of a sound-suppression helmet the noise was awesome, a thunder that numbed the ears and vibrated the soul.

Unwilling to wait for Skidmore's response, the air boss now roared over the radio at Jake Grafton : 'We got you, son. Kill those engines! You aren't going anywhere now.'

Long seconds ticked by before the pilot complied. When he did, finally, the air boss remembered Skidmore:

'*El Ss Oh*, if you ever, *ever*, wave off another airplane in close on this fucking boat I will personally come down there and throw your silly ass into the goddamn wake. Do you read me, you mindless bastard?'

Skidmore found his voice. 'The deck went foul, Boss.'

'We'll cut up the corpse later. Wave off the guy in the groove so we can get this squashed A-6 out of the gear and clean the shit out of the cockpit.'

The plane in the groove was still a half mile out, but Skidmore obediently triggered the wave-off lights. As he did so he heard the engines of the A-6 in the gear die as the pilot secured the fuel flow.

Already the arresting gear officer had his troops on deck stripping the pennant from number-three engine. The rest of the recovery would be accomplished with only three engines on line.

Skidmore turned to the Real McCoy. 'I guess I screwed the pooch on that one.'

McCoy was still looking at the A-6 up forward. The yellow shirts were hooking a tow tractor to the nose wheel. He turned his gaze on Skidmore, who was looking into his face.

He had to say something. 'Looks like the boss is safety-wired to the pissed-off position.'

Skidmore nodded toward the stern. 'I thought he could make it. I didn't think he was *that* close.'

'Well . . .'

'Oh, hell.'

Jake Grafton stood rubbing his neck in Flight Deck Control, the room in the base of the carrier's island superstructure where the aircraft handler directs the movement of every plane on the ship. Flap Le Beau stood beside him. Someone was talking to the handler on the squawk box, apparently someone in Air Ops. The handler listened awhile, then leaned toward Jake and said, 'You need two more traps. The in-flight engagement was your fourth.'

'Yeah.'

'If you're feeling up to it, we'll give you another plane and send you out for your last two. Or you can wait until we get to Hawaii and we'll do the whole night bit again. It's up to you. How do you feel?'

Jake used a sleeve to swab the sweat from his forehead and eyes. 'What about tomorrow night?' he asked.

'The captain won't hold the ship in here against this coast just to qual one pilot. We have to transit to Hawaii.'

Jake nodded. That made sense. He flexed his shoulders and pivoted his head slowly.

The fear was gone. Okay, panic. But it was gone. He was still feeling the adrenaline aftershock, which was normal.

'I'm okay,' he told the handler, who turned to relay the message into the squawk box.

Flap pulled at Jake's sleeve. 'You don't have to do this tonight. There's no war on. It doesn't matter a whit whether you get qualled tonight or a week from now in Hawaii.'

Jake stared. The flippant, kiss-my-ass cool dude he had flown with all day was gone. The man there now was serious and in total control, with sharp, intelligent eyes. This must be the Flap Le Beau that was the legend.

'I can hack it. Are you okay?'

'I am if you are.'

'I am.'

'I gave you a load of shit today just to see if you could handle a little pressure. You can. You don't have anything to prove to anybody.'

82

Jake shook his head from side to side. 'I have to go now so the next time I'll know I can.'

A trace of a smile crossed Le Beau's face. He nodded, just the tiniest dip of the head, and turned toward the handler.

'What plane do they want us to aviate, Handler-man? Ask the grunts in Ready Four and have them send up the book.'

'Please, *sir!*'

'Of course, *sir.* Did I leave the please out? What's come over me? I must still be all shook up. You know, we came within two inches of being chocolate and vanilla pudding out there. If we'd fell another two inches you'd be cleaning us up with spoons. I'm gonna write a thank-you letter to Jesus. Praise *God*, that was a religious experience, Amen! I feel born again, Amen! The narrowness of our escape and my ecstasy must have made me the eensiest bit careless in my military manners. I apologize. You understand, don't you, sir?'

'Ecstasy! What crap! Go sit over there in that corner with your Amens and keep your mouth shut until your fellow jarheads get the maintenance book up here for your pilot to read. He can read, can't he?'

'Oh yes, sir. He's Navy, not Marine. He's got a good, solid, second-grade education. His mamma told me he did just fine in school until . . .'

Jake Grafton decided he was thirsty and needed to take a leak. He wandered away to attend to both problems.

He was slurping water from a fountain in the passageway outside the hatch to Flight Deck Control when he realized that Lieutenant Colonel Haldane was standing beside him. Haldane was wearing his uniform tonight, not his flight suit. His I-been-there decorations under his gold aviator wings made an impressive splotch of color on his left breast.

'What happened?' he asked Jake.

'They gave me a late wave-off, sir. I was almost at the ramp, or at it. Somebody said something about the deck going foul. Whatever, at the time all I knew was that the red lights were flashing and the LSO was shouting. So I did my thing. I was just too close.'

Haldane was watching his eyes as he spoke. When he finished speaking the colonel gave him another five seconds of intense scrutiny before he asked, 'Did you do everything right?'

Jake Grafton swallowed hard. This just wasn't his day. 'No, sir. I didn't. I knew we had passed the wave-off point, so I was concentrating on the ball and lineup. When the wave-off lights came on, I guess I was sorta stunned there for a tenth of a second. Then I reacted automatically – nose up, boards in, full power. I should have given her the gun and got the boards in, but I should have just held the nose attitude. Should have rode it into a bolter.'

Haldane's head bobbed a millimeter. 'Are you up to two more?' he asked.

'I think so, sir.'

'If you don't want to go I'll back you up. No questions asked.'

'I'd like to go now, sir, if we can get a bird.'

'How many carrier landings do you have?'

'Before today, sir, three hundred twenty-four.'

'How many at night?'

'One hundred twenty-seven, I believe.'

Haldane nodded. 'Whenever I have a close call,' he said, 'the first thing to go afterward is my instrument scan. I get way behind the plane, fixate on just one instrument. Really have to work to keep the eyeballs moving.'

'Yessir,' Jake said, and grinned. He liked the way Haldane used himself as an example. That was class. 'I'll keep it safe, Skipper,' Jake added.

'Fine,' said the colonel, and went into Flight Deck Control to see the handler.

'A thank-you letter to Jesus, huh?'

'That was the best I could do on the spur of the moment. Don't hold it against me.'

'Amen to that.' Jake sighed and tried to relax. They were sitting behind the jet-blast deflector for Cat One, waiting for the A-7 ahead to do his thing. Jake tugged at the VDI reflexively and wriggled to get his butt set in the seat.

He was still feeling the aftereffects of adrenaline shock, but he knew it, so he forced himself to look at everything carefully. Wings locked, flaps and slats out, stabilator shifted, roger the weight board, ease forward into the shuttle, throttles up and off brakes, cat grip up, wipe out the controls, check fuel flow, RPM, EGT . . . Lights on and bam! they were hurling down the catapult into the blackness.

Off the pointy end, nose up, gear up, climbing . . .

It went well until he got onto the ball, then he couldn't get stabilized. Too nervous. Every correction was too big, every countercorrection overdone. The plane wobbled up and down on the glide slope and went from fast to slow to fast again. He was waggling the wings trying to get properly lined up as he went across the ramp and that, coupled with not quite enough power, got him a settle into the two-wire.

The last one was more of the same. At this point Jake realized he was totally exhausted.

'Settle down,' Flap told him in the groove.

'I'm trying. Let's just get this fun over with, okay?' Crossing the ramp he lowered the nose and eased the power a smidgen to ensure he wouldn't bolter. He didn't. One wire.

He had to pry himself from the cockpit. He was so tired he had trouble plodding across the deck.

'Another day, another dollar,' Flap said cheerfully.

'Something like that,' Jake mumbled, but so quietly Flap didn't hear it. No matter.

'It was a late wave-off, and I'm sorry,' Hugh Skidmore told Jake in the ready room. The LSOs were waiting for Jake when he came in. The television monitor mounted high in the corner of the room was running the PLAT tape of the in-flight engagement, over and over and over. Colonel Haldane was there, but he stood silently without saying anything. Jake and the LSOs watched the PLAT tape twice.

'You owe me, Skidmore.'

'Other than that little debacle, your first one – the touch-and-go – was okay, the first trap okay, the second fair, the third okay. The fifth trap was a fair and the last one a no-grade. I almost waved you off. I don't want to see any more of that deck spotting—' After a glance at the skipper Skidmore ran out of words. He contented himself with adding, 'I think you were a little wrung out on the last one.'

Jake nodded. He had sinned there at the end and wasn't too proud to admit it. 'I spotted the deck on the last one. Sorry!' He tried to shrug but didn't have the energy. 'What about the in-flight?'

'Gave you a fair.'

'Fair? Now wait just a minute—' Jake knew the futility of arguing with the umpire, but that pass had cost him too much. 'I had a good pass going until everything went to hell.'

'Not all that good. You were carrying a little too much power in the middle and went fast. You made the correction but you overdid it. Approaching the ramp you were slow and settling into a two-wire when I waved you off.'

'How do you figure that?'

The Real McCoy spoke up. 'Jake, if you had been right on a centered ball when the wave-off came, you would have missed all the wires on the wave-off. Smacking on a big wad of power should have just carried you across the wires into a bolter. Hugh's right. You were a half ball low going lower when you gunned it. That pass would have been a fair two-wire. Look at that PLAT tape again. Carefully.'

Jake surrendered. 'I bow to the opinion of the experts.'

'Next time keep the ball centered, huh?'

Flap Le Beau spoke up. 'There had better not be a next time. If there is, you two asshole mechanics better swim for it before I get out of the plane.' He was apparently oblivious of the presence of Richard Haldane.

Jake glanced at the colonel to see how he was taking all this. Apparently without a flicker of emotion.

'No, I'm serious,' Skidmore said. 'If you ever get a wave-off in close like that, Jake, slam the throttles up and run the boards in, but don't rotate. Just ride her into a bolter.'

'But don't go into the water waiting for the wheels to hit,' the Real added.

Now Richard Haldane spoke. 'May I have a word with you gentlemen?'

Skidmore and McCoy went over to where the colonel was standing. Flap asked Jake, 'How are you supposed to know that it's an in-close wave-off if the LSOs can't figure it out?'

'The guy with the stick in his hand is always responsible,' Jake told the bombardier. 'He's the dummy who signed for the plane.'

After Jake and Flap debriefed both the planes they had flown that evening, Jake asked Flap if he wanted a drink.

'Yeah. You got any?'

'A little. In my stateroom. One drink and I'm into my rack. See you in a bit.'

Ten minutes later Flap asked, 'So Skidmore should not have waved us off, even though the cable might have parted on number three if we had caught it?'

'Yeah. That's right. The in-close position is defined as the point where a wave-off cannot be safely made. From that point on, in to touchdown, you are committed, like the pig. The LSO has to take you aboard no matter what. It's a practical application of the lesser of two evils theory.'

'Like the pig?'

'Yeah. A chicken lays eggs, she's dedicated. A pig gives his life, he's committed.'

'Where you from, anyway?'

'Virginia. Rural Virginia, down in the southwest corner. And you?'

'Brooklyn.'

'All that crap you gave me this morning about Louisiana and you're from Brooklyn?'

'Yep. Born in the ghetto to a woman who didn't know who my daddy was and raised on the streets. That's me.'

'So how did you get into the Corps?'

Flap Le Beau finished off his straight whiskey and grinned. He held up the glass. 'Got any more?'

'Help yourself.'

When he finished pouring, Flap said, 'Did you ever hear of a guy named Horowitz who funded scholarships for ghetto children?'

'No. Don't think so.'

'Well, it's sorta the in-thing for a millionaire to do these days. Publicly commit yourself to funding a college education for ten ghetto kids, or fifty, a hundred if you have the bucks. Sol Horowitz was the first. He promised to pay for the college education of a hundred first-graders in a public school in Brooklyn if they graduated from high school. I was one of the hundred. It's sort of amazing, but I actually got through high school. Then I got caught stealing some cars and the probation officer told the judge I had this college scholarship waiting, if I would only go. So the judge sentenced me to college. I kid you not.'

Flap sipped, remembering. Finally he continued. 'I screwed around at the university. Drank and came real close to flunking out, or getting thrown out. Miracle number two, I graduated. So somebody arranged for me to meet Horowitz. I don't know exactly what I expected. Some wizened old Jew with money sticking out of every pocket sitting in a mansion – I don't know. Well, Solomon Horowitz was none of that. He lived in a walk-up flat off Flatbush, a real dump. He looked me up and down and told me I was nothing.

' "You have learned nothing," he said. "You barely passed your courses – I hear you continued to steal cars. Oh yes, I have my sources. They tell me. I know." What could I say?

'Horowitz asked, "Who do you think gave you a chance to make something of yourself? Some oil baron? Some rich Jew asshole whose daddy left him ten million? I will tell you who."

'He rolled up his sleeve. He had a number tattooed on the inside of his wrist. He had been in Dachau. And you know something else? When he made the promise to send those kids to college, *he didn't have any money*. He made the promise because then he would have to work like hell to earn the money.'

'Why?' Jake asked.

'That was my question. I'll level with you, Jake. I was twenty-two years old and I'd never met anybody in my life who wasn't in it for himself. So I asked.

'Horowitz thought about it for a little bit and finally said he guessed I was entitled to know. The Nazis castrated him. He could never have any children. When he got out of Dachau after the war weighing ninety-one pounds, he came to America. He wanted his life to make a difference to somebody, he said, so he promised to send a hundred kids to college, blacks and Puerto Ricans who would never have a chance otherwise. He worked three jobs, seven days a week, saved his money, invested every dime. And he did it. Actually sent thirty-two, who were all of the hundred that finished high school and could read and write well enough to get into a college. Thirty-two. He paid board, room, books and tuition and sent a little allowance every month. Twenty-three of us graduated.'

Flap tossed off the last of the liquor and set the glass in the small metal sink jutting out from the wall.

'I thought long and hard about the interview. I decided I wanted my life to make a difference, to make Horowitz's life make a difference . . . you see what I mean. But I'm not Solomon Horowitz. All I knew how to do was drink, screw, do burglaries and fight. I wasn't so good at stealing cars – I got caught a lot. So I picked the fightin'est outfit of them all and joined up.

'They wouldn't send me to officer candidate school because of my record. I enlisted anyway. I was full of Horowitz's fire. I went to boot camp and finished first in my class, went to mortar school and came out first, so they made me an instructor. Got to be a pretty fair hand with a mortar and a rifle and led PT classes in my spare time. Finally they decided I might make a Marine after all, so they sent me to OCS.'

'How did you do there?' Jake asked, even though he thought he knew the answer.

'Number one,' Le Beau said flatly, without inflection. 'They gave me a presentation sword.'

'Going to stay in?'

'There's nothing for me in Brooklyn. My mother died of a drug overdose years ago. I've been in ten years now and I'm staying until they kick me out. The Corps is my home.'

'Don't you get tired of it sometimes?'

'Sometimes. Then I remember Horowitz and I'm not tired anymore. I've got his picture. Want to see it?' The Marine dug out his wallet.

Jake looked. Flap towered over Horowitz – a younger Flap togged out in the white dress uniform of a Marine officer. The old, old man had wispy white hair and stooped shoulders. His head was turned and he was looking up into the beaming face of the handsome black man. They were smiling at each other.

'Horowitz came to Parris Island for the graduation ceremony,' Flap explained. 'They gave me the sword and I walked over to where he was sitting and gave it to him.'

'He still alive?'

'On no. He died six months after this picture was taken. This is the only one of him I have.'

After Flap left, Jake slowly unlaced his flight boots and pulled them off. It took the last of his energy.

If the whole cruise goes like this day has, I'm not going to make it. Russian frigates, in-flight engagements . . . Jesus!

He eyed his bunk, the top one, and worked himself up to an effort. He didn't even pull off his flight suit. Sixty seconds after his head hit the pillow he was asleep.

CHAPTER SIX

The ships sailed across a restless, empty ocean. Jake saw no ships other than those of the task group whenever he went on deck, which he managed to do three or four times a day. Many sailors never went topside; they spent every minute of their day in their working spaces, their berthing areas, or on the mess deck, and saw sunlight only when the ship pulled into port. Jake Grafton thought he would go stir-crazy if he couldn't see the sea and sky and feel the wind on his face every few hours.

He would stroll around the deck, visit with Bosun Muldowski if he ran into him, chat with the catapult crews if they were on deck, and examine planes. His eyes seemed naturally drawn to airplanes. His destination on these excursions was usually the forward end of the flight deck, where he would stand between the catapults looking at the ocean. The wind was usually vigorous here. It played with his hair and tugged at his clothes and cleaned the below-decks smells from his nostrils.

The first morning he saw a school of whales to starboard. Knots of sailors gawked and pointed. The whales spouted occasionally and once one came soaring out of the water, then crashed down in a magnificent cloud of spray. Mostly the view was of black backs glistening amid the swells.

When he went below this first morning at sea, reentered the world of crowded passageways, tiny offices, and never-ending paperwork, the squadron maintenance officer cornered him. 'That plane you flew last night – well, we haven't found any airframe damage yet. Maybe we dodged the bullet.' If there was no damage there would be no official report assessing blame. 'The avionics took a helluva lot bigger lick than they're designed for, though. Radar and computer and VDI are screwed up.'

Jake threw himself into the problem assigned to him by Colonel Haldane. How would you attack a Soviet ship? Since the Soviets had all kinds of ships, he soon focused on the most capable, the guided missile cruisers that were the mainstay of their task forces, Kyndas and Krestas. After preliminary research of classified material in the Air Intelligence spaces, he paid a visit to the EA-6B Prowler squadron in their small ready room on the 0-3 level, near the number-four arresting gear room.

This squadron had only four aircraft, but they were Cadillacs. A stretched version of the A-6, the Prowler held a crew of four: one pilot and three electronic warfare specialists. The airplane's sole mission was to foil enemy radars. The electronic devices it used for this task were mounted in pods slung on the weapons stations. Other than the pilot's instruments, the panels of the cockpit were devoted to the displays and controls necessary to detect enemy radar transmissions and render the information they gave the enemy useless. Since it was a highly modified version of the A-6, the plane was popularly referred to as a Queer Six.

The Prowler crews in Ready Eight greeted Jake with open arms. They too were stationed on Whidbey Island when ashore, and two or three of the officers knew Jake. When he finally got around to explaining his errand, they were delighted to help. The capabilities of Soviet warships were their stock in trade.

Jake had already known that Soviet ships were heavily armed, but now he found out just how formidable they really were. Radar capabilities were evaluated, weapons envelopes examined. Finally Jake Grafton gave his conclusion:

'A single plane doesn't have much of a chance against one of these ships.' This comment drew sober nods from the two electronic warfare experts at his elbows.

Nor, he soon concluded, did a flight of planes have much of a chance if the weapons they had to use were free-falling bombs, technology left over from World War II. Oh, free-falling bombs had been adequate in Vietnam when attacking stationary targets ashore – barely adequate – but modern warships were another matter entirely. Ships would detect the aircraft on radar while they were still minutes away. Radar would allow antiaircraft missiles to be fired and guided long before the attacker reached the immediate vicinity of the ship. Then, in-close, radar-directed guns would pour forth a river of high explosives.

If our lucky attack pilot survived all that, he was ready to aim his free-fall weapons at a maneuvering, high-speed target. Even if he aimed his bombs perfectly, the bombs were unguided during their eight to ten seconds of fall, so if the ship's captain reversed the helm or tightened a turn, or if the pilot had miscalculated the wind, the bombs would miss.

And now our frustrated aerial warrior had to turn his fanny to the fire and successfully avoid on the way out all the hazards he had penetrated on the way in.

What the attack pilot desperately needed was a missile he could shoot at the ship, Jake concluded, the farther away the better. Alas, the US Navy's antiship missiles were still in the development stage, victims of Vietnam penny pinching, so the attack crews would have to make do with what they had. What they had were some short-range guided missiles like Bullpup, which unfortunately carried only a 250-pound warhead – enough to cripple a warship but not to sink it.

If the weather was good enough, the attacking planes could use laser-guided bombs, preferably two-thousand pounders. Although these weapons were unpowered, the laser seeker and guidance assembly on the nose of the weapon could steer it into the target if the attack pilot made a reasonably accurate delivery, and if the spot of laser light that the guidance system was seeking was indeed on the target. The weak point of the system was the beam of laser light, which was scattered by visible moisture in the air. Alas, over the ocean the sky was often cloudy.

With or without laser-guided bombs, the attackers were going to have to penetrate the enemy ship's radar-directed defenses. Here was where the EA-6B came in. The electronic warfare (EW) plane could shield the attack force electronically if it were in the middle of it or placed at the proper angle to the attack axis.

What about overloading the enemy's defenses with planes? Perhaps a coordinated attack with as many planes as we can launch, saturating the enemy's defenses with targets, one prays too many targets. Some would inevitably get through.

And our coordinated attack should come in high and low at the same time. Say A-6s at a hundred feet and A-7s and F-4s diving in from thirty thousand.

Jake made notes. The EA-6 crews had a lot of ideas, most of which Jake thought excellent. When he said his good-bye two hours after he came, he shook hands all around.

Back in his stateroom staring at his notes, Jake wondered what a war with the Soviets would be like. An exchange of intercontinental ballistic missiles would make for a loud, almighty short war, but Jake didn't think there would be much reason for the surviving warships to try to sink one another. Without countries to go back to, the sailors and the ships were all doomed anyway. Could there be a war without nuclear weapons, in 1973?

Really, when one is contemplating the end of civilization the whole problem becomes fantastic, something out of a sweaty nightmare. Could sane men push the button, thereby destroying themselves, their nations, most of the human race? He got bogged down at this point. The politicians would have to figure it out.

One thing he knew for sure – if there was a war without a nuclear Armageddon, the American admirals would go for the Soviet ships like bulldogs after raw meat.

It wouldn't be easy. He knew well that a strike on a single ship would be a fluke, an ambush of a straggler. Like every other navy, the Soviets would arrange their ships in groups for mutual support. Any attack would have to be against a task force.

Staring at his notes on detection ranges, missile and flak envelopes, Jake could envision how it would be. The ships would be rippling off missiles – the sky would be full of Mach 3 telephone poles. If that weren't enough, Soviet warships were covered with antiaircraft guns. American ships these days didn't have many, but then the Soviet Navy had no aircraft carriers to launch strikes against them. The flak from the Soviet ships would be fierce, would literally be a steel curtain the attacking planes would have to fly through.

An Alpha strike – everything the ship could launch, coming in high and low and in the middle, shielded by EA-6B Prowlers and coordinated as well as possible by an E-2 Hawkeye orbiting safely out of range a hundred miles away – that was the answer he would give Colonel Haldane.

Wouldn't ever happen, of course. America and Russia weren't about to fight a war. Planning an attack on a Soviet task force was just another peacetime military what-if exercise. Yet if it *did* happen, few of those planes would survive. And of those crews who successfully penetrated the cordon of missiles and flak, only the most fiercely determined would successfully drive the thrust home. For Jake Grafton knew that it was neither ships nor airplanes that won battles, but men.

Were there men like that aboard this ship? By reputation Flap Le Beau was one, but were there any more?

Disgusted with the whole problem, he began to think of home. He had visited his parents on their farm in southwestern Virginia this spring. In May, with the leaves on the trees coming out, the grass in the meadows growing green and tender, the cows nursing new-born calves.

His parents had been so glad to see him. Dad, well, his pride in his son had been visible, tangible. And Mother, smiling through her tears at her man-son come home.

He had helped his father with the cattle, once again felt the morning chill and smelled the aroma of warm bovine bodies, manure, sweet hay . . . Just the memory of it made him shiver here in his small stateroom aboard this giant steel ship. The dew in the grass that recorded every step, the sun slanting up over the low ridges and shining into the barn, his father's voice as he talked to the cattle, reassuring, steady . . . all of it came flooding back.

Why are you here, aboard this steel ship on this wilderness of ocean, worried about Russian flak and missiles, contemplating the ultimate obscenity? Why aren't you there, where you grew up, feeling the warmth of the sun on your back and helping your father in the timeless rituals that ensure life will go on, and on . . . as God intended? Why aren't you there to help your mother in her old age? Answer me that, Jake Grafton. You never hated the farm as your elder brother did – you loved it. Loved everything about it. Your parents – you love them. You are of them and they are of you. Why are you here?

Why?

Life aboard ship quickly assumed its natural rhythm, which was the rhythm dictated by two hundred years of naval tradition and regulations. Everyone worked, meals were served, the ship's laundry ran full blast, and every after-noon at precisely 13:30 the PA system came to life and announced a general quarters drill. 'This is a drill, this is a drill. General quarters, general quarters. All hands man your battle stations. Go up and forward on the starboard side and down and aft on the port side. General quarters.'

The aviators' battle stations were their ready rooms. While the damage control parties fought mock fires and coped with flooding, nuclear, chemical and biological attack, the aviators took NATOPS exams, listened to lectures, and generally bored one another. It was during these drills that Jake gave his lectures on shipboard operations. In addition to the material in the CV NATOPS, he added every tip he could recall from his two previous combat cruises. The lectures went well, he thought. The Marines were attentive and asked good questions. To his amazement, he found he actually enjoyed standing in front of the room and talking about his passion, flying.

After secure from general quarters the officers scattered to squadron spaces throughout the ship to do paperwork, to which there was no end in this life. The evening of the second day at sea Jake found an opportunity to discuss his Soviet ship project with the skipper, Colonel Haldane, who knew as much about the subject as Jake did. After they had spent an hour going over the problem, the colonel took him to the air wing spaces to meet the air wing ops officer, a lieutenant commander. Here the subject was aired again. The upshot of it was that Jake was assigned to help Wing Ops put together realistic exercises for the ship's air wing.

Officers could eat dinner in either of the two wardrooms aboard – the formal wardroom on the main deck, right beside Ready Four, where uniforms were required, or in the dirty-shirt wardroom up forward in the 0-3 level between the bow catapults where flight suits and flight deck jerseys were acceptable. In practice the formal wardroom was the turf of the ship's company officers who were not aviators, invaded only occasionally by aviation personnel on their best behavior. Here in the evening after dinner a movie was shown, one watched with proper decorum by congressionally certified gentlemen.

The aviators congregated in their ready rooms for their evening movies, here to whistle, shout, offer ribald suggestions to the characters, moan lustily at the female lead, and throw popcorn at the screen and each other. If a flyer didn't like the movie in his ready room, he could always wander off to another squadron's, where he would be welcome if he could find a seat.

And in the late evening somewhere in the junior officers' staterooms there was a card game under way, usually nickel-dime-quarter poker because no one had much money. Although alcohol was officially outlawed aboard ship, at a card game a thirsty fellow could usually find a drink. Or several. As long as one didn't appear in any of the ship's common spaces drunk or smelling of liquor, no one seemed to care very much.

Of course, a junior officer could skip the movie and card game and retire to his stateroom to listen to music or write letters. Since a lot of the junior officers were very much in love, a lot of them did this almost every night, Jake Grafton among them. Of course the lonely lovers had roommates, which sometimes presented problems.

'It's so damned unfair,' the Real McCoy lamented. 'I could get more information about the markets if I were sitting in a mud hut in some squalid village in the middle of India. Anywhere but here.' He turned his woeful gaze on his roommate. 'There are telephones everywhere on this planet except here. Everywhere.'

Jake Grafton tried to look sympathetic. He did reasonably well, he thought.

'It's the not knowing,' the LSO continued. 'I bought solid companies, with solid prospects, nothing speculative. But I am just completely *cut off*. Condemned to the outer darkness.' He gestured futilely. 'It's maddening.'

'Maybe you should put your investments in a trust or something. Give someone a power of attorney.'

'Who? Anyone who can do as well as I have in the market is doing it, not fooling around with someone else's portfolio for a fee.'

'We'll be in Hawaii in a week. I'll bet you'll find that you're doing great.'

The Real McCoy groaned and glanced at Jake Grafton with a look that told him he was hopeless. The LSO took a deep breath, then exhaled slowly. He looked so forlorn that Jake decided to try to get him talking.

A question. He should ask a question. After thinking about it for a moment, Jake said, 'Hey, what's the difference between stocks and shares? In the newspapers they talk about stockholders and shareholders and—'

He stopped because the Real gave him a withering look and stomped for the door. He slammed it shut behind him.

Dear Callie,

We are three days out of San Francisco on our way to Pearl Harbor. We are making about twenty knots. We tried to go faster but the escorts were taking a pounding in heavy swells, so we slowed down. The swells are being kicked up by a typhoon about fifteen hundred miles to the southwest. I got requalified on carrier landings, day and night, the first day out of port, but we haven't flown since.

My bombardier-navigator is a guy named Flap Le Beau. He's from Brooklyn and has been in the Marines for ten years. I'm still trying to figure him out. He appears to be a good BN and a fine officer. He wasn't too sure about me the first time we flew together and gave me a lot of gas to see if I could take it. What he didn't know is that I've learned to take gas from experts, so his little performance was just a minor irritation. I think he's a pretty neat guy, so I was lucky there. I think you'd like him too.

My roommate is a character, fellow called the Real McCoy. He is in a tizzy worrying about what is happening in the stock market while we are out of touch. He's made a lot of money in stocks and wants to make a lot more. If I knew anything about stocks I would too, but I don't. I couldn't make easy money if I owned the mint.

The skipper is a lieutenant colonel – same rank as a commander – named Richard Haldane. Don't know where he is from but he doesn't have an accent like I do. Neither does Flap, for that matter.

Jake didn't know he had an accent until Callie told him he did. She was a linguist, with a trained ear. Since she made that remark he was listening more carefully to how other people talked. Just now he said a few words to see if he could detect some flaw in his pronunciation. 'My name is Jake Grafton. I work for the government and am here to save you.'

Nope.

She wouldn't kid about a thing like that, would she?

Colonel Haldane has me giving lectures to the flight crews on flight operations around the ship. It's easy and sort of fun. It used to be that I didn't like standing in front of a crowd and saying anything, but now I don't mind it if I know the material I am going to talk about. I must have a little ham in me.

The colonel also has me doing some research on how to attack Soviet ships, just in case we ever have to. The research is difficult, especially when you realize that if the necessity ever arises, a lot of American lives are going to depend on how well you did your homework.

As I mentioned, the first day out of port I got requalified day and night. The day traps went okay, but the night ones were something else. On the fourth one I had an in-flight engagement, which means I caught a wire during a wave-off and the plane fell about four feet to the deck. The impact almost destroyed the airplane. It appears to have survived with only damage to the avionics, which is the electronic gear. Why a wheel didn't come off I'll never know.

Everyone says the in-flight wasn't my fault, but in a way it was. The LSO gave me a wave-off too late, and I shouldn't have rotated as much as I did when I poured the power to her. It's a technique thing. I did it by the book and got bitten, yet if I had deviated from approved wave-off procedure *in this particular case*, things would have probably worked out better.

All you can do is hope that when the challenge comes, you will do the right thing through instinct, training, or experience, or some combination of these. The one thing you know is that when the crunch comes you won't have time to think about how you should handle it. The hard, inescapable reality is that anyone who flies may die in an airplane.

I suppose I have accepted this reality on some level. Still, the in-flight shook me up pretty good. As the airplane decelerated, still in the air, we were thrown forward into the straps that hold us to the seat. At moments like that every perception is crystal clear, every thought arrives like a bell ringing. You are so totally alive that the events of seconds seem to happen so slowly that later you can recall every nuance. As I felt the plane decelerating, I knew what had happened.

In-flight!

I could feel her slowing, saw the needle of the angle-of-attack gauge swing toward a stall, saw the engine RPM still winding up . . . and knew that we were in for it. For an instant there we hung suspended above the deck. Then we fell.

The jolt of falling about four feet stunned me. I knew exactly what had happened, yet I didn't know whether or not we were safely arrested. I couldn't see too well. I didn't know if the hook had held, or if the cross-deck pennant had held together. Or if the airplane was in one piece – if the fuel tank had ruptured we were only seconds away from blowing up.

It was a bad scare.

I've had a few of those through the years and one more isn't headline stuff, but still, with the war over and all and me thinking about getting out, that moment was a hard, swift return to cold reality.

I have been thinking a lot about you these last few days. Our time together in Chicago was something very special. Although the visit didn't wind up quite the way I planned, everything else was super. Theron is a great guy and your folks seem like they would be very pleasant once I got to know them a little better.

He stopped and reread that last paragraph. That bit about the parents wasn't strictly true, but what could he say? *Your dad's a royal jerk but I like them like that.*

Diplomacy. This letter had some diplomacy in it.

When you stop and think about it, life is strange. Some people believe in preordination, although I don't. Still, you grow up knowing that somewhere out there is the person you are going to fall in love with. So you wonder what that person will be like, how she will look, how she will walk, talk, what she will think, how she will smile, how she will laugh. There's no way of knowing, of course, until you meet her. The realization that you have finally met her comes as a wondrous discovery, a peek into the works of life.

Maybe a guy could fall instantly in love, but I doubt it. I think love sort of creeps over you – like a warm feeling on a clear blue fall day. This person is in your thoughts most of the time – all the time, actually. You see her when you close your eyes, when you look off into the distance, when you pause from what you are doing and take a deep breath. You remember how her eyes looked when she laughed, how she threw her head back, how her fingers felt when they touched you . . .

The loved one becomes a part of you, the most valuable part.

At least it is that way with me when I think of you.

As ever,
Jake

CHAPTER SEVEN

Visual dive-bombing really hadn't changed much since the 1930s, even though the top speeds of the aircraft had tripled and their ordnance-carrying capacity had increased fifteenfold. The techniques were still the same.

Jake Grafton thought about that as the flight of four A-6s threaded their way upward through a layer of scattered cumulus clouds. The four warplanes, spread in a loose finger-four formation, passed the tops at about 8,000 feet and continued to climb into the clear, open sky above.

Perhaps it was the touch of the romantic that he tried with varying degrees of success to keep hidden, but the link to the past was strong within him. On a morning like this in June 1942, US Navy dive bomber pilots from *Enterprise* and *Yorktown* topped the clouds and searched across the blue Pacific for the Japanese carriers then engaged in hammering Midway Island. They found them, four aircraft carriers plowing the broad surface of that great ocean, pushed over and dove. Their bombs smashed *Kaga*, *Akagi* and *Soryu*, set them fatally ablaze and turned the tide of World War II.

This morning thirty-one years later this group of bombers was on its way to bomb Hawaii, actually a small island in the Hawaiian archipelago named Kahoolawe.

The oxygen from the mask tasted cool and rubbery. Jake eyed the cockpit altimeter, steady at ten thousand feet, and unsnapped the left side of his mask. He let it dangle from the fitting on the other side as he devoted most of his attention to holding good formation. His position today was number three, which meant that he flew on the skipper's, Colonel Haldane's, right side. Number four was on Jake's right, number two on Haldane's left.

He glanced at his BN, Flap Le Beau, who had his head pressed against the radar hood. He was using both hands to twiddle knobs and flip switches, but he never took his eyes from the radar. Excellent. He knew the location and function of every knob, button and switch without looking. When the going got tough there would be no time to look, no time to fumble for this or that, no time to think.

The colonel's BN, Allen Bartow, was similarly engaged. From his vantage point twenty feet out from the colonel's wingtip, Jake could see every move Bartow made in the cockpit, could see him pull his head aft a few inches and eye the computer readouts on the panel just to the right of the radar screen, could see him glance down occasionally, referring to the notes on his kneeboard.

He had gotten to know Bartow fairly well the last few days. A major with twelve years in the Corps, Bartow was addicted to French novels. He read them in French. Just now he was working his way through everything that Georges Simenon had ever written. He had books stacked everywhere in his stateroom and carried one in his flight suit, which he pulled out whenever he had a few minutes to kill.

'I'm retiring as soon as I get my twenty years in,' he told Jake. 'On that very day. Then I'm going to get a doctorate in French literature and spend the rest of my life teaching.'

'Sounds dull,' Jake said, grinning, just to needle him.

To his surprise Bartow had considered that remark seriously. 'Maybe. Academic life won't be like the Corps, like life in a squadron. Yet we all have to give this up sooner or later. I enjoy it now, but when it's over I have something else I'll enjoy just as much. Something different. So now I've got the flying and the guys and the anticipation of that something else. I'm a pretty rich man.' And he returned Jake's grin.

Bartow *was* rich, Jake reflected ruefully as he watched the bombardier sitting hunched over his scope. Richer than Jake, anyway. All Jake had was the flying and the camaraderie. He didn't even have Callie – he had screwed that up.

Le Beau – he apparently didn't want anything else. Or did he?

'You got a gal waiting for you?' Jake asked his bombardier without taking his eyes off the lead plane.

'You can fly this thing and think about women too?'

'I always have time to think about women. You got one stashed somewhere?'

'Dozens.'

'A special one?'

'Naw. The ones I want to get serious about don't want me after they've had a good look. I'm just tempered, polished steel, a military instrument. How we doing on fuel, anyway?'

Jake glanced at the gauges. He punched the buttons to get a reading on his remaining wing fuel, then finally said, 'We're okay.'

'Umph. We're only fifty miles out.' Le Beau went back to the radar. 'Don't embarrass me. Try to get some decent hits.'

The bombs hanging under the wings were little blue twenty-five-pound practice bombs. Each one contained a small pyrotechnic cartridge in the nose that would produce a puff of smoke when the bomb struck, allowing the hit to be spotted. Each A-6 carried a dozen of these things on their bomb racks.

The planned drill was for the pilot of each plane to drop the first half-dozen manually, using the visual bomb sight à la World War II, then the second six using the aircraft's electronic system. Jake carefully set the optical sight to the proper mil setting for a forty-degree dive with a six-thousand-foot release. Releasing six thousand feet above the target, the slant range was about nine thousand feet. To drop a bomb nine thousand feet from a target and hit it was difficult, of course – nearly impossible when you considered the fact that the wind would affect the bomb's trajectory throughout its fall. Yet *that* was the dive bomber's art.

Hitting the target was the payoff. Five thousand men at sea for months, the treasure spent on ships, planes and fuel, the blood spilled in training, all to set up that moment when the bomb struck the target. If the pilot could get it there.

Colonel Haldane expected his pilots to do their damnedest. Last night he taped a poster to the ready room bulkhead with the names of all his pilots on it. The poster was just as large, just as prominent as the one on the bulkhead that recorded each pilot's landing grades. You had to be able to get aboard ship safely to be a carrier pilot, but you weren't much use in combat unless you could hit the target when the chips were down. Haldane said as much. He went further:

'In this squadron, after the upcoming Hawaiian ops period, the pilots who are going to lead sections and flights are the pilots with the best bombing scores. I guarantee you, your bombing scores will appear on your fitness report. I expect each and every one of you to earn your pay on the bombing range.'

First Lieutenant Doug Harrison couldn't resist. 'Hey, Skipper. You can fly on my wing.'

'If you can out-bomb me, I will,' Haldane shot back.

Harrison was number four today, flying on Jake's right wing. You had to admire Harrison, for his chutzpah if nothing else. Haldane had spent years in Vietnam dive-bombing under fire and Harrison was just a year out of flight school. No fool, Harrison well knew how good the experienced professionals were and risked ignominy anyway.

Although he was less vocal about it, Jake Grafton took a backseat to no one when it came to pride in his own flying skills. He had seen his share of flak and dropped his share of bombs. His name would be at the top of that ready room poster if it were humanly possible to get it there.

Major Bartow pumped his fist at Jake, who scooted farther away from the lead plane. Number two, Captain Harry Digman, came under the lead, his canopy just a few feet below Haldane's exhausts, and surfaced where Jake had been. Now the formation was in right echelon.

Colonel Haldane did the talking on the radio. Cleared into the target area as a flight of F-4s were leaving, he led his echelon down in a gentle, sweeping left turn to 15,000 feet, then straightened out for the run up the bearing line. Over the target he broke to the left. Ten seconds later the second plane broke, and Jake ten seconds after that.

Around they came, now strung out, each pilot verifying his clearance from other airplanes, then concentrating on the target and flying his own plane.

The first essential for a successful run is to get to the proper roll-in point. This is that location in space from which you can roll in and arrive on the proper run-in heading at the preselected dive angle, today forty degrees. Practice targets, with run-in lines bulldozed into the earth and marks gouged out as reference points, help the pilots develop a feel for that correct, perfect place to roll in.

And 'roll in' describes the maneuver. Today Jake approached the bearing line obliquely, at about forty-five degrees off, waiting, watching the target get nearer and nearer as he ran the trim to one degree nose-down, the 500-knot setting, while he held the plane level with back stick.

Now!

He slaps the stick sideways and in a heartbeat has the

A-6 past the vertical, in 135 degrees of bank. Now the stick comes sharply back and the G's smash them into their seats as the pilot pulls the nose of the aircraft to just below the target while he adjusts the throttles. Since he is carrying low-drag practice bombs today, Jake sets the throttles at about eighty percent RPM.

G off, stick right to roll her hard to the upright position.

Flap flips on the master armament switch and makes the radio call: 'War Ace Three's in hot.'

If the pilot has rolled in properly, the plane is now in a forty-degree dive, the pipper in the bombsight below the target and tracking toward it. This is where Jake finds it now, although just a little too far right. He corrects this instantly by forcing the stick to the left, then jerking the wings back level. This is no place to try to be smooth – it is imperative that he quickly get the lane into the proper dive with the pipper tracking so that he will have as many seconds as possible to solve the drift problem. Jake flies his dives with both hands on the stick, muscling the plane to the position he wants.

A glance at the airspeed – over 400 and increasing – now the altimeter. Flap is calling the altitudes: 'Fourteen . . . thirteen . . . forty-one degrees . . . twelve . . .'

The wind is drifting the pipper leftward. Jake rolls right and forces the pipper back to the right. He wants the pipper to the right of the bearing line and drifting left toward it, yet at the moment of release it must still be slightly right of the bull's-eye. The bomb will continue to drift during its fall.

And he is steep. He must release with the pipper just a smidgen short of the target to compensate for that.

'. . . Ten . . . nine . . . eight . . .'

Coming down with the pipper tracking toward the bull's-eye, today a painted white spot in the middle of a white circle, he glances at the G-meter. Steady on one. He releases his death grip on the stick so that he can feel the

110

effect of the trim. Coming toward neutral, which means he is getting toward 500 knots true airspeed, 465 indicated. The briefest glance at the airspeed indicator – 445 and increasing . . .

'Seven . . .'

And since the target is several hundred feet above sea level and he has synchronized the movement of the pipper with the descent, he releases the bomb two hundred feet above six thousand feet with the pipper at a five o'clock position on the bull.

And pulls.

Wings level and throttles forward to the stops, pull until the G-meter needle hits four, then hold it there. He reaches for the master arm switch with his right hand – his arm weighs a ton with all this G on – and toggles it off.

Flap again on the radio: 'War Ace Three's off safe.'

With his nose passing the horizon Jake Grafton relaxes the G and scans the sky for the airplane in front of him. There! And farther around, the skipper. Okay. Nose on up and let her soar, converting that diving airspeed back into altitude.

The spotters on the ground are calling the hits. The skipper's first one was seventy-five feet at seven o'clock. His wingman gets a called score of a hundred-ten feet at twelve. Jack gets a score of fifty feet at five.

'Overcompensated for the wind,' he mutters to Flap, who has no comment.

Now they are back at 15,000 feet and he pulls the throttles back, steers a little wider as he makes his turn. He glimpses the flashing wings of the plane ahead as it rolls into its dive.

'War Ace Four, your hit seventy-five feet at nine o'clock.'

'Harrison's holding his own with the colonel,' Jake tells Flap, and chuckles.

He checks the drift of the puffs of smoke from the

practice bombs. He eyes the clouds, glances behind to see where Harrison is, checks his fuel, checks the annunciator panel for warning lights, then eyes the target to see where he should go to get to the roll-in.

Master Arm switch on, roll and pull!

'Don't you just love this shit?' Flap says between altitude calls on their second dive.

'Bull's-eye,' the target spotter says as Jake soars upward after release, and he reaches over and slaps Flap on the thigh.

'With a spoon, Flapjack!' He slams the stick sideways and the aircraft spins on its longitudinal axis. He stops it after precisely 360 degrees of roll.

'Okay, okay, you're the best in the west,' Flap says. 'Just keep popping them in there.'

After their sixth dive, it was Flap's turn. He had the radar and computer ready. This time as Jake rolled he had to point the fixed reticle of the bombsight exactly at the target. Then he squeezed the commit trigger on the stick and began to fly the steering commands on the vertical display indicator, the VDI, in the center of the instrument panel in front of him.

Squeezing the commit trigger told the computer where the target was and told the radar to track it. While Flap monitored the velocities the computer was getting from the inertial, the computer providing steering commands, wind-compensated of course, to guide Jake to the proper release point, which was that point in space where the bomb could be released to fall upon the target.

Jake concentrated upon the steering commands and followed them as precisely as he could. When the computer gave him a pull-up command he laid on the G while concentrating fiercely on keeping the wings level. The computer released the weapon and he kept the nose coming up.

'Seventy-five feet at six o'clock.'

He went around to do it again.

'You know,' he said to Flap, 'it's like they invented a machine to hit a baseball.'

'Just follow steering, Babe Ruth. This gizmo is smarter than you are.'

'Yeah, but I'm an *artiste!*'

'We ain't dodging flak today, Jake.'

This was the eternal war – the pilot wanted to drop them all visually and the bombardier wanted to use the system every time. Both men knew the system was better and they both knew Jake would never admit it. Today at this practice target the pilot had ideal conditions: a stationary target with a known elevation, a plowed run-in line, visual cues on the ground, no flak, the luxury of repeated runs that allowed him to properly dope the wind. The system of this A-6E was a first-time, every-time sure thing.

But a machine is hard to love.

The four A-6s rendezvoused off target and Harrison, the number-four man, slid under the other three checking them for hung bombs. Then Jake checked Harrison. Harrison and number two each had one little blue bomb still handing on the racks.

The skipper led them up to 20,000 feet and Flap dialed in the ships TACAN, a radio navigation aid. The mileage readout refused to lock – they were still too far out – but Flap soon had the ship on radar. One hundred thirty-two miles.

After checking the cockpit altitude – stable at 10,000 feet – Jake took his mask off and hung it on the left side mirror on the canopy rail. He swabbed the sweat off his face.

The planes were in parade formation, only about fifteen feet from the cockpit to the wing tip of the next man. Flying this close to another plane was work, but Jake

Grafton enjoyed it. The restless air always affected the planes differently as they sliced through it, so constant adjustments were required from the wingman. The lead just flew his own machine.

If you were the wingman, you kept the wing tip of the lead plane just below and behind the canopy. This look must be maintained with continuous small adjustments of stick and throttles, occasionally rudder. If you did it right, you could hang here no matter what the lead plane was doing – flying straight and level, banking, climbing, diving, executing wingovers, loops; whatever.

Jake settled in and concentrated. Doing this on a sunny morning in clear, fairly calm air was merely drill. Doing it on a stormy, filthy night with the planes bouncing in turbulence over an angry ocean demanded a high level of skill and confidence. With an emergency and a low reading on the fuel gauge, your ability to hang on someone's wing became your lifeline.

Bartow was motioning him out. A pushing motion.

'We're opening it up,' he told Flap, who glanced at Bartow, then gave the identical signal to Harrison, on Jake's right wing.

When he had opened the gap to about sixty or seventy feet, Jake stabilized and checked Harrison. He looked at the skipper's wingman, on the skipper's left wing. Everybody about right. Okay.

Flap had written down all the scores and now he was tallying them, figuring each crew's CEP – circular error probable. He did this by finding the sixth best hit. Half the bombs would hit within a circle with this radius.

In the skipper's cockpit Bartow was looking at his radar. Jake glanced at the mileage readout on the radar repeater between his legs: 126. Then his eyes flicked across the instrument panel. Airspeed 295 indicated, altitude 20,040 feet, warning lights out, hydraulic pressures okay. Fuel – about 7,600 pounds remaining.

He looked straight ahead, saw nothing, then glanced again across that gap toward Bartow.

He had his eyes focused on Bartow when an F-4 Phantom crossed his line of vision. Between him and the skipper. Flashed by going in the opposite direction, and at the same time another Phantom went by the skipper's left side, between him and his wingman.

They were there only long enough to register on Jake's brain, then they were gone. The A-6 jolted as it flew into the edges of the wash of the Phantom's wings.

'What was that?' Flap asking, raising his head and looking around.

Jake grabbed his oxygen mask and snapped it on. 'You won't believe this,' he said on the ICS, 'but a Phantom just went between us and the skipper. And another went down the skipper's left side, between him and Digman.'

'What?'

'Yeah, a flight of Phantoms just went through our flight. I shit you not. The skipper went between the lead and his wingman and one of them went between us and the skipper. We missed by *inches*.'

Jake stared across the gap that separated him from Bartow. Bartow was looking back at him. Had he seen the F-4s?

'If we had been still in parade formation,' Jake told Flap, 'you and me would be tapping on the pearly gates right now.'

Say the fighters were also going 300 indicated – that's a closing speed of 600 knots indicated, over 800 knots true. Almost a thousand miles per hour!

He had looked straight ahead just a second or two before they got here – and seen nothing.

But they were *there*, coming head-on, like guided missiles.

And he didn't see them. Of course the distance was over a half mile two seconds before they arrived, but still . . . He should have seen something!

He broke into a sweat. His mouth and lips were dry. He tried to swallow.

At those speeds, if his plane had collided with that Phantom . . .

He wouldn't have felt a thing. Not a single thing. He would have been just instantly dead, a spot of grease trapped in the exploding fireball.

'Well, Ace,' Flap said, 'you will be delighted to hear we have a fifty-foot CEP.'

Jake tried to reply but couldn't.

'If World War III comes, you and I will be among the very first to die,' Flap informed him. 'How about them apples? We've earned it.'

Those Phantoms – he wondered if the pilots of the fighters had even seen the A-6s.

'Gives you goose bumps, huh? Ain't life something else?'

'Did anybody see those Phantoms?' Jake asked.

Silence. Blank looks. They were debriefing the flight in the ready room. Seven blank faces.

'You mean I was the only one to see them?'

Later, in the solitude of his stateroom, he thought about miracles. About how close to the abyss he had come, how many times. What was that quote – something about if you stared into the abyss long enough, the abyss stared back.

That was true. He could feel it staring back just now.

No one doubted his word when he told them about the fighters. But no one else had seen them.

To be told later that you had a close call was like learning that your mother had difficulty when you were born. It meant nothing. You shrugged and went on.

The Phantoms must have been from this ship. That was easy enough to check. He examined the air plan and found the fighter squadron that had the target time immediately after the A-6 outfit, then paid a visit to their ready room.

'Hey, did any of you guys have a near midair today?

Anybody almost trade paint with four A-6s? On your way into the target?'

They stared at him like he was a grotesque apparition, a leering reminder of their own mortality. No one had seen anything. All must have been looking elsewhere, thinking of something else, because unless they were looking in exactly the right place, they would have missed it. Just as the other seven Intruder crewmen had.

Here in his stateroom he worked out the math. An F-4 was about fifty feet long. At a combined speed of 800 knots it would pass the eye in thirty-seven thousandths of a second. Less than an eye blink.

When death comes, she will come quick.

But you've always known that, Jake Grafton.

He got out of his chair and examined his face in the mirror over the sink. The face in the glass stared back blankly.

'A ship under way is a very difficult target,' Jake said.

Lieutenant Colonel Haldane didn't reply. He knew as well as Jake did that once free-falling bombs were released, a well-conned ship would turn sharply. Probably into the wind, although the attacker certainly couldn't count on that.

'Ideally we should drop as close to the ship as possible to minimize the time he has to turn,' Jake said. Such a choice would also minimize the effect of any errors in the computer, errors in velocity, drift angle, altitude, etc.

'That would be the ideal,' Haldane agreed, 'but it wouldn't be smart to get all our airplanes shot down trying for the perfect attack. We're going to have to pick an attack that maximizes our chances of hitting yet gives us a half-decent chance of getting to the drop point. Let's look again at the weapons envelopes we'll have to penetrate.'

Jake was briefing the skipper on the progress of the

planning efforts under way in the air wing offices. He had been attending these meetings for several days. Now he spread out several graphs he had constructed and explained them to his boss, Lieutenant Colonel Haldane.

As the attackers approached a Soviet task force, the first weapons that they would face would be SA-N-3 Goblet missiles, which could engage them up to twenty miles away at altitudes between 150 and 80,000 feet. These Mach 2.5 missiles would probably be fired in pairs, the second one following the first by a few seconds. Then the launcher would be reloaded and another pair fired – each launcher had the capacity to shoot thirty-six missiles. The number of launchers present would depend on the makeup of the task group, but for planning purposes figure there were ten. That's a possible 360 missiles in the air.

The next threat would be encountered at a range of nine or ten miles, when the attackers penetrated the envelope of the Mach 3.5 SA-N-1 Goa missiles. The weak point in the Goa system was the fire control director, which could engage only one target at a time. Yet since the missiles were carried on twin launchers, presumably two would be fired at the target, then a second target could be acquired while the launcher was reloaded. The magazine capacity for each launcher was sixteen missiles. Unfortunately the Soviets placed these weapons on destroyers as well as Kynda and Kresta cruisers, so one could expect a lot of launchers. Plan for twenty and we have another possible 320 missiles to evade.

If our harried attack crews were still alive seven miles from the target, they would enter the envelope of the Mach 2+ SA-N-4. This weapon was also fired from twin launchers, each with a magazine capacity of twenty missiles. Figure a task group with twenty launchers and we have a possible 400 missiles of this type.

Finally, after a weapons release, the attacker could expect surviving ships to fire a cloud of SA-N-5 Grail heat-seeking missiles, the naval version of the Soviet Army's Strela. Grail carried a one-kilogram warhead over a slant range of only 4.4 kilometers and needed a good hot tailpipe signature to guide, but just one up your tailpipe would ruin your day. Within the Grail envelope the attacker could expect to see dozens in the air.

Yet missiles were only half the story. There would also be flak, an extraordinary amount of it. Soviet ships bristled with guns. The larger guns would fire first, as soon as the attacking force came in range. As the distance between the attackers and the defenders closed, the smaller calibers would open fire.

The smaller the gun, the faster the rate of fire, so as the range closed, the sheer volume of high explosive in the air would increase exponentially. In close, that is within a mile and a quarter, the attacker would fly into range of six-barreled 30-mm Gatling guns, each capable of firing at a sustained rate of a thousand rounds per minute or squirting bursts of up to three times that volume.

'Since I started putting this data together,' Jake told the colonel, 'I've become a big fan of attack submarines.'

'Why don't you say what you really think?'

'Yes, sir. Attacking a Soviet task group with free-fall bombs will be a spectacular way to commit suicide.'

'If the balloon goes up, we'll go when we're told to go, suicide or not.'

'Yessir.'

'So we had better have a realistic plan, just in case.'

'The air wing is planning Alpha strikes. Two strikes, Blue and Gold, half the planes on each one.' An Alpha strike was a maximum effort, with fighters escorting the attackers and the entire gaggle diving the target in close order. The ideal was to get all the bombs on target and everyone exiting the area within sixty seconds.

'Okay,' Colonel Haldane said.

'That will only work on a daytime, good weather

launch,' Jake continued. 'In my opinion, skipper, we can figure on losing half our planes on each strike.'

Haldane didn't say anything.

'At night or in bad weather, they'll just send the A-6s. We're the only planes with the capability.'

CHAPTER EIGHT

Steam catapults make modern aircraft carriers possible. Invented by the British during World War II, catapults freed designers from the necessity of building naval aircraft that could rise from the deck under their own power after a run of only three hundred feet. So wings could shrink and be swept as the physics of high speed aerodynamics required, jet engines that were most efficient at high speeds could be installed, and airframes could be designed that would go supersonic or lift tremendous quantities of fuel and weapons. A luxury for most of the carrier planes of World War II, the catapult now was an absolute requirement.

The only part of the catapult that can be seen on the flight deck is the shuttle to which aircraft are attached. This shuttle sticks up from a slot in the deck that runs the length of the catapult. The catapult itself lies under the slot and consists of two tubes eighteen inches in diameter arranged side by side like the barrels of a double-barreled shotgun. Inside each tube – or barrel – is a piston. There is a gap at the top of each barrel through which a steel lattice mates the two pistons together, and to which the shuttle on deck attaches.

The pistons are hauled aft mechanically into battery by a little cart called a 'grab.' Once the pistons are in battery, the aircraft is attached to the shuttle, either by a linkage on the nose gear of the aircraft in the case of the A-6 and A-7, or by a bridle made of steel cable in the case of the F-4 and

RA-5. Then the slack in the bridle or nose-tow linkage is taken out by pushing the pistons forward hydraulically – this movement is called 'taking tension.'

Once the catapult is tensioned and the aircraft is at full power with its wheel brakes off, the firing circuit is enabled when the operator pushes the 'final ready' button.

Firing the catapult is then accomplished by opening the launch valves, one behind each tube, simultaneously, which allows superheated steam to enter the barrels behind the pistons.

The amount of acceleration given to each aircraft must be varied depending on the type of aircraft being launched, its weight, the amount of wind over the deck, and the outside air temperature. This is accomplished by one of two methods. Either the steam pressure is kept constant and the speed of opening of the launch valves is varied, or the launch valves are always opened at the same rate and the pressure of the steam in the accumulators is varied. Aboard *Columbia*, the steam pressure was varied and the launch valves were opened at a constant rate.

Although the launch valves open quickly, they don't open instantaneously. Consequently steam pressure rising on the back of the pistons must be resisted until it has built up sufficient pressure to move the pistons forward faster than the aircraft could accelerate on its own. This resistance is provided by a shear bolt installed in the nose gear of the aircraft to be launched, to which a steel hold-back bar is attached. One end of the bar fits into a slot in the deck. The bolt used in the A-6 was designed to break cleanly in half under a load of 48,000 pounds, only then allowing the pistons in the catapult, and the aircraft, to begin forward motion.

The superheated steam expanding behind the pistons drove them the length of the 258-foot catapults of the *Columbia* in about 2.5 seconds. Now up to flying speed, the aircraft left the deck behind and ran out into the air sixty feet above the ocean, where it then had to be rotated to the proper angle of attack to fly – in the A-6, about eight degrees nose-up.

Meanwhile, the pistons, at terminal velocity and quickly running out of barrels, had to be stopped. This was accomplished by means of water brakes, tubes welded onto the end of each of the catapult barrels and filled with water. The pistons each carried a tapered spear in front of them, and as the pistons reached the water brakes the spears penetrated the open ends, forcing water out around the spears. Water is incompressible, yet as the spears were inserted the escape openings for the water got smaller and smaller. Consequently the deeper the spears penetrated the higher the resistance to further entry. The brakes were so efficient that the pistons were brought to a complete stop after a full-power shot in only nine feet of travel.

The sexual symbolism of the tapered spears and the water-filled brakes always impressed aviators – they were young, lonely and horny – but the sound a cat made slamming into the brakes was visceral. The stupendous thud rattled compartments within a hundred feet of the brakes and could be felt throughout the ship.

Tonight as he sat in the cockpit of an A-6 tanker waiting for the cat crew to retract the shuttle, Jake Grafton ran through all the things that could go wrong with the cat.

The launching officer, Jumping Jack Bean, was wandering around near the hole in the deck that contained the valves and gauges that allowed him to drag steam from the ship's boilers to the catapult accumulators. The enlisted man who always sat on the edge of the hole wearing a sound-powered telephone headset that enabled him to talk to the men in the catapult machinery spaces was already in his place, staring aft at the two planes on the cats. The luminescent patches on his helmet and flight deck jersey were readily visible in the dim red glow of the lights from the ship's island superstructure, almost a hundred yards aft.

If anything goes wrong with the machinery below-decks, Jake Grafton knew, the probable result would be less end speed for the plane being launched. A perfect shot gave the launching aircraft a mere fifteen knots above stall speed. A couple knots less and the pilot would never notice. Five off, the plane would be sluggish. Ten off, a ham-handed pilot could stall it inadvertently. Fifteen or more off, the plane was doomed.

Bad, or 'cold,' cat shots were rare, thank God. The catapult was very reliable, more so than the aircraft that rode it. They could have an engine flame out under the intense acceleration, dump a gyro, lose a generator, spring a hydraulic or fuel leak . . . or the pilot could just become disoriented during the sudden, intense transition from sitting stationary on deck to instrument flight fifteen knots above a stall, at night. The blackness out there beyond the bow was total, a void so vast and bleak that one wanted to avert his eyes. Look at something else. Think about something else.

The hell of it was that there was nothing else to look at – nothing else to think about. Tonight Jake was flying a tanker, which was going to be flung off the pointy end of the boat in just a few minutes right into that black void, climb to 5,000 feet and tank a couple Phantoms, climb up to 20,000 and circle the ship for an hour and a half, then come back and trap. That was it, the whole damn mission. Go around and around the ship. Orbit. At max conserve airspeed. On autopilot. The challenge would be staying awake.

No, the challenge was this goddamn night cat shot. The worst part of the whole flight was right at the start – the blindfolded ride on the rabid pig . . .

The cat crewmen were now taking the rubber seal out of the catapult slot. Steam wisped skyward from the open slot, steam leaking from some fitting somewhere in the cat. They kept the slot seal in between launches, Jake knew, to help maintain the temperature of those eighteen-inch tubes.

The handler had parked the tanker here on the cat, probably so that the miserable peckerhead pilot would have to sit in the cockpit watching the steam wisp up from the cat against the backdrop of the black void while he thought about dying young.

And his life wasn't going so good just now. First Callie's jerk father, then Tiny Dick Donovan, the in-flight engagement, that near-midair . . .

Maybe God was trying to tell him something.

Or maybe those Phantoms this morning hadn't been there at all.

What if he had just imagined them? Of course the planes passed each other quickly, but there were at least two Phantoms and four A-6s, two guys in each plane. A total of twelve men, and *he* was the *only* one who had seen the varmint.

Really doesn't make sense.

Does it?

'What are you staring at through that windshield?' Flap Le Beau asked.

'There's a naked woman out there. If you look real careful you can see her nipples.'

'You look like you're mentally composing your will. That isn't good leadership. You are supposed to be impressing me with *your* self-confidence, calming *my* fears. The stick's on your side, remember?'

'What if those F-4s weren't really there this morning? What if I just imagined it?'

'Are you still on that? You saw 'em. They were there.'

'How come no one else is in a sweat?'

'What do you want me to do, fill my drawers? Slit my wrists? Fate fired a bullet and it missed.'

'You could have the common courtesy to look nervous, sweat it a little.'

'You're making me nervous.'

'That'll be the day,' Jake Grafton replied disgustedly.

'Okay, I'm sweating It's dripping out of my armpits. Every jerk pilot I ever met has tried to kill me. I'm waiting for you to give it a whirl.'

'How come you got into aviation anyway?'

'Jungle rot. Pretty bad case. They tell me I'm now a paragraph and photo in a medical textbook. Little did I know when I signed up for this glamorous flying life how much jungle I still had to visit.'

The brown-shirt plane captain standing beside the aircraft waved his wands to get Jake's attention, then signaled for a start.

Time to do it.

'It could have been worse,' Flap told Jake as he started the left engine. 'I could have made medical history with a spectacular social disease. Wouldn't that have been a trip? For a hundred years every guy going overseas would have had to watch a movie featuring my diseased, ulcerated pecker.'

Six minutes later Jake rogered the weight board and eased the plane forward into the shuttle. He felt the nose-tow bar drop into the shuttle slot and came off the brakes and added power at the yellow-shirt's signal.

The engines began winding up. Another small jolt as the hydraulic arm shoved the cat pistons into tension, taking all the slack out of the hold-back bar. Now just the shear-bolt was holding them back.

Full power, wipe out the controls, check the gauges, cat grip up . . . 'You ready?' he asked Flap.

'I'm really really ready.'

He could feel the vibration as the engines sucked air and blasted it out the exhausts against the jet black deflector, feel rather than hear the ear-splitting roar. He swept his eyes across the annunciator panel – all warning lights out. The exterior light master switch was on the end of the cat grip, right beside his left thumb. He flicked it on.

The cat officer took a last look at the island, looked up the cat at the void, then swept his yellow wand down in a fencer's lunge until he touched the deck, then he came up to a point.

The catapult fired. The G's slammed him back . . . and both fire warning lights illuminated.

They were big red lights, one on each side of the bomb-sight on the top of the instrument panel. Labeled L FIRE and R FIRE, both lights shone into his eyes like spotlights as the acceleration pressed him deeper into the seat back.

Oh, God, he thought, trying to take it in as the adrenaline whacked him in the heart.

His eyes went to the engine instruments, white tapes arranged vertically in front of his left knee. They looked—

The acceleration stopped and the plane was off the cat, the nose coming up. A glance at the airspeed – not decaying. Angle-of-attack gauge agreed. He grabbed the stick and slapped the gear handle up. Wings level, check the nose . . .

His left hand rose automatically toward the emergency jettison button above the gear handle. If he pushed it and held it down for one second the five drop tanks, each containing two thousand pounds of fuel, would be jet-tisoned from the aircraft. She would instantly be five tons lighter and could then fly on one engine. He was sorely tempted but he didn't push it. His hands came back to the throttles.

Which engine was it?

Both lights were screaming at him!

Which fucking engine?

Engine tapes still okay . . . airspeed okay . . . eight degrees nose up. He was squinting against the glare of the red fire lights. He had let the left wing sag so he picked it up. Climbing through two hundred feet, 160 knots . . .

Both fire lights – the book said to pull the affected engine to idle, but he had *both* lights on!

Fire!

Was he on fire? If he was it was time to eject. Jettison this fucking airplane. Swim for it. He looked in the mirrors. Black. Nothing to see.

He became aware that Flap was on the radio. '... both fire lights ... declaring an emergency ... Boss, can you see any fire?'

The reply was clear in his ears. 'Off the bow, you look fine. You say you have both fire lights on?'

Jake cut in on Flap. 'Both of them. We'd like a dump charley.'

'Your signal dump. It'll be about eight more minutes until we have a ready deck. We'll call you.'

'Roger.'

His heart was slowing. She didn't seem to be on fire. Thank you, thank you, thank you.

Accelerating through 185 knots, he raised the flaps and slats, then toggled the switches for the wing and main dump valves. They were carrying 26,000 pounds of fuel and the max he could take aboard the ship was 6,000. He needed to dump ten tons of fuel into the atmosphere.

And as he reached for the switch that would isolate a portion of the combined hydraulic system, he looked at the hydraulic gauges. For the first time. He had forgotten to look at the hydraulic gauges before. Now, squinting against the glare of the fire lights, he saw the needle on the right combined system pump flickering.

Uh-oh. A fire could be melting hydraulic lines. Hydraulic fluid itself was nonflammable, but the lines could melt.

'We have hydraulic problems,' he told Flap.

'How come those fire lights are so bright?' Flap asked. 'I can barely see the gauges.'

'Dunno.' Jake was too busy to cuss out that comfortable, anonymous bureaucrat who had specified the wattage of the bulbs in the fire warning lights. They were certainly impossible to miss. You are about to die, they screamed.

128

'Maybe you better stop dumping the main tank.'

Flap was right. Jake secured the main tank dump. Still 8,500 pounds there.

By now he had the plane at 2,500 feet headed downwind, on the reciprocal of the launch bearing, steady at 250 knots. When he pulled the power back the fire lights stayed on.

Did they have a fire? Modern jet aircraft utilized every cubic inch of space inside the fuselage for fuel, engines, pumps, switches, hydraulic lines, electronic gear, wires, etc., and the spars and stringers that held the whole thing together. A fire anywhere within the plane had to be burning something critical. And if it got to the tanks . . . well, the explosion would be spectacular.

Jake again checked the rearview mirrors for a glow. Nothing.

'Get out the checklist,' he told Flap as he turned off the cabin pressurization system. Unfortunately the ducts carrying bleed air from the engines had failed on a half-dozen occasions in the past: the resulting fires had cost the Navy men and airplanes. Jake had no desire to add his name to that list. If there was a leak downstream of the valve that controlled cabin pressurization, closing the valve should isolate it.

'Got it right here. You ready?'

'Yeah.'

Flap read the comments and recommended procedure over the ICS. One of the comments read, If a fire warning light stays illuminated, secure the affected engine.

He only had two engines and both fire lights were lit. So much for that advice.

The right combined hydraulic system gauge read zero. The needle on the left one was sagging, twitching. And a hydraulic leak was a secondary indication of fire! But did he have one?

'Marine airplanes are shit,' he groused to Flap, who shot back:

'Yeah, the Navy gives us all the crap they don't want.'

Flap got busy on the radio and reported the hydraulic failure. Soon he was talking to Approach. The controller put them in an orbit ten miles aft of the ship. Jake slowed to 220 knots and checked the fuel quantity remaining in the wings. Still a few thousand. In the glow of the left wing-tip light he could just make out the stream from the dump pipe gushing away into the slipstream.

Well, he had it under control. Other than the nuisance glare of the fire lights, everything would be fairly normal. He would blow the gear down, lower the flaps electrically and just motor down the glide slope. He could hack it.

He released the left side of his oxygen mask. He sniffed carefully, then swabbed the sweat from his face. His heart rate was pretty much back to normal and the adrenaline was wearing off. There was no fire – he was fairly confident of that.

Wing fuel read zero. OK. He would leave the dump open a moment or two longer to purge the tank, then secure it. He reached down and punched the button to make the needle on the fuel gauge register main tank fuel. And stared, unable to believe his eyes. Only 3,500 pounds.

Holy . . . !

Yes, the main dump switch was off. But the valve never closed! All the fuel in the main tank had dumped, right down to the top of the standpipe, which prevented the last 3,600 pounds from going overboard. And he had already burned a hundred pounds of that 3,600.

He slapped on the mask and spoke to the controller. 'Uh, Approach, War Ace Five Two One has another problem out here. The main dump valve didn't close. We're down to Three Point Five. How soon can you give us a charley?'

'Standby, War Ace.'

Flap leaned across the center consol and stared at the offending fuel gauge for several seconds, then straightened up. He didn't say anything.

'How far is it to Hickam Field?' Jake asked.

Flap consulted the notes on his kneeboard. 'About a hundred fifty miles.'

'We're almost to bingo!' Jake exclaimed, his horror evident in his voice. 'We've got to have a tanker *right now!*'

Flap Le Beau keyed the radio: 'Approach, War Ace Five Two One, our state is Three Point Five. We're eight hundred pounds above bingo. Apparently the fuselage dump valve stuck open. Request a tanker ASAP.'

'Negative, War Ace. We'll take you aboard in about eight or ten more minutes.'

A sense of foreboding seized Jake Grafton. They were in deep and serious trouble. 'How's the spare tanker?' he asked.

'We're still trying to launch it,' was the reply. 'We should have it off in a few minutes.'

Jake couldn't help himself. 'Is there some problem with the spare?' He felt like a condemned man asking if he could have one more cigarette.

'Yes.' One word.

'They're digging us a hole,' Flap told Jake.

The pilot glumly examined the instruments. What else can go wrong? Bingo was the fuel state that required he depart for the shore divert field on a max range profile flight. Bingo was a low fuel emergency. And he was eight hundred pounds above that state. He had to leave for the shore field before his fuel reached that level or he would flame out before he got there.

Without additional fuel which only a tanker could provide, Jake had to trap or eject. Well, he still had some time. Right now he was burning four thousand pounds of fuel per hour. When he blew the gear down he would be unable to raise them again. And his fuel consumption would immediately jump to six thousand pounds per hour in level flight. More in a climb. At this moment he had three thousand four hundred.

Why had he switched the fuel gauge from the fuselage

tank to the wings? So he could monitor dumping. Of course, there was a totalizer there under the needle, but it was usually unreliable. Over the years he had developed a habit of ignoring it. What a fool he was! The lash stung and he laid it on hard.

He could stand the glare of the fire warning lights no longer. He took the L-shaped flashlight hanging on the webbing of his survival vest and pounded the offending lights until they shattered. The cockpit was darker, a lot darker, and that calmed him.

At least the weather was good tonight. Ceiling was high, maybe ten thousand feet, and the visibility underneath was ten miles or so. He could see the lights of the carrier eight miles away, just a little collection of red and white lights in the dark universe, and here and there, the little globs of light that were her escorts. At least he could fly alongside a destroyer or frigate when he had to eject. Then he and Flap wouldn't have to depend on the rescue helicopter to find them.

That was something. A straw to grasp.

Exasperated, his thoughts turned to Callie. It was four-thirty in the morning in Chicago; she was probably in bed asleep.

Thirty-one hundred pounds on the fuel gauge. A-6s had been known to flame out with as much as seven hundred pounds showing on the gauge. He could have as little as twenty-four hundred.

He got a pen from the sleeve pocket of his flight suit and did some figuring on the top card on his kneeboard, which as usual he wore strapped to his right thigh. The numbers told him he was burning sixty-seven pounds of fuel a minute, about ten gallons. Every six seconds a gallon of gas went into the engines. Twenty-four hundred divided by sixty seven – hell, he could dangle here twisting slowly in the wind for thirty-five more minutes. What's the problem? What's the sweat? Well, when he lowered the gear the power requirements would go up. He might bolter. The deck could stay fouled. The weather could go to hell. Something else could go wrong with the plane – like the gear might not come down or the hook might stay up. Or . . . He felt frustrated and outraged. The plane had betrayed him!

The second hand on the clock caught his eye. It swept around and around and around.

'Did I ever tell you about the time I stole a police car?' Flap asked.

'No, and I don't need to hear it now.'

'Stole a cruiser, with a bubble-gum machine on top, siren, police radio, even a shotgun on a rack in the front, the whole deal. Fellow in Jersey wanted it for a farm truck. He wanted to take the trunk lid off and weld up a pickup bed. Was gonna use it to haul manure. He was a retired Mafia soldier. Now I didn't know Mafia guys ever retired, but this one apparently had. He was out of the rackets and had him a little farm in north Jersey. A brother I knew told me there was five hundred bucks in it for me if I could come up with a police car. Luckily I knew another bro who was screwing a cop's daughter pretty regular, so I got to thinking. Five hundred bucks was real money to me back then. Anyway . . .'

Jake could hear pilots in other planes checking into marshal. It all sounded pretty normal. Well, the weather was good, no one was shooting . . .

'Ninety-nine planes in marshal, ninety-nine planes in marshal, this is Approach.' Ninety-nine meant 'all.' 'Your signal, max conserve. Add ten minutes to your commence times. Add ten minutes to push times.'

Now what?

Should he ask? He waited a minute, waited while another sixty-seven pounds of fuel went into the engines. Then he said, 'Approach, War Ace Five Two One. Does that ten minutes apply to me too?'

'Affirm.'

'Uh, what's the problem?'

Silence. Then, 'The nose gear collapsed on a Phantom on Cat Three. The deck is foul.' Cat Three was on the waist, in the landing area.

'War Ace Five Two One has Two Point Eight. Any word on Texaco?' Texaco was the tanker.

'We're working on it, War Ace.'

Flap left his story unfinished. Jake stared at the offending fuel gauge. Should he just say Bingo and go?

The ship was headed northwest, into the prevailing wind. Hickam was northeast. As the minutes passed they were getting no closer to Hickam, but on the other hand, they were getting no farther away. Without more fuel, what did it matter?

The minutes ticked by. Five, six, seven . . .

The needle on the fuel gauge passed twenty-four hundred pounds and kept descending. One pass – that was it. They would get one lousy pass at the deck. If he boltered for any reason, he and Flap were going to have to swim for it.

The crew fidgeted.

The hell of it was that they were betting everything on the emergency gear extension system. Compressed nitrogen would be used to blow the gear down since hydraulic fluid was no longer available to do the job. If any one of the three wheels failed to lock down, they could not trap aboard the ship. They would have to eject.

Betting your ass on any one system in an airplane with a variety of other problems is not the recommended path to a long and happy life.

Jake Grafton sat monitoring the instruments and thinking about the black ocean beneath him. At least the water was warm. With warm water came sharks. He hated sharks, feared them unreasonably. Sharks were his phobia. If he went into the water he would have to fight back the panic, have to keep functioning somehow.

He had never told anyone about the sharks. The thought of being down there with them made him nauseated. And at night, when he couldn't see. Of course he would be bleeding somewhere. Nobody ever ejected without getting cut somehow. Blood in the water, trying to keep from drowning . . .

'War Ace Five Two One, your signal charley.'

'Five Two One,' Jake acknowledged bitterly, then bit his lip. He should have told the brass to go to hell and bingoed.

First came ten degrees of flaps, which had to be lowered electrically. Linked to the flaps were the slats on the leading edge of the wing; they also came out. The flaps and slats changed the shape of the wings and allowed them to develop lift at lower airspeeds. They also added drag, slowing the plane.

Next came the hook. Jake merely pulled the handle and made sure the transition light disappeared.

The Intruder was slowing . . . 170 . . . 160 . . . 150 . . . 'Here goes nothing,' he told Flap as he lowered the gear handle to the gear down position, then rotated the knob on the end ninety degrees and pulled it out. The up-up-up indications on the panel barber-poled.

He waited. He could feel the drag increasing on the plane, could see his airspeed decreasing, and added power. The fuel-flow tapes surged upward.

C'mon, baby. Give me three down indications. Please!

The nose gear locked down first. Two seconds later the mains locked down. Seventeen hundred pounds of fuel left in the main bag.

'They're down' he announced to Flap and God and whoever else was listening.

Approach controller was giving him a steer.

'Hell!' Flap exclaimed disgustedly between calls from the controller, 'it wasn't even close. We don't even have a low fuel light.' The low fuel warning light would come on at about 1,360 pounds.

'We aren't down yet,' Jake pointed out.

'Oh ye of little faith, take note. We're almost down.'

Jake concentrated on flying the plane, staying on speed, smoothly intercepting the glide path. He was carrying less power than normal since the speed brakes were inoperative after the hydraulic failure, and while this saved a few gallons of gasoline, it caused its own problems. If he got high, retarding the throttles would be less effective than usual – the plane would tend to float.

He saw the ball two miles out. At a mile he called, 'Five Two One, Intruder ball, One Point Four.'

'Roger ball. Paddles has you. Looking good . . . fly the ball!'

The meatball began to rise above the datums and he pulled power aggressively while watching that angle-of-attack needle.

Paddles was talking to him. 'Power back on . . . too much, off a little . . . No, little more . . . lineup . . .'

Any second would come the burble, the swirl of air disturbed by the ship's island. He anticipated it just a smidgen on the power and didn't have to slam on too much, then he was quick to get it off.

Coming across the ramp the airspeed decayed a tad and the ball began to sink.

'Power!' shouted the LSO.

Slam! The wheels hit. Throttles to the stops . . . and the welcome, tremendous jerk as the hook snagged a wire.

'Two wire, I think,' Flap told him.

Jake didn't care. A huge sigh of relief flooded through him.

Here came the yellow-shirts. He raised the flaps and slats electrically while they chocked the plane, then cut the engines.

They were back.

Walking across the flight deck with their helmet bags in

their hands, with the warm sea wind on their wet hair, the firm steel deck beneath their flight boots, Flap repeated, 'It wasn't even close.'

No, Jake Grafton acknowledged to himself, it wasn't. Not tonight. But a man can't have luck all the time, and someday when he reached into that tiny little bag where he kept his luck, the bag would be empty. A hold-back bolt would break at the wrong time, a taxiing plane would skid into another, the airborne tanker would go sour, the weather would be bad . . . some combination of evil things would conspire against the man aloft and push him over the edge. Jake Grafton, veteran of more than 340 cat shots and arrested landings, knew that it could happen to him. He knew that as well as he knew his name.

The brass had taken the net from under the tightrope when they didn't let him bingo, and he was infuriated and disgusted with himself for letting them do it.

I think, Jake wrote to Callie that night, *that a man's fate is not in his control. We are under the illusion that we can control our destinies, that the choices we make do make a difference, but they don't. Chance rules our lives Chance, fate, fortune — whatever you wish to call it — sets the hook and pulls the string and we quiver and flail, jerk and fight. Maybe pray.*

I don't think praying helps very much. I do it anyway, just in case. I ask Him to be with me when I fall.

CHAPTER NINE

There are few things in life more satisfying than to be accepted as an equal in a fraternity of fighting men. Jake Grafton was so accepted now, and this morning when he entered the ready room he was greeted by name by the men there, who asked him about his adventures of the previous evening and listened carefully to his comments. They laughed, consoled him, and joked about the predicament he had found himself in last night. Several refused to believe, they said, that the main dump valve had failed: he had forgotten to secure it and was now trying to cover his sin by appealing to their naivete. All this was in good fun and was cheerfully accepted as such by Jake Grafton. He belonged. He was a full member of this aristocracy of merit, with impeccable credentials. His mood improved with each passing minute and soon he was his usual self.

He and his Marine colleagues inspected the board that recorded the pilots' landing grades. Jake's grades for his qualification landings were not displayed there, so like most of them, he had only two landings so far this cruise, an OK 3-wire and a fair 2-wire.

The bombing poster was more complicated, displaying the CEP of each crew, and to settle ties, the number of bull's-eyes. Jake ranked fourth in the squadron here. Today he was scheduled to go to the target with twelve five-hundred pounders, so perhaps he could better his standing.

He had a secret ambition to be the best pilot in the

squadron in landings and bombing and everything else, but he shared that ambition with everyone so it wasn't much of a secret. Still, it wasn't a thing that you talked about. You tried your very best at everything you did, glanced at the rankings, fiercely resolved to do better, and went on about your business. The rankings told you who was more skilled – 'more worthy' was the phrase used by the Real McCoy a day or two before – than you were.

The LSO regarded intrasquadron competition with good-natured contempt. 'Games for children,' he grumped. But Jake noticed now that McCoy's name was in the top half of the rankings on both boards.

This morning there was mail, the first in six days. A cargo plane brought it out from Hickam Field, trapped aboard, then left with full mail sacks from the ship's post office. Two hours later the mail was distributed throughout the ship.

Jake got three letters from Callie, one from his folks, and something from the commanding officer of Attack Squadron 128 in an official, unstamped envelope. He shuffled Tiny Dick Donovan's missive – probably some piece of official foolscap from a yeoman third in the Admin Office – to the bottom of the pile. Callie's letters came first.

She was taking classes at the University of Chicago, working on her master's degree. Her brother and her parents were fine. The weather was hot and muggy. She missed him.

I think that it is important for you to decide what you wish to do with your life. This is a decision that every man must make for himself, and every woman. To make this decision because you hope to please another is to make it for the wrong reason. We each owe duties to our families, when we acquire them, but we also owe a duty to ourselves to make our lives count for something. To love another person is not enough.

139

I have thought a great deal about this these last few weeks. Like every woman, I want to love. I feel as if I have this great gift to give – myself. I want to be a wife and mother. Oh, how I could love some man!

And I want the man I love to love me. To have a man who would return the love I have to give is my great ambition.

I have dated boys, known boys of all ages, and I do not want to marry one.

I want to marry a man. I want a man who believes in what he is doing, who goes out the door every day to make a contribution – in business, in academia, in government, somewhere. I want a man who will love not just me, but life itself. I want a man who will stand up to the gales of life, who won't bend with every squall, who will remain true to himself and those who believe in him, a man who can be counted on day after day, year after year.

An hour later, after he had reread Callie's letter three times and lingered over the one from his parents, he opened the official letter. In it he found a copy of his last fitness report, bearing Donovan's signature. In the text Donovan wrote:

Lieutenant Grafton is one of the most gifted aviators I have ever met in my years in the naval service. In every facet of flying, he is the consummate professional. As a naval officer, Lieutenant Grafton shows extraordinary promise, yet he has not made the commitment to give of himself as he must if he is to fulfill that promise.

There was more, a lot more, most of it the usual bullshit required by custom and instruction, such as a comment upon his support of the Navy's equal opportunity goals and programs. Jake merely skimmed this treacle, then

140

returned to the meat: '. . . has not yet made the commitment to give of himself as he must if he is to fulfill that promise.'

A pat on the back immediately followed by a kick in the pants. His first reaction was anger, which quickly turned to cold fury. He stalked from the ready room and went to his stateroom, where he opened his desk and seized pen and paper. He began a letter to Commander Donovan. He would write a bullet that would skewer the son of a bitch right through the heart.

What kind of half-assed crack was that? Not committed to being a good naval officer? Who the hell did that jerk Donovan think he was talking about anyway?

Even before he completed his first sentence, the anger began leaking from him. Donovan had said nothing about the Sea-Tac adventure, didn't even mention that the promising Lieutenant Grafton had punched out a windy blowhard and thrown him ass over tea kettle through a plate glass window, then spent a weekend in jail. Perhaps his comments dealt strictly with the performance of Jake's duties at the squadron. No, he *must* have meant that comment to cover the Sea-Tac debacle in addition to everything else. Worse, Donovan was right – a more committed, thinking officer would not have done it. A wiser man . . . well, he wouldn't have either.

Jake threw down the pen and rubbed his face in frustration.

Were Callie and Dick Donovan talking about the same thing?

'Man, you should have seen ol' Jake last night,' Flap Le Beau told his fellow Marines. 'Both the you're-gonna-die lights pop on bright as Christmas goin' down the cat, and this guy handled it like he was in a simulator. Cool as ice. Just sat there doin' his thing. Me – I was shakin' like a dog shittin' razor blades. I ain't been so scared since the teacher caught me with my hand up Susie Bulow's skirt back in the sixth grade.'

There were eight of them, four crews, and they had just finished a briefing for another flight to the Kahoolawe target. This time they were carrying real ordnance, twelve five-hundred-pound bombs on each plane. After they had reviewed how the fuses and arming wires should look on the bomb racks, the crews stood and stretched. That was when Flap took it on himself to praise his pilot to the heavens.

Jake was embarrassed. He had been frightened last night, truly scared, and Flap's ready room bull puckey struck a sour note. Still, Jake kept his mouth shut. This was neither the time nor place to brace Flap about his mouth.

He got out of his chair and went over in the corner to check his mailbox. Nothing. He gazed at the posters on the wall as if interested, trying to shut out Flap, who was expanding upon his theme: Jake Grafton was one cool dude.

One of the pilots, Rory Smith, came over and dug a sheet of official trash out of his mailbox, something he was supposed to read and initial. 'Flap gets on your nerves, does he?' he asked, his voice so soft it was barely audible. He scribbled his initials in the proper place and shoved the paper into someone else's box.

'Yeah.'

'Don't sweat it. To hear him tell it, every guy he flies with is the best who ever stroked a throttle. He was saying that in the ready room about his last stick five minutes before he was down in the skipper's stateroom complaining that the guy was dangerous. You just have to take him with a grain of salt.'

Jake grinned at Rory.

'Everybody else does,' the Marine said, then wandered off toward the desk where the maintenance logs on each aircraft were kept. Jake followed him.

Smith helped himself to the book for 511, the plane Jake had flown into an in-flight engagement.

'Gonna fly it today, huh?' Jake said.

'Yeah,' Smith said. 'The gunny says it's fixed. We'll see.'

'It'll probably go down on deck,' Jake pointed out. 'Down' in this context meant a maintenance problem that precluded flight. 'Since I bent it,' he continued, 'I'll fly it if you want to trade planes.'

'Well, I'm one of the maintenance check pilots and they gave it to me.'

'Sure.'

Meanwhile Flap had progressed to his favorite subject, women. Jake looked up from the maintenance book on his plane when Flap roared, 'Oh, my *God*, she was *ugly!*'

'*How* ugly?' three or four of his listeners wailed in unison.

'She was *so* ugly that paint peeled off the walls when she walked into a room.'

'*How* ugly?'

'So ugly that strong men fainted, children screamed, and horses ran away.'

'*How* ugly?' This refrain had become a chorus. Even Rory Smith joined in from the back of the room.

'Women tore their hair, the sky got black, and the earth trembled.'

'*That's* not ugly.'

'I'm telling you guys, she was *so* dingdong ugly that mirrors cracked, dogs went berserk, fire mains ruptured and one man who had smiled at her at night dropped stone cold dead when he saw her in the daylight. That, my friends, is the gospel truth.'

It was a typical afternoon in the tropics – scattered puffy clouds drifting on the balmy trade winds, sun shining through the gaps. Hawaii was going to be wonderful. Two more days, then Pearl Harbor! Oh boy.

Jake inspected the Mark 82 five-hundred-pounders

carefully. He hadn't seen deadly green sausages like this since the night he was shot down, seven months ago. Talk about a bad trip!

Well, the war was over, this was a peacetime cruise . . . He could probably spend another twenty years in the Navy and would never again have to drop one of these things for real. World War III? Get serious.

Up into the cockpit, into the comfortable seat, the familiar instruments arranged around him just so. The truth was he knew this cockpit better than he knew anything else on earth. Just the thought of never getting back into one bothered him. How do you turn your back on six years of your life?

Flap settled into the seat beside him as the plane captain climbed the ladder on Jake's side and reached in to help with the Koch fittings.

He had lived all this before – it was like living a memory. And somehow that was good.

Rory Smith preflighted his aircraft, 511, very carefully indeed. That four- or five-foot fall couldn't have done this thing any good. The main concern was the landing gear. If anything cracked . . . Well, the airframes guys hadn't found a single crack. They had scraped the paint from the parts, fluoroscoped them and pronounced them perfect. What can a pilot doe? Just fly it.

The radar, computer and inertial were seriously messed up. All the component boxes of those systems had been replaced, as had the radar dish and drive unit in the nose. The vertical display indicator – the VDI – and the radio were also new.

When Smith and his BN – Hank Davis – were strapped in, they turned on each piece of gear and checked it carefully. The inertial was slow getting an alignment, but it did align. Make a note for the debrief.

They were the last A-6 to taxi toward a cat, number two

on the bow. The others were airborne and in a few minutes, Smith would join them at nine thousand feet. That altitude should be well above the tops of this cumulus, he thought, taking three seconds to scan the sky.

Roger the weight board, check the wing locks, flaps and slats down, stabilizer shifted, into the shuttle, off the brakes and power up. Check the controls.

'You ready?'

'Yep,' Hank Davis told him cheerfully.

Rory Smith saluted and placed his head back into the headrest. He watched the bow cat officer give his fencer's lunge into the wind as his arm came down to the deck. Out of the corner of his eye he saw the catapult deck edge operator lower both hands as he reached for the fire button.

In the space of a second the launching valves dropped open, 450 pounds of steam hit the back of the pistons, and the hold-back bolt broke. The G's slammed Smith back into his seat as War Ace Five One One leaped forward. And the VDI came sliding out of the center of the instrument panel.

Rory Smith reached for the black box with both hands, but too late. The front of it tilted down and came to rest in his lap. Jammed the stick back. All this in the first second and a half of the shot.

Desperately Smith heaved at the box against the G. He had to free to stick!

And then they were off the bow, the nose coming up. And up and up as he struggled to lift the fucking box!

With his right hand he reached under and tried to shove the stick forward. Like pushing against a building.

He felt the stall, felt the right wing go down. He was trying to lift the box with his left hand and push the stick forward with his right when Hank Davis ejected. The horizon was tilting and the nose was slewing right.

Oh, *damn!*

*

145

On the bridge of *Columbia* the captain saw the whole thing. The nose of the Intruder off of Cat Two rose and rose to almost thirty degrees nose up, then her right wing dropped precipitously. Passing thirty or forty degrees angle-of-bank he saw a man in an ejection seat come blasting out. The wing kept dropping past the vertical and the nose came right and the A-6 dove into the ocean. A mighty splash marked the spot.

Galvanized, the captain roared, 'Right full rudder, stop all engines.'

The officer of the deck immediately repeated the order and the helmsman echoed it.

The captain's eyes were on the ejection seat. The drogue streamed as the seat arched toward the sea. The seat was past the apogee when the captain saw a flash of white as the parachute began to deploy. He blossomed, but before the man on the end of the shrouds could complete a swing he hit the water. Splat.

This 95,000-ton ship was making twenty-five knots. The A-6 went in a little to the right of her course, and the survivor splashed a little right of that. All he could hope to do was swing the stern away. The stern with its thrashing screws.

There, the bow was starting to respond to the helm.

The rescue helicopter, the angel, was already coming into a hover over the survivor. His head was just visible bobbing in the water as the carrier swept by, still making at least twenty knots.

Missed him.

'War Ace Five Oh Five, Departure.'

'Go ahead, Departure.'

'Five Oh Five, your last playmate will not be joining you. Switch to Strike and proceed with your mission, over.'

'Roger that.' Major Sam Cooley gave the radio frequency change signal by hand to Jake on his left wing and the Real McCoy on his right. He waited until the formation came around to the on-course heading, then leveled his wings and added power for the climb. They were on top of the cumulus layer. Above them was sunny, deep blue open sky.

So Rory Smith didn't get that plane airborne, Jake thought. He should have accepted that offer to switch planes. It's a good day to fly.

'Rory Smith's dead.'

They heard the news in the ready room, after they landed.

'He never got out. When Hank Davis punched Rory was sitting there wrestling the VDI. Hank's okay. He said the VDI came out on the cat shot. Came clean out of the panel right into Rory's lap. Jammed the stick aft. They stalled and went in.'

'Aww . . . ,' Flap said.

When Jake found his voice he muttered, 'He must not have checked to see that it was screwed in there.'

'Huh?'

'Yeah,' he told Flap. 'You gotta tug on the thing to make sure the screws that hold it are properly screwed in. Doesn't matter except on a catapult shot. If the VDI isn't secured right on a cat shot, it can come back into your lap. The damn thing weighs seventy pounds.'

'I never knew that.'

'I thought *everybody* knew that.'

'*I* never knew that. I wonder if Smith did.'

Jake Grafton merely stared in horror at the BN. *He* was the one tasked to cover everything these Marines needed to know about shipboard operations. He had forgotten to mention checking the VDI before the shot. Flap didn't know. Maybe Rory didn't either. And now Rory Smith was *dead!*

He sagged into a nearby chair. He had forgotten to tell

them about the VDI on the cat! What else had he forgotten to tell them? *What else?*

The television camera on the ship's island super-structure had caught the whole accident on videotape. The tape was playing now on the ready room television. Jake stared at the screen, mesmerized.

The shot looked normal, but the horizontal stabilizer – the stabilator – was really nose up. Too much? Hard to tell. There he went, off the bow, nose up rapidly, way too high, the stall and departure from controlled flight, a spin de-veloping as the plane went in. One ejection. The whole thing happened very quickly. The A-6 was in the water twelve seconds after the catapult fired.

Just twelve seconds.

The show continued. The angel hovered, a swimmer leaped from about four feet into the water . . . lots of spray from the rotor wash . . .

Jake rose and walked out. In sick bay he asked the first corpsman he saw, 'Captain Hank Davis?'

'Second door on the left, sir.'

The skipper came out of Hank's room before Jake got to the door. He told Jake, 'He doesn't need any visitors just now. He swallowed a lot of seawater and he's pretty shook.'

'I need to ask him a question, sir.'

'What is it?'

Jake explained about the VDI, how the screws might not engage when the box was installed, how the pilot must check it. 'I need to know, Colonel, if Rory tugged on the VDI to check it before he got to the cat.'

The colonel said nothing. He listened to Jake, watched his eyes, and said nothing.

'I'll ask him,' Haldane said finally, then opened the door and passed through.

Minutes passed. Almost five. When Haldane reappeared, he closed the door firmly behind him and faced the pilot, who was leaning against the bulkhead on the other side of the passageway.

'He doesn't remember.'

'Did he know about the possibility of the VDI coming out?'

'No. He didn't.'

Jake turned and walked away without another word.

He was sitting in his stateroom at his desk when the Real McCoy came in. The only light was the ten-watt fluorescent tube above Jake's desk. McCoy seated himself on his bunk.

'Take a hike, will ya, Real? I need some time alone.'

McCoy thought about it for a few seconds. 'Sure,' he said, and left.

Summer in Virginia was his favorite time of year. Everything was growing, the deer were lazy and fat, the squirrels chattered in the trees. The sun there would be hot on your back, the sweat would dampen your shirt. You would feel good as you used your muscles, accomplished tangible work that stood as hard evidence of the effort that had been put into it. The folks up and down the road were solid, hard-working people, people to stand with in good times and bad. And he had given that up for this . . .

Sitting in his stateroom Jake Grafton could hear the creaks and groans of the ship, the noises made by the steel plates as she rode through the seaway. And man-made noises, lots of them, trapping and hammering, chipping, pinging, clicking, grinding . . . slamming as doors and hatches were opened and closed.

Responsibility – they give you a tiny little job and you fuck it up and someone dies. In twelve seconds. Twelve lousy seconds . . .

And he had tried hard. He had taken the time, made the effort to do it right. He had written point after point, gone through the CV NATOPS page by page, paragraph by paragraph. He had covered every facet of carrier operations that he knew about. And had forgotten one item, a scintilla of information that he had heard once, somewhere, about an improperly secured VDI that slid four inches out of the tray in which it sat when the plane went down the catapult. Probably there were messages about it, several years ago, but the Marines didn't take cat shots then and the info apparently went in one official grunt ear and out the other. Now, when they needed to know that tidbit, he had forgotten to tell them.

Luck is really a miserable bitch. Just when you desperately need her to behave she sticks the knife in and twists it, leering at you all the while.

Rory Smith was dead. No bringing him back. All the teeth gnashing, hair pulling, hand wringing and confessions in the world won't raise him from the Pacific and breathe life back into his shattered body. The cockpit of War Ace 511 was his coffin. He was in it now, down there on the sea floor. The sea will claim his body and the airplane molecule by molecule, until someday nothing remains. He will then be a part of this ocean, a part of the clouds and the trade winds and the restless blue water.

Jake opened his safe and got out a bottle of whiskey. He poured himself a drink, raised it to Rory Smith, and swallowed it down.

The liquor made him sleepy. He climbed into the top bunk.

This guilt trip was not good. Yet at least it gave him the proper perspective to view the flying, the ship, the Navy, and all those dead men. Morgan McPherson, the Boxman, Frank Allen, Rory Smith, all those guys. All good dead men. All good. All dead. All dead real damn good.

He was going to get out of the Navy, submit a letter of resignation.

Never again. I'm not going to stand in the ready room any more helplessly watching videotapes of crashes. I'm not going to any more memorial services. I'm not packing any more guys' personal possessions in steel footlockers and sending them off to the parents or widow with any more goddamn little notes telling them how sorry I am. I'm not going to keep lying to myself that I am a better pilot than they were and that is why they are dead and I'm not. I've done all that shit too much. The guys that still have the stomach for it can keep doing it until they are each and every one of them as dead as Rory Smith but I will not. I have had enough.

CHAPTER TEN

Jake and Flap flew a tanker hop the next afternoon, which was the last scheduled flying day before the ship entered Pearl Harbor. They were in the high orbit, flying the five-mile arc around the ship at 20,000 feet, when Flap said, 'I hear you are putting in a letter of resignation.'

Since it wasn't a question, Jake didn't reply. He had talked to the first-class yeoman in the air wing office this morning, and apparently the yeoman talked to the Marines.

'That right?' Flap demanded.

'Yeah.'

'You know, you are one amazing dude. Yesterday afternoon you dropped six five-hundred-pounders visually and got four bull's-eyes, then did six system bore-sights and got three more. Seven bull's-eyes out of twelve bombs. That performance put you first in the squadron, by the way.'

This comment stirred Jake Grafton. In the society of warriors to which he belonged it was very bad form to brag, to congratulate yourself or listen placidly while others congratulated you on your superb flying abilities. The fig leaf didn't have to cover much, but modesty required that he wave it. 'Pure luck,' Jake muttered. 'The wind was real steady, which is rare, and—'

Flap steamed on, uninterested in fig leaves. 'Then you motor back to the ship and go down the slide like you're riding a rail, snag an okay three-wire, find out a guy crashed, announce it's all your fault because you knew something he didn't, and submit a letter of resignation. Now is that weird or what?'

'I didn't announce anything was my fault.'

'Horse shit. You announced it to yourself.'

'I didn't—'

'I had a little talk with the Real McCoy last night,' Flap explained. 'You were moping down in your room. You sure as hell weren't crying over Rory Smith – you hardly knew the guy. You were feeling sorry for yourself.'

'What an extraordinary insight, Doctor Freud! I can see now why I'm so twisted – when I was a kid my parents wouldn't let me screw my kitty cat. Send me a bill for this consultation. In the meantime *shut the fuck up!*'

Silence followed Jake's roar. The two men sat staring into the infinity of the sky as the shadow cast by the canopy bow walked across their laps. This shadow was the only relief from the intense tropic sunshine which shone down from the deep, deep blue.

'Hard to believe that over half the earth's atmosphere is below us,' Flap said softly. 'Without supplemental oxygen, at this altitude, most fit men would pass out within thirty minutes. You know, you've flown so many times that flying has probably become routine with you. That's the trap we all fall into. Sometimes we forget that we are really small blobs of protoplasm journeying haphazardly through infinity. All we have to sustain us are our little lifelines. The oxygen will keep flowing, the engines will keep burning, the plane will hold together, the ship will be waiting . . . Well, listen to the news. The lifelines can break. We are like the man on the tightrope above Niagara Falls: the tiniest misstep, the smallest inattention, the most minuscule miscalculation, and disaster follows.'

Flap paused for a moment, then continued: 'A lot of people have it in their heads that God gave them a guarantee when they were born. At least seventy years of vigorous life, hard work will earn solid rewards, your wife

153

with be faithful, your sons courageous, your daughters virtuous, *justice* will be done, *love* will be enough — in the event of problems, the manufacturer will set things right. Like hell! The truth is that life, like flying, is fraught with hazards. We are all up on that tightrope trying to keep our balance. Inevitably, people fall off.'

In spite of himself Jake was listening to Flap. That was the problem with the bastard's monologues – you couldn't ignore them.

'I think you're worth saving, Grafton. You're the best pilot I've met in the service. You are very very good. And you want to throw it all away. That's pretty sad.'

Flap paused. If he was giving Jake a chance to reply, he was disappointed. After a bit he continued:

'I never had much respect for you Navy guys. You think the military is like a corporation – you do your job, collect your green government check, and you can leave any time you get the itch. Maybe the Navy *is* that way. Thank God, the Corps *isn't.*'

Stung, Jake broke his silence. 'During our short acquaintance, you haven't heard one snotty remark out of me about the Holy Corps. But if you want to start trading insults, I can probably think up a few.'

Flap ignored Jake. 'We Marines are all in this together,' he said, expanding on his thesis. 'When one man slips off the rope, we'll grab him on the way down. We'll all hang together and we'll do what we have to do to get the job done. The Corps is bigger than all of us, and once you are a part of it, you are a part of it forever. Semper Fidelis. If you die, when you die, the Corps goes on. It's sorta like a church . . .'

Flap fell silent, thinking. The Corps was very hard to explain to someone who wasn't a Marine. He had tried it a few times in the past and always gave up. His explanations usually sounded trite, maybe even a little silly. 'Male bonding bullshit,' one woman told him after he had delivered himself of a memorable attempt. He almost slapped her.

For you see, the Corps was *real*. The feelings the Corps aroused in Flap and his fellow Marines were as real, as tangible, as the uniforms they wore and the weapons they carried. They *would* be loyal, they *would* be faithful, even unto death. Semper Fi. They belonged to something larger than themselves that gave their lives a meaning, a purpose, that was denied to lesser men, like civilians worried about earning a living. To Marines like Flap civilians concerned with getting and spending, getting and spending, were beneath contempt. They were like flies, to be ignored or brushed away.

'I'm trying to explain,' he told Jake Grafton now, 'because I think you could understand. You're a real good aviator. You're gifted. You owe it to yourself, to us, to hang tough, hang in there, keep doing what you know so well how to do.'

'I've had enough,' Jake told him curtly. He had little patience for this sackcloth and ashes crap. He had fought in one war. He had seen its true face. If Flap wanted to wrap himself in the flag that was his business, but Jake Grafton had decided to get on with his life.

'Rory Smith knew,' Flap told him with conviction. 'He was one fine Marine. He knew the risks and did his job anyway. He was all Marine.'

'And he's dead.'

'So? You and I are gonna die too, you know. Nobody ever gets out of life alive. Smith died for the Corps, but you're gonna go be a civilian, live the soft life until you check out. Some disease or other is going to kill you someday – cancer, heart disease, maybe just plain old age. Then you'll be as dead as Rory Smith. Now I ask you, what contribution will you have made?'

'I already made it.'

'Oh no! Oh no! Smith made *his* contribution – he gave all

that he had. You've slipped one thin dime into the collection plate, Ace, and now you announce that dime is your fair share. Like hell!'

'I've had about two quarts more than enough from you today, Le Beau,' Jake spluttered furiously. 'I did two cruises to the Nam. I dropped my bombs and killed my gooks and left my friends over there in the mud to rot. For what? For not a single goddamn thing, that's for what. You think you're on some sort of holy mission to protect America? The idiot green knight. Get real – those pot-smoking flower-power hippies don't *want* protection. You'd risk your life for them? If they were dying of thirst I wouldn't piss in their mouths!'

Jake Grafton was snarling now. 'I've paid my dues in blood, Le Beau, *my* blood. Don't give me any more *shit* about *my fair share!*'

Silence reigned in the cockpit as the KA-6D tanker continued to orbit the ship 20,000 feet below, at max conserve airspeed, each engine sucking a ton of fuel per hour, under the clean white sun. Since the tanker had no radar, computer or inertial navigation system, there was nothing for Flap to do but sit. So he sat and stared at that distant, hazy horizon. With the plane on autopilot, there was also little for Jake to do except scan the instruments occasionally and alter angle-of-bank as required to stay on the five-mile arc. This required almost no effort. He too spent most of his time staring toward that distant, infinite place where the sky reached down to meet the sea.

The crazy thing was that the horizon looked the same in every direction. In all directions. Pick a direction, any direction, and that uniform gauzy junction of sea and sky obscured everything that lay beyond. Yet intelligence tells us that direction is critical – life itself is a journey *toward something, somewhere* . . .

Which way?

Jake Grafton sat silently, looking, wondering.

Hank Davis was still in a private room in sick bay when Jake dropped by to see him. He looked pale, an impression accentuated by his black-as-coal, pencil-thin mustache.

'Hey, Hank, when they gonna let you out of here?'

'I'm under observation. Whenever they get tired of observing. I dunno.'

'So how you doing?' Jake settled into the only chair and looked the bombardier over carefully.

Davis shrugged. 'Some days you eat the bear, some days the bear eats you. He got a big bite of my butt yesterday. A big bite.'

'Well, you made it. You pulled the handle while you still had time, so you're alive.'

'You ejected once, didn't you?'

'Yeah,' Jake Grafton told him. 'Over Laos. Got shot up over Hanoi.'

'Ever have second thoughts?'

'Like what?'

'Well, like maybe you were too worried about your own butt and not enough about the other guy's?'

'I thought the VDI came out on the shot? Went into Smith's lap?'

'Yeah.'

'Hank! What could you do? The damned thing weighs seventy pounds. Even with your help, Smith couldn't have got it back into its tray. No way. If you'd crawled across to help, you'd both be dead now. It's not like you guys had a half hour to dick with this problem.'

Davis didn't reply. He looked at a wall, swallowed hard.

Jake Grafton racked his brains for a way to reach out. *I should have told you guys about checking the VDI's security.* Although he felt that, he didn't say it.

Hank related the facts of his ejection in matter-of-fact tones. The chute had not completely opened when he hit the water. So he hit the water way too hard and had trouble getting out of his chute. The swimmer from the helicopter had been there in seconds and saved his bacon. Still, he swallowed a lot of seawater and almost drowned.

'I dunno, Jake. Sometimes life's pretty hard to figure. When you look at it close, the only thing that makes a difference is luck. Who lives or who dies is just luck. "The dead guy screwed up," everybody says. Of course he screwed up. Lady Luck crapped all over him. And if that's true, then everything else is a lie – religion, professionalism, everything. We are all just minnows swimming in the sea and luck decides when it's your turn. Then the shark eats you and that's the fucking end of that.'

'If it's all luck, then these guilt trips don't make much sense, do they?' Jake observed.

'Right now the accident investigators are down in the avionics shop,' Hank Davis told him. 'They are looking for the simple bastard who didn't get the VDI screwed in right. All this *shit* is gonna get dumped right on that poor dumb son of a bitch! "Rory Smith is dead and it's *your* fault." Makes me want to puke some more.'

Squadron life revolves around the ready room, ashore or afloat. Since the A-6 squadrons always had the most flight crewmen, they always got the biggest ready room, in most ships Ready Five, but in *Columbia*, Ready Four. The ready room was never big enough. It was filled with comfortable, padded chairs that you could sink into and really relax in, even sleep in, but there weren't enough of them for all the officers.

In some squadrons when all the officers assembled for a meeting – an AOM – chairs were assigned by strict seniority. In other outfits the rule was first come, first served. How it was done depended on the skipper, who always got a chair up front by the duty desk, the best seat in the house. Lieutenant Colonel Haldane believed that rank had its privileges – at least when not airborne – so seniority reigned here. Jake Grafton ended up with a seat four rows back. The nuggets, first lieutenants on their first cruise, stood around the back of the room or sat on metal folding chairs.

AOMs were social and business events. Squadron business was thrashed out in these meetings, administrative matters dealing with the ship and the demands of the amorphous bureaucracies of the Navy and the Marine Corps were considered, lectures delivered on NATOPs and flying procedures, the 'word' passed, all manner of things.

At these soirees all the officers in the squadron got to know each other well. Here one got a close look at the department heads – the 'heavies' – watched junior officers in action, here the commanding officer exerted his leadership and molded the flight crews into a military unit.

In addition to the legal authority with which he was cloaked, the commanding officer was always the most experienced flyer there and the most senior. How he used these assets was the measure of the man, for truly, his responsibility was very great. In addition to the aircraft entrusted to him, he was responsible for about 350 enlisted men and three dozen officers. He was legally and morally responsible for every facet of their lives, from the adequacy of their living quarters to their health, professional development and performance. And he was responsible for the squadron as a military unit in combat, which meant the lives of his men were in his hands.

The responsibility crushed some men, but most commanding officers flourished under it. This was the professional zenith that they had spent their careers working to attain. By the time they reached it they had served under many commanding officers. The wise ones adopted the best of the leadership styles of their own former skippers and adapted it as necessary to suit their personalities. Leadership could not be learned from a book: it was the most intangible and the most human of the military skills.

In American naval aviation the best skippers led primarily by example and the force of their personalities – they intentionally kept the mood light as they gave orders, praised, cajoled, hinted, encouraged, scolded, ridiculed, laughed at and commented upon whatever and whomever they wished. The ideal that they seemed to instinctively strive for was a position as first among equals. Consequently AOMs were normally spirited affairs, occasionally raucous, full of good humor and camaraderie, with every speaker working hard to gain his audience's attention and cope with catcalls and advice – good, bad, indifferent and obscene. In this environment intelligence and good sense could flourish, here experience could be shared and everyone could learn from everyone else, here the bonds necessary to sustain fighting men could be forged.

This evening Rory Smith's death hung like a gloomy pall in the air.

Colonel Haldane spoke first. He told them what he knew of the accident, what Hank Davis had said. Then he got down to it:

'The war is over and still we have planes crashing and people dying. Hard to figure, isn't it? This time it wasn't the bad guys. The gomers didn't get Rory Smith in three hundred and twenty combat missions, although they tried and they tried damned hard. He had planes shot up so badly on three occasions that he was decorated for getting the planes back. What got him was a VDI that slid out of its tray in the instrument panel and jammed the stick.

'Did he think about ejecting? I don't know. I wish he had ejected. I wish to God we still had Rory Smith with us. Maybe he was worried about getting his legs cut off if he pulled the handle. Maybe he didn't have time to punch. Maybe he thought he could save it. Maybe he didn't realize how quickly the plane was getting into extremis. Lots of maybes. We'll never know.'

He picked up the blue NATOPs manual lying on the podium and held it up. 'This book is the Bible. The engineers that built this plane and the test pilots that wrung it out put their hearts and souls into this book – for you. Telling you everything they knew. And the process didn't stop there – as new things are learned about the plane the book is continually updated. It's a living document. You should know every word in it. That is the best insurance you can get on this side of hell.

'But the book doesn't cover everything. Sooner or later you are going to run into something that isn't covered in the book. Whether you survive the experience will be determined by your skill, your experience, and your luck.

'There's been a lot of mumbling around here the last twenty-four hours about luck. Well, there is no such thing. You can't feel it, taste it, smell it, touch it, wear it, fuck it, or eat it. It doesn't exist!

'This thing we call luck is merely professionalism and attention to detail, it's your awareness of everything that is going on around you, it's how well you know and *understand* your airplane and your own limitations. We make our own luck. Each of us. None of us is Superman. Luck is the sum total of your abilities as an aviator. If you think your luck is running low, you'd better get busy and make some more. Work harder. Pay more attention. Study your NATOPs more. Do better preflights.

'A wise man once said, "Fortune favors the well prepared." He was right.

'Rory Smith is not with us here tonight because he didn't eject when he should have. Hank Davis is alive because he did.

'We're going to miss Rory. But every man here had better resolve to learn something from his death. If we do, he didn't die for nothing. Think about it.'

*

The best way to see Hawaii is the way the ancient Polynesians first saw it, the way it was revealed to whalers and missionaries, the way sailors have always seen it.

The islands first appear on the horizon like clouds, exactly the same as the other clouds. Only as the hours pass and your vessel gets closer does it become apparent that there is something different about these clouds. The first hints of green below the churning clouds imply mass, earth, land, an *island*, where at first there appeared to be only sea and sky.

Finally you see for sure – tawny green slopes, soon a surf line, definition and a crest for that ridge, that draw, that promontory.

Hawaii.

Jake Grafton stood amid the throng of off-duty sailors on the bow watching the island of Oahu draw closer and closer. She looked emerald green this morning under her cloud-wreath. The hotels and office buildings of Honolulu were quite plain there on the right. Farther right Diamond Head jutted from the sea haze, also wearing a cumulus buildup.

The sailors pointed out the landmarks to one another and talked excitedly. They were jovial, happy. To see Hawaii for the first time is one of life's great milestones, like your first kiss.

Jake had been here before – twice. On each of his first two cruises the ship had stopped in Pearl on its way to Vietnam. As he watched the carrier close the harbor channel, he thought again of those times, and of the men now dead whom he had shared them with. Little fish. Sharks.

He went below. Down in the stateroom the Real McCoy was poring over a copy of the *Wall Street Journal*. 'Are you rich enough to retire yet?'

'I'm making an honest dollar, Grafton. Working hard at it and taking big risks. We call the system capitalism.'

'Yeah. So how's capitalism treating you?'

'Think I'm up another grand as of the date of this paper, four days ago. I'll get something current as soon as I can get off base.'

'Uh-huh.'

'Arabs turned off the oil tap in the Mideast. That will send my domestic oil stocks soaring and melt the profits off my airline stocks. Some up, some down. You know, the crazy thing about investing – there's really no such thing as bad news. Whether an event is good or bad depends on where you've got your money.'

Jake eyed his roommate without affection. This worm's-eye view of life irritated him. The worms had placed bets on the little fish. Somehow that struck him as inevitable, though it didn't say much for the worms. Or the little fish.

'You going ashore?' McCoy asked.

'Like a shot out of a gun, the instant the gangway stops moving,' Jake Grafton replied. 'I have got to get off this tub for a while.'

'Liberty hounds don't go very high in this man's Navy,' McCoy reminded him, in a tone that Jake thought sounded a wee bit prissy.

'I really don't care if Haldane uses my fitness report for toilet paper' was Jake Grafton's edged retort. And he didn't care. Not one iota.

'Hello.'

'Hello, Mrs McKenzie? This is Jake Grafton. Is Callie there?'

'No, she isn't, Jake. Where are you?'

'Hawaii.'

'She's at school right now. She should be back around six this evening. Is there a number where she can reach you?'

'No. I'll call her. Please tell her I called.'

'I'll do that, Jake.'

The pilot hung up the phone and put the rest of the

163

quarters from his roll back into his trouser pocket. When he stepped out of the telephone booth, the next sailor in line took his place.

He trudged away looking neither right nor left, ignoring the sporadic salutes tossed his way. The palm trees and frangipani in bloom didn't interest him. The tropical breeze caressing his face didn't distract him. When a jet climbing away from Hickam thundered over, however, the pilot stopped and looked up. He watched the jet until the plane was out of sight and the sound had faded, then walked on.

About a ship's length from the carrier pier was a small square of grass complete with picnic table adjacent to the water. After brushing away pigeon droppings, Jake Grafton seated himself on the table and eased his fore-and-aft cap farther back onto his head. The view was across the harbor at the USS *Arizona* memorial, which he knew was constructed above the sunken battleship's superstructure. *Arizona* lay on the mud under that calm sheet of water, her hull blasted, holed, burned and twisted by Japanese bombs and torpedoes. Occasionally boats ferrying tourists to and from the memorial made wakes that disturbed the surface of the water. After the boats' passage, the disturbance would quickly dissipate. Just the faintest hint of a swell spoiled the mirror smoothness of that placid sheet, protected as it was from the sea's turbulence by the length and narrowness of the channel. The perfect water reflected sky and drifting cumulus clouds and, arranged around the edge of the harbor, the long gray warships that lay at the piers.

Jake Grafton smoked cigarettes while he sat looking. Time passed slowly and his mind wandered. Occasionally he glanced at his watch. When almost two hours had passed, he walked back toward the telephone booths at the head of the carrier pier and got back into line.

'Hey, Callie, it's me, Jake.'

'Well, hello, sailor! It's great to hear your voice.'

'Pretty nice hearing yours too, lady. So you're back in school?'

'Uh-huh. Graduate courses. I'm getting so educated I don't know what I'll do.'

'I like smart women.'

'I'll see if I can find one for you. So you're in Pearl Harbor?'

'Yep. Hawaii. Got in a while ago. Gonna be here a couple days, then maybe Japan or the Philippines or the IO.' Realizing that she probably wouldn't recognize the acronym, he added belatedly, 'That's the Indian Ocean. I don't know. Admirals somewhere figure it out and I go wherever the ship goes. But enough about me. Talk some so I can to listen to your voice.'

'I got your letter about the in-flight engagement. That sounded scary. And dangerous.'

'It was exciting all right, but we lost a plane yesterday on a day cat shot. An A-6. Went in off the cat. The pilot was killed.'

'I'm sorry, Jake.'

'I'm getting real tired of this, Callie. I've been here too long. I'm a civilian at heart and I think it's time I pulled the plug. I've submitted a letter of resignation.'

'Oh,' she said. After a pause, she added, 'When are you getting out?'

'Won't be until the cruise is over.'

'Are you sure about this?'

'Yeah.'

He twisted the telephone cord and wondered what to say. She wasn't saying anything on her end, so he plunged ahead. 'The plane that went in off the cat was the one I had the in-flight engagement in, ol' Five One One. The in-flight smacked the avionics around pretty good, and when they reinstalled the boxes one of the technicians didn't get the VDI properly secured. So the VDI box came out on

165

the cat shot, jammed the stick. The BN punched and told us what happened, but the pilot didn't get out.'

'You're not blaming yourself, are you?'

'No.' He said that too quickly. 'Well, to tell the truth, I am a little bit responsible. With better technique I might have avoided the in-flight. That's spilled milk. Maybe it was unavoidable. But I was briefing these Marines on carrier ops – everything you need to know to be a carrier pilot in four two-hour sessions, and I forgot to mention that you have to check the security of the VDI.'

'I see.'

'Do you?'

'Not really. But aren't these risks a part of carrier aviation?'

'Not a part. This is the main course, the heart of it, the very essence. In spite of the very best of intentions, mistakes will be made, things will break. War or no war, people get killed doing this stuff. I'm getting sick of watching people bet their lives and losing, that's all.'

'Are you worried about your own safety?'

'No more than usual. You have to fret it some or you won't be long on this side of hell.'

'It seems to me that the dangers would become hard to live with—'

'I can handle it. I think. No one's shooting at me. But see, that's the crazy part. The war is over, yet as long as men keep flying off these ships there are going to be casualties.'

'So what will you do when you get out?'

'I don't know, Callie.'

Seconds passed before she spoke. 'Life isn't easy, Jake.'

'That isn't exactly news. I've done a year or two of hard living my own self.'

'I thought you liked the challenge.'

'Are you trying to tell me you want me to stay in?'

'No.' Her voice solidified. 'I am not suggesting that you do anything. I'm not even hinting. Stay in, get out, whatever, that's your choice and yours alone. You must live your own life.'

'Damn, woman! I'm trying.'

'I know,' she said gently.

'You know me,' he told her.

'I'm beginning to.'

'How are your folks?'

'Fine,' she said. They talked for several more minutes, then said good-bye.

The vast bulk of the ship loomed high over the bank of telephone booths. Jake glanced up at the ship, at the tails of the planes sticking over the edge of the flight deck, then lowered his gaze, stuffed his hands into his pockets and walked away.

The problem was that he had never been able to separate the flying from the rest of it – the killing, bombing, dying. Maybe it couldn't be separated. The My Lai massacre, Lieutenant William Calley, napalm on villages, burning children, American pilots nailed to trees and skinned alive, Viet Cong soldiers tortured for information while Americans watched, North Vietnamese soldiers given airborne interrogations – talk or we'll throw you from the helicopter without a parachute: all of this was tied up with the flying in a Gordian knot that Solomon couldn't unravel.

He thought he had cut the knot – well, Commander Camparelli and the Navy had cut it for him – last winter in Vietnam. He had picked an unauthorized target, the North Vietnamese capitol building in Hanoi, attacked and almost got it, then faced some very unhappy senior officers across a long green table. They knew what their duty was: *obey orders from the elected government.* What they couldn't fathom was how he, Lieutenant Jake Jackass from Possum Hollow, had lost sight of it.

We're all in this together. *We must keep the faith.* Wasn't that what you and your friends were always telling one another when the shit got thick and the blood started flowing?

We do what we must and die when we must *for each other*.

The faith was easier to understand then, easier to keep. Now the war was over. Although some people want to keep fighting it, by God, it's *over*.

Now the Navy was peacetime cruises, six- to eight-month voyages to nowhere, excruciating separations from loved ones, marriages going on the rocks under the strain, kids growing up with a father who's never there; it's getting scared out of your wits when Lady Luck kisses your ass good-bye; it's seeing people squashed into shark food; it's knowing – knowing all the time, every minute of every day – that you may be next. The life can be smashed out of you so quick that you'll inhale in this world and exhale in hell.

Lieutenant Jake Grafton, farmer's son and history major, was going to get on with his life. Do something safe, something sane. Something with tangible rewards. Something that allowed him to find a good woman, raise a family, be a father to his children. He would bequeath this flying life to dedicated half-wits like Flap Le Beau.

Yet he would miss the flying.

This afternoon as Jake Grafton walked along the boulevard that led into downtown Honolulu, huge, benign cumulus clouds were etched against the deep blue sky, seemingly fixed. He would like to fly right now – to strap on an airplane and leave behind the problems of the ground.

We are, he well knew, creatures of the earth. Its minerals compose our bodies and provide our nourishment. Our cells contain seawater, legacies of ancestors who lived in the oceans. Yet on the surface man evolved, here where there are other animals to kill and eat, edible plants, trees with nuts and fruits, streams and lakes teeming with life. Our bodies function best at the temperature ranges, atmospheric pressures and oxygen levels that have prevailed on the earth's surface throughout most of the age of mammals. We need the protection from the sun's radiation that the atmosphere provides. Our senses of smell and hearing use the atmosphere as the transmitting medium. The earth's gravity provides a reference point for our sense of balance and the resistance our muscles and circulatory systems need to function properly. The challenges of surviving on the dry surface provided the evolutionary stimulus to develop our brains.

Without the earth, we would not be the creatures we are. And yet we want to leave it, to soar through the atmosphere, to voyage through interplanetary space, to explore other worlds. And to someday leave the solar system and journey to another star. All this while we are still trapped by our physical and psychological limitations here on the surface of the mother planet.

Sometimes the contradictions inherent in our situation hit him hard. Last fall, while he was hunting targets in North Vietnam as he dodged the flak and SAMs, Americans again walked on the moon. Less than seventy years after the Wright brothers left the surface in powered flight, man stood on the moon and looked back at the home planet glistening amid the infinite black nothingness. They looked while war, hunger, pestilence and man's inhumanity to man continued unabated, continued as it had since the dawn of human history.

It was a curious thing, hard to comprehend, yet worth pondering on a balmy evening in the tropics with the air laden with fragrant aromas and the surf flopping rhythmically on the beach a few yards away.

Jake Grafton walked along the beach, stared at the hotels and the people and the relentless surf and thought of all these things.

An hour later, as he walked back toward the army base with traffic whizzing by, the tops of the lazy large clouds were shot with fire by the setting sun.

The problem, he decided, was keeping everything in proper perspective. That was hard to do. Impossible, really. To see man and his problems, the earth and the universe, as they really are one would have to be God.

The officers' club was full of people, music, light, laughter. Jake stood in the entrance for several seconds letting the sensations sink in. He tucked his hat under his belt, then strolled for the bar.

He heard them before he got to the door.

'How ugly was she?' three or four voices asked in a shaky unison.

'She was ugly as a tiger's hairball.' Flap's soaring baritone carried clearly. People here in the lounge waiting to be called for dinner looked at each other, startled.

'How ugly?'

'Ugly as a mud wrestler's navel.' Eyebrows soared.

'How ugly?' Eight or ten voices now.

'Ugly as a pickled pervert's promise.' Women giggled and whispered to each other. Several of the gentlemen frowned and turned to stare at the door to the bar. Jake saw one of the men, in his fifties, with short, iron gray hair, wink at his companion.

'*That's* not ugly!'

'She was so damn ugly that the earth tried to quake and couldn't – it just shivered. So ugly that five drunken sailors pretended they didn't see her. The city painted her red and put a number on her – two dogs relieved themselves on her shoes before I got to the rescue, that's how ugly she was. She was so desperately ugly that my zipper welded itself shut. And that, my gentle friends, is the gospel truth.'

Jake Grafton grinned, squared his shoulders, and walked into the bar.

CHAPTER ELEVEN

The air was opaque, the sun hidden by the moisture in the air. Two or three miles from the ship in all directions the gray sea and gray sky merged. *Columbia* was in the midst of an inverted bowl, three days northwest of Pearl laboring through fifteen-foot swells. The wind was brisk from the west.

From his vantage point in the cockpit of a KA-6D tanker spotted behind the jet blast deflector – the JBD – for Cat Three, Jake Grafton could see a frigate a mile or so off the port beam. Just ahead, barely visible on the edge of the known universe, he could make out the wake and super-structure of another.

Jake and Flap were standing the five-minute alert tanker duty, which meant that for two hours they had to sit in the cockpit of this bird strapped in, ready to fire up the engines and taxi onto the catapult as soon as the F-4 Phantom that was parked there – also on five-minute alert – launched. There was another fighter on five-minute status sitting just short of the hook-up area on Cat Four, and an airborne early warning aircraft, an E-2 Hawkeye, parked with its tail against the island. Sitting on the waist catapult tracks was a manned helicopter, the angel, which would have to launch before the catapults could be fired. A power unit with its engine running was pugged into each aircraft, instantly ready to deliver air to turn the engines. All five of the alert birds had been serviced and started, checked to make sure all their systems worked, then shut down.

The crews were strapped into the airplanes. The pilot of

the Phantom on Cat Four was reading a paperback novel, Jake could see, but he couldn't make out the title.

On the deck behind the waist catapults sat two more fighters and a tanker on alert-fifteen status, which meant that their crews were flaked out in their respective ready rooms wearing all their flight gear, ready to run for the flight deck if the alarm sounded.

Alert duty kept flight crews busy any time that planes were not aloft. Except in waters just off the shore of the United States, it was rare for a carrier to be below alert-thirty status. Alert-fifteen was the usual status for the high seas, with alert-five reserved for the South China Sea during the war just ended or other locations where a possible threat existed. Today a possible threat existed. Intelligence expected the Soviets to try to overfly the carrier task group as it transited to Japan with land-based naval bombers from Vladivostok or one of the fields on Sakhalin Island or the Kamchatka peninsula.

The Russkis were going to have their work cut out for them overflying the ship in this low visibility, Jake thought, if they came at all. He sat watching the frigate on the port beam labor into the swells, ride up and then bury her bow so deep that white spray was flung aft all the way to the bridge.

Columbia's ride was definitely more pleasant, but Jake could feel her pitching and see the leading edge of the angled deck rise and fall as she rode the restless sea.

To Jake's right, in the bombardier-navigator's seat, Flap Le Beau was reading a book by Malcolm X. Every time he got to the bottom of a page, he lowered the paperback and glanced around, his eyes scanning several times while he turned the page.

On one of Flap's periscope sweeps, Jake asked, 'That book any good?

'Guy sure is interesting,' Flap said, and resumed his reading.

'What's it about?

'You don't know Malcolm X?'

'Uh-uh.'

'Hated honkeys. Believed the races should have their own enclaves, no mixing, that kind of stuff.'

'Do you believe that?' Jake asked tentatively. Flap was only the second or third black naval aviator Jake had ever met, and he had never discussed race with one.

'He had some good ideas,' Flap said, glancing at Jake. 'But no, I think the races should be integrated. America is for Americans — black, white, brown, yellow, green or purple. But what about you? You're from rural Virginia, nigger-hating redneck heaven, one-party bigot politics, pot-gutted klagel sheriffs — what d'ya think?'

'Ol' X should've had you writing his speeches.'

Jake Grafton wasn't stupid enough to proclaim himself a true believer in racial equality and brotherly love, certainly not to a black man probably capable of forcing him into the bigot cesspool with just a little effort.

'Who knows, if this Marine Corps gig goes sour, I might go into politics,' Flap allowed, then resumed reading his book.

His father had two black employees on his farm during the years Jake was growing up. They were both huge men, with hands like pie plates and upper arms larger than Jake's thighs. They were barely able to sign their names but they could work any four white men into the dirt. In their younger days they had worked on railroad track-repair gangs swinging sledge-hammers. 'Georgia niggers,' his father, Sam, had called them. How they came to end up on the Grafton farm Jake never quite understood, but Isaiah and Frank allowed from time to time that they had absolutely no intention of crossing the Virginia line south-bound. Then they would shake their heads and laugh at some private joke, creating the vision in the boy's mind of blood-thirsty southern sheriffs eager to avenge spectacular, unmentionable crimes.

His father treated the two blacks like the whites he hired occasionally, worked alongside them, shared food and smokes and jokes. Young Jake liked the men immensely.

Yet, like most of the boys of his generation in south-western rural Virginia, he accepted racial segregation as natural, as unremarkable and logical as the deference men showed women and the respect accorded the elderly. That is, he did until 1963, the year he turned eighteen. One evening while watching the network news show footage of Negro children in Birmingham being blasted with streams from high-pressure fire hoses, his father had let out an oath.

'I guess it's a damn good thing that I'm not colored,' Sam Grafton declared. 'If I were, I'd get me a gun and go to Birmingham and start shooting some of those sons of bitches. And I'd start with that bastard right there!' His finger shot out and Jake found himself staring at the porky visage of Bull Connor.

'Sam!' exclimed his mother disgustedly.

'Martha, what the hell do they have to do to get treated decent by whites? The colored people have put up with a hell of a lot more crap than any Christian should ever have to deal with. Those sons of bitches laying the wood to them aren't Christians. They're Nazis. It's a miracle the colored people haven't started shooting the damned swine.'

'Do you have to cuss like that?'

'It's high time some white people got mad at those bigots,' Sam Grafton thundered. 'I wish Jack Kennedy would get his ass out of his rocking chair and kick some butt. The President of the United States, saying there's nothing he can do when those rednecks attack children! By God, if Bull Connor was black and those kids were white he'd be singing a different tune. He's just another gutless politician scared of losing the bigot vote. Pfft!'

174

That evening had been an eye-opener for Jake. He started paying attention to the civil rights protests, listening to the arguments. His father had always been a bit different than his neighbors, marching to a different drummer. And he was usually right. He was that time, too, his son concluded.

Remembering that evening, he sighed, then glanced around the flight deck. People were lying on the deck beside their equipment, napping.

He was in the middle of a yawn when he heard the hiss of the flight deck loudspeaker system coming to life. 'Launch the alert-five. Launch the alert-five. We have bogies inbound.'

The lounging men on the flight deck sprang into action. Jake Grafton twirled his fingers at the plane captain, received a twirl in response. He turned on the left engine-fuel master switch and pushed the start button. With a low moan the engine began to turn. When the RPM was high enough he came around the horn with the throttle, then sat watching the temperatures and RPMs rise while he pulled his helmet on.

By the time he got the second engine started and the canopy closed, the chopper on the cat tracks was engaging its rotors. The ship was turning – Jake could see the list on the flight deck – coming about forty degrees left into the wind. Now the deck leveled out. The *Columbia*'s rudder was centered. Thirty seconds later the angel lifted off. It left the deck straight ahead. When it was safely past the bow the chopper pilot laid it into a right turn.

Now the catapult shuttles were dragged back out of the water brakes into battery while the final checkers inspected the two fighters and gave their thumbs-up. Red-shirted ordnancemen pulled the safety pins from the missile racks and showed them to the pilots. The yellow-shirted taxi director gave the pilot of the plane in front of Jake a come-ahead signal and let him inch the last two feet forward onto Cat Three while the green-shirted catapult hook-up men crawled underneath with the bridle and two more greenies installed the hold-back bar, on the Phantom a ten-foot-long hinged strap with the hold-back shear-bolt attaching to the airplane's belly and the other end going into a slot in the deck. The weight-board man flashed his board at the pilot and got a thumbs-up, then showed it to the cat officer, who also rogered. The whole performance was a ballet of multicolored shirts darting around, near and under the moving fighter, each man intent on doing his job perfectly.

As the taxiing fighter reached the maximum extent of the hold-back bar, the JBDs came up, three panels that would deflect the exhaust of the launching aircraft from the plane behind.

Now Jake saw the Phantom lower its tail – actually the nose-gear strut was extended eighteen inches to improve the angle-of-attack. He saw the cat officer twirl his fingers above his head for full power and heard the thunderous response from the Phantom, saw the river of black smoke blasted upward by the JBD, felt his plane tremble from the fury of those two engines. The fighter pilot checked his controls, and the stabilator and rudder waggled obediently. Thumbs-up flashed from the squadron final checkers.

The cat officer signaled for afterburners, an opening hand on an extended arm. The river of smoke pouring skyward off the JBDs cleared, leaving hot, clear shimmering gases. Incredibly, even here in the cockpit of the tanker the noise level rose. Jake got a good whiff of the acrid stench of jet exhaust.

My oxygen mask must not be on tight enough. Fix it when I'm airborne.

The last of the catapult crewmen came scurrying out from under the fighter. This was the man who swung on the bridle to ensure it was on firmly. He flashed a thumbs-up at the cat officer, the shooter.

The shooter saluted the F-4 pilot, glanced down the deck, and lunged. One potato, two potato, and wham, the fighter shot forward trailing plumes of fire from its twin exhausts. It hadn't gone a hundred feet down the track when the JBD started down and a taxi director gave Jake Grafton the come-ahead signal.

After he watched the Phantom clear the deck, the shooter turned his attention to the fighter on Cat Four, which was already at full power. He gave the burner sign. Fifteen seconds later this one ripped down the cat after the first one, which was out of burner now and trailing a plume of black smoke that showed quite distinctly against the gray haze wall.

Jake taxied forward and ran through his ritual as the wind over the deck swirled steam leaking from the catapult slot around the men on deck. Their clothes flapped in the wind.

Power up, control check, cat grip, engine instruments, warning lights, salute.

One potato, two pota – he felt just the tiniest jolt as the hold-back bolt broke, then the acceleration smashed him backward like the hand of God.

The strike controller told Jake to go on up to 20,000 feet. 'Texaco take high station.'

Flap rogered, then Jake said on the ICS, 'They must not be going to launch the alert-fifteen.'

'Why do you say that?'

'Surely they'll want us to tank the second section of fighters immediately after launch, if they launch them.'

'Maybe not.'

'Ours is not to reason why, our is but to do or die.'

'Noble sentiment. But let's *do* today, not die.'

'Aye aye, sir.'

'Don't get cute.'

Jake Grafton gave a couple of pig grunts.

'I thought you said you weren't going to insult the Corps?' Flap sounded shocked.

'I lied.'

The sea disappeared as they climbed through 3,000 feet. Jake was on the gauges. There was no horizon, no sky, no sea. Inside this formless, featureless void the plane handled as usual, but the only measure of its progress through space was movement of the altimeter, the TACAN needle, and the rotating numbers of the distance measuring equipment – DME.

Jake kept expecting to reach an altitude where the goo thinned perceptibly, but it was not to be. When he leveled at 20,000 feet he could see a blob of light above him that had to be the sun, yet the haze seemed as thick as ever. Just what the visibility might be was impossible to say without another object to focus upon.

Flap reported their arrival at high station. The controller rogered without apparent enthusiasm.

Jake set the power at max conserve and when the airspeed had stabilized, engaged the autopilot. He checked the cockpit altitude and loosened one side of his oxygen mask from his helmet. Flap sat silently for a moment or two, looking here and there, then he extracted his book from a pocket of his G-suit and opened it to a dog-eared page.

Jake busied himself with punching buttons to check that the fuel transfer was proceeding normally. The tanker carried five 2,000-pound drop tanks. The transfer of fuel from these drops was automatic. If transfer didn't occur, however, he wanted to know it as soon as possible because he would have that much less fuel available to give to other aircraft or burn himself. Today the transfer seemed to be progressing as advertised, so he had 26,000 pounds of fuel to burn or give away.

They were almost eight hundred miles northwest of Midway Island alone in an opaque sky. Other than flicking his eyes across the instruments and adjusting the angle-of-bank occasionally, he had nothing to do except scan the blank whiteness outside for other airplanes that never came.

The fighters were being vectored out to intercept the incoming Russians, the E-2 was proceeding away from the ship to a holding station – those were the only other airplanes aloft. There was nothing in this sky to see. Yet if an aircraft did appear out of the haze, it would be close, very close, on a collision course or nearly so, a rerun of the Phantom incident a week ago. He sure as hell didn't want to go through *that* again.

In spite of his resolution to keep a good lookout, boredom crept over him. His mind wandered.

He had signed the letter of resignation from the Navy yesterday and submitted it to Lieutenant Colonel Haldane. The skipper had taken the document without comment. Well, what was there to say?

Haldane wasn't about to try to argue him into staying – he barely knew Jake. If Jake wanted out, he wanted out. What he could expect was a form letter of appreciation, a handshake and a hearty 'Have a nice life.'

That *was* what he wanted, wasn't it?

Why not go back to Virginia and help Dad with the farm? Fishing in the spring and summer, hunting in the fall . . . He would end up joining the Lions Club, like his father. Lions meeting every Thursday evening, church two or three Sundays a month, high school football games on Friday nights in September and October . . .

It would be a chance to settle down, get a house of his own, some furniture, put down roots. He contemplated that future now, trying to visualize how it would be.

Dull. It would be damn dull.

Well, he had been complaining that the Navy was too challenging, the responsibility for the lives and welfare of other people too heavy to carry.

One life offered too much challenge, the other too little. Was there something, somewhere, more in the middle?

'Texaco, Strike.'

'Go ahead.'

'Take low station. Buster.' Buster meant hurry, bust your ass.

'We're on our way.'

Jake Grafton disengaged the autopilot and rolled the Intruder to ninety degrees angle-of-bank. The nose came down. Speed brakes out, throttles back, shallow the bank to about seventy degrees, put a couple G's on . . . the rate-of-descent needle pegged at 6,000 feet per minute down. That was all it would indicate. A spiral descent was his best maneuver because the tanker had a three-G limitation, mandated by higher authority to make the wings last longer. He was right at three G's now, the altimeter unwinding at a dizzying rate.

Low station was 5,000 feet, but it could be lowered if the visibility was better below this crud. Maybe he should ask. 'Ah, Strike, Texaco. How's the visibility and ceiling underneath?'

'A little worse than when you took off. Maybe a mile viz under an indefinite obscuration.'

'Who's our customer?'

'Snake-eye Two Oh Seven. He's got an emergency. Switch to button sixteen and rendezvous on him.'

Jake was passing ten thousand feet, still turning steeply with G on. Bracing himself against the G, Flap changed the radio channel and called.

'Snake-eye Two Oh Seven, this is Texaco. Say your posit, angels, and heading, over.'

'Texaco, I'm on the Three One Zero radial at nine miles, headed inbound at four grand. Better hurry.'

Jake keyed the radio transmitter. 'Just keep going in and we'll join on you.'

The fighter pilot gave him two clicks in reply.

Jake eyed the TACAN needle on the HSI, the horizontal situation indicator, a glorified gyroscopic compass. He had a problem here in three-dimensional space and the face of the instrument was an aid in helping him visualize it.

He rolled the wings level and stuffed the nose down more. His airspeed was at 400 knots and increasing.

'Snake-eye, Texaco, what's your problem?'

'We're venting fuel overboard and the pull-forward is going to take more time than we've got.'

'Posit again?'

'Three One Zero at five, angels four, speed three hundred, heading One Three Zero.'

'Are you in the clear?'

'Negative.'

'Let's go on down to three grand.'

Jake was passing six thousand feet, on the Three Three Zero radial at nine miles. He was indicating 420 knots and he was raising the nose to shallow his dive. He thumbed the speed brakes in and added some power. 'We're going to join fast,' he muttered at Flap, who didn't reply.

The problem was that he didn't know how much visibility he would have. If it was about a mile, like the controller on the ship said, and he missed the F-4 by more than that margin, he would never see him. Unlike the Phantom, the tanker had no radar to assist in the interception.

He was paying strick attention to the TACAN needle now. The seconds ticked by and the distance to the ship closed rapidly.

'There, at one o'clock.' Flap called it.

Now Jake saw the fighter. He was several hundred feet below Jake, which was good, at about a mile, trailing a plume of fuel. Grafton reduced power and deployed the speed brakes.

Uh-oh, he had a ton of closure. He stuffed the nose down to underrun the Phantom.

'*Look out!*'

The wingman! His tailpipes were *right there*, coming in the windscreen! Sweet Jesus!

He jammed the stick forward and the negative G lifted him and Flap away from their seats. In two heartbeats he was well under and jerked the stick back. He had forgotten about the wingman.

Still indicating 350, he ran under the Phantom in trouble and pulled the power to idle. 'At your one o'clock, Snake-eye. We'll tank at two seventy. Join on me.'

At 280 knots he got the power up and the speed brakes in. He quickly stabilized at 270 indicated. After checking to ensure that he was level headed directly for the ship, Jake turned in his seat to examine the Phantom closing in as Flap deployed the refueling drogue.

The three-thousand-pound belly tank the F-4 usually carried was gone. Fuel was pouring from the belly of the aircraft.

'Green light, you're cleared in,' Flap announced on the radio.

Jake turned back to his instruments. He wanted to provide a stable drogue for the fighter to plug. 'What's your problem, Snake-eye?'

'Belly tank wouldn't transfer. We jettisoned it and now we are pumping fuel out the belly. The check valve must be damaged. We're down to one point seven.'

'Strike, Texaco, how much does Two Oh Seven get?'

'All he needs, Texaco. We should have a ready deck in six or seven minutes. Pulling forward now.' This meant all the planes parked in the landing area were being pulled forward to the bow.

The green light on the refueling panel went out and the fuel counter began to click over. 'You're getting fuel,' Flap told the fighter.

They were crossing over the ship now. Jake Grafton eased the tanker into a descent. If he could get underneath

182

this haze he could drop the Phantom at the 180-degree position, only thirty seconds or so from the deck.

When the fuel-delivered counter registered two thousand pounds, Jake told the fighter pilot.

'Keep it coming. We're up a grand in the main bag. At least we're getting it faster than it's going over the side.'

At two thousand feet Jake saw the ocean. He kept descending. At fifteen hundred feet he spotted the carrier, on his left, turning hard. The ship was coming into the wind. From this distance Jake could only see a couple airplanes still to go forward. Very soon.

He leveled at twelve hundred feet and circled the ship in a left turn at about a mile.

Five thousand pounds transferred . . . six . . . seven . . . the ship was into the wind now and the wake was streaming straight behind her, white as snow against the gray sea as the four huge screws bit hard to drive her faster through the water.

'Snake-eye Two Oh Seven, this is Paddles. We're going to be ready in about two minutes. I want you to drop off the tanker on the downwind, dirty up and turn into the groove. Swells still running about fifteen feet, so the deck is pitching. Average out the ball and fly a nice smooth pass.'

'Two Oh Seven.'

Jake was crossing the bow now, the fuel counter still clicking. Eight thousand five hundred pounds transferred so far.

'Texaco, hawk the deck.'

'Roger.' Hawk the deck meant to fly alongside so that the plane on the bolter could rendezvous and tank.

This was going to work out, Jake told himself. This guy is going to get aboard.

The fuel-delivered counter stopped clicking over at 9,700 pounds. The fighter had backed out of the basket. Jake took a cut to the right, then turned back left and looked over his shoulder. The crippled fighter was descending and slowing, his hook down and gear coming out. And the fuel was still pouring from his belly in a steady, fire-hose stream. The wingman was well behind, still clean.

When the fighter pilot jettisoned the belly tank, Jake thought, the quick-disconnect fitting must have frozen and the plumbing tore loose inside the aircraft. There was a one-way check valve just upstream of the quick-disconnect; obviously it wasn't working. So the pressure in the main fuel cell was forcing fuel overboard through the broken pipe.

Jake slowed to 250 knots and cycled the refueling hose in and back out to reset the reel response. Now to scoot down by the ship, Jake thought, so that if he bolters, I'll be just ahead where he can quickly rendezvous.

He dropped to a thousand feet and turned hard at a mile to parallel the wake on the ship's port side.

The landing fighter was crossing the wake, turning into the groove, when Jake saw the fire.

The plume of fuel streaming behind the plane ignited. The tongue of flame was twice as long as the airplane and clearly visible.

'*You're on fire!*' someone shouted on the radio.

'*In the groove, eject, eject, eject!*'

Bang, bang, two seats came out. Before the first chute opened the flaming fighter went nose-first into the ship's wake. A splash, then it was gone.

'Two good chutes.' Another voice on the radio.

In seconds both the chutes went into the water. As Jake went over he spotted the angel coming up the wake.

'Boy, talk about luck! It's a wonder he didn't blow up,' Jake told Flap.

He was turning across the bow when the air boss came on the frequency. You always knew the boss's voice, a God-like booming from on high. 'Texaco, your signal, charley. We're going to hot spin you.'

Jake checked his fuel quantity. Nine thousand pounds left. He opened the main dump and dropped the hook, gear and flaps.

As advertised, the ball was moving up and down on the optical landing system, which was gyroscopically stabilized in roll and pitch, but not in heave, the up and down motion of the ship.

He managed to get aboard without difficulty and was taxied in against the island to refuel. He kept the engines running.

In moments the helicopter settled onto the deck abeam the island. Corpsmen with stretchers rushed out. The stretchers weren't needed. The two Phantom crewmen walked across the deck under their own power, wet as drenched rats, grinning broadly and flashing everyone in sight a thumbs-up.

Jake and Flap were still fueling five minutes later when two Soviet Bear bombers, huge, silver, four-engine turbo-props, came up the wake at five hundred feet. The bombers were about a thousand feet apart, and each had an F-4 tucked in alongside like a pilot fish.

The flight deck crew froze and watched the parade go by.

'We could have done a better job up there today,' Jake told Flap. 'We should have had the second radio tuned into Strike. Then we would have known what Two Oh Seven's problem was without asking. And we should have asked about that wingman. Phantoms always go around in pairs, like snakes.'

'Those tailpipes in our windscreen,' Flap said, sighing. 'Man, that was a leemer.'

Jake knew what a leemer was – a shot of cold urine to the heart. 'We gotta get with the program,' he told the BN.

'I guess so,' Flap said as he tucked Malcolm X into his G-suit pocket and zipped it shut.

The air wing commander was Commander Charles 'Chuck' Kall, a fighter pilot. He was known universally as CAG, an acronym that rhymed with *rag* and stood for Commander Air Group. This acronym had been in use in the US Navy since it acquired its first carrier.

CAG Kall made careful notes this evening as he listened to the air intelligence officer brief the threat envelopes that could be expected around a Soviet task force. Lieutenant Colonel Haldane, his operations officer Major Bartow, and Jake Grafton were the A-6 representatives at this planning session. Jake sat listening and looking at the projected graphics with a sense of relief – The AI's presentation sounded remarkably like his homemade presentation for Colonel Haldane several weeks ago. An attacking force could expect to see a *lot* of missiles and stupendous quantities of flak, according to the AI.

'They aren't gonna shoot all those missiles at the first American planes they see,' CAG said softly. He always spoke softly so you had to listen hard to catch his words. 'It wouldn't surprise me to find out that half those missile launchers are out of service for lack of maintenance. Be that as it may, these numbers should dispel any notions anybody might have that smacking the Russians is going to be easy. These people aren't rice farmers – they are a first-class blue-water Navy. Putting them under with conventional, free-fall bombs is going to be really tough. We're going to lose a lot of people and airplanes getting it done.'

'We'll probably never have to,' someone said, and three or four heads bobbed in agreement.

'That's right,' Kall said, almost whispering. 'But if the order comes, we're going to be ready. We're going to have a plan and we're going to have practiced our plan. We're not going to try to invent the wheel after war is declared.'

There were no more comments about the probability of war with the Soviet Union.

'We'll plan Alpha strikes,' CAG said. 'When we get to the Sea of Japan we'll schedule some and see how much training we need to make that option viable. At night and in bad weather, however, the A-6s are going to have to go it alone. I'd like to have the A-6 crews run night attacks against our own destroyers to develop a profile that gives them the best chance of hitting the target and surviving. Colonel Haldane and his people can work out a place to start and we'll go from there.'

'Aye aye, sir,' Haldane said.

CHAPTER TWELVE

One morning when Jake came into the ready room the duty officer, First Lieutenant Doug Harrison, motioned to him. 'Sir, the skipper wants to see you in his stateroom.'

'*Sir!* What is this, the Marines?'

'Well, we try.'

Jake sighed. 'You know what it's about?'

'No, sir.'

'For heaven's sake, my name is Jake.'

'Yes, sir.'

'You try too hard. Let your hair grow out to an inch. Take a day off from polishing your shoes. Do twenty-nine pushups instead of thirty. You can overdo this military stuff, Doug.'

The skipper's stateroom was on the third deck, the one below the ready room deck. Entry to the skipper's sub-division was gained by lowering yourself through a water-tight hatch, then going down a ladder.

Jake knocked. The old man opened the door. 'Come in and find a seat.'

The pilot did so. Colonel Haldane picked up a sheaf of paper and waggled it, then tossed it back on his desk. 'Your letter of resignation. I have to put an endorsement on it. What do you want me to say?'

Jake was perplexed. 'Whatever you usually say, sir.'

'Technically your letter is a request to transfer from the regular Navy to the Naval Reserve and a request to be ordered to inactive status. So I have to comment about whether or not you would be a good candidate for a reserve commission. Why are you getting out?'

'Colonel, in my letter I said—'

'I read it. "To pursue a civilian career." Terrific. Why do you want out?'

'The war's over, sir. I went to AOCS because it was that or get drafted. I got a regular Navy commission in 1971 because it was offered and my skipper recommended me, but I've never had the desire to be a professional career officer. To be frank, I don't think I'd be a very good one. I like the flying, but I don't think I'm cut out for the rest of it. I'll be the first guy to volunteer to come back to fight if we have another war. I just don't want to be a peacetime sailor.'

'You want to fly for the airlines?'

'I don't know, sir. Haven't applied to any. I might, though.'

'Pretty boring, if you ask me. Take off from point A and fly to point B. Land. Taxi to the gate. Spend the night in a motel. The next day fly back to A. You have to be a good pilot, I know, but after a while, I think a man with your training and experience would go quietly nuts doing something like that. You'd be a glorified bus driver.'

'You're probably right, sir.'

'So what are you going to do?'

'I don't know, Skipper.'

'Hells bells, man, why resign if you don't have something to go to? Now if you had your heart set on going to grad school or into your dad's business or starting a whorehouse in Mexicali, I'd say *bon voyage* – you've done your bit. That doesn't appear to be the case, though. I'll send this in, but you can change your mind at any time up to your release date. Think it over.'

'Yessir.'

'Oh, by the way, the skipper of the Snake-eyes had some nice words for the way you tanked Two Oh Seven and dropped him off on the downwind. A quick, expeditious rendezvous, he said, a professional job.'

'Too bad Two Oh Seven caught fire.'

'As soon as he slowed to landing speed the gas seeped into the engine bays around the edges of the engine-bay doors. The engines ignited the fuel. From the time the fire first appeared visually, it was a grand total of two and a half seconds before the hydraulic lines burned through. The pilot punched when the nose started down. He pulled back stick and there was nothing there.'

Jake Grafton just nodded.

'This is a man's game,' Haldane said. He shrugged. 'There's no glamour, no glory, the pay's mediocre, the hours are terrible and the stakes are human lives. You bet your life and your BN's every time you strap on an airplane.'

The carrier and her escorts sailed west day after day. *Columbia*'s airplanes remained on deck in alert status as her five thousand men maintained their machinery, coped with endless paperwork, and drilled. They drilled morning, afternoon, and evening: fire drills, general quarters, nuclear, biological and chemical attack, collision, flooding, engine casualty, and flight deck disasters. The damage control teams were drilled to the point of exhaustion and the fire fighting teams did their thing so many times they lost count.

The only breaks in the routine came in the wee hours of the night when underway replenishments – UNREPS – were conducted. The smaller escorts came alongside the carrier every third day to top their tanks with NSFO – Navy standard fuel oil – from the carrier's bunkers.

Nowhere was seamanship more on display than during the hours that two or three vastly dissimilar ships steamed side by side through the heavy northern Pacific night seas joined by hoses and cables.

The destroyers and frigates were the most fun to watch, and Jake Grafton was often on the starboard catwalk to look and marvel. The smaller warship would overtake the carrier from astern and slow to equal speed alongside. The huge carrier would be almost rock-steady in the sea, but the small ship would be pitching, rolling, and plunging up and down as she rode the sea's back. Occasionally the bow would bite so deep into the sea that spray and foam would cascade aft, hiding the forward gun mount from view and dousing everyone topside.

As the captain of the destroyer held his ship in formation, a line would be shot across the seventy-five-foot gap between the ships to be snagged by waiting sailors wearing hard hats and life jackets. This rope would go into sheaves and soon a cable would be pulled across the river of rushing water. When the cable was secured, a hose would go across and soon fuel oil would be pumping. Three hoses were the common rig to minimize the time required to transfer hundreds of tons of fuel. Through it all the captain of the small boy stood on the wing of the bridge where he could see everything and issue the necessary orders to the steersman and engine telegraph operator to hold his ship in formation.

One night a supply ship came alongside. While Jake watched, a frigate joined on the starboard side of the supply ship, which began transferring fuel through hoses and supplies by high-line to both ships at once. Now both the frigate and carrier had to hold formation on the supply ship. To speed the process a CH-46 helicopter belonging to the supply ship lifted pallets of supplies from the stern of the supply ship and deposited them on the carrier's flight deck, a VERTREP, or vertical replenishment.

Here in the darkness on the western edge of the world's greatest ocean American power was being nakedly exercised. The extraordinary produce of the world's most advanced economy was being passed to warships in stupendous quantity: fuel, oil, grease, bombs, bullets, missiles, toilet paper, movies, spare parts, test equipment, paper, medical supplies, canned soft drinks, candy, meat, vegetables, milk, flour, ketchup, sugar, coffee – the list went on and on. The supply ship had a trainload to deliver.

The social organization and hardware necessary to produce, acquire and transport this stupendous quantity of wealth to these powerful warships in the middle of nowhere could be matched by no other nation on earth. The ability to keep fleets supplied anywhere on the earth's oceans was the key ingredient in American sea power, power that could be projected to anyplace on the planet within a thousand miles of saltwater. For good or ill, these ships made Washington the most important city in the world; these ships made the US Congress the most important forum on earth and the President of the United States the most powerful, influential person alive; these ships enforced a global Pax Americana.

The whole thing was quite extraordinary when one thought about it, and Jake Grafton, attack pilot, history major and farmer's son, did think about it. He stood under a A-6's tail on the flight deck catwalk wearing his leather jacket with the collar turned up against the wind and chill, and marveled.

'I hear you're going to get out,' the Real McCoy said one evening in the stateroom.

'Yeah. At the end of the cruise.' Jake was in the top bunk reading his NATOPS manual.

McCoy had the stock listing pages of the *Wall Street Journal* spread across the floor, his cruise box, bunk and desk. He was sitting cross-legged on the floor with his notebook full of charts on his lap. He had fallen into the habit of annotating his charts each evening after the ship received a mail delivery. He leaned back against his locker, stretched out his legs, and sighed.

'I've thought about it,' he said. 'Getting exiled to the Marines got the wheels spinning. Being ten days behind the markets makes them spin faster. But no.' He shrugged. 'Maybe one of these days, but not now.'

Jake put down his book. 'What's keeping you in? I thought you really liked that investment stuff?'

'Yeah, makes a terrific hobby. I think my problem is I'm a compulsive gambler. Stocks are the best game around – the house percentage is next to nothing – just a brokerage fee when you trade. Yet it's just money. On the other hand, you take flying – that's the ultimate gamble: your life is the wager. And waving – every pass is a new game, a new challenge. All you have is your wits and skill and the stakes are human lives. There's nothing like that in civilian life – except maybe trauma medicine. If I got out I'd miss the flying and the waving too much.'

Jake was slightly stunned. He had never before heard flying described as a gamble, a game, like Russian roulette. Oh, he knew the risks, and he did everything in his power to minimize them, yet here was a man for whom the risks were what made it worth doing.

'If I were you,' Jake told the Real, 'I wouldn't make that crack about waving down in the ready rooms.'

'Oh, I don't. A lot of these guys are too uptight.'

'Yeah.'

'They think the LSO is always gonna save them. And that's what we want them to think, so they'll always do what we tell them, when we tell them. If they get the notion in their hard little heads that we might be wrong, they'll start second-guessing the calls. Can't have that now, can we?'

'Ummm.'

'But LSOs are human too. Knowing that you can make a mistake, that's what keeps you giving it everything you've got, all the time, every time.'

'What if you screw up, like the CAG LSO did with

me? Only somebody dies. How are you going to handle that?'

'I don't know. That's the bad thing about it. You do it for the challenge and you *know* that sooner or later the ax will fall and you're going to have to live with it. That's why flying is easier. If you screw up in the cockpit, you're just dead. There's a lot to be said for betting your own ass and not someone else's.'

'Aren't many things left anymore that don't affect someone else,' Jake muttered.

'I suppose,' said the Real McCoy, and went back to annotating his stock charts.

Columbia and her retinue of escorts entered the Sea of Japan one morning in late July through the Tsugaru Strait between the islands of Hokkaido and Honshu. Transiting the strait, the five-minute alert fighters were parked just short of the catapults with their crews strapped into the cockpits, but a mob of sailors stood and sat around the edge of the flight deck wherever there was room between the planes. Some were off-duty, others had received their supervisors' permission to go topside for a squint, many worked on the flight deck.

Land was visible to the north and south, blue, misty, exotic and mysterious to these young men from the cities, suburbs, small towns and farms of America. That was Japan out there – geisha girls, kimonos, rice and raw fish, strange temples and odd music and soft, lilting voices saying utterly incomprehensible things. And they were here looking at it!

Several large ferries passed within waving distance, and the Japanese aboard received the full treatment – hats and arms and a few shirts. Fishing vessels and small coasters rolling in the swells were similarly saluted as the gray warships passed at fifteen knots.

This was the first cruise beyond America's offshore

waters for many of these young men. More than a few sniffed the wet sea wind and thought they could detect a spicy, foreign flavor that they had never whiffed before in the nitrogen-oxygen mixture they had spent their lives inhaling back in the good ol' US of A. Even the homesick and lovelorn admitted this was one hell of a fine adventure. If the folks at home could only see this . . .

So steaming one behind the other, the gray ships transited the strait while the young men on deck soaked up impressions that would remain with them for as long as they lived.

Those men standing on the carrier's fantail saw something else: two thousand yards astern the thin sail of a nuclear-powered attack submarine made a modest bow wave. How long she had been there, running on the surface, no one on the flight deck was sure, but there she was. Those with binoculars could just make out a small American flag fluttering from the periscope.

Once through the strait, the ship went to flight quarters and the tourists cleared the flight deck. Except for the few pilots who had launched in the interception of the Russian Bears, most of the aviators had not flown for nine days. This layoff meant that they needed a day catapult shot and trap before they could legally fly at night. With this requirement in mind, the staff had laid on a series of surface surveillance missions in the Sea of Japan. These missions would also show the flag, would once again put carrier-borne warplanes over the merchantmen and warships that plied these waters just in case anyone had become bored listening to American ambassadors. By the time the carrier hurled her first planes down the catapults, the submarine had quietly slipped back into the depths.

Jake was not scheduled to fly today. He was, however, on the flight schedule – two watches in Pri-Fly and one after dark in the carrier air traffic control center, CATCC, pronounced cat-see. During these watches he was the squadron representative, to be called upon by the powers that be to offer expert advice on the A-6 should such advice become necessary. There was an A-6 NATOPS manual in each compartment for him to refer to, and before each watch he found it and checked it to make sure it was all there. Then he stood with observers from the other squadrons with the book in his hand, watching and listening.

In addition to ensuring the air boss and Air Ops officer had instant access to knowledgeable people, these watches were a learning experience for the observers. Here they could observe how the aircraft were controlled, why problems arose, and watch those problems being solved. In CATCC they could also watch the air wing commander, known as CAG, and their own skippers as they sat beside the Air Ops officer on his throne and answered queries and offered advice. Air Ops often conferred with the skipper of the ship via squawk box. Every facet of night carrier operations was closely scrutinized and heavily supervised. While the junior officer aloft in the night sweated in his cockpit, he was certainly not alone. Not as long as his radio worked.

During the day the seas became rougher and the velocity of the wind increased. By sunset the overcast was low and getting lower. Below the clouds visibility was decreasing. A warm front was coming into the area.

Jake watched the first night recovery on the ready room PLAT monitor as he did paperwork. The deck was moving and there were three bolters. The second night recovery Jake spent in CATCC with the NATOPS book in his hand. It was raining outside. Two pilots were waved off and four boltered, one of them twice. One of the tankers was sour and a flailex developed when the spare tanker slid on the wet catapult track during hook-up and had to be pushed back with a flight deck tractor. While this mess kept the deck foul, the LSOs waved off three planes into the already-full bolter pattern.

When the last plane was aboard – the recovery took thirty-eight minutes – Jake headed for his stateroom to work on a training report.

He was still at it half an hour later when the Real McCoy came in, threw his flight deck helmet and LSO logbook onto his desk and flopped into his bunk. 'Aye yei yei! What a night! They're using those sticks to kill rats in the cockpits and the weather is getting worse.'

'You were on the platform?' Jake meant the LSO's platform on the edge of the flight deck.

'Yep. I'm wavin' 'em. Another great Navy night, I can tell you. A real Chinese fire drill. Three miles visibility under a thousand-foot overcast, solid clag up to twenty-one grand, ten-foot swells – why didn't I have the sense to join the Air Force? The boys in blue would have closed up shop and gone to the club three hours ago.'

'The next war,' Jake muttered.

'Next war, Air Force,' McCoy agreed. 'So, wanna stand on the patform with me for the next act?'

Jake regarded his half-finished report with disgust, got out of his chair and stretched. 'Why not? I've listened to you wavers preach and moan for so long that I could probably do it myself.'

McCoy snorted. 'That'll be the day!'

Jake did a clumsy tap dance for several seconds, then struck a pose. 'He looked good going by me.'

McCoy groaned and closed his eyes. He was a self-proclaimed master of the short catnap, so Jake timed it. Sixty-five seconds after the LSO closed his eyes he was snoring gently.

They came out of the skin of the ship by climbing a short ladder to the catwalk that surrounded the flight deck, yet was about four feet below flight deck level.

The noise of twenty jet engines at idle on the flight deck was piercing, even through their ear protectors. Raindrops swirling in the strong wind displaced by the ship's structure came from every direction, seemingly almost at once, even up through the gridwork at their feet. The wind blew with strength, an ominous presence, coming from total darkness, blackness so complete that for a second or two Jake felt as if he had lost his vision. This dark universe of wind and water was permeated by the acrid stench of jet exhaust, which burned his nose and made his eyes water.

Gradually his eyes became accustomed to the red glow of the flight deck lights and he could see things – the outline of the catwalk, the rails, the round swelling shapes of the life raft canisters suspended outboard of the catwalk railing, and in the midst of that void beyond the rail, several fixed lights. The escorts. Above his head were tails of airplanes. He and McCoy crouched low as they proceeded aft toward the LSO platform to avoid those invisible rivers of hot exhaust that might be flowing just above their heads. Might be. The only sure way to find one was to walk into it.

Somewhere aloft in the night sky, high above the ship, were airplanes. With men in them. Men sitting strapped to ejection seats, studying dials and gauges, riding the turbulence, watching fuel gauges march mercilessly toward zero.

Jake and the Real McCoy climbed a ladder to the LSOs' platform as the first of the planes on deck rode a catapult into the night sky. Both men watched the plane's lights as it climbed straight ahead of the ship. There – they were getting fuzzy . . . And then they were gone, swallowed up by the night.

'Six or seven hundred feet, a couple of miles viz. That's it,' McCoy roared into Jake's ear.

The petty officer who assisted the LSOs was already on the platform getting out the radio handsets, plugging in cords, checking the PLAT monitor, donning his sound-powered headset and checking in with the enlisted talkers in Pri-Fly and Air Ops.

*

The platform was not large, maybe six feet by six feet, a wooden grid that jutted from the port side of the flight deck. To protect the signal officers from wind and jet blast, a piece of black canvas stretched on a steel frame was rigged on the forward edge of the platform, like a wall. So the platform was an open stage facing aft, toward the glide slope.

Under the edges of the platform, aft and on the seaward side, hung a safety net to catch anyone who inadvertently fell off the platform. Or jumped. Because if a pilot lost it on the glide slope in close and veered toward the platform, going into the net was the only way for the LSOs to save their lives.

Jake Grafton glanced down into the blackness. And saw nothing. 'Relax, shipmate,' McCoy told him. 'The net's there. Honest Injun.'

The platform was just aft of the first wire, about four hundred feet away from the ship's center of gravity, so it was moving. Up and down, up and down.

As McCoy checked the lights on the Fresnel lens, which was several hundred feet forward of the platform, Jake watched. McCoy triggered the wave-off lights, the cut lights, adjusted the intensity of the lens. The lights seemed to behave appropriately and soon he was satisfied.

The Fresnel lens was, in Jake's mind, one of the engineering triumphs that made carrier aviation in the jet age possible. In the earliest days, aboard the old *Langley*, pilots made approaches to the deck without help. One windy day one of the senior officers grabbed a couple signal flags and rushed to the fantail to signal to a young aviator who was having trouble with his approach. This innovation was so successful that an officer was soon stationed there to assist all the aviators with signal flags, or paddles. This officer helped the pilot with glide slope and lineup, and since the carriers all had straight decks, gave the vital engine 'cut' signal that required the aviator to pull his throttle to idle and flare.

When angled decks and jets with higher landing speeds came along, it became obvious that a new system was required. As usual, the British were the innovators. They rigged a mirror on one side of the deck and directed a high-intensity light at it. The light was reflected up the glide slope. By rigging a set of reference lights midway up on each side of the mirror, a datum was established. A pilot making his approach would see the light reflected on the mirror – the ball – rise above the datum lights when he was above glide slope, or high, and descend below it when he was low. The landing signal officer was retained to assist the pilot with radio calls, and to give mandatory wave-offs if an approach became unsafe.

The Fresnel lens was the mirror idea carried one step further. The light source was now contained within five boxes, stacked one on top of the other. The datum lights were beside the middle, or third, box. Due to the way the lens on each light was designed, a horizontally wide but vertically narrow beam of light was directed up the glide slope by each box. Crossing the fantail, the beam from the middle box, the 'centered ball,' was a mere eighteen inches in height.

This was the challenge: a pilot must fly his jet airplane through turbulent air into an eighteen-inch-thick window in the sky. At night, with the deck moving as the ship rode a seaway, hitting this window became extraordinarily difficult, without argument the most difficult challenge in aviation. That anyone other than highly skilled, experienced test pilots could do it on a regular basis was a tribute to the training the Navy gave its aviators, and was the reason those who didn't measure up were ruthlessly weeded out.

You could do it or you couldn't – there was no in between. And yet, no one could do it consistently every time. The task was too difficult, the skills involved too perishable. So night after night, in fair weather and foul, they practiced, like they were doing on this miserable night in the Sea of Japan, eighty miles west of Honshu.

As Jake Grafton stood on the platform staring into the darkness as the wind swirled rain over him, he was glad that tonight was not his night. It felt so good to be *here*, not up *there* sweating bullets aa the plane bounced around, trying to keep the needles steady, watching the fuel, knowing that you were going to have to fly that instrument approach to the ball, then thread the needle to get safely back aboard. To return to the world of the living, to friends, to food, to letters from loved ones, to a bunk to sleep in, to a world with a past *and* a future. There in that cockpit when you were flying the ball there was only the present, only the airplane, only the stick in your right hand and the throttles in your left and the rudder beneath your feet. There was only the *now*, *this* moment for which you had lived your whole life, *this* instant during which you called upon everything within you to do this thing.

Oh, yes. He was glad.

Other LSOs were climbing to the platform now, so Jake moved as far back as he could to stay out of the way. All these specialists were here to observe, to see another dozen landings, to polish their skills, to learn. This was normal. The platform was packed with LSOs on every recovery.

The last airplane to be launched was upon the catapult at full power when the lights of the first plane on the glide slope appeared out of the gloomy darkness astern. In secopnds the catapult fired and the deck became unnaturally silent.

The Real was already three feet out onto the deck holding the radio headset against his ear with his left hand while he held the Fresnel lens control handle in his right over his head, a signal to his colleagues that he was aware the deck was foul. Jake leaned sideways and looked forward around the edge of the canvas screen. The waist catapult crewmen were working furiously to put the protector plate over Cat Three's shuttle and clear the launching gear from the flight deck. Until they were out of the landing area, the deck would remain foul.

'Come on, people,' the air boss roared over the flight deck loudspeaker. He seemed to believe that his troops worked best when properly stimulated. In any event, he didn't hesitate to stimulate them. 'We've got a Phantom in the groove. Let's clear the deck.'

The last flight deck tractor zipped across the foul line near the island, yet three cat crewmen were still struggling with the protector plate.

Jake lifted one side of his mouse ears away from his head. He heard McCoy roger the ball call.

The air boss on the loudspeaker again: 'He's called the ball. Let's get this deck clear *now*, people!'

There, the cat crewmen were running for the catwalk. Jake looked aft. The Phantom was within a half mile, about two hundred feet high, coming fast. On his nose-gear door was a stop-light arrangement of little lights, red, yellow and green, that was operated by the angle-of-attack instrument in the cockpit. Red for slow, yellow for on speed, and green for fast. The yellow light was lit, but even as Jake saw it, the red light flickered.

'You're going to go slow,' Real told the pilot. 'Little power.'

The red foul deck light went out and the green light came on.

'Clear deck,' shouted the LSO talker.

'Clear deck,' McCoy echoed, and lowered his right arm.

The jet was slamming through the burble causd by the island, his engines winding up, then decelerating. In seconds the Phantom crossed the ramp with its engines wailing, its hook reaching for a wire. Then the hook struck in a shower of sparks and the main gear thumped down. The hook snagged the second wire as the engines wound up to their full fury – a futile roar, because the big fighter was quickly dragged to a quivering halt. The exterior lights went out. The hook runner raced across the foul line with his wands signaling 'hook up.' Seconds later the Phantom was taxiing out of the landing area and the wings were folding.

Meanwhile McCoy was giving the grade to another LSO, who was writing in the log. 'Little slow in the middle, OK Two.'

McCoy glanced at Jake. 'Nice pass. Pitching deck and reduced visbility and he handled it real well. I bet I couldn't do as well on a shitty night like this.'

Then he was back out into the landing area listening to the radio. In seconds another set of lights came out of the goo. Another Phantom. This guy had more difficulty with the pass than the first fighter, but he too successfully trapped. The third Phantom boltered and McCoy waved off the fourth one. It was going to be a long recovery.

One of the LSOs handed Jake his radio. He put it to his ear in time to hear the RA-5C Vigilante call the ball.

The Vigilante was the most beautiful airplane the Navy owned, in Jake's opinion. It was designed as a supersonic nuclear bomber back when nuclear bombs were big. The weapon was carried in an internal bay and was ejected out a door in the rear of the plane between the tailpipes. The Navy soon discovered this method of delivery didn't work: the bomb was trapped in the airplane's slipstream and trailed along behind – sometimes for seconds at a time before it fell free. The weapon's impact point could not be predicted and there was a serious danger that the bomb would strike the aircrft while it was tagging along behind, damaging the plane and the weapon. So the Vigilantes were converted to reconnaissance aircraft. Fuel tanks were installed in the bomb bays and camera packages on the bellies.

With highly swept wings and empennage, a needle nose, and two huge engines with afterburners, the plane was extraordinarily fast, capable of ripping through the heavens at an honest Mach 2+. And it was a bitch to get aboard the ship. Jake thought the Vigie pilots were supermen, the best of the best.

Yet it was the guys in back who had the biggest *cojónes*, for they rode the beast with no control over their fate. Even worse, they rode in a separate cockpit behind the pilot that had only two tiny windows, one on each side of the fuselage. They could not see forward or aft and their view to either side was highly restricted. A-6 BNs with their seats beside the pilot and excellent view in all quadrants regarded the Vigie backseaters with awe. 'It's like flying in your own coffin,' they whispered to one another, and shuddered.

Tonight the Vigie pilot was having his troubles. 'I got vertigo,' he told McCoy on the platform.

'Fly the ball and keep it coming,' the LSO said. 'Your wings are level, the deck is moving, average out the ball. You're slightly high drifting left . . . Watch your lineup!' The Vigilante was a big plane, with a 60-foot wingspan – the foul lines were 115 feet apart.

'Pick up your left wing, little power . . . right for lineup.'

Now the Vigie was crossing the ramp, and the right wing dropped.

'*Level your wings*,' McCoy roared into the radio.

The Vigilante's left wing sagged and the nose rose. Jake shot a glance at the PLAT monitor: the RA-5 was way too far right, his right wingtip almost against the foul line.

His gaze flipped back to the airplane, just in time to hear the engines roar and see the fire leap from the afterburners, two white-hot blowtorches fifteen feet long. The light ripped the night open, casting a garish light on the parked planes, the men standing along the right foul line, and the ship's superstructure.

With her hook riding five feet above the wires and her left wing slightly down, the big swept-wing jet crossed the deck and rose back into the night sky. Only then did the fire from the afterburners go out. The rolling thunder continued to wash over the men on the ship's deck, then it too dissipated.

An encounter with an angry dragon, Jake thought, slightly awed by the scene he had just witnessed.

'A nugget on his first cruise,' McCoy told his colleagues, then dictated his comments to the logbook writer.

The motion of the ship was becoming more pronounced, Jake thought, especially here on the platform. When the deck reached the top of its stroke, he felt slightly light on his feet.

McCoy noticed the increased deck motion too, and he switched the lens to a four-degree glide slope, up from the normal three and one half. The talker informed the controllers in Air Ops.

In seconds there was another plane on the ball, this time an A-7 Corsair. 'Three One Zero, Corsair ball, Three Point Two.'

'Roger ball, four-degree glide slope. Pitching deck.'

This guy was an old pro. McCoy gave him one call, a little too much power, and that was all it took. He snagged a three.

The next plane was the Phantom that boltered, and this time he was steadier. Yet the steeper glide slope fooled him and he was fast all the way, flattened out at the ramp and boltered again.

The next plane, a A-7, took more coaching, but he too caught a wire. So did the Phantom that followed him, the one that had waved off originally. The next A-7 had to be waved off, however, because the deck was going down just before he got to the in-close position, while he was working off a high and slightly fast. If he had overdone his power reduction he would have been descending through the glide slope just as the deck rose to meet him: a situation not conducive to a long life.

An A-6 successfully trapped, then the Phantom came around for his third pass. Clear sky and the tanker were twenty-one thousand feet above, so the pressure was on. McCoy looked tense as a coiled spring as he stood staring up the glide slope waiting for the F-4's lights to appear out of the overcast.

There!

'One Zero Two, Phantom ball, Four Point Two, trick or treat.' Trick or treat meant that he had to trap on this pass or be sent to tank.

'Roger ball, four-degree glide slope, it'll look steep so fly the ball.'

A dark night, a pitching deck, rain . . . these were the ingredients of fear, cold, clutching, icy as death. A carrier pilot who denied he ever experienced it was a liar. Tonight, on this pass, this fighter pilot felt the slimy tentacles of fear play across his backbone. As he crossed the ramp he reduced power and raised the nose. The heavy jet instantly increased its rate of descent.

'No,' screamed McCoy.

The hook slapped down and the main mounts hit and the number one wire screamed from its sheaves.

'There's one lucky mother,' McCoy told the writer and the observing signal officers when the blast of the Phantom's two engines had died to an idling whine. 'Spotted the deck and should have busted his ass, but the deck was falling away. Another military miracle. Who says Jesus ain't on our side?'

More A-7s came down the chute. The first one got aboard without difficulty but the second announced he had vertigo.

'Roger that. Your wings are level and you're fast. Going high. Steep glide slope, catch it with power. More power.'

He was getting close and the red light on his nose gear door winked on. He was slow. 'Power. Power! *Power!*

At the third power call the Real McCoy triggered the wave-off lights, but it was too late. Even as the Corsair's engine wound up, the wheels hit the very end of the flight deck and there was a bright flash. With the engine winding up to full screech the plane roared up the deck, across all the wires, and rotated to climb away. McCoy shouted 'Bolter, bolter, bolter,' on the radio.

Now McCoy handed the radio and Fresnel lens pickle to the nearest LSO. He began running toward the fantail. Jake Grafton followed.

The dim light made seeing difficult. The deck was really moving here, 550 feet aft of the ship's center of gravity. The ship was like a giant seesaw. Keeping your knees bent helped absorb the thrusts of the deck.

McCoy took a flashlight from his hip pocket and played it on the ramp, the sloping end of the flight deck. The ramp dropped away at about a thirty-degree angle, went down ten or twelve feet, then ended. That was the back end of the ship. The flashlight beam stopped three feet right of the centerline stripe, at the deep dent.

'Hook strike,' Jake shouted.

'No, that's where his main mount hit.' Real scanned with the flashlight and stopped at another dent, the twin of the first. 'There's where the other wheel hit. His hook hit below the ramp.' Then McCoy turned and ran for the LSO platform, with Jake following.

Back on the LSO platform McCoy told the sailor wearing the sound-powered phones, 'His hook hit the back end of the ship and disintegrated. He doesn't have a hook now. Tell Air Ops.'

Without a hook, the plane could be trapped aboard only with the barricade, a huge nylon net that was rigged across the landing area like a giant badminton net. Or it could be sent to an airfield in Japan.

Air Ops elected to send the crippled plane to Japan.

McCoy got back to the business of waving airplanes. He had the Vigilante on the ball, with an A-6 and EA-6B behind him, then the E-2 Hawkeye and KA-6 tanker to follow.

This time the Vigie pilot drifted right of centerline and corrected back toward the left. He leveled his wings momentarily, so McCoy let him keep coming. Then, passing in close, the left wing dropped. The Vigilante slewed toward the LSOs' platform as McCoy screamed 'Wave-off' and dived to the right.

Jake had his eyes on the approaching plane, but McCoy was taking everyone on the platform with him. Jake was almost to the edge when the RA-5 swept overhead in burner, his hook almost close enough to touch. Instinctively Jake ducked.

That was close! Too close. Now Jake realized that he and McCoy were the only two people still on the platform. He looked down to his right. Two hands reached up out of the darkness and grabbed the edge by Jake's foot. *Everyone else went into the net.*

They clambered back up, one by one. The talker picked up his sound-powered headset where he had dropped it and put it back on.

McCoy leaned toward the talker. 'Tell Air Ops that I recommend he send the Vigie to the beach for fuel and a turnaround. Give that guy some time to calm down.'

And that is what Air Ops did.

The last plane was still two miles out when a sailor brought a lump of metal to the platform and gave it to McCoy. 'We found this down on the fantail. There's a lot of metal shards down there but this was the biggest piece. I think it's a piece of hook point.'

McCoy examined it by flashlight, then passed it to Jake.

It was a piece of the A-7's hook point, all right. About a

pound of it. The point must have shattered against the structure of the ship and the remnants rained down on the fantail.

When the last plane was aboard, Jake followed McCoy down the ladder to the catwalk, then down another flight into the ship.

'That was exciting,' Jake Grafton told the LSO.

'You dum ass. You should have gone into the net.'

'Well, I didn't think—'

'That Vigie about got us. No shit.'

'Hell of a recovery.'

'That's no lie. Did you hear about the A-7 that had the ramp strike?'

'No.'

'The talker told me. The guy had a total hydraulic failure on the way to the beach and ejected. He's in the water right now.'

'You're kidding.'

'The rebound of the hook shank probably severed his hydraulic lines. He's swimming for it. Just another great Navy night.'

The pilot of the RA-5C Vigilante who had so much trouble with lineup on this recovery landed in Japan and refueled. He returned to the ship for the last recovery of the evening and flew a fair pass into a three-wire.

The A-7 pilot with the hydraulic failure wasn't rescued until ten o'clock the next morning. He spent the night in his life raft, buffeted by heavy seas, overturned four times, though each time he regained the safety of the raft. He swallowed a lot of seawater and did a lot of vomiting. He vomited and retched until blood came up. Still retching when the helicopter deposited him back on the carrier, he had to be sedated and given an IV to rehydrate him. He was also suffering from a serious case of hypothermia. But he was alive, with no bones broken. His shipmates trooped to sick bay in a steady procession to welcome him back to the company of living men.

CHAPTER THIRTEEN

The Soviet intelligence ship *Reduktor* joined the task group during the night and fell in line astern. At dawn she was two miles behind the carrier wallowing heavily. When the sun came up she held her position even though the task group raised its speed to twelve knots. When the sea state eased somewhat the Soviet ship rode steadier.

Jake came up on deck for the first launch of the day only to find that the AGI was dropping steadily astern. Her captain knew the drill. The carrier had been running steadily downwind, but to launch she would turn into the wind, toward the AGI. So now the Soviet ship was slowing to one or two knots, just enough to maintain steerageway.

At the brief the air intelligence officers showed the flight crews file photos of this Okean-class intelligence collector. She was a small converted trawler. Had she not been festooned with a dazzling array of radio antennas that rose from her superstructure and masts, one would assume her crew was still looking for fish.

So there they were. Russians. In *Reduktor*'s compartments they were busy with their reel-to-reel tape drives – probably all made in Japan – recording every word, peep or chirp on every radio frequency that the US Navy had ever been known to use. Doubtlessly they monitored other frequencies occasionally as well, just in case. These tapes would be examined by experts who would construct from them detailed analyses of how the US Navy operated and what its capabilities were. Encrypted transmissions would be turned over to specialists who would try to break the codes.

In short, the crew of *Reduktor* were spies. They were going about their business in a lawful manner, however, in plain sight upon the high seas, so there was nothing anyone in the US Navy could do about it. In fact, the American captains and watch officers had to make sure that their ships didn't accidentally collide with the Soviet ship.

There was one other possibility, not very probable, but possible. *Reduktor* might be a beacon ship marking the position of the American task group for Soviet forces. Just in case, American experts aboard the US ships monitored, recorded and analysed every transmission that *Reduktor* made.

Anticipating the coming of a Soviet AGI, the US task group had already reduced its own radio transmissions as much as possible. During the day the aircrews from *Columbia* operated 'zip-lip,' speaking on the radio only when required. Specialists from the Communications Security Group – COMSEGRU – had visited every ready room to brief the crews.

This morning Jake Grafton spent a moment watching the old trawler, then went on with his preflight. He would, he suspected, see a lot of that ship in the next few months.

After four days of operations in the Sea of Japan, *Columbia* and her escorts called at Sasebo and stayed for a week. *Reduktor* was waiting when they came out of port.

The first week of August was spent operating off the southern coast of Korea, then the task group steamed south and spent a week flying in the South China Sea. The Soviet AGI was never far away.

Here, for the first time, the air wing began flying the Alpha strikes that Jake had helped plan with CAG Ops. Jake didn't get to go on the first one, when Skipper Haldane led the A-6s. Due to his bombing scores, however, he was scheduled to lead the A-6s the next day. He and Flap spent half the night in Strike Planning with the other element leaders making sure they had it right.

CAG Kall sat in a corner and sipped coffee during the entire session. He didn't say much, yet when he did you listened carefully because he had something to say worth listening to. He also smiled a lot and picked up names easily. After an hour you thought you had known the man all your life. That night in his bunk the thought tripped through Jake Grafton's mind that he would like to lead the way Chuck Kall did.

Well, tomorrow he would get his chance. Six Intruders were scheduled to fly and the maintenance gunny said he would have them. The target was an abandoned ship on a reef a few miles off the western coast of Luzon, the northernmost of the Philippine Islands. Today's strike had pretty well pulverized the ship, but there were enough pieces sticking out of the water to make an aiming point. The water was pretty shallow there. To make sure there were no native fishing boats in the target area tomorrow before live bombs rained down, an RA-5C was scheduled to make a prestrike low pass.

Jake had so many things on his mind that he had trouble falling asleep. He took the hop minute by minute, the climb-out, the rendezvous, frequency changes, formation, airplane problems, no-radio procedures, the letdown to roll-in altitude . . . he drifted off to sleep and dreamed about it.

The morning was perfect, a few puffy low clouds but widely scattered. The brisk trade wind speckled the sea with whitecaps and washed away the haze.

After a quick cup of coffee and check of the weather, Jake met with the element leaders for two hours. Then he went to the ready room for the crew briefs, briefed the A-6's portion of the mission, read the maintenance logbook on his assigned plane and donned his flight gear. By the time he walked out onto the flight deck with Flap Le Beau he had been working hard for four hours.

The escort ships looked crisp and clean upon a living blue sea. The wind – he inhaled deeply.

He and Flap took the time to inspect the weapons carefully. For today's mock attack they had live bombs, four Mark-84 two-thousand-pounders. A hit with one of these bombs would break the back of any warship that was cruiser-size or smaller. The multiple ejector racks that normally carried smaller bombs had been downloaded so the one-ton general purpose bombs could be mated to the parent bomb racks. There were two of these on each wing. As usual, the centerline belly station carried a two-thousand-pound drop tank. One of the bombs, the last one to be dropped, had a laser-seeker in the nose. The other three were fused with a mechanical nose fuse and an electrical tail fuse.

The mechanical nose fuse was the most reliable fuse the Navy possessed, which made it the preferred way to fuse bombs. A bare copper wire ran from a solenoid in the parent rack forward across the weapon to the nose, where it went through a machined hole in the fuse housing and then through the little propeller at the very front of the fuse. The wire physically prevented the propeller from turning until the weapon was ejected from the rack. The wire then pulled out of the fuse and stayed on the rack, which freed the propeller. As the bomb fell the wind spun the propeller for a preset number of seconds and armed the fuse. When the nose of the bomb struck its target, the fuse was triggered. After a small delay – one hundredth of a second to allow the weapon to penetrate the target – the fuse detonated the high explosive in the bomb.

If the mechanical fuse was defective, the electric tail fuse would set the bomb off. That fuse was armed by a jolt of electricity in the first two feet of travel as the bomb fell away from the parent rack, then its arming wire, an insulated electrical cable, pulled loose.

The BN's job on preflight was to check to ensure the ordnancemen had rigged bombs, fuses and arming wires correctly. Since any error here could ruin the mission, Jake Grafton always checked too. Today he and Flap stood side by side as they examined each weapon. Everything was fine.

The bomb with the laser-seeker in the nose was the technology of the future, the technology that had already made unguided free-fall bombs obsolete and would itself be made obsolete by guided missiles. One had to aim a laser-light generator at the target and hold the light on it as the bomb fell. If the bomb was dropped into the proper cone above the target, the seeker would guide it to the reflected spot of laser light by manipulating small canards on the body of the device.

In two or three years the A-6 would have its own laser-light generator in the nose of the aircraft. Now the generators, or 'designators,' were hand-held. Today a radar-intercept officer in the backseat of an F-4 orbiting high above the target would aim the designator while Intruders, Corsairs and other Phantoms dropped the bombs. This system worked. Navy and Air Force crews used it with devastating effect on North Vietnamese bridges in the last year of the war.

Due to the cost of the seekers, each plane had only one for today's training mission. Dropping three unguided weapons in addition to the guided one had an additional benefit – the pilot had to try for a perfect dive to put all four on the target. If one bomb was a bull's-eye and the other three went awry, he screwed up.

The plane looked good. Strapped in waiting for the engine start, Jake Grafton arranged his charts in the cockpit, then paused for a few seconds to savor the warmth of the sun and the wind playing with his hair. The moment was over too soon. Helmet on, canopy closed, crank engines.

The cat shot was a hoot, an exhilarating ride into a perfect morning. His airplane flew well, all the gear worked as advertised, none of the other A-6s had maintenance problems and all launched normally.

The A-6s rendezvoused at 9,000 feet. When Jake had his gaggle together, he led them upward to 13,000 feet and slowly eased into position on the right of the lead division, today four Corsairs. When all the other divisions were aboard, the strike leader, the CO of one of the A-7 squadrons, rolled out on course to the target and initiated a climb to 23,000 feet.

The climb took longer than usual. The bombers were heavily loaded. At ninety-eight percent RPM all Jake could coax out of his plane was 280 knots indicated. He concentrated on flying smoothly so his wingmen would not have to sweat bullets to stay with him.

The six-plane division was broken up into two flights of three. Jake had one wingman on each side. Out farther to the right flew another three-plane flight, but its leader was also flying formation on Grafton. Just before the time came to dive, the man on each leader's left would cross over, then the two flights would join so that there were six airplanes in right echelon. The plan was for Jake to roll in and the others to follow two seconds apart, so that all six were diving with just enough separation between the planes that each pilot could aim his own bombs. If they did it right, all six would be in the enemy's threat envelope together and divide the enemy's antiaircraft fire. And all would leave together. That was the plan, anyway.

Flap had the radar and computer fired up, so Jake was getting steering to the target. He was merely comparing it to the course the strike leader was flying, however.

The radio frequency was crowded. The strike leader was talking to the E-2 Hawkeye, the RA-5C was chattering about a fishing boat that he had chased away from the target and the cloud cover, someone had a hydraulic problem, the tankers wanted to change the poststrike rendezvous position because the carrier wasn't where it was supposed to be when this evolution was put together, and one of the EA-6s was late getting launched and was going to be late getting to its assigned position. Situation normal, Jake thought.

He checked the position of his wingmen regularly, yet he spent most of his time scanning the sky and staying in proper position in relation to the strike leader. When he had a spare second he brought his eyes back into the cockpit to check his engine instruments and fuel.

The cumulus clouds below thickened as the strike group approached the coast of Luzon. The bases were at 4,000 feet, but the tops were building. From 23,000 feet the clouds seemed to cover about fifty percent of the sea below.

Would there be holes over the target big enough to bomb through?

The twenty-six bombers and their two EA-6 escorts began their descent toward their roll-in altitude of 15,000 feet. The leader left his throttle alone, so the airspeed began to increase. The faster the strike could close a Soviet task group, the fewer missiles and less flak it would encounter. In aerial warfare, speed is life.

Now CAG was on the radio. He was at 30,000 feet over the target in an F-4. 'Where are the Flashlights?'

Flashlight was the F-4 that would illuminate the target with the laser designator. Actually there were two F-4s, both carrying hand-held laser designators. The pilots would have to find a hole in the clouds so the RIOs – radar intercept officers – could aim the designators, then they would have to maneuver to keep the target in sight and avoid colliding with one another. In a real attack on Soviet ships, the pilots would also be dodging missiles and flak.

'Uh, Flashlight is trying to find the target.'

The F-4's electronic system was designed to find and

track other airborne targets, not find the remnants of a wrecked ship resting on a reef. The A-6s' systems, however, were working fine. Flap had the target and Jake was getting steering and distance. In the planning sessions he had argued that A-6s should carry the designators but had been overruled.

'Ten miles to roll-in,' Flap told Jake. The strike was passing 20,000 feet. Now the strike leader dropped his nose farther, giving the group about 4,000 feet a minute down. Three hundred twenty knots indicated and increasing.

Passing 18,000 feet Jake pumped his arm at the A-6 on his left side. Flap did the same to the man on his right. The Intruder formation shifted to echelon.

The tops of the clouds were closer. Still some holes, but the target wasn't visible through them.

The situation was deteriorating fast. Without holes in the clouds, the F-4s carrying bombs could not find the target. The A-7s might be able to, but not in formation since the pilots could not fly formation and work their radars and computers too. The A-6s could break off at any point and make a system attack on the target, individually or in pairs. This was the edge an all-weather, two-man airplane gave you.

The strike leader, Gold One, knew all this. He had only seconds to decide.

'This is Gold One. Let's go to Plan Bravo. Plan Bravo.'

Jake Grafton lowered his nose still farther. Now he wanted to descend below the formation The A-7s were shallowing their dive, which helped.

Flap was on the ICS: 'Target's twenty degrees left. Master Arm on.'

'Kiss off,' Jake told him, and Flap took a few seconds to splay his fingers at the wingman on his right as Jake turned left to center steering and dropped his nose still more. Fifteen degrees down now, going faster than a raped ape, the plane pushing against the sonic shock wave and vibrating slightly, nothing but clouds visible in the windscreen dead ahead. The other A-6s would continue on course for four seconds each, then turn toward the target. All six would run the target individually.

'We're in attack,' Flap announced, and sure enough, the attack symbology apeared on the VDI in front of Jake.

'War Ace One's in hot,' he announced on the radio.

He took one more quick look around to ensure the other airplanes in this gaggle were clear.

Something on his left wing caught his eye. His eyes focused.

The bomb on Station One, the station nearest the left wing tip – *the propeller on the mechanical fuse was spinning!* The fuse was arming.

He gaped for half a second, unwilling to believe his eyes. The propeller was spinning.

One bomb in a thousand, they say, will detonate at the end of arming time. The propeller will spin for 8.5 seconds to line up the firing circuit.

He could drop it now!

His thumb moved toward the pickle. The master armament switch was already on. All he had to do was squeeze the commit trigger and push the pickle. The bomb would fall away and be clear of the plane when the fuse finished arming. If it blew then . . .

He would still be within the blast envelope.

All these thoughts shot through his mind in less than a second. Even while he was considering he scanned the instruments to ensure he was tracking steering with his wings level.

He looked outside again. The propeller was stopped.

The bomb was armed! And it hadn't exploded. Okay, we've dodged the first bullet.

He pushed the radio transmit button as he retarded the throttles and raised the nose. 'War Ace One has an armed bomb on the rack. Breaking off the attack and turning north at . . .' He looked at the altimeter. He was descending through 12,000 feet. '. . . At twelve thousand.'

He grabbed the stick with his left hand and used his right to move the Master Arm switch to the safe position.

Everyone was talking on the radio – A-6s calling in hot, and A-7s breaking up for dives, F-4s looking for holes – probably no one heard Jake's transmission.

'Station One,' he told Flap on the ICS when he had his left hand back on the throttles, talking over the gabble on the radio. 'The bomb is armed.'

He concentrated on flying the plane, on getting the nose up and turning to the north. He was in the clouds now, bouncing around in turbulence. A northerly heading should take him out from under the strike gaggle, which was circling the target to the south.

'The arming wire pulled out of the fuse somehow,' he told Flap. 'I saw the propeller spinning. The fucking thing is armed.'

He looked again at the offending weapon. Now he saw that the thermal protective coating was peeled back somewhat. The Navy sprayed all its weapons with a plastic thermal coating after experiencing several major flight-deck fires in which bombs cooked off. The coating must have had a flaw in it, something for the slipstream to work on. The slipstream peeled the coating, which pulled the arming wire.

A two-thousand-pound bomb . . . if it detonated under the wing, the airplane would be instantly obliterated. The fuel in the plane would probably explode. So would the other three weapons hanging on the plane. Not that he or Flap would care. They would already be dead, their bodies crushed by the initial blast and torn into a thousand pieces.

And this turbulence . . . it could set off that fuse.

He retarded the throttles. Almost to idle. Cracked the speed brakes to help slow down.

'Let's climb out of this crap,' Flap suggested.

Jake slipped the speed brakes back in and raised the nose. He added power.

Finally he stabilized at an indicated 250 knots.

'Cubi?' Flap asked.

'Yeah.'

Flap hit a switch and the computer steering went right. Jake looked at the repeater between his legs. The steering bug was at One Six Zero degrees, eighty miles. Flap dialed in the Cubi TACAN station.

'It could go at any time,' Jake said.

'I know.'

'Let's get off this freq and talk to Black Eagle.'

Flap got on the radio as they climbed free of the clouds. The turbulence ceased.

Left turn. Fly around the target and the strike group to seaward.

No. Right turn. Go around on the land side. The other planes would be leaving the garget to seaward. Maybe at this altitude. No sense taking any more chances than—

An F-4 shot across the windscreen going from right to left. Before Jake could react the A-6 flew into his wash. Wham! The plane shook fiercely, then it was through.

'If that didn't set the damned thing off, nothing will,' Flap said.

Like hell. The jolts and bumps might well be cumulative.

Jake concentrated on flying the plane. He was sweating profusely. Sweat stung his eyes. He stuck the fingers of his left hand under his visor and swabbed it away.

Black Eagle suggested a frequency switch to Cubi Point Approach. Flap rogered and dialed the radio.

They were at 18,000 feet now and well above the cloud tops.

Jake glanced at the armed bomb from time to time. If he pickled it the shock of the ejector foot smacking into the weapon to push it away from the rack might set it off.

221

If the bomb detonated he and Flap would never even know it.

One second they would be alive and the next they would be standing in line to see St Peter.

What a way to make a living!

Just fly the airplane, Jake. Do what you can and let God worry about the other stuff.

'Cubi Approach, War Ace Five Oh Seven. We have an armed Mark Eighty-Four hanging on Station One. We're carrying three more Mark Eighty-Fours, but they are unarmed. After we land we want to park as far away from everything as possible. And could you have EOD meet us?' EOD stood for explosive ordnance disposal.

'Roger live weapon. We'll roll the equipment and call EOD.'

Cubi Point was the US naval air station on the shore of Subic Bay, the finest deep-water port in the western Pacific. It had one concrete runway 9,000 feet long. Today Jake Grafton flew a straight-in approach over the water, landing to the northeast.

He flared the Intruder like he was flying an Air Force jet. He retarded the engines to idle, pulled the nose up and greased the main mounts on. He held the nose wheel off the runway until the airspeed read 80 knots, then he lowered it as gently as possible. Only then did he realize that he had been holding his breath.

The tower directed him to taxi back to the south end of the runway and park on the taxiway. As he taxied he raised his flaps and slats and shut down his left engine. Then he opened the canopy and removed his oxygen mask. He wiped his face with the sleeve of his flight suit.

A fire truck was waiting when Jake turned off the runway. He made sure he was across the hold-short line, then eased the plane to a stop. One of the sailors on the truck came over to the plane with a fire bottle, a fire extinguisher on wheels. Jake chopped the right engine. On shutdown the fuel control unit dumped the fuel it contained overboard, and this fuel fell down beside the right main wheel. If the brake was hot the fuel could ignite, hence the fire bottle. The danger was nonexistent if you shut down an engine while taxiing because you were moving away from the jettisoned fuel. But there was no fire today.

One of the firemen lowered the pilot's boarding ladder. Jake safetied his ejection seat and unstrapped. He left the helmet and mask in the plane when he climbed down.

The thermal casing on the armed bomb had indeed been peeled back by the blast of the slipstream, pulling the arming wire and freeing the fuse propeller.

Jake Grafton was standing there looking at it when he realized that a chief petty officer in khakis was standing beside him.

'I'm Chief Mendoza, EOD.'

Jake nodded at the weapon. 'We were running an attack. I just happened to look outside for other planes just before we went into a cloud and saw the propeller spinning.'

Flap came over while Jake was speaking. His put his hands on his hips and stood silently examining the bomb.

'If you'd dropped it like that, sir, it might have gone off when the ejector foot hit it,' the chief said.

Neither airman had anything to say.

'Guess you guys were lucky.'

'Yeah.'

'Well, I gotta screw that fuse out. We'll snap a few photos first because we'll have to do a bunch of paperwork and the powers that be will want photos. I suggest you two fellows ride on the fire truck. You don't want to be anywhere around when I start screwing that fuse out.'

'I'll walk,' Jake said.

Flap Le Beau headed for the fire truck.

The chief turned his back on the weapon while the

firemen took photos. He was facing out to sea, looking at the sky and the clouds and the shadows playing on the water when Jake Grafton turned away and began walking.

The pilot loosened his flight gear. He was suddenly very thirsty, so he got out his water bottle and took a drink. The water was warm, but he drank all of it. His hands were shaking, trembling like an old man's.

The heat radiated from the concrete in waves.

He wiped his face again with his sleeve, then half turned and looked back at the plane. The chief was still standing with his arms folded, facing out to sea.

As he walked Jake got a cigarette from the pack in his left sleeve pocket and lit it. The smoke tasted foul.

CHAPTER FOURTEEN

A week after Jake and Flap visited Cubi Point for three whole hours, *Columbia* maneuvered herself against the carrier pier.

Subic Bay, Olongapo City across the Shit River, the BOQ pool, the Cubi O Club with its banks of telephone booths and the Ready Room Bar out back – Jake Grafton had seen it all too recently and it bruoght back too many memories.

He got a roll of quarters and sat in a vacant telephone booth with a gin and tonic, but he didn't make a call. Callie wasn't in Hong Kong – she was in Chicago. Mail was arriving regularly but there were no letters from her; in fact, she hadn't written since he called her from Hawaii.

Somehow he had screwed it up. He sat in the phone booth smoking a cigarette and sipping the drink and wondered where it had gone wrong.

Well, you can't go back. That's one of life's hard truths. The song only goes in one direction and you can't run it backward.

Morgan McPherson, Corey Ford and the Boxman were gone, gone forever. Tiger Cole was undergoing rehab at the Naval Aeromedical Institute in Pensacola and working out each day in the gym where the AOCS classes did their thing, in that converted seaplane hangar on the wharf. Sammy Lundeen was writing orders at the Bureau of Naval Personnel in Washington, Skipper Camparelli was on an admiral's staff at Oceana. Both the Augies had gotten out of the Navy – Big was going to grad school someplace and Little was in dental school in Philadelphia.

And he was here, sitting in fucking Cubi Point in a fucking phone booth with the door open, listening to a new crop of flyers get drunk and talk about going across the bridge tonight and argue about whether the whores of Po City were worth the risk.

They're up there now near the bar, roaring that old song:

> '*Here I sit in Ready Room Four,*
> *Just dreaming of Cubi and my Olongapo whore,*
> *Oh Lupe, dear Lupe's the gal I adore,*
> *She's my hot-fucking, cock-sucking Olongapo whore . . .*

All his friends were getting on with their lives and he was stuck in this shithole at the edge of the known universe. The war was over and he had no place to go. The woman he wanted didn't want him and the flying wasn't fun anymore. It was just dangerous. That might be enough for the Real McCoy, but it wasn't for Jake Grafton.

He finished his first drink and began on his second – he always ordered his drinks two at a time in this place – and lit another cigarette.

He was just flat tired of it – tired of all of it. He was tired of the flying, tired of the flyers, tired of the stink of the ship, the stink of the sailors, the stink of his flight suit. He was tired of Navy showers, tired of floating around on a fucking gray boat, tired of sitting in saloons like this one, tired of being twenty-eight years old with not prospect one.

'Hey, whatcha doin' in there?' Flap Le Beau.

'What's it look like, dumb ass? I'm waiting for a phone call.'

'From who?'

'Miss June. The Pentagon. Hollywood. Walter Crankcase. The commissioner of baseball. Whoever.'

'Hmmm.'

226

'I'm getting drunk.'

'You look pretty sober to me.'

'Just got started.'

'Want any company, or is this a solo drunk?'

'Are you waiting for a call?'

'No. The only one who could conceivably want to talk to me would be the Lord, and I ain't sure about Him. But He knows where to find me if and when.'

'That's comforting, if true. But you say you're not sure?'

'No, I'm not.'

'Life's like that.'

'Come on up to the bar. I'll buy the next round.'

'Some of that Marine money would be welcome,' Jake admitted. He pried himself from the booth and followed Flap along the hallway and up the short flight of stairs into the bar room.

Flap ordered a beer and Jake acquired two more gin and tonics. 'Only drink for the tropics,' he told Flap, who cheerfully paid the seventy-five-cent tab and tossed an extra dime on the counter for the bartender. These Americans were high rollers.

'Miss June, huh?'

'Yeah,' said Jake Grafton. 'I wrote her a fan letter about her tits. Gave her the number of that booth. Told her when I was gonna be in Cubi. She'll call anytime.'

'Let's go play golf. We got enough time before dark.'

'Golf's a lot of work. Whacking that ball around in this heat and humidity . . .'

'Come on,' Flap said. 'Bring your drinks. You can drive the golf cart.'

> *'Oh Lupe, dear Lupe's the gal I adore,*
> *She's my hot-fucking, cock-sucking Olongapo whore . . .'*

There was a line of taxis in front of the club. Jake and Flap went to the one at the head of the line. Jake took huge slurps of both his drinks before he maneuvered himself into the tiny backseat, so he would be less likely to spill any.

And away they went in a cloud of blue smoke, the little engine in the tiny car revving mightily, the Filipino driver hunched over the wheel and punching the clutch and slamming the shift lever around like Mario Andretti.

The golf course was in a valley. Hacked out of the jungle were long, rolling fairways and manicured greens with sand traps and fluttering hole flags. Somewhere up there in the lush tropical foliage beyond the rough was the base fence, a ten-foot-high chain-link affair topped by barbed wire. Beyond the base fence were some of the world's poorest people, kept in line by a Third World military establishment and ruled by a corrupt, piss-pot tyrant. The native laborers who maintained this golf course, and were of course not allowed to play on it, were paid the magnificent sum of one US dollar a day as wages.

The whole damned scene was ludicrous, especially if you were working on your forth drink of the hour. The best thing was not to think about it, not to contemplate that vast social chasm between the men running lawnmowers and raking sand traps and the half-tanked fool driving this shiny little made-in-Japan golf cart. Best not to dwell on the shared humanity or the Grand Canyon that sepraated their dreams and yours.

The heat and humidity made the air thick, oppressive, but it was tolerable here in the golf cart with the faded canvas top providing shade. Jake stuck to piloting the cart while Flap drove, chipped and putted.

'Hotter than hell,' Jake told Flap.

'Yeah. Fucking tropical rain forest.'

'Jungle.'

'Rain forest. Nobody gives a shit about jungle, but they bleed copious dollars over rain forest.'

'Why is that?'

'I dunno. I got a seven on that last hole.'

'That's a lot of strokes. You aren't very good at this.'

'When I play golf, I play a *lot* of it. The object of the game is whacking the ball.'

'Keep your own score. I"m just driving.'

'Driver has to keep score. That's the way it's done at all the top clubs. Pebble Beach, Inverness, everywhere. Gimme a six on the first hole and a seven on this one.'

'You wouldn't cheat, would you?'

'Who? Me? Of course I'd cheat. I'm a nigger, remember?'

Jake wrote down the numbers and put the cart in motion. 'You shouldn't call yourself a nigger. It isn't right.'

'What do you know about it? I'm the black man.'

'Yeah, but I have to listen to it. And I don't like the word.'

'Bet you used it some yourself.'

'When I was a kid, yeah. But I don't like it.'

'Just drink and drive. It's too damn hot to think.'

'Don't use that word. I mean it.'

'If it'll make you happy.'

'I'm out of booze.'

'Well, you can get drunk tonight. Right now you can sit half-tanked and enjoy the pleasure of watching the world's greatest black colored Negro African-American golfer while you contemplate your many heinous sins.'

'It seemed like a good day for a drunk.'

'I've had days like that.'

The problem was, Jake finally admitted to himself, somewhere along the fourth fairway, that he had no dreams. Everyone needs dreams, goals to work toward, and he didn't have any. That fact, and the gin, depressed him profoundly.

He didn't want to be skipper of a squadron, or an admiral, or a farmer. Nor did he want to be an executive vice president in charge of something or other for some grand, important corporation, luxuriating in his new Buick and his generous expense account and his comfortable semi-custom house in an upscale real estate development and his blond wife with the big smile, big tits and purse full of supermarket coupons. He didn't want a stock portfolio and he didn't want to spend his mornings poring over the *Wall Street Journal* to see how rich he was. Just for the record, he also didn't give a damn about French novels and doubted if he ever could.

He didn't want *anything*. And he didn't want to *be* anything.

What in hell do people do who don't have any dreams?

True, he had once wanted to be a good attack pilot. To walk into the ready room and be accepted as an equal by the best aerial warriors in the world. He had achieved that ambition. And found it wasn't worth a mouthful of warm spit.

He had worked awful hard to get there, though.

That was something. He had wanted something and worked hard enough to earn it. And he was still alive. So many of them weren't. He was.

That was something, wasn't it?

He was still thinking about that two holes later when Flap dropped into the right seat of the cart after a tee shot and said, 'There's somebody in the jungle up by the next hole.'

'How do you know?'

'Two big birds flew out of there while I was in the tee box.'

'Birds fly all the time,' Jake pointed out. 'That's the jungle. There's zillions of 'em.'

'Not like that.'

Jake Grafton looked around. He and Flap were the only people in sight. There weren't even any Filipino grounds-keepers. 'So?'

'So I'm going to hit this next one over into the jungle on that side, then go in there to look for the ball. You just sit in the cart and look stupid.'

'I've heard that some locals like to crawl under the fence and rob people on this course.'

'I've heard that too.'

'Let's get outta here. You don't need to play hero.'

'Naw. I'll check 'em out.'

'I hear they carry guns.'

'I'll be careful. Just stop up there by my ball and let me slap it over into the jungle.'

'Don't go killing anybody.'

'They're probably just groundskeepers working on the perimeter fence or something.'

'I mean it, Le Beau, you simple green machine shit. Don't kill anybody.'

'Sure, Jake. Sure.'

So Flap addressed his ball in the fairway and shanked it off into the rough. He said a cuss word and flopped into the cart. Jake motored over to the spot where the ball had disappeared into the foliage and stopped the cart. They were still sixty yards or so short of the green.

'I think this is the spot.'

'Yeah.'

Flap Le Beau climbed out and headed for the jungle, his wedge in his left hand.

Jake examined his watch – 5:35 P.M. The shadows were getting longer and the heat seemed to be easing. That was something, anyhow. Damned Le Beau! Off chasing stickup guys in this green shit – if there were any stickup guys. Probably just a couple of birds that saw a snake or something.

He waited. Swatted at a few bugs that decided he might provide a meal. Amazing that there weren't more bugs, when you thought about it. After all, this was the jungle, the real genuine article with snakes and lizards and rain by the mile and insects the size of birds that drank blood instead of water.

Jake had seen enough jungle to last a lifetime in jungle

survival school in 1971, on the way to Vietnam that first time. They held the course in the jungle somewhere around here. He ate a snake and did all that Tarzan shit, back when he was on his way to being a good attack pilot.

For what?

That had been a stupid goal.

It had been a stupid war, and he had been stupid. Just stupid.

He was still sitting in the cart five minutes later trying to remember why he had wanted to be an attack pilot all those years ago when Flap came out of the jungle up by the green and waved at him to come on up. He was carrying something. As Jake got nearer he saw that Flap had a submachine gun in his right hand and his golf club in his left. The shaft of the club was bent at about a sixty-degree angle six inches or so up from the head.

He pulled the cart alongside Flap and stopped. 'Is that a Thompson?'

'Yeah. There were two guys. One had a machete and one had this.' Flap tossed the bent club in the bin in back of the cart.

'Is it loaded?'

Flap eased the bolt back until he saw brass, then released it. 'Yep.'

'Did you kill them?'

'Nope. They're sleeping like babies.'

Jake got out of the cart. 'Show me.'

'What do you want to see?'

'Come on, Le Beau, you moron. I want to see that these dumb little geeks are still alive and that you didn't kill them just for the fucking fun of it.'

Jake took three steps and entered the foliage. Flap trailed along behind.

The vegetation was extraordinarily thick for the first five or six feet, then it thinned out somewhat and you could see. For about ten feet.

'Well, where are they?'

Flap elbowed by him and led the way. One man lay on his face and the other lay sprawled ten feet away, on his back.

Jake rolled the first man over and checked his pulse. A machete lay a yard away. Well, his heart was still beating.

Jake picked up the machete and went over to the second man. He was obviously breathing. As Jake stood there staring down at him, taking in the sandals, the thin cotton shirt and dirty gray trousers, the short hair and brown skin and broken teeth, the man's eyes opened. Wide. In terror. He tried to sit up.

'Hey. You doing okay?'

His eyes left Jake and went behind him. Jake glanced that way. Flap was standing nonchalantly with the Thompson cradled in his left arm, peering lazily around. Yet his right hand was grasping the stock and his forefinger was on the trigger.

The man slowly got to his feet. He almost fell, then caught himself by grabbing a tree.

'Grab your buddy and get back across the fence.'

The Filipino worked on his friend for almost a minute before he stirred. When he had him sitting up, he looked at the two Americans. Jake jerked his head at the fence, then turned and headed for the fairway. Flap followed him.,

Jake tossed the machete into the bin beside Flap's rented golf bag and the bent club. Flap dumped the Tommy gun there too and sat down in the passenger seat.

'You're really something else, Grafton.'

'What do you want to do? Play golf or discuss philosophy?'

'I've heard it said that golf is philosophy.'

'It's hot and I'm thirsty and a little of your company goes a hell of a long way.'

'Yeah. Tell you what, let's go see what the rest of this course looks like. Drive on.' He flipped his fingers and Jake pressed the accelerator. The cart hummed and moved. 'Just drive the holes and we'll ride along like Stanley and Dr Livingston touring Africa. Nothing like an evening drive to settle a man's nerves and put everything into perspective. When we get back to the clubhouse, I'll buy you a drink. Maybe later we can go find two ugly women.'

'How ugly?'

'Ugly enough to set your nose hair on fire.'

'That's not ugly.10

'Maybe not,' Flap said agreeably. 'Maybe not.

CHAPTER FIFTEEN

The days at sea quickly became routine. The only variables were the weather and the flight schedule, but even so, the possible permutations of light and darkness, storms and clouds and clear sky and the places your name could appear on the flight schedule were finally exhausted. At some point you'd seen it all, done it all, and tomorrow would be a repetition of some past day. So, you suspected, would all the tomorrows to come.

Not that the pilots of the air wing flew every day, because they didn't. The postwar budget crunch did not permit that luxury. Every third day was an off day, sprinkled with boring paperwork, tedious lectures on safety or some aspect of the carrier aviator's craft, or – snore! – another NATOPS quiz. Unfortunately, on flying days there were not enough sorties to allow every pilot to fly one, so Jake and the rest of them took what they could get and solaced themselves with an occasional ugly remark to the schedules officer, as if that harried individual could conjure up money and flight time by snapping his fingers.

On those too-rare occasions when bombs were the main course – usually Mark 76 practice bombs, but every now and then the real thing – Jake Grafton managed to turn in respectable scores. Consequently he was a section leader now, which meant that when two A-6s were sent to some uninhabited island in the sea's middle to fly by, avoid the birds, and take photographs, he got to lead. He led unless Colonel Haldane was flying on that launch, then he got to fly the colonel's wing. Haldane *was* the skipper, even if his CEP was not as good as Jake's. Rank has its privileges.

Of course Doug Harrison reminded the skipper of his earlier commitment to letting the best bomber lead. Haldane's response was to point to the score chart on the bulkhead. 'When *you* get a better CEP than *mine*, son, I'll fly your wing. By then my eyes will be so bad I'll need someone to lead me around. Until that day . . .'

'Yessir,' Harrison said as his squadron mates hooted.

Jake had been spending at least half his time in the squadron maintenance department, and now the skipper made it official. Jake was to assist the maintenance officer with supply problems.

The squadron certainly had supply problems. Spare parts for the planes were almighty slow coming out of the Navy supply system. The first thing Jake did was to sit down with the book and check to see if the requisitions were correctly filled out. He found a few errors but concluded finally that the supply sergeant knew what he was doing. Then he sat down for a long talk with the sergeant.

Armed with a list of all the parts that were on back order, he went to see the ship's aviation supply officer, a lieutenant commander in the Supply Corps, a staff corps that ranked with law and medicine. Together they went over Jake's list, a computer printout, then sorted through the reams of printouts that cluttered up the supply office. Finally they went to the storerooms, cubbyholes all over the ship crammed with parts, and compared numbers.

When Jake went to see Colonel Haldane after three days of this, he had several answers. The erroneous requisitions were easily explained – there were actually fewer than one might expect. Yet the Marine sergeant was the odd man out with the Navy supply clerks, who were giving him no help. The system would not work if the people involved were not cooperating fully and trying to help each other.

The most serious problem, Jake told the colonel, was the shortages on the load-out manifest when the ship put to sea. Parts that should be aboard the ship weren't. Related to this problem was the fact that the supply department had stored some of its inventory in the wrong compartments, effectively losing a substantial portion of the inventory that was aboard. This, he explained, was one reason the clerks were less than helpful with the squadron supply sergeant – they didn't want to admit that they couldn't find spare parts that their own records showed they had.

Lieutenant Colonel Haldane went to see CAG, the air wing commander, and together they visited the ship's supply officer, then the executive officer. Jake didn't attend these meetings but he read one of the messages the captain of the ship sent out about shortages in the load-out manifest. Sparks were flying somewhere. Two chief petty officers in the supply department were given orders back to the States. Soon parts began to flow more freely into the squadron's maintenance department. One evening the supply sergeant stopped Jake in the passageway and thanked him.

It was a pleasant moment.

One day the flight schedule held a surprise. From the distant top branches of the Pentagon aviary came tasking for flights to photograph estuaries along the coast of North Vietnam. Told to stay just outside the three-mile limit, the aircrews marveled at these orders. They knew, even if the senior admirals did not, that even if the North Viets were preparing a mighty fleet to invade Hawaii and they managed to get photographs of the ships, with soldiers marching aboard carrying signs saying WAIKIKI OR BUST, the politicians in Washington would not, could not renew hostilities with the Communists in Hanoi. Still, orders were orders. In Ready Four the A-6 crews loaded 35-mm cameras with film, hung them around the BNs' necks, and went flying.

There were no enemy warships lurking in the estuaries. Just a few fishing boats.

It was weird seeing North Vietnam again, Jake told himself as he flew along at 3,000 feet, 420 knots, dividing his attention between the coast and his electronic counter-measures – ECM – alarms as Flap Le Beau busied himself with a hand-held 35-mm camera. The gomers were perfectly capable of squirting an SA-2 antiaircraft missile out this way, even if he was over international waters. Or two or three missiles. He kept an eye on the ECM and listened carefully for the telltale sounds of radar beams painting his aircraft.

And heard nothing. Not even a search radar. The air was dead.

The land over there on his right was partially obscured by haze, which was normal for this time of year. Yet there it was in all its pristine squalor – gomer country, low, flat and half-flooded. The browns and greens and blues were washed out by the haze. The place wasn't worth a dollar an acre, and certainly not anybody's life. That was the irony that made it what it was, a miserable land reeking of doom and pointless death.

Looking at it from this angle four miles off the coast, from the questionable safety of a cockpit, he could feel the horror, could almost see it, as if it were as real and tangible as fog. All those shattered lives, all those terrible memories . . .

They had fuel enough for thirty minutes of this fast cruising, then they planned to turn away from the coast and slow down drastically to save fuel. First Lieutenant Doug Harrison was somewhere up north just now, taking a peek into Haiphong Harbor. Grafton would meet him over the ship.

They were fifteen minutes into their mission when Jake first heard it – three different notes in his ears, notes with a funny rhythm. Da-de-duh . . . da-de-duh . . .

238

He reached for the volume knob on the ECM panel. Yes, but now there were four notes.

'Hear that?' he asked Flap.

'Yeah. What is it?'

'Sounds like a raster scan.'

'It's a MiG or F-4, man. Look, the A1 light is illumin—'

He got no more out because Jake Grafton had rolled the plane ninety degrees left and slapped on five G's as he punched out some chaff.

When the heading change was about ninety degrees, Jake rolled out some of the bank and relaxed the G somewhat. The coast was behind him and he was headed out to sea. The Air Intercept light remained illuminated and the tone continued in their ears, although it was back to three notes, a pause, then the three notes again.

'We're on the edge of his scan, but he sees us all right,' Flap said.

'Hang on.'

Throttles forward to the stops, Jake lowered the left wing and pulled hard until he had turned another ninety degrees. Now he was heading north. He let the nose drop and they slanted down toward the ocean. Meanwhile Flap was craning his head to see behind. Jake was looking too, then coming back inside to scan the instruments. Outside again . . . too many puffy clouds. He saw nothing.

The adrenaline was really pumping now.

'See anything?' he demanded of Flap.

'You'll be the first to hear if I do. I promise.'

Probably a Phantom, but it could be a MiG! Out over the ocean, in international waters. If it shot them down, who would know?

Or care?

Goddamn!

This A-6 was unarmed. Sidewinders could be fitted but Jake had never carried one, not even in training. This was an *attack* plane, not a fighter. And there was no gun. For reasons known only to God and Pentagon cost efficiency experts, the Navy had bought the A-6 without any internal guns. Against an enemy fighter it was defenseless.

The raster beat was tattooing their eardrums. Now they had a two-ring-strength strobe on the small Threat Direction Indicator – TDI. Almost directly aft.

He did another square corner, turning east again, then retarded the throttles to idle to lower the engines' heat signature and kept the plane in a gentle descent to maintain its speed. The enemy plane extended north, then turned, not as sharply. Now it was at five o'clock behind them.

Jake looked aft. Clouds. Oh, sweet Jesus! Dit-da-de-duh, dit-da-de-duh, dit-da-de-duh . . . the sound was maddening.

He was running out of sky. Passing eleven hundred feet. The ocean was down here.

He slammed the throttles full forward. As the engines wound up he pushed the nose over to convert what altitude he had into airspeed. He bottomed out at four hundred feet on the altimeter with 500 knots on the airplane. He pulled, a nice steady four-G pull.

He was climbing vertically, straight up, when he entered the clouds. Concentrating on the gauges, trying to ignore the insane beat of the enemy radar, he kept the stick back but eased out most of the G. Still in the clouds with the nose up ten degrees, he rolled upright and continued to climb.

The sound of the enemy's radar stopped. The MiG must have sliced off to one side or the other, be making a turn to reacquire him. But which way? He had been concentrating so hard on flying the plane that he hadn't had time to watch the TDI.

'Right or left?' he asked Flap.

'I dunno.'

The clouds were thinning. Lots more sunlight. Then the A-6 popped out on top.

Jake looked left, Flap right.

The pilot saw him first, three or four thousand feet above, turning toward them. An F-4.

'It's a fucking Phantom,' he roared over the ICS to Flap.

Flap spun and craned over Jake's shoulder. Then he flopped back in his seat and held up middle fingers to the world.

Jake raised his visor and swabbed his face. Now the strobe reappeared on the TDI and the music sounded in his ears. He reached with his right hand and turned the ECM equipment off.

The plane was climbing nicely. He engaged the autopilot, then turned to watch the F-4. It tracked inbound for several seconds, then turned away while it was still a half mile or so out.

Jake took off his oxygen mask and helmet and used his sleeve to swab the perspiration from his face. He was wearing his flight gloves, so he used them to wipe his hair. The sweat made black stains on his gloves and sleeve. Then he took off one glove and used his fingers to clean the stinging, salty solution from his eyes.

'Think he did that on purpose?' Flap demanded when he had his helmet back on and could again hear the ICS.

'How would I know?'

One evening as Jake entered the stateroom, his room-mate, the financier, glanced at him and groaned. 'Not another haircut! For heaven's sake, Jake, why don't you just shave your head and be done with it?'

Grafton surveyed his locks in the mirror over the sink. 'What are you quacking about? Looks okay to me.'

'Is this the third haircut this week?'

'Well, I admit, watching these Marines parade off to the barbershop on an hourly basis has had a corrosive effect on my morals. I feel like a scuz bucket if I don't go along. What are you caterwauling about? It's my head and it'll all grow out, sooner or later.'

'You're ruining my image, Grafton. Already they are giving me the evil eye. I feel like a spy in the house of love.'

'You've been reading Anaïs Nin, haven't you?'

'Bartow loaned me an edition in English. Wow, you ought to read some of that stuff! Ooh la la. It's broadening my horizons.'

'What are you working on this evening?' The Real had paper strewn all over his desk, but there wasn't a stock market listing in sight.

McCoy frowned and flipped some of the pages upside down so that Jake couldn't see them. Then he apparently thought better of his actions and sat back in his chair surveying Grafton. The frown faded. In a moment he grinned. 'We're going to cross the line in two days.'

The line – the equator. The task group was heading south-east, intending to sail around the island of Java and reenter the China Sea through the Sunda Strait. Of necessity the ship would cross the equator twice.

'So?'

'I'm the only officer shellback in the squadron. Everyone else is a pollywog, including you.'

A pollywog was a sailor who had never crossed the equator. A shellback was one who had previously crossed and been duly initiated into the Solemn Mysteries of the Ancient Order of Shellbacks. It was easy enough to find out who was and who wasn't. In accordance with naval regulations, all shellbacks had the particulars of their initiation recorded in their service records – ship, date and longitude.

'Too bad you'll miss out on all the fun,' Jake said carelessly.

McCoy chuckled. 'I ain't gonna miss a thing, shipmate, believe you me. I'm coming to the festivities as Davy Jones. But if you're willing, I could use a little help.'

Jake was aghast. 'Help from a lowly pollywog?'

'We'll have to keep this under our hats. Can't have scandalous things like this whispered around, can we? This would be help on the sly, for the greater glory of King Neptune.' He picked up the documents on his desk that he had turned over to keep Jake from seeing and passed them to his roommate.

The next two days passed quickly and pleasantly. Then the great day arrived. There was, of course, no flying scheduled. All morning people – presumably shellbacks – bustled around the ship on mysterious errands, with lots of giggling.

The pollywogs were given strict orders over the ship's loudspeaker system. They were to go to their staterooms or berthing compartments after the noon meal and remain there until summoned into the august presence of Neptunus Rex, Ruler of the Raging Main. Actually there were over two dozen Neptunes, selected strictly on seniority, i.e., the number of times they had crossed the line. Initiation ceremonies would be held simultaneously in ready rooms, berthing areas and mess decks throughout the ship, and each ceremony would be presided over by Neptunus Rex.

In his stateroom, Jake took off his uniform and pulled on a pair of civilian shorts. He donned a T-shirt and slid his feet into shower thongs. Then he settled back to wait for his summons.

It wasn't long in coming. The telephone rang. The duty officer. 'Pollywog Grafton, come to the ready room.'

'Aye aye, sir.'

Jake took off his watch and dog tags. After he checked to ensure that his stateroom key was in his pocket, he went out and locked the door behind him.

The ready room was rapidly filling with his fellow wogs. Jake slipped into his regular seat. Colonel Haldane was lounging in his seat near the duty officer's desk, chatting quietly with the executive officer. Alas, both officers were also wogs and were decked out for the festivities to come in jeans and Marine Corps green T-shirts. Standing everywhere around the bulkheads were officers from the air wing and other squadrons in uniform. Shellbacks. They immediately began to heckle the Marines, and Grafton.

'You're in for it now, wogs . . . Just you wait until King Neptune arrives . . . You slimy wogs are in deep and serious . . .'

The public address system crackled to life. Ding ding, ding ding, ding ding, ding ding, ding ding. Ten bells. 'Ruler of the Raging Main, arriving.'

A howl of glee arose from the onlookers, who laughed and pointed at the assembled victims, many of whom were making faces at their tormentors. Now Flap Le Beau stood in his chair, his arms folded across his chest. He was wearing a pillowcase on top of his head, held on with a band. His face was streaked with paint. As the onlookers hooted, he explained that he was an African king, ruler of the ancient kingdom of Boogalala, and he demanded deferential treatment from this Rex guy.

The shellbacks successfully shouted him down. Finally he sat, promising that he would renew his demands when the barnacled one arrived. One row behind him, Jake Grafton grinned broadly.

They didn't have long to wait. The door was flung open and the Real McCoy stalked in. 'Attention on deck,' he roared. The Marines snapped to attention like they were on parade. When everyone was erect and rigid, McCoy continued, 'All hail, Neptunus Rex, Ruler of the Ragin' Main.'

'Hail,' the assembled shellbacks shouted lustily.

Here they came, the royal party, led by the air wing commander, the CAG, who was decked out in a bedsheet. Behind him came Neptunus Rex, wearing a gold crown that looked suspiciously like it had been crafted of cardboard and spray painted. He wore swimming trunks and tennis shoes, but no shirt. His upper arms each bore a tattoo of a well-endowed, totally naked woman and on his chest was a screaming eagle in flight. A bedsheet cape flowed behind him. In his hand he carried a cardboard trident. As he seated himself on his throne – a chair on a platform so that everyone had a good view – Jake recognized him, as did half the men in the room. Bosun Muldowski.

The Real McCoy – Davy Jones – took his place at the podium and adjusted the microphone. He was wearing long underwear, which he and Jake had decorated with a bottle of iodine last night in a vain attempt to paint fish, octopi and other sea creatures. Alas, the outfit just looked like a bloody mess, Jake decided now. McCoy was enjoying himself immensely, and it showed on his face.

Flap Le Beau stood up again in his chair. 'Hey, King! How's it going?'

McCoy frowned, CAG frowned, Neptune frowned.

'Sit down, wog! Show some respect in the royal presence.'

'Uh, Davy, you don't seem to understand. I'm King Flap of Boogalala. Being a king my very own self, I shouldn't be here in the company of these slimy pollywogs. I should be up there on a throne beside ol' Neptune discussing the many mind-boggling mysteries of the deep and how he's making out these days with the mermaids.'

'Well pleaded, King Flap.' The onlookers seemed to disagree, and hooted their displeasure. Davy looked over at Neptune. 'What say you, oh mighty windy one?'

Neptune scowled fiercely at the upstart Le Beau. 'Have you wogs no respect? The dominions of the land are irrelevant here upon the briny deep, where I am sovereign. I suggest, Davy, that the loud-mouth pretender kiss the royal baby three times.'

'Wog Le Beau, you heard the royal wish. Thrice you shall kiss the royal baby. Now sit and assume a becoming humility or you will again face the awesome wrath of mighty Neptune.'

Le Beau sat. He screwed up his face and tried to cry. And almost made it. A gale of laughter swept the room.

It was good to be a part of this foolishness, Jake Grafton thought, good to have a hearty laugh with your shipmates, fellow voyagers on this journey through life. He and the Real had worked hard to get some laughs, and they succeeded. Many of the wogs were hailed individually before the royal court and their sins set forth in lurid detail. Major Allen Bartow was confronted with a book labeled *S'il Vous Plaît* really a NATOPS manual with a suitable cover – from which spilled a dozen Playmate-of-the-Month foldouts.

'Reading dirty books, slobbering over dirty pictures . . . shame, shame!' intoned Davy Jones, and King Neptune pronounced the sentence: three trips through the tunnel of love.

After about an hour of this nonsense the wogs were led up to the hangar deck, then across it to an aircraft elevator, which lifted the entire Ready Four pollywog/shellback mob to the flight deck. There the remainder of the initiation ceremonies, and all of Neptune's verdicts, were carried out.

The tunnel of love was a canvas chute filled with garbage from the mess decks. All the wogs crawled through it at least once, the more spectacular sinners several times. At the exit of the tunnel were shellbacks with saltwater hoses to rinse off the garbage, but the wogs were only beginning their odyssey.

Next was the royal baby, the fattest shellback aboard, who sat on a throne without a shirt. His tummy was liberally coated with arresting gear grease. Victims were thrust forward to kiss his belly button. He enthusiastically assisted the unwilling, grabbing ears and smearing handfuls of grease in the supplicants' hair. After kisses from every three or four victims, able assistants regreased his gut from a fifty-five-gallon drum that sat nearby. A messy business from any angle . . .

A visit to the royal dentist was next on the list. This worthy squirted a dollop of a pepper concoction into his victim's mouths from a plastic ketchup dispenser. Expectoration usually followed immediately.

After a visit to the royal barber – more grease – and the royal gymnasium, the wogs ended their journey with a swim across the royal lagoon, a canvas pool six inches deep in water. No, Jake learned as he looked at the victims splashing along, the water was only about one inch deep. It floated on at least five inches of something green, something with a terrible smell. Shellbacks arranged around the lagoon busily offered opinions about what the noisome stuff might be. The wogs slithered through this mess to the other side, where shellbacks helped them out, wiped them down, and congratulated them heartily. Without hesitation Jake flopped down and squirmed his way through the goo while his squadron-mates on the other side – the ones who had beat him over – cheered and offered impractical advice.

Jake joined Flap Le Beau on the fantail, where they stood watching the proceedings and comparing experiences as they wiped away the worst of the grease with paper towels.

The ship wasn't moving, Jake noticed. She lay dead in the water on a placid, gently heaving sea. Around her at distances ranging from one to three miles her escorts were similarly still. All the ships were conducting crossing-the-line initiation ceremonies. Painted ships upon a painted ocean, Jake thought.

With a last glance at the sea and the sky and the merry group still cavorting on the flight deck, he headed below for the showers.

'Getting shot down was a real bad scene,' Flap le Beau told Jake. They were on a surface surveillance mission along the southern coast of Java, photographing ships. To their right was the mountainous island with its summits wreathed in clouds, to the left was the endless blue water. They had just descended to 500 feet to snap three or four shots of a small coaster bucking the swells westward and were back at 3,000 feet, cruising at 300 knots. The conversation had drifted to Vietnam.

Perhaps it was inevitable, since both men had been shot down in that war, but neither liked to talk about their experiences, so the subject rarely came up. If it did, it was in an oblique reference. Somehow today, in a cockpit in a tropic sky, the subject seemed safe.

'It was just another mission, another day at the office, and the gomers got the lead right and let us have it. I hadn't even seen flak that morning until we collected a packet. Goose was killed instantly – one round blew his head clean off, the left engine was hit, the left wing caught fire. All in about the time it takes to snap your fingers.'

'What were you doing?'

'Dive-bombing, near the Laotian border. We were the second plane in a two-plane formation, working with a Nail FAC.' A FAC was a forward air controller, who flew a small propeller-driven plane.

'We were on our second run. Oh, I know, we shouldn't have been making more than one, but the FAC hadn't seen any shit in the air and everything was cool during our first run. Then whap! They shot us into dog meat going down the chute. I grabbed the stick, pickled the bombs and pulled out, but the left engine was doing weird things and the wing was burning like a blowtorch and Goose was smeared all over everything, including me. Wind howling through the cockpit – all the glass on his side was mashed out. Real bad scene. So I steered it away from the target a little and watched the wing burn and told Goose good-bye, then I boogied.'

'How long did you wait before you ejected?'

'Seemed like an hour or so, but our flight leader told me

later it was about a minute. All the time he was screaming for me to eject because he could see the fire. But we were at about six thousand feet at that point and I wanted a little distance from the gomers and I wanted the plane slowed down so I wouldn't get tore up going out. There was so much noise I never heard anything on the radio.'

Jake remembered his own ejection, at night, over Laos. Just thinking about it brought back the sweats. He didn't say anything.

'When I got on the ground,' Flap continued, 'I got out my little radio and started talking. Now I'd checked the battery in that jewel before we took off, but I could barely hear the FAC. I found a place to settle in where I could keep an eye on the chute. Then the rescue turned to shit. The gomers were squirting flak everywhere and it was late in the afternoon and darkness was coming. What I didn't know until way afterward was that the guy flying the rescue chopper got a case of cold feet and decided his engine wasn't right or something. Anyway, he never came. It got dark and started raining and I decided I was on my own.'

'So how'd you feel?'

'Well, I felt real bad about Goose. He was a good guy, y'know? Tough getting it like that.'

'I mean how did *you* feel?'

'Like I had never left Marine recon. At least my jungle rot wasn't itching. That was something. I skinned out of all that survival gear and kept only what I needed and decided to set up an ambush. What I really wanted was a rifle. All I had was the forty-five. And my knife.'

'Didn't you think they might catch you?'

'No way, man. I knew they wouldn't. Couldn't. Not unless they shot me or something. I was on the ground for two weeks and had people walk by within six feet of me and they never saw me.'

'So what did you do?'

'Do? Well, I found a guy who had a rifle and took it, and his food. Ball of rice, with a lot of sand mixed in. You sort of have to develop a taste for it.'

'Uh-huh.'

'Checked in on the emergency freq about once a day, when the gomers weren't close. Didn't want to overwork the batteries in that radio. But they never heard me. A patrol found me on the fourteenth day. It was a good thing, because my jungle rot was starting to itch by then. You can never really cure that shit, you know.'

'So how many gomers did you kill?'

'A dozen that I know about.'

'Know about?'

'Yeah. I kept busy building booby traps and such. With a little luck the traps got a few more of 'em. In a way, it sort of made up for losing Goose. Not really, I guess. But it helped.'

'Uh-huh.'

'A fucked-up war, that's what it was. A hell of a mess.'

'Yeah,' Jake said, and checked the fuel and the clock on the instrument panel. 'I think we're going to have to turn around.'

'Okay,' Flap Le Beau said. 'Boy, it sure is pretty out here today.'

'There's a decision point for every career officer,' Lieutenant Colonel Haldane said, 'one day when you wake up and decide that you want to make a contribution. And for pilots, that doesn't mean driving an airplane through the sky every day.'

He and Jake were sitting in the ready room. Jake had the duty and sat at the duty desk and Haldane was in his chair just behind it. There was only one other officer in the room, doing paperwork near the mailboxes. Haldane's voice was low so that only Jake could hear it.

'True, some officers merely decide to stay until retirement, and I suppose that's okay. We need those people too. But the people we want are those who dedicate themselves to making the service better, to being leaders, people who try to grow personally and professionally every day. Those folks are few and far between but we need them desperately.'

Jake merely nodded. Haldane had read the latest classified messages and handed the board back to Jake just before he began this monologue. Apparently Jake's letter of resignation was on his mind, although he hadn't mentioned it.

Haldane went on, almost thinking out loud: 'In every war America fought before Vietnam, the people who led the military to victory were never the people in charge when the shooting started. US Grant and William T. Sherman weren't even in the army when the Civil War started. Phil Sheridan was a captain. Eisenhower and George Patton were colonels at the start of World War II, Halsey and Nimitz were captains. Curious, don't you think?'

Before Jake could reply, he continued, 'In peacetime the top jobs go to politicians, men who can stroke the civilians and oil the wheels of the bureaucracy. During a war the system works the way it is supposed to – men who can lead other men in combat are pulled to the top and given command. In Vietnam this natural selection process was stymied by the politicians. It was a political war all the way and the last thing they wanted was to relinquish the controls to war fighters. So we lost. And you know something funny? We could afford to lose because we didn't have anything important at stake in the first place.

'Someday America is going to get into a fight it has to win. I don't know when it will come or who the fight will be with. That war may come next year, or twenty years from now, or fifty. Or a hundred. But it *will* come. It always has in the past and evolution doesn't seem to be improving the human species anywhere near fast enough.

'The question is, who will be in the military when that war comes? Will the officer corps be full of glorified clerks, efficiency experts and computer operators putting in their time to earn a comfortable retirement? Or will there be some military leaders in that mix, men who can lead other men to victory, men like Grant, Patton, Halsey?'

Haldane rose from his chair and adjusted his trousers. 'Interesting question, isn't it, Mr Grafton?'

'Yessir.'

'The quality of the people in uniform – such a little thing. And that may make all the difference.'

Haldane turned and walked out. The officer doing paperwork had already left. Jake pulled out the top drawer of the desk and propped his feet up on it.

That Haldane – a romantic. Blood, thunder, destiny . . . If he thought that kind of talk cut any ice anymore he was deluding himself. Not in this post-Vietnam era. Not with the draft dodgers who didn't want to go and not with the veterans who weren't so quick.

Jake Grafton snorted. He had had his fill of this holy military crap! His turn expired when this boat got back to the States in February. Then somebody else could do it.

And if the United States goes down the slop chute someday because no one wants to fight for it, so be it. No doubt the Americans alive then will get precisely what they deserve, ounce for ounce and measure for measure.

What was that quote about the mills of the gods? They grind slowly?

CHAPTER SIXTEEN

Singapore lies at the southern end of the Malay peninsula, a degree and a half north of the equator. This city is the maritime crossroads of the earth. Ships from Europe by way of Suez and the Red Sea, India, Pakistan, Africa and the Middle East transit the Strait of Malacca and call here before entering the South China Sea. Ships from America, Japan, China, Taiwan, Korea and the Soviet Far East call here on their way west. The city-state is close enough to the Sunda Strait that it makes a natural port call for ships from the Orient bound for South Africa or South America via the Cape of Good Hope.

Although it is one of the world's great seaports, Singapore doesn't have a harbor. The open roadstead is always crammed with ships riding their anchors, except on those rare occasions when a typhoon threatens. There are few piers large enough for an oceangoing vessel, so the majority of the cargo being off- or on-loaded in Singapore travels to and from the ships in lighters. The squadrons of these busy little boats weaving their way through the anchored ships from the four corners of the earth and all the places in between make Singapore unique.

As befits a great seaport, the city is a racial melting pot. The human stew is composed mostly of Malay, Chinese, Thai, Hindu, Moslem, and Filipino, with some Japanese added for seasoning, but there are whites there too. British, primarily, because Singapore was one of those outposts of empire upon which the sun never set, but also people from most of the countries of Europe, Australia, New Zealand, and, inevitably, America.

Visitors who have always considered their place, their nation, as the zenith of civilization here receive a shock. Vibrant, cosmopolitan Singapore is a major vortex, one of those rare places where the major strains of the human experience come crashing together and swirl madly around until something new is created.

To the delight of visiting American sailors, the British still had a military base there, Changi, and shared it with those stout lads from Down Under, the Australians, who naturally came supplied with Down Under lassies. Australian women were the glory of Singapore. These tall, lithe creatures with tanned, muscular legs and striking white teeth that were forever being displayed in dazzling smiles somehow completed the picture, made it whole. You ran into them at Raffles, the old hotel downtown with ceiling fans and rattan chairs and doddery old gentlemen in white suits sipping gin. You ran into them in the lobbies and restaurants of the new western hotels and in the bazaars and emporiums. You saw them strolling the boulevards and haggling with small Chinese women in baggy trousers for sapphires and opals. You saw them everywhere, young, tan, enjoying life, the center of attention wherever they were. It helped that their colorful tropical frocks contrasted so vividly with the drab trousers and white shirts that seemed to be the Singaporean national costume. They were like songbirds surrounded by sparrows.

'If Qantas didn't bring them here, the United Nations should supply them as a gesture of good will to all human kind.'

Flap Le Beau stated this conclusion positively to Jake Grafton and the Real McCoy as they stood outside Raffles Hotel surveying the human parade on the sidewalk.

'I think I'm in love,' the Real McCoy told his companions. 'I want one of those for my very own.'

The three of them had ridden the liberty boat two miles across the anchorage an hour ago. They had walked for an hour, taking it all in and had developed a terrible thirst. Just now they were contemplating going into Raffles to see if their need could be quenched somewhat.

'After forty-five days at sea, everything female looks mighty good to me,' Flap Le Beau said, then smiled broadly at an elderly British lady coming out of the hotel. She nodded graciously in reply and seated herself in a waiting taxi.

'Well, gentlemen,' Jake Grafton said, and turned to face the white antique structure, 'shall we?'

'Let's.'

The temperature inside was at least ten degrees cooler. The dark interior and the ceiling fans apparently had a lot to do with that, but the very Britishness of the place undoubtedly helped. The heat and humidity could stay outside – it wouldn't dare intrude.

The American aviators went to the bar and ordered – of all things – Singapore slings. The waiter, a Chinese, didn't bat an eye. He nodded and moved on. He had long ago come to terms with the curious taste of liquor that seemed to afflict most Americans.

'You sort of expect to see Humphrey Bogart or Sidney Greenstreet sitting around under a potted palm,' the Real commented as he tilted his chair back and crossed his legs.

Jake Grafton sipped his drink in silence. Forty-five days at sea riding the catapults, night rendezvouses above the clouds, instrument approaches to the ball, mid-rats sliders, ready room high jinks, lying in his bunk while the ship moved ever so gently in the sea as he listened to the creaks and groans . . . then to be baptized with a total immersion in *this*. Cultural shock didn't begin to describe it. The sights and sounds and smells of Singapore were sensory overload for a young man from a floating monastery.

He sat now trying to take it all in, to adjust his frame of reference. He had been here once before, on one of his cruises to Vietnam. He tried to recall some details of that visit, but the memories were vague, blurred scenes just beyond the limits of complete recall. He had sat here in this room with Morgan McPherson . . . at which table? He couldn't remember. Morgan's face, laughing, he could see that, but the room . . . Who else had been there?

Oh, Morg! If you could only be here again. To sit here and share a few moments of life. We wouldn't waste it like we did then. If only . . .

So many of those guys were dead. And he had forgotten. That the moments he had spent with them were fuzzy and blurred seemed a betrayal of what they had been, what they had given. Life goes on, but still . . . All that any man can leave behind are the memories that this friends carry. He isn't really gone until they are. But if the living quickly forget, it is as if the dead man never was.

'. . . we oughta go buy some souvenirs,' the Real was saying. 'The folks at home would really like . . .'

Jake polished off the last of his drink and stood. He threw some Singapore dollars on the table, money he had acquired this morning from the money changers aboard ship. 'See you guys later.'

'Where are you going?'

He was going back to the ship, but he didn't want to say that. 'Oh, I dunno. Gonna just walk. See you later.'

Outside on the street he stuffed his hands into his pockets and turned toward the wharves. He walked along staring at the sidewalk in front of him, oblivious of the traffic and the sights and the human stream that parted to let him past, then immediately closed in behind him.

The next day Jake stood an eight-hour duty officer watch in the ready room. About two in the afternoon the Real McCoy came breezing in.

'Today's your lucky day, Grafton. You are blessed to have Flap and me for friends. Truly blessed.'

'I know,' Jake told him dryly.

'We met some Brits. What a bunch they are! How we ever kicked them out of the good ol' US of A is a mystery I'll never understand.'

'A military miracle.'

'These are *good* guys.'

'I'm sure.'

'They've invited us to a party at Changi this evening. A party! And they swore that some Aussie women would be there! Quantas stews. Can you beat that?' Without pausing to let Jake wrestle with that question, he steamed on. 'When do you get off?'

'Uh, two hours from now.'

The Real consulted his watch. 'I'll wait. Flap is taking the next boat in, but I'll wait for you. I've got directions. We'll grab a cab and tootle on over to *party hearty*. Maybe, just maybe, we'll get a glorious opportunity to lower the white count. Oooh boy!'

McCoy strode up the aisle between the huge, soft chairs, past the silent 16-mm movie projector, and blasted through the door into the passageway.

Jake sat back in his chair and opened the letter from his parents yet again. It had been two weeks since the last mail delivery, via a cargo plane out of Cubi Point, and this was the current crop, delivered this morning – one letter from his mother. She signed it 'Mom and Dad,' but she wrote every word. Nothing from Callie McKenzie.

Maybe that was for the best. It had been a hell of a romance, but now it was over. She was from one world, he was from a completely different one. Presumably she was doing her own thing there in Chicago, going to class and dating some long-haired hippie intellectual who liked French novels. What was it about French novels?

But he desperately wished she had written. Even a Dear

John letter would be preferable to this vast silence, he told himself, wanting to believe it but not quite sure that he did.

Oh well. Like most of the things in his life, this relationship was out of his control. Have a nice life, Callie McKenzie. Have a nice life.

Darkness comes quickly in the tropics. Twilight is an almost instantaneous transition from daylight to darkness. Jake, Flap and the Real had just arrived at Changi by taxi and found the outdoor pavilion when the transition occurred. Whoom, and the lanterns in the pavilion were flickering bravely against the mighty darkness.

The Brit and Aussie soldiers had indeed not forgotten their invitation of the afternoon. They led the three Americans around and introduced them, but Flap was the only surefire hit with the ladies. Soon he had all five of the women gathered around him.

'The Aussies aren't used to black men wearing pants,' the Real whispered to Jake. 'Those stews will get over the novelty in a while and we'll get a chance to cut a couple out.'

Jake wasn't so sure. The soldiers seemed to be eyeing the crowd around Flap with a faint trace of dismay. Nothing obvious, of course, but Jake thought he could see it.

'Hey, mate. How about a beer?' The Australian who asked held out a couple of cold bottles of Fosters.

'Thanks. Real hard duty you guys got here.'

'Beats the outback. Beats that scummy little war you Yanks gave in the Nam, too. Saigon was a bit of all right but the rest of it wasn't so cheery. This is mighty sweet after that busman's holiday, I can tell you.'

'It was the only war we had,' the Real explained, then poured beer down his throat. Jake Grafton did the same.

Two beers later Jake Grafton was sitting at a table in the corner listening to Vietnam War stories from a couple of the Aussies when one of the stews came over to join them. 'Mind if I join you chaps?'

'Not at all, not at all. Brighten up the party. How long are you in for this time, Nell?'

'Off to Brisbane and Sydney tomorrow. Then back here via Tokyo the following day.' Nell winked at Jake. 'Girl has to keep herself busy now, doesn't she?'

Grafton nodded and grinned. Nell returned it. She was a little above medium height, with fair hair and a dynamite tan. Several gold bracelets encircled each of her wrists and made tiny tinkly noises when she moved her arms.

'My name's Jake,' he told her.

'Nell Douglas,' she said, and stuck out her hand. Jake shook it. Cool and firm. And then he looked around and realized the Aussies had drifted and he and Nell were alone.

'So what do you do for the Yanks?'

'I'm a pilot.'

'Oh, God!' Not another one. I've sworn off pilots for at least three months.' She smiled again. He liked the way her eyes smiled when she did.

'Better tell me about it. Nothing like a sympathetic listener to ease a broken heart.'

'You don't look like the sympathetic type.'

'Don't be fooled by appearances. I'm sensitive, sympathetic, charming, warm, witty, wonderful.' He shrugged. 'Well, part of that's true, anyway. I'm warm.'

Now her whole face lit up. Her bracelets tinkled.

'How long have you been flying with Qantas?'

'Five years. My father has a station in Queensland. One day I said to myself, Nell old girl, if you stay here very much longer one of these jackeroos will drag you to the altar and you'll never see any more of the world than you've seen already, which wasn't very much, I can tell you. So I applied to Qantas. And here I am, flying around the globe with my little stew bag and makeup kit, serving whiskey to Japanese businessmen, slapping pilots, giving lonely soldiers the hots, and wondering if I'm ever going back to Queensland.'

'What's a jackeroo?'

'You Yanks call them cowboys.'

This could be something nice, Jake thought, looking at the marvelous, open, tanned female face and feeling himself warmed by her glow. There are a lot of pebbles on the beach and some of them are nuggets, like this one.

'So a station's a ranch?'

'Yes. Sheep and cattle.'

'I was raised on a farm myself. Dad ran a few steers, but mainly he raised corn.'

'Ever going back?' Nell asked.

'I dunno. Never say never. I might.'

She told him about the station in Queensland, about living so far from anything that the world outside seemed a fantasy, a shimmering legend amid the heat and dust and thunderstorms. As she talked he glanced past the lanterns into the darkness beyond, at that place where the mown grass and the velvet blackness met. The night was out there as usual, but here, at least, there was light.

An hour or so later someone turned on the radio and several of the women wanted to dance. To Jake's surprise Flap 'Go Ugly Early' Le Beau proved good at dancing, slow or fast, so good that he did only what his partner could do. You had to watch him with three or four of the sheilas before you realized that he sensed their skill level almost instantaneously and asked of them only what they had to give. Nell pointed that out to Jake, who saw it then. She danced a fast number with Flap – she was very good – as the Aussies and Brits watched appreciatively. They applauded when the number ended.

Nell rejoined Jake and led him out onto the floor for the next slow number. 'I don't dance very well,' he told her.

'That's not the point,' she said, and settled in against him to the beat of the languid music.

It was then that Jake Grafton realized he was in over his head. The supple body of the woman against his chest, the caress of her hair on his cheek, the faint scent of a cologne he didn't recognize, the touch of her hands against his – all this was having a profound effect and he wasn't ready.

'Relax,' she whispered.

He couldn't.

The memory of his morning in bed with Callie four months ago came flooding back. He could see the sun coming through the windows, feel the clean sheets and the sensuous touch of her skin . . .

'You're stiff as a board.'

'Not quite.'

'Oops. Didn't mean it quite that way, love.'

'I'm not a very good dancer.'

She moved away a foot or so and looked searchingly into his face. 'You're not a very good liar either.'

'I'm working on it.'

She led him by the hand through the crowd and out of the pavilion into the darkness. 'Why is it all the good ones come with complications?'

'At our age virgins are hard to find,' Jake told her.

'I quit looking for virgins years and years ago. I just want a man who isn't too scarred up.'

She led him to a wall and hopped up on it. 'Okay, love. Tell Ol' Nell all about it.'

Jake Grafton grinned. 'How is it that a fine woman like you isn't married?'

'You want the truth?'

'If you feel like it.'

'Well, the truth is that I didn't want the ones who proposed and the ones I wanted didn't propose. Propose marriage, that is. They had a lot of things in mind but a trek to the altar wasn't on the list.'

'That sounds like truth.'

'It is that, ducky.'

The music floating across the lawn was muted but clearly audible. And she was right there, sitting on the wall. Instinctively he moved closer and she put an arm around his shoulder. Their heads came together.

Before very long they were kissing. She had good, firm lips, a lot like Callie's. Of course Callie was . . .

His heart was thudding like a drum when they finally parted for air. After a few deep breaths, he said, 'There's another woman.'

'Amazing.'

'I'm not married or anything like that. And I haven't asked her to marry me, but I wanted to.'

'Uh-huh.'

'I think she gave up on me. Hasn't written in a couple months.'

'You like your women dumb, then?' she asked softly, and put her lips back on his.

Somehow she was off the wall and they were entwined in each other's arms, their bodies pressed together. When their lips parted this time, a ragged breath escaped her. 'Whew and double whew. You Yanks! Sex-starved maniacs, that's what you are.'

She eased away from him. 'Well, that was my good deed for today. I've given another rejected, love-starved pilot hope for a brighter future. Now I think it's time for this Sheila to trek off to her lonely little bed. Must fly tomorrow, you know.'

'Going to be back in Singapore day after tomorrow?'

'Yes.'

'What hotel? Maybe I can stop by and take you to dinner.'

'The Intercontinental.'

'I'll walk inside with you.'

'No, just stay where you are, mate. I've had quite enough

tonight. One more good look at you in the light and I might drag you off to my lonely little bed for a night of sport. Can't have that, can we, not with you pining your heart out for that other silly girl.'

'With that she was gone. Across the lawn and into the crowd.

Jake Grafton leaned on the wall and lit a cigarette. His hands were trembling slightly.

He didn't know quite what to think, so he didn't think anything. Just inhaled the cut-grass smell and looked into the darkness and let his heart rate subside to its normal plodding pace.

At least half an hour passed before Jake went back into the pavilion. Three half-potted Aussies were huddled around the piano watching Flap dance with the three stews who were still there. Le Beau had them in a line and was teaching them new steps to the wailing of a Japanese music machine. Everyone else had left, including the Real McCoy. Tomorrow was a working day for most of them.

Jake decided one more beer for the road wouldn't hurt, so he picked a bottle out of the icy water of the tub and joined the piano crowd.

'Hey, mate.'

'How you guys doing tonight?'

'Great.'

'Sure nice of you fellows to invite us to your wing ding. Makes a good break after forty-five days at sea.'

'Don't know how you blokes manage.'

'Prayer,' Jake told them, and they laughed.

The biggest of them was a brawny man three or four inches taller than Jake and at least forty pounds heavier. Most of his bulk was in his chest, shoulders and arms. He hadn't said anything yet, but now he gestured to Flap. 'Wish your bleedin' nigger mate would pick his bird and let us at the other two.'

Jake Grafton carefully set his beer on the piano. This was getting to be a habit. The last time they had sent him to the Marines.

Wonder where they'll send me this time?

He stepped in front of the big Aussie, who still had one giant mitt wrapped around a bottle of beer.

'What did you say?'

'I said, I wish your bleedin' nigger mate would—'

As Jake drew back his right fist for a roundhouse punch he jabbed the Aussie in the nose with his left. This set the man momentarily off balance, so when the right arrived on his chin with all Jake's weight behind it, it connected solidly with a meaty thunk that rocked Jake clear to the shoulder. The Aussie went backward onto the floor like he was pole-axed. And he stayed there.

'Nice punch, mate, but you—' said the one to the left, but his words stopped when Jake's fist arrived. The man took it solidly on the side of the head and sent a right at Jake that connected and shook him badly.

Stars swam before Grafton's eyes. He waded in swinging furiously. Some of his punches missed, some hit. That was the lesson he had learned as a boy on the grade school playground – keep swinging and going forward. Most boys don't really like to fight, so when you keep swinging they will fall back, and ultimately quit. Of course, these soldiers weren't boys and worse, they *liked* to fight.

His attack worked for several seconds, then the third Aussie, who was now behind him, grabbed him and spun him around. Before Jake could get set he took a shot on the cheekbone that put him down.

Dazed, he struggled to rise. When he got to his feet it was too late. All three of the Aussies were asleep on the floor and Flap Le Beau was standing there calmly scrutinizing him.

'What was that all about?'

Jake swayed and caught himself by grabbing the piano.

'They insulted Elvis.'

Flap sighed. 'I guess we've worn out our welcome.' He took Jake's arm and got him started for the door. 'Ladies,' he said, addressing the three stews gaping at them, 'it's been a real treat. The pleasure of your company was sweeter than you will ever know.'

He beamed benignly at them and steered Jake out into the night.

The base was quiet. No taxi at the main gate. They waved at the sentry and kept walking. Jake's right hand throbbed and so did his head. The hand was the important thing, though. He rubbed it as he walked.

'What really happened back there?' Flap asked.

'The big stud called you a nigger.'

'You hit him for *that*?'

'Yeah. The asshole deserved it.'

Flap Le Beau threw back his head and laughed. 'Damn, Jake, you are really something else.'

'He was peeved because you were monopolizing the women.'

Flap thought this was hilarious. He roared with laughter.

'Want to tell me what's so damn funny?'

'You are. You nitwit! All of them are bigots. Even the women. I wasn't getting anywhere with them. Not a one of those women would have gone to bed with me, not even if I was the richest nigger in America and had a cock eighteen inches long. They'll go back to Australia and tell all about their big adventure, talking to and dancing with an American *nigger*. "Oh, Matilda, you won't believe this, but I even let him *touch* me."'

Jake didn't know what to say, so he said nothing.

After a bit Flap asked, 'Think you broke your hand?'

'Dunno. Don't think so. Maybe stoved it. Man, I got that big guy with a perfect shot. Had everything behind it and drove it right through his chin.'

'He never moved after you hit him. Bet it's the first time anybody ever knocked him out.'

'Thanks for coming to the rescue, Kemo Sabe.'

'Any time, Tonto. Any time. But you could have broken your hand hitting that guy that hard.'

'Had to. He outweighed me by forty pounds. If I had just given him a you-piss-me-off social punch he would have killed me.'

'You're a violent man, Jake.'

'I had a lot of trouble with potty training.'

The next morning he realized the dimensions of the quandary he faced. Nell Douglas was a fine woman, passionate, level-headed, intelligent, thoughtful ... And Callie McKenzie was one fine woman, also passionate and level-headed, intelligent, educated, well spoken ... He was in love with one and could easily fall in love with the other. But the woman he loved hadn't written in two months and had made it clear that he wasn't measuring up.

The woman he could love wasn't being quite so picky. No doubt when he knew her better she would get more picky – women were like that. But she wasn't being picky *now!* And if you couldn't take the heat there was always celibacy to fall back on.

Alas, celibacy didn't seem very attractive to Jake Grafton. Not when you are in your twenties, in perfect health, when the sight, smell and touch of a woman makes the blood pound in your temples and your knees turn to jelly.

He sat in his chair in his stateroom savoring the memories of last night. Of how her lips had felt against his, how her hot, wet tongue had speared between his teeth and stroked his tongue, how her breasts had heaved against his chest, how her thighs had pressed against his while her hands stroked his back. Gawd Almighty!

He liked the way she talked, too. That flat Australian

twang was sexy as hell. Just made shivers run up your spine when you recalled how the words sounded as she said them. '. . . I might drag you off to my lonely little bed for a night of sport.' Well, lady, I wish . . .

I don't know what I wish! Damnation.

He was writhing on the horns of this dilemma when the door opened and the Real McCoy staggered through. He flopped into his bunk and groaned. 'Wake me up next week. I am spent. Wrung out like a sponge. That woman turned me every way but loose. There are hot women and there are *hot* women. That one was a thermonuclear.'

'Tough night, huh?'

'She was after me every hour! I didn't sleep a wink. Every *hour!* I'm so sore I can hardly walk.'

'Lucky you escaped her evil clutches.'

'Never in my born days, Jake, did I even contemplate that there might be women like *that* walking the surface of the earth. Australia is merely the greatest nation on the planet, that's all. That they breed women like *that* down there is the best-kept secret of our time.'

Jake nodded thoughtfully and flexed his right fist. It was sore and a little swollen.

'I'm getting out of the Nav, arranging to have my subscription to the *Wall Street Journal* sent to me Down Under, and I am going south. May the cold, blue light of Polaris never again meet my weary gaze. It's the Southern Cross for me, Laddie Buck. I'm going to Australia to see if I can fuck myself to death before I'm forty.'

With that pronouncement the Real McCoy turned on his side and curled his pillow under his head. Jake looked at his watch. The first gentle snore came seventy-seven seconds later.

Were the women bigots? Well, Flap should know. If he said those three stews were prejudiced, they probably were. But what about Nell?

And what about you, Jake? Are you?

Aaugh! To waste a morning in port fretting about crap like this.

He pulled a table around and started a letter to his parents.

The liberty boat for the enlisted men was an LCI – landing craft infantry – a flat-bottomed rectangular-shaped boat with a bow door that flopped down to let troops run through the surf onto the beach. Jake often rode it from the beach to the ship. This evening, however, he was dressed in a sports coat and a tie and didn't want to get soaked with salt spray, so he headed for the officers' brow near Elevator Two. The captain's gig and admiral's barge had been lowered into the water from their cradles in the rear of the hangar bay. In ten minutes he was descending the ladder onto the float, then he stepped into the gig.

Jake knew the boat officer, a jaygee from a fighter squadron, so he asked if he could stand beside the coxswain on the little midships bridge. Permission was granted with a grin and a nod. The rest of the officers went below into either the fore or aft cabin.

With the stupendous bulk of the carrier looming like a cliff above them, the sailors threw the lines aboard and the coxswain put the boat in motion. It stood out from the ship and swung in a wide circle until it was on course for fleet landing.

The water was calm this evening, with merely a long, low swell stirring the oily surface. The red of the western sky stained the water between the ships, gave it the look of diluted blood.

The roadstead was full of ships: freighters, coasters, tankers, all riding on their anchors. Lighters circled around a few of the ships, but only a few. Most of them sat motionless like massive steel statues in a huge park lake.

But there were people visible on most of the ships. As the gig threaded its way through the anchorage Jake could see them sitting under awnings on the fantails, sometimes cooking on barbecue grills, talking and smoking on after-decks crowded with ship's gear. Most of the sailors were men, but on one Russian ship he saw three women, hefty specimens in dresses that reached below their knees.

'Pretty evening,' the jaygee said to Jake, who agreed.

Yes, another gorgeous evening, the close of another good day to be alive. It was easy to forget the point of it all sometimes, easy to lose sight of the fact that the name of the game was to stay alive, to savor life, to live it day to day at the pace that God intended.

One of Jake Grafton's talents was to imagine himself living other lives. He hadn't been doing much of that lately, but riding the gig through the anchorage, looking at the ships, he could visualize sitting on one of those fantails, smoking and chatting and watching the sun sink closer and closer to the sea's rim. To go to sea and work the ship and spend quiet evenings in port in the company of friends – it could be very good. *I could live that way*, he reflected.

Maybe in my next incarnation.

The Intercontinental was a huge, modern hotel built on a slight hill. The lobby was a cavern seven or eight stories high. Marble floors accented with giant potted plants, a raised bar with easy chairs in the middle, all the accents a plush burgundy, polyester fabric glued to the walls – yuck!

Jake settled into one of the bar's overstuffed polyester chairs and tilted his head back. You could almost get dizzy looking up at the balconies, which were stacked closer and closer together until they met at the ceiling. Tropical plants hung from planters along each balcony, so the view upward was green. Dark green, because the lighting up there was very poor.

'Grotesque, isn't it?'

He dropped his gaze from the green canopy above to the young woman walking toward him. he stood and grinned. 'Yep.'

'The interior designer was obviously demented.' Nell Douglas settled into the chair opposite. A waiter appeared and hovered.

'Something to drink?' Jake asked her politely.

'A glass of white wine, please.'

'Scotch on the rocks.'

The waiter broke hover and disappeared behind a large potted leafy green thing.

'So how was your flight in?'

'Bumpy. Storms over the South China Sea. How's your hand?'

'You heard about that, huh?'

'The other girls were all atwitter. Your black friend really impressed them.'

'Flap can move pretty fast when he wants to. He's handy to have around.'

'If the necessity arises to knock people senseless. Is he lurking nearby now, just in case?'

Vaguely uneasy, Jake flashed a polite smile. 'No, I think he came ashore earlier today hoping to cheat some opal merchants. And my hand's fine.' He wiggled his fingers at her, pretending she cared.

Their drinks came and they sat sipping them in silence, both man and woman trying to sense the mood of the other.

After a bit Nell said, 'He's some kind of trained killer, isn't he?'

That comment was like glass shattering. Amazingly, Jake Grafton felt a tremendous sense of relief. It had been a nice fantasy, but this woman was not Callie.

'I guess everyone in combat arms is,' he said slowly, 'if you want to look at it that way. I deal in high explosives myself. I fly attack planes, not airliners.'

He took the plastic stir stick from his drink and chewed at it. Why do they put these damn things in a drink that is nothing but whiskey and ice? He took it out of his mouth and broke it between his fingers as he examined her face.

'I started the fight,' he continued, now in a hurry to end it. 'One of the soldiers referred to Captain Le Beau as a nigger. He happens to be my BN and a personal friend. He is also a fine human being. The fact that his skin is black is about as important as the fact that my eyes are gray. That word is an insult in America and here. The man who said it knew that.'

'The only black people in Australia are aborigines.'

'I guess you have to be an American to understand.'

'Perhaps.'

The waiter reappeared with his credit card and the invoice. Jake added a tip, signed it and pocketed the card and his copy.

Her face was too placid. Blank. Time to get this over with. 'Would you like to go to dinner?'

Nell Douglas looked this way and that, apparently searching for something to say.

Finally she sat her wineglass on the table and leaned forward slightly. She looked him in the eye. 'It was wonderful the other night, and I am sure you are a fine person, but let's leave it at that.'

He nodded and finished his drink.

'We grew up on opposite sides of the world.' She stood and held out her hand. 'Thanks for the drink.'

'Sure.'

Jake stood and shook. She threaded her way through the potted jungle and made for the elevators.

'Did you get laid?' the Real McCoy asked late that night in their stateroom aboard ship.

'She said we grew up on opposite sides of the world.'

'You idiot. You're suppose to fuck 'em, not discuss philosophy.'

'Well, it probably turned out for the best,' Jake said,

thinking of Callie. He desperately wished she would write. She could write anything – if she would just put *something* in an envelope and stick a stamp on it.

He decided to write her.

He got a legal pad, climbed into the top bunk and adjusted the light just so. Then he began. He went through their relationship episode by episode, almost thought by thought, pouring out his heart. After eight pages he ground to a halt.

Every word was true, but he wasn't going to send it. He wasn't going to take the chance that he cared more than she did.

You aren't going to get very far with the fairer sex if you aren't willing to take some risks.

I'm tired of taking risks. Someone else can take a few.

Faint heart never won—

If she cared, she'd write. End of story.

The night before the ship weighed anchor Lieutenant Colonel Haldane asked Jake to come to his stateroom. According to the duty officer. Jake went.

Flap was already there sitting in the only chair. Jake sat on the colonel's bed and Flap passed him a sheet of paper. It was a letter from the commander at Changi. Fight in the pavilion. Jake scanned it quickly and passed it back to Flap, who handed it to Haldane, who tossed it on his desk.

'The skipper of the ship got this. He wants me to investigate, take action, and draft a reply for his signature. What can you tell me?'

Jake told the colonel about the incident, withholding nothing.

'Any comments, Captain Le Beau?'

'No, sir. I think Mr Grafton covered it.'

Haldane made a face. 'Okay. That's all. We're having a

back-in-the-saddle NATOPS do in the ready room at zero seven-thirty. See you there.'

Both the junior officers left. Jake closed the door behind him.

Twenty frames down the passageway he asked Flap, 'Was that it? We aren't in hack or candidates for keelhauling?'

'Naw. Haldane will apologize profusely to our allies, tell them that he's ripped us a new one, and that's that. It was just a friendly little social fight. What more could there be?'

Jake shrugged. 'My hand's still sore.'

'Next time kick 'em in the balls.'

CHAPTER SEVENTEEN

At dawn one morning the task group weighed anchor and entered the Strait of Malacca. With Sumatra on the left and the Malay peninsula on the right, the ships steamed at 20 knots for the Indian Ocean, or the IO as the sailors called it, pronouncing each letter.

In the narrows the strait was a broad watery highway with land on each horizon. The channel was dotted with fishing boats and heavily traversed by tankers and freighters. As many as a half dozen of the large ocean-going ships were visible at any one time.

As usual in narrow waterways, the carrier's flight deck and island superstructure were crowded with sightseeing sailors. Typically, Jake Grafton was among them, standing on the bow facing forward. With all of the great ship behind him the sensation was unique, almost as if one were a seabird soaring along at sixty feet above the water into the teeth of a 20-knot wind.

This morning Jake watched the steady stream of civilian ships and marveled. He had flown enough surface surveillance missions over the open ocean to appreciate how empty the oceans of the earth truly were. Often he and Flap flew a two-hour flight and saw not a single ship, just endless vistas of empty sea and sky. Yet here the ships plowed the brown water like trucks thundering along an interstate highway.

A hundred years ago these waters hosted sailing ships. As he stood on the bow watching the ships and boats this morning he thought about those sailing ships, for Jake Grafton had a streak of romance in him about a foot wide. Clipper ships bound for China for a load of tea left England and the eastern ports of the United States and sailed south to round the Cape of Good Hope on the southern tip of Africa. The sailors would have gotten close enough to land for a glimpse of Africa only in good weather. Then they crossed the vast Indian Ocean and entered this strait, where they saw land for the first time since leaving England or America. Months at sea working the ship, making sail, reefing in storms, watching the officers shoot the sun at noon and the stars at night when the weather allowed, then to hit this strait after circumnavigating half the globe – it was a great thing, a thing to be proud of, a thing to remember for the rest of their lives. Exotic China still lay ahead, but here the sailors probably saw junks for the first time, those flat-bottomed Chinese sailing ships that carried the commerce of the Orient. Here two worlds touched.

Jake looked at the freighters and tankers with new interest. Perhaps he should look into getting a mate's license, consider the merchant marine after the Navy. It was a thing to think on.

Standing on the bow with the moist wind in his hair and the smell of the land filling his nostrils as the task group transited this narrow passage between two great oceans, he was struck by how large the earth really was, how diverse the human life, how many truths there must be. The US Navy was a tiny part of it, surely, but only a tiny part. He had been confined long enough. He needed to reach out and embrace the whole.

The Indian Ocean lay ahead, beyond that watery horizon. The flying there would be blue water ops, without the safety net of a divert field ashore. The ship would be hundreds of miles from land, so when the planes burned enough fuel to get down to landing weight there would be no dry spot on earth they could reach with the fuel remaining in their tanks. They had to get abroad. Airborne tankers could provide fuel for another handful of attempts, but their presence would not change the scenario – every pilot would have to successfully trap or eject into the ocean.

Carrier aviation never gets easier. The challenge is to develop and maintain skills that are just good enough. In this war without bullets the stakes were human lives. Each pilot would have only his skill and knowledge to keep him alive in the struggle against the weather, chance, the vagaries of fate. Some would lose. Jake Grafton knew that as well as he knew his name. He might be one of them.

Thinking about that possibility as he stood here on the bow, he took a deep breath of the moist sea air and savored it.

A man never knows.

Well, he would do his best. That was all he could do. God had the dice, He would make the casts.

Jake was standing the squadron duty officer watch in the ready room one night when first Lieutenant Doug Harrison came in from a flight. He gave Jake his flight time figure and handed him the batteries from his emergency radio – the batteries were recharged in a unit above the duty officer's desk – then dropped into the skipper's empty chair as Jake annotated the flight schedule. Only then did Grafton turn and take a good look at the first-cruise pilot. His face was pasty and covered with a sheen of perspiration.

'Tough flight, huh?'

Harrison dropped his eyes and massaged his forehead with a hand. 'No . . . Got a cigarette?'

'Sure.' Jake passed him one, then held out a light.

After Harrison had taken three or four puffs, he took the cigarette from his mouth and said softly, 'After we landed, I almost taxied over the edge.'

'It's dark out there.'

'I've never seen anything like it. No light at all, the deck greasy, rain on top of the grease . . . it was like trying to taxi on snot.'

'What happened?'

'Taxi director took me up to the bow on Cat One, then turned me. Wanted me to taxi aft on Cat Two. It was that turn on the bow. Sticking out over the fucking black ocean. I was *sure* I was going right off the bow, Jake. I about shit myself. I kid you not. Pure, unadulterated terror, two-hundred proof. I have *never* had a feeling like that in an airplane before.'

'Uh-huh.'

'I was turning tight, I could feel the nose wheel sliding, the yellow-shirt was giving me the come-ahead signal with the wands, and the edge was *right there!* And there isn't even a protective lip. You know how the bow just turns down, same as the stern?'

'So what did you do?'

'Locked the left wheel and goosed the right engine. The plane moved about a foot. I could feel the left wheel sliding. To make things perfect I could also feel the deck going up and down, up and down. Every time it started down the vomit came up my throat. Then the yellow-shirt crossed his wands and had the blue-shirts chock it right where it sat. When I climbed down from the cockpit I couldn't believe it – the nose wheel was like *six inches* from the edge! It was so dark up there that I had to use my flashlight to make sure. There was *no way* the nose wheel was going around that corner. Even if it had, the right main wouldn't have made the turn – it would have dropped off the edge.'

Harrison took a greedy drag on his cigarette, then continued: 'My BN couldn't even get out of the cockpit. The plane captain didn't have room to drop his ladder. He had to stay in the cockpit until they towed the plane to a decent parking place.'

'Why'd you keep taxiing when you knew you were that close to the edge?'

Harrison closed his eyes for a second, then shook his head. 'I dunno.'

'I know,' Jake Grafton told him positively. 'You jarheads are spring-loaded to the yessir position. Doug, if it doesn't feel right, don't do it. You have only one ass to lose.'

Harrison nodded and sucked on the cigarette. The color was slowly coming back to his face. After a bit he said, 'Did you ever watch those RA-5 pilots taxi at night? The nose wheel is way aft of the cockpit. They are sitting out over the ocean when they taxi that Vigilante to the deck edge and turn it. I couldn't do that. Not in a million years. Just watching them gives me the shivers.'

'Don't obey a yellow-shirt if it doesn't look right,' Jake said, emphasizing the point. 'It isn't the fall that kills you, Doug, or the stop at the bottom – it's the sudden realization that, indeed, you *are* this fucking stupid.'

When Doug wandered off Jake went back to the notes of his talks on carrier operations. He was expanding and refining them so he could have them typed. He thought he would send them back to the senior LSO at the West Coast A-6 training squadron, VA-128 at Whidbey Island. Maybe there was something in there that the LSOs could use for their lectures.

Boy, if he wasn't getting out, it would sure be nice to go back to VA-128 when this cruise was over. Rent a little place on a beach or a bluff overlooking the sound, fly, teach some classes, kick back and let life flow along. If he wasn't getting out . . . If Tiny Dick Donovan was willing to take him back. Forgive and forget.

But he was getting out! No more long lonely months at sea, no more night cat shots, no more floating around the IO quietly rotting, no more of this—

Allen Bartow came up to the desk. 'When you get off

here tonight, we're having a little game down in my room. We need some squid money in the pot.'

'I've still got a lot of jarhead quarters from the last game. I'll bring those.'

'The last of the high rollers . . .'

He wasn't going to miss it, he assured himself, for the hundredth time. Not a bit.

One of the most difficult tasks in military aviation is a night rendezvous. On a dark night under an overcast the plane you are joining is merely a tiny blob of lights, flashing weakly in the empty black universe. Without a horizon or other visual reference, the only way the trick can be done is to keep your instrument scan going inside your cockpit while you sneak peeks at the target aircraft. The temptation is to look too long at the target, to get too engrossed in the angles and closure rate, and if that happens, you are in big trouble.

On this particular night Jake Grafton thought he had it wired. He was rendezvousing on the off-going tanker at low station, 5,000 feet over the ship on the five-mile arc. There it was, its lights winking weakly.

'Ten o'clock,' Flap said.

'Roge, I got it.'

'He'll be doing two-fifty.'

Jake glanced at his airspeed. Three hundred knots indicated. He would have to work that off as he closed. But not quite yet.

The tanker would be in a left-hand turn. Jake cranked his plane around until he had his nose in front of it and was looking at it through the right quarter panel, across the top of the radar scope-hood. He eased in a little left rudder and right flaperon to help keep his plane in a position where he could see the tanker.

With the target plane on the right side the A-6 was difficult to rendezvous because the cockpit was too wide – the BN sat on the pilot's right. This meant that the right glareshield and canopy rail were too high and, as the planes closed, would block the pilot's vision of the target aircraft if he allowed himself to get just a little behind the bearing line or get a tad high. Jake knew all this. He had accomplished several hundred night rendezvous and knew the problems involved and the proper techniques to use without even thinking about it. Tonight he was busy applying that knowledge.

Yet something was wrong. Jake checked his instruments. All okay. Why was the tanker moving to the right? Instinctively he rolled more wings level, rechecked his attitude gyro, the altimeter, the airspeed . . . All okay. And still the sucker is moving right!

'Texaco, say your heading.'

'Zero Two Zero.'

Hell! Now Jake understood. He was still on the outside of the tanker's turning radius, not on the inside as he had assumed. He leveled his wings and flew straight ahead to cross behind the tanker, feeling slightly ridiculous. He had *assumed* that he was on the inside . . .

Now, indeed, he was on the inside of the tanker's turn. He turned to put the nose in the proper position and started inbound. Checking the gauges, watching the bearing, slowing gently . . . 280 knots would be perfect, would give him 30 knots of closure . . .

And the tanker was . . . Jesus! Coming in awful fast – *way too fast!* Power back, boards out, and . . .

'Look at your altitude.' Flap.

Jake looked. He was at ninety-degrees angle-of-bank, passing 4,500 feet, descending.

He leveled the wings and got the nose up. The tanker shot off to the left.

'I'm really screwed up tonight,' he told the BN.

'Turn hard and get inside of him, then close.'

Jake did. He felt embarrassed, like a neophyte on his first night formation hop. Yet only when he got to within two hundred yards and could make out the tanker's position lights clearly was he sure of the tanker's direction of flight. Only then was he comfortable.

He wasn't concentrating hard enough. Attempting to rendezvous on a single, flashing light, in a dark universe devoid of any other feature . . . it was difficult at best and impossible if you weren't completely focused.

Flap extended the drogue as Jake crossed behind the tanker and surfaced on his right side. 'You got the lead,' said the tanker pilot, Chance Malzahn. Jake clicked his mike twice in reply as Chance slid aft. He dropped slightly and disappeared from sight behind. Jake concentrated on flying his own plane, staying in this steady, twenty-degree angle-of-bank turn, keeping on the five-mile arc, holding altitude perfectly.

In seconds the green ready light on the refueling panel went out and the counter began to click off the pounds delivered. The refueling package worked.

'Five Twenty-Three is sweet,' Flap told the ship.

The green ready light appeared again. Malzahn had backed out of the drogue. Now he came up on Jake's left side.

'You got the lead,' Jake told him as Malzahn's drogue streamed aft.

The drogue looked like a three-foot-wide badminton birdie. It dangled on the end of a fifty-foot-long hose aft and slightly below the wash of the tanker. To get fuel, Jake would have to insert his fuel probe, which was permanently mounted on the nose in front of his windscreen, into the drogue and push it in about five feet. When the take-up reel on the tanker had turned the proper amount, electrical switches would mate and begin pumping fuel down the hose into the receiver aircraft.

The trick was getting the probe into the drogue, the basket. If the basket was new, with all the feathers in good shape, it was usually almost stationary and fairly easy to plug. If it was slightly damaged, however, it tended to weave back and forth in the windstream and present a moving target. Turbulence that bounced the tanker and receiver aircraft added to the level of difficulty. And, of course, there was the 'pucker factor' – extensive experience has proven that the tension of a pilot's sphincter is directly proportional to the level of his anxiety, ie, higher makes tighter, etc.

Tonight, needing only to hit the tanker to 'sponge' the excess fuel, Jake's anxiety level was normal, or even slightly below. He was fat, had plenty of fuel. And the air was fairly smooth. The only fly in the ointment was the condition of that Marine Corps drogue. Tonight it weaved in a small, erratic figure-eight pattern.

Jake stabilized his plane about ten feet behind the drogue and watched it bob and weave for a moment. Flap Le Beau kept his flashlight pointed at it.

'Little Marine bastard is bent.'

'Yeah.' Flap was full of sympathy.

Flopping drogues had cracked bullet-proof windscreens, shattered Plexiglas and fodded engines. Tonight Jake Grafton eyed this one warily, waited for his moment, then smartly added power and drove his probe in. Drove it at that spot where the drogue would be when he got there. He hoped.

Miraculously he timed it right. The probe captured the drogue and locked in. He kept pushing until the green light above the hose chute in the tanker came on. Now he was riding about fifteen feet below the tanker's tail and ten feet aft. As long as he stayed right here, held that picture, he would get fuel.

'You get twelve hundred pounds,' Chance Malzahn told him.

Two clicks in acknowledgement.

'Nice,' Flap said, referring to the plug, the flashlight never wavering.

When the last of the gas was aboard Jake backed out. He came up on Malzahn's left side and took the lead as Malzahn reeled in his hose. After a word with Tanker Control, Malzahn cut his power and turned away, headed down on a vector for an approach.

Jake and Flap were now Texaco. Soon two F-4s came to take a ton of fuel each, then they turned away and disappeared in the vast darkness.

Jake took the tanker on up to high station, 20,000 feet, and settled it on autopilot at 220 knots. Around and around the ship, orbiting. Flap got out a paperback book and adjusted his kneeboard light. Jake loosened one side of his oxygen mask and let it dangle.

'Do you ever see the faces of the men you killed?' Jake asked. They had been orbiting the ship at high station for almost half an hour.

'What do you mean?'

Jake Grafton took his time before he answered. 'I got shot down last December. We ended up in Laos. Had to shoot three guys before they got us out. They were trying to kill us – me and my BN – and one of them shot me. That's how I ended up with this scar on my temple.'

'Uh-huh.'

'Had to do it, of course, or they would have killed us. Still, I see them sometimes in dreams. Wake up feeling rotten.'

Flap Le Beau didn't say anything.

'Dropping bombs, now, I did that for a couple cruises. Bound to have killed a lot of people. Oh, most of the time we bombed suspected truck parks and crap like that – probably killed some ants and lizards and turned a lot of trees into toothpicks. That's what we called them, toothpick missions – but occasionally we went after better targets. Stuff where there would be people. Not just trees in the jungle and mud roads crossing a creek.'

'Yeah.'

'Toward the end there we were really pounding the north, hitting all the shit that Johnson and McNamara didn't have the brains or balls to hit six years before.'

'It was fucked up, all right.'

'One mission, close air support of some ARVN, they told me I killed forty-seven of 'em. Forty-seven. That bothered me for a while, but I don't see them at night. Forty-seven men with one load of bombs . . . it's like reading about it in a newspaper or history book . . . doesn't seem real now. I still see those three NVA though.'

'I still see faces too.'

Below them an unbroken cloud deck stretched away in all directions. The sliver of moon was fuzzy and there weren't many stars – they were trying to shine through a gauzy layer of high cirrus.

'Wonder if it'll ever stop? If they'll just fade out or something.'

'I don't know.'

'Doesn't seem right somehow, to lose fifty-eight thousand Americans, to kill all those Vietnamese, all for nothing.'

Flap didn't reply.

'I don't like seeing those faces and waking up in a cold sweat. I had to do it. But damn . . .'

He wanted to forget the past, forget all of it. The present was okay, the flying and the ship and the men he shared it with. Yet the future was waiting out there, somewhere, hidden in the mists and haze. He was reaching out for *something*, something that lay ahead along that road into the unknown. Just what it would be he didn't know. He was ready to make the journey though.

Under the overcast it was raining. At five thousand feet visibility was down to two or three miles and the oncoming tanker had trouble finding them, even with vectors from tanker control. It was that kind of night, with nothing going right. Once he was there Jake slipped in behind, eyed the basket, and went for it. He got it with only a little rudder kick in close and pushed it in.

Nothing. The green light over the hose hole did not illuminate.

'Are we getting any?' Flap asked the other crew.

'No. Back out and let us recycle.'

Jake retarded the power levers a smidgen and let his plane drift aft. The basket came off the probe. He moved out to the right and Flap told the other crew to recycle. They pulled the hose all the way in, then ran it out again.

This time Jake missed the basket on the first try. He stabilized and slipped in on his second attempt.

'Still no gas.'

'Tanker Control, this is Five Two Two, we're sour.'

'Roger, Two Two. Your signal is dump. Steer Two Two Zero and descend to One Point Two, over.'

'Five Two Two, Two Two Zero and down to One Point Two.'

'Texaco, Tanker Control, you steer Two Zero Zero and descend to One Point Two, over.'

Jake slid left and the other tanker went right. It was already streaming fuel from the main and wing-tip dumps. Nine tons of fuel would have to be dumped into the atmosphere. Too bad, but there it was.

Jake settled onto his desired course and popped his speed brakes. The nose went over. When he stabilized he looked to the right for the other A-6, which was already fading into the rain and darkness. He came back into the cockpit and concentrated on his instruments.

This little world of needles and dials illuminated by red lights had always fascinated him. Making the needles behave didn't seem all that difficult, until you tried it. And on nights like this, when he felt about half in the bag, when he was having trouble concentrating, then it was exquisite torture. Everything he did was either too little or too much. It was maddening.

The perverse needles taunted him. *You are too high*, they whispered, *too fast, off course, now you are low* . . . He had to work extremely hard to make them behave, had to pay strict attention to their message. The slightest inattention, the most minute easing of his concentration would allow the needles to escape his grasp.

The controller worked him into a hole in the bolter pattern, which was rapidly filling up. The voices on the radio told him the story as he struggled to make the needles behave. The weather was worse than forecast. Rain was ruining the visibility, the sea was freshening, and one of the F-4s had already boltered twice. Nearest land was 542 miles to the northwest. There were no sweet tankers in the air.

'Ain't peace wonderful?' Flap muttered.

'Landing checklist,' Jake said, and they went through it. They were too heavy so they dumped fifteen hundred pounds of fuel to get to landing weight. Crazy, that the only good tanker was dumping to land instead of hawking the deck to help that Phantom crew, but ours is not to reason why, ours is but to do or . . .

At a mile and a half he saw the ship, a tiny smear of red light enlivening the dead universe.

Flap called the ball at Six Point Oh.

'Roger Ball.'

Jake recognized the Real McCoy's voice, but just in case he didn't the Real continued. 'Deck's dancing, Jake. Watch your lineup.'

He had the ball centered, nailed there, and with just a little dip of the wings he chased the landing centerline to the right, working the throttles individually so as not to over-control. The rain flowed around the canopy in a continuous sheet, but the engine bleed air kept the pilot's windscreen clear.

There was an art to throttle-work on the ball, moving each individual lever ever so slightly, yet knowing when to move them both. Tonight Jake got it just right. He deck got closer and closer, the ball stayed centered, the lineup was good, the angle-of-attack needle behaved . . . and they caught a three-wire.

'Luck,' Jake told Flap as they rolled out of the landing area.

They taxied him to a stop abeam the island where a half-dozen purple-shirts – grapes – waited with a fuel hose. Jake opened the canopy as the squadron's senior troubleshooter climbed the ladder. The wind felt raw and the rain cold against his skin.

'We're going to hot pump you and shoot you again,' the sergeant shouted over the whine of the engines. 'This is the only up tanker.'

Jake stuck his thumb up to signify his understanding.

The sergeant went back down the ladder and raised it as Jake closed the canopy. Might as well keep the rain out. The sergeant flashed a thumbs-up and went around to the BN's side of the plane to watch the refueling operation. Jake moved the switch to depressurize the tanks.

Refueling took a while. They needed twenty thousand pounds for a full load and the ship's pumps could only deliver it at about a ton a minute.

He was tired and his butt felt like dead meat, yet it was very pleasant sitting here in the warm, comfortable cockpit. From their vantage point here beside the foul line they had a grandstand seat. The planes came out of the rain and darkness and slammed into the deck. The first two trapped, then a Phantom boltered, his hook ripping a shower of sparks the length of the landing area. This was the guy who had already boltered twice before.

Ah yes, this comfortable cockpit, with everything working just the way it was supposed to, the rain pattering on the Plexiglas and collecting into rivulets that smeared the light.

He was tired, but not too much so. Just pleasantly tired.

Jake unhooked his oxygen mask and laid it in his lap. He took off his helmet and massaged his face and head. He used his sleeves and gloves to swab away the perspiration, then pulled the helmet back on.

The minutes ticked by as the fuel gauges faithfully reported the fuel coming aboard.

They were still fueling when the errant F-4 came out of the gloom and snagged a two-wire. The pilot stroked the afterburners on the roll out. The white-hot focused flames poured from the tailpipes for about a second, then went out, leaving everyone on deck half-blinded.

Two minutes later an A-7 carrying a buddy store, a tanking package hung on a weapon's station under one wing, was taxied from the pack up to Cat Two and launched. Apparently the brain trust in Air Ops wanted more gas aloft.

At last Jake and Flap were ready. Pressurize the tanks. Boarding ladders up, refueling panel closed, seats armed, and they were taxiing toward Cat Two, the left bow catapult.

Spread the wings, flaps to takeoff, slats out, wipe out the cockpit, ease into the shuttle. There, the jolt as the hold-back reached full extension, then another jolt as the shuttle went forward into tension. Off the brakes, throttles up.

He watched the engines come up to full power as he pulled up the catapult grip and arranged the heel of his hand behind the throttles, felt the airplane tremble as the engines sucked in vast quantities of that rainy air and slammed it out the tailpipes into the jet blast deflector – the JBD. Fuel flow normal, temperatures coming up nicely, RPM at 100 percent on the left engine, a fraction over on the right. Hydraulics normal, everything okay.

Jake wiped out the cockpit, glanced at the panel, ensured Flap had his flashlight on the standby gyro . . . 'You ready?'

'Let it rip.'

He flipped on the exterior light master switch on the end of the cat grip with his left thumb.

The hold-back bolt broke. *He felt it break.* Then came the shot, a stiff jolt of terrific acceleration, which lasted about a quarter of a second. Then it ceased. *Sweet Jesus fucking Christ the airplane was still accelerating but way too god-damn slow!*

He was doing maybe 30 knots when he released the cat grip and closed the throttles. Automatically he extended the wing-tip speed brakes. He jammed his feet down on the top of the rudder pedals, locking both brakes.

They were still going forward, sliding on the wet, greasy deck. Thundering toward the bow, the round-down, the edge of the cliff . . .

Jake pulled the left throttle around the horn to idle cutoff, stopping the flow of fuel to that engine.

He released the left brake and engaged nose-wheel steering. Slammed the rudders to neutral, then hard right. That should capture the nose wheel and turn it right, if the shuttle wasn't holding it. But the nose wheel refused to respond.

Still going forward, but slower. The edge was there, coming toward them . . . only seconds left.

He released both brakes, and engaged nose-wheel steering and slammed the rudder full left. He felt something give. The nose started to swing left.

On the brakes hard. *Is there enough deck left, enough—?*

An explosion beside him. Flap had ejected. The air was filled with shards of flying Plexiglas.

Sliding, turning left and still sliding forward . . . he felt the left wheel slam into the deck-edge combing, then the nose, now the tail spun toward the bow, the whole plane still sliding . . .

And he stopped.

Out the right he could see nothing, just blackness. The right wheel must be almost at the very edge of the flight deck.

He took a deep breath and exhaled explosively.

His left hand was holding the alternate ejection handle between his legs. He couldn't remember reaching for it, but obviously he had. He gingerly released his grip.

The Plexiglas was gone on the right side of the canopy. Flap had ejected through it. Where his seat had been there was just an empty place.

Was Flap alive?

Jake closed the speed brakes and raised the flaps and slats, watched the indicator to make sure they were coming in properly, exterior lights off. Out of the corner of his eye he saw people, a mob, running toward him. He ignored them.

When he had the flaps and slats up, he unlocked the wings, then folded them. The wind was puffing through the top of the broken canopy . . . rain coming in. He could feel the drops on the few inches of exposed skin on his neck.

Was the plane moving? He didn't think so. Yet if he opened the canopy he couldn't eject. The seat was designed to go through the glass – if the canopy was open, the steel bow would be right above the seat and would kill him if he tried to eject. And if this plane slid off the deck he would have to eject or ride it into that black sea.

Now the reaction hit him. He began to shake.

A yellow-shirt was trying to get his attention. He kept giving Jake the cut sign, the slash across the throat.

But should he open the canopy?

Unable to decide, he chopped the right throttle and sat listening as that engine died.

Someone opened the canopy from outside. Now a sergeant was leaning in. 'You can get out now, sir. Safe your seat.'

'Have they got it tied down?'

'Yes.'

He had to force himself to move. He safetied the top and bottom ejection handles on the seat and fumbled with the

Koch fittings that held him to the seat. Reached down and fumbled in the darkness with the fittings that attached to his leg restraints. There. He was loose.

He started to get out, then remembered his oxygen mask and helmet leads. He disconnected all that, then tried to stand.

He was still shaking too badly. He grabbed a handhold and eased a leg out onto the ladder, all the while trying to ignore the blackness yawning on the right side, and ahead. Here he was, ten feet above the deck, right against the edge. He felt like he was going to vomit.

Hands reached up and steadied him as he descended the boarding ladder.

With his feet on deck, he looked at the right main wheel. Maybe a foot from the edge. The nose-wheel was jammed against the deck-edge combing and the nose-tow bar was twisted.

Jake asked the yellow-shirt, 'Where's my BN?'

The sailor pointed down the deck, toward the fantail. Jake looked. He saw a flash of white, the parachute, draped over the tail of an A-7. So Flap had landed on deck. Didn't go into the ocean.

Now the relief hit him like a hammer. His legs wobbled. Two people grabbed him.

His mask was dangling from the side of his helmet, and he swept it out of the way just in time to avoid the hot raw vomit coming up his throat.

He started walking aft, toward the island and the parachute draped over that Corsair a hundred fifty yards aft. He shook off two sailors who tried to assist him. 'I'm all right, all right, okay.'

An A-7 came out of the rain and trapped.

There was Flap, walking this way. Now he saw Grafton, spread his arms, kept walking.

The two men met and hugged fiercely.

*

291

Lieutenant Colonel Richard Haldane watched the PLAT tape of the cat shot gone awry five or six times as he listened to Jake Grafton and Flap Le Beau recount their experience in the ready room.

They were euphoric – they had spit in the devil's eye and escaped to tell the tale. In the ready room they went through every facet of their adventure for their listeners, who shared their infectious glee.

Isn't life grand? Isn't it great to still be walking and talking and laughing after a trip to the naked edge of life itself?

After a half hour or so, Haldane slipped away to find the maintenance experts. He listened carefully to their explanations, asked some questions, then went to the hangar deck for a personal examination of 523's nose-tow bar.

Apparently the hold-back bolt had failed prematurely, a fraction of a second before the launch valves fully opened, perhaps just as they began to open. The KA-6D at full power had begun to move forward, creating a space – perhaps an inch or two – between the T-fitting of the nose-tow bar and the catapult shuttle. Then the shuttle shot forward as steam slammed into the back of the catapult pistons. At this impact of shuttle and nose-tow bar, the nose-tow bar probably cracked. It held together for perhaps thirty feet of travel down the catapult, then failed completely.

Now free of the twenty-seven-ton weight of the aircraft, the pistons accelerated through the twin catapult barrels like two guided missiles chained together. Superheated steam drove them through the chronograph brushes five feet short of the water brakes at 207 knots.

With a stupendous crash that was felt the length of the ship, the pistons' spears entered the water brakes, squeezed out *all* the water and welded themselves into the brakes. Brakes, spears, and pistons were instantly transformed into one large lump of smoking, twisted, deformed steel. Cat Two was out of action for the rest of the cruise.

Colonel Haldane was less interested in what happened to the catapult than the sequence of events that took place inside 523 after the catapult fired. Careful analysis of the PLAT tape showed that the plane came to a halt just 6.1 seconds later. Total length of the catapult was 260 feet, and it ended twenty feet short of the bow. The plane had used all 280 feet to get stopped. The bombardier ejected 3.8 seconds into that ride.

That Jake Grafton had managed to get the plane halted before it went into the ocean was, Colonel Haldane decided, nothing less than a miracle.

Seated at his desk in his stateroom, he thought about Jake Grafton, about what it must have felt like trying to get that airplane stopped as it stampeded toward the bow and the black void beyond. Oh, he had heard Grafton recount the experience, but already, while it was still fresh and immediate, Grafton had automatically donned the de rigueur cloak of humility: 'In spite of everything I did wrong, miraculously I survived. I was shot with luck. All you sinners take note that when the chips are down clean living and prayer pays off.'

Most pilots would have ejected. Haldane thought it through very carefully and came to the conclusion that he would have been one of them. He would have grabbed that alternate ejection handle between his legs and pulled hard.

Yet Grafton hadn't done that, and he had saved the plane. Luck, Haldane well knew in spite of Grafton's ready room bullshit, had played a very small part.

Should he have ejected? After all, the Navy Department could just order another A-6 from Grumman for $8 million, but it couldn't buy another highly trained, experienced pilot. It took millions of dollars and years of training to produce one of those; if you wanted one combat experienced, you had to have a war, which was impractical to do on a regular basis since a high percentage of the liberal upper crust frowned upon wars for training purposes.

Yep, Grafton should have punched. Just like Le Beau.

Sitting here in the warmth, safety, and comfort of a well-lit stateroom nursing a cup of coffee, any sane person would reach that obvious conclusion. Hindsight is so wonderful.

And the same person would be wrong.

Great pilots always find a way to survive. Almost by instinct they manage to choose a course of action – sometimes in blatant violation of the rules – that results in their survival.

The most obvious fact here was probably the most important: Jake Grafton was still alive and uninjured.

Had he ejected . . . well, who can say how that would have turned out? The seat might have malfunctioned, he might have gone into the ocean and drowned, he might have broken his neck being slammed down upon the flight deck or into the side of an airplane. Le Beau had been very lucky, and he freely admitted it, proclaimed it even, in the ready room afterward: 'I'd rather be lucky than good.'

Grafton was good. He had saved himself and the plane. Yet there was more. In the ready room afterward he hadn't been the least bit defensive, had stated why he did what he did clearly and cogently, then listened carefully to torrents of free advice – the what-you-should-have-done variety. He wasn't embarrassed that Flap ejected. He blamed no one and expressed no regrets.

Haldane liked that, had enjoyed watching and listening to a man whose rock-solid self-confidence could not be shaken. Grafton believed in himself, and the feeling was contagious. One wondered if there were anything this man couldn't handle.

Now the colonel dug into the bottom drawer of his desk. In a moment he found what he was looking for. It was a personal letter from the commanding officer of VA-128, Commander Dick Donovan. Haldane removed the letter from its envelope and read it, carefully, for the fourth or fifth time.

> I am sending you the most promising junior officer in the squadron, Lieutenant Jake Grafton. He is one of the two or three best pilots I have met in the Navy. He seems to have an instinct for the proper thing to do in a cockpit, something beyond the level that we can teach.
> As an officer, he is typical for his age and rank. Keep your eye on him. He has a temper and isn't afraid of anything on this earth. That is good and bad, as I am sure you will agree. I hope time and experience will season him. You may not agree with my assessment, but the more I see of him, the more I am convinced that he is capable of great things, that someday he will be able to handle great responsibilities.
> I want him back when your cruise is over.

Colonel Haldane folded the letter and put it back into its envelope. Then he pulled a pad of paper around and got out his pen. He hadn't answered this letter yet, and now seemed like a good time.

Donovan wasn't going to be happy to hear that Grafton was resigning, but there wasn't anything he or Donovan could do about it. That decision was up to Grafton. Still, it was a shame. Donovan was right – Grafton was a rare talent of unusual promise.

When the adrenaline rush had faded and the ready room crowd had calmed down, Jake and Flap went up to the forward 'dirty shirt' – wardroom between the bow cats. Flap had already been to sick bay and had several minor Plexiglas cuts dressed. 'Iodine and Band-Aids,' he told Jake with a grin. 'I've been hurt worse shaving. Man, talk about luck!'

In the serving line each man ordered a slider, a large

cheeseburger so greasy that it would slide right down your throat. With a glass of milk and a handful of potato chips, they sat on opposite sides of a long table with a food-stained tablecloth.

'I didn't think you could get it stopped,' Flap said between bites.

'You did the right thing,' Jake told him, referring to Flap's decision to eject. 'If I hadn't managed to get it sliding sideways I would have had to punch too.'

'Well, we're still alive, in one piece. We did all right.'

Jake just nodded and drank more milk. The adrenaline had left his stomach feeling queasy, but the milk and slider settled it. He leaned back in his chair and belched. Yep, there's a lot to be said for staying alive.

Down in his stateroom he stood looking around at the ordinary things, the things he saw every day yet didn't pay much attention to. After a glimpse into the abyss, the ordinary looks fresh and new. He sat in his chair and savored the fit, looked at how the light from his desk lamp cast stark shadows into the corners of the room, listened to the creaks and groans of the ship, examined with new eyes the photos of his folks and Callie that sat on his desk.

He twiddled the dial of the desk safe, then pulled it open. The ring was there, the engagement ring he had purchased for her last December aboard *Shiloh*. He took it from the safe and held it so the light shone on the small diamond. Finally he put it back. Without conscious thought, he removed his revolver from a pocket of his flight suit and put that in the safe too, then locked it.

He was going to have to do something about that woman.

But what?

It wasn't like he had her hooked and all he had to do was reel her in. The truth of the matter was that she had him hooked, and she hadn't decided whether or not he was a keeper.

So what is a guy to do? Write and pledge undying love? Promise to make her happy? Worm your way into her heart with intimate letters revealing your innermost thoughts?

No. What he had to do was speak to her softly, tell her of his dreams . . . if only he had any dreams to tell.

He felt hollow. Everyone else had a destination in mind: they were going at different speeds to get there, but they were on their way.

It was infuriating. Was there something wrong with him, some defect in him as a person? Was that what Callie saw?

Why couldn't she understand?

He thought about Callie for a while as he listened to the sounds of the ship working in a seaway, then finally reached for a pad and pen. He dated the letter and began:

'Dear Mom and Dad . . .'

When he finished the letter he didn't feel sleepy, so he took a hot shower and dressed in fresh, highly starched khakis and locked the door behind him. There weren't many people about. The last recovery was complete. The enlisted troops were headed for their bunks and the die-hard aviators were watching movies. He peered into various ready rooms to see who was still up that he knew. No one he wanted to talk to. He stopped in the arresting gear rooms and watched a first-class and two greenies pulling maintenance on an engine. He stopped by the PLAT office and watched his aborted takeoff several more times, wandered through the catapult spaces, where greenies supervised by petty officers were also working on equipment. In CATCC the graveyard shift had a radar consol torn apart.

In the Aviation Intermediate Maintenance avionics shop the night shift was hard at repairing aircraft radars and computers. This space was heavily air-conditioned and the lights burned around the clock. The technicians who worked here never saw the sun, or the world of wind and sea and sky where this equipment performed.

Finally, on a whim, Jake opened the door to the Air Department office. Warrant Officer Muldowski was the only person there. He saw Jake and boomed, 'Hey, shipmate. Come in and drop anchor.'

Jake helped himself to a cup of coffee and planted his elbows on the table across from the bosun, who had a pile of paper spread before him.

'You did good up there on that cat.'

'Thanks.'

'Kept waiting for you to punch. Thought you had waited too long.'

'For a second there I did too.'

They chewed the fat for a while, then when the conversation lagged Jake asked, 'Why did you stay in the Navy, Bosun?'

The bosun leaned back in his chair and reached for his tobacco pouch. When he had his pipe fired off and drawing well, he said, 'Civilians' worlds are too small.'

'What do you mean?'

'They get a job, live in a neighborhood, shop in the same stores all their lives. They live in a little world of friends, work, family. Those worlds looked too small to me.'

'That's something to think about.' Jake finished his coffee and tossed the Styrofoam cup in a wastebasket.

'Don't you go riding one of those pigs into the water, Mr Grafton. When you gotta go, you go.'

'Sure, Bosun.'

CHAPTER EIGHTEEN

A Soviet task group came over the horizon one Sunday in late November. *Columbia* had no flying scheduled that day, so gawkers packed the flight deck when Jake Grafton came up for a first-hand look. A strong wind from the south-west was ripping the tops off the twelve- to fifteen-foot swells. Spindrift covered the sea, all under a clear blue sky. *Columbia* was pitching noticeably. The nearest destroyer was occasionally taking white water over the bow.

Up on deck Jake ran into the Real McCoy. 'Where are they?'

McCoy pointed. Jake saw six gray warships in close formation, closing the American formation at an angle from the port side, still four or five miles away. The US ships were only making ten knots or so due to the sea state, but the Soviets were doing at least twice that. Even from this distance the rearing and plunging of the Soviet ships was quite obvious. Their bows were rising clear of the water, then plunging deeply as white water cascaded across the main decks and smashed against the gun mounts.

On they came, seemingly aiming straight for *Columbia*, which, as usual, was in the middle of the American formation.

Gidrograf, the Soviet Pamir-class AGI that had been shadowing the Americans' for the last month, was trailing along behind the Americans, at least two miles astern. Her speed matched the Americans' and she made no move to join the oncoming Soviet ships.

'What do you think?' McCoy asked.

'Unless Ivan changes course, he's going to run his ships smack through the middle of our formation.'

'I think that is exactly what he intends to do,' McCoy said after a bit, when the Russians were at least a mile closer.

'Sure looks like it,' Jake agreed. The angle-of-bearing hadn't changed noticeably, which was the clue that the ships were on collision courses. He glanced up at *Columbia*'s bridge. Reflections on the glass prevented him from seeing anyone, but he imagined that the captain and the admiral were conferring just now.

'Under the rules of the road, we have the right of way,' McCoy said.

'Yeah.' Somehow Jake suspected that paper rules didn't count for much with the Russian admiral, who was probably on the bridge of his flagship with one eye on the compass and the other on the Americans.

The Soviet ships were gorgeous, with sleek, raked hulls and superstructures bristling with weapons and topped with radar dishes of various types. The biggest one was apparently a cruiser. A couple were frigates, and the other three looked like destroyers. All were armed to the teeth.

The American destroyer on the edge of the formation gave way to the Russians. On they came. Now you could see the red flags at their mastheads as dots of color and tiny figures on the upper decks, like ants.

'Big storm coming,' McCoy said, never taking his eyes off the Russians. 'Up from the southwest. Be here this evening.'

Jake looked aft, at the carrier's wake. It was partially obscured by parked aircraft, but he saw enough. The wake was straight as a string. He turned his attention back to the Soviet ships. About that time the collision alarm sounded on *Columbia*'s loudspeaker system. Then came the announcement: 'This is not a drill. Rig for collision port-side.'

The Soviet destroyers veered to pass ahead and behind *Columbia* but the cruiser stayed on a collision course. Now you could plainly see the sailors on the upper decks, see the red flag stiff in the wind, see the cruiser's bow rise out of the water as white and green seawater surged aft along her decks, see that she was also rolling maybe fifteen degrees with every swell.

But she was a lot smaller than the carrier. The American sailors on the flight deck were well above the Russians' bridge. In fact, they could see the faces of the Russian sailors at the base of the mast quite plainly. The Russians were hanging on for dear life.

The Russian captain was going to veer off. He had to. Jake jumped into the catwalk so he could see better as the cruiser crossed the last fifty yards and the carrier's loud-speaker boomed, 'Stand by for collision portside. All hands brace for collision.'

The Soviet captain misjudged it. He swung his helm too late and the sea carried his ship in under the carrier's flight deck overhang. The closest the two hulls came was maybe fifteen feet, but as the cruiser heeled her motion in the sea pushed her mast and several of the radar antennae into the underside of the flight deck overhang. The Russian sailors clustered around the base of the mast saw that the collision was inevitable only seconds in advance and tried to flee. Two didn't make it. One fell to the cruiser's main deck, but the other man fell into that narrow river of white water between the two ships and instantly disappeared from view.

The top of the mast hit the catwalk forward of the Fresnel lens and ripped open three of the sixty-man life raft containers. The rafts dropped away. One ended up on the cruiser and the others went into the sea. The Russians' mast and several radar antennae were wiped off the super-structure and her stack was partially smashed.

Then the cruiser was past, surging ahead of *Columbia* with her mast trailing in the water on her portside.

Jake bent down and stuck his head through the railing under the life raft containers so that he could keep the cruiser in sight. If the Russian captain cut across *Columbia*'s bow he was going to get his ship cut in half.

He did cut across, but only when he was at least six or seven hundred yards ahead, still making twenty knots.

The Soviet ships rejoined their tight formation and continued on course, pulling steadily away.

An American destroyer dropped aft to look for the lost Soviet sailor as the air boss ordered the flight deck cleared so he could launch the alert helo.

The helo searched for half an hour. The destroyer stayed on the scene for several hours, yet the Russian sailor wasn't found.

By evening a line of thunderstorms formed a solid wall to the southwest, a wall that seemed to stretch from horizon to horizon. As the dusk deepened lightning flashed in the storms continually. Jake was on deck watching the approaching storms and savoring the sea wind when the carrier and her escorts slowly came about and pointed their bows at the lightning.

The ships rode better on the new course. Apparently the heavies had decided to sail through the storm line, thereby minimizing their time in it. Unfortunately the weather on the back side of the front was supposed to be bad; heavy seas, low ceilings and lots of rain. Oh well, no flying tomorrow either.

When the darkness was complete and the storms were within a few miles, Jake went below. This was going to be a good night to sleep.

The ringing telephone woke Jake. The Real McCoy usually answered it since all he had to do was roll over in his bunk and reach, and he did this time. The motion of the ship was less pronounced than it had been when Jake and Real went to bed about 10 P.M., during the height of the storm.

'McCoy, sir.'

Jake looked at his watch. A little after 2 A.M.

After a bit, he heard his roommate growl, 'This had better not be your idea of a joke, Harrison, or your ass is a grape . . . Yeah, yeah, I'll tell him . . . In a minute, okay?'

Then McCoy slammed the receiver back on the hook.

'You awake up there?'

'Yeah.'

'They want us both in the ready room in five minutes, ready to fly.'

'Get serious.'

'That's what the man said. Must be World War III.'

'Awww . . .'

'If Harrison is jerking our chains he'll never have another OK pass as long as he lives. I promise.'

But Harrison wasn't kidding, as Jake and the Real found out when they went through the ready room door. The skipper and Allen Bartow were standing near the duty desk talking to CAG Kall. Flap Le Beau was listening and sipping a cup of coffee. All of them were in flight suits.

'Good morning, gentlemen,' CAG said. He looked like he had had a great eight hours sleep and a fine breakfast. He couldn't have had, Jake knew. Things didn't work like that in this Navy.

''Morning, CAG,' McCoy responded. 'So it's war, huh?'

'Not quite. Pull up a chair and we'll sort this out.'

Apparently the admiral and CINCPACFLT had been burning the airways with flash messages. The Soviet ambassador in Washington had delivered a stiff note to the State Department protesting the previous day's naval incident in the Indian Ocean, which he called 'a provocation.'

The powers that be had concluded that the US Navy had to serve notice on the Russians that it couldn't be bullied.

'The upshot is,' CAG said, 'that we have been ordered to make an aerial demonstration over the Soviet task group, tonight if possible.'

'What kind of demonstration, sir?'

'At least two airplanes, high-speed passes, masthead height if possible.'

Eyebrows went up. McCoy got out of his chair and went to the television, which he turned to the continuous weather display. Current weather was three to four hundred feet broken to overcast, three-quarters of a mile visibility in rain. Wind out of the northwest at twenty-five knots.

CAG was still talking. '. . . it occurred to me that this would be a good time to try our foul weather attack scheme on the Russians. I thought we could send two A-6s and three EA-6Bs. We'd put a Hummer up to keep it safe. The admiral concurred. The Prowler crews and Hummer crews will be here in a few minutes for the brief. What do you think?'

'Sir, where are the Russians?'

'Two hundred miles to the east. Apparently the line of thunderstorms went over them several hours ago and they are also under this system.'

As he finished speaking the ship's loudspeaker, the 1-MC, came to life: 'Flight quarters, flight quarters, all hands man your flight quarters stations.'

In minutes the Prowler and Hawkeye crews came in and found seats and the brief began. CAG did the briefing, even though he wouldn't be flying. Forget the masthead rhetoric from Washington – the lowest any of the crews could go was five hundred feet.

The three senior pilots of the Prowler squadron would fly their planes, and the CO of the E-2 squadron would be in the left seat of the Hawkeye. Lieutenant Colonel Haldane and the Real McCoy would fly the go A-6s and Jake Grafton would man the spare.

'Uh, skipper,' Flap said, 'if I may ask, why McCoy?'

'He's got the best landing grades in the squadron. Grafton is second. As it happens, they have more traps than anyone else in the outfit and getting back aboard is going to be the trick. As for me, this is my squadron.'

'Yessir, but I was wondering about McCoy. Let's face facts, sir. When the landing signal officer has the best landing scores – well, it's like an umpire having the top batting average. There's just a wee bit of an odor, sir.'

Laughter swept the room as McCoy grinned broadly. He winked at Jake.

'What say you and I flip for the go bird,' Jake suggested to McCoy.

'Forget it, shipmate. If my plane's up, I'm flying it. Tonight or any other night.'

'Come on! Be a sport.'

The Real was having none of it. And Jake understood. Naval aviation was their profession. Given the weather and sea state, this would be a very tough mission. When you began ducking the tough ones, you were finished in this business. Maybe no one else would know, but *you* would.

In flight deck control Jake looked at the airplane planform cutouts on the model ship to see where his plane was spotted. Watching the handler check the weight chits as rain splattered against the one round, bomb-proof window and the wind moaned, Jake Grafton admitted to himself that he was glad he had the spare. He wasn't ducking anything – this was the bird the system gave him and he wasn't squawking.

All he had to do was preflight, strap in and start the engines, then sit and watch Haldane and McCoy ride the catapult into the black goo. After that he could shut down and go below for coffee. If he went to the forward mess deck galley he could probably snag a couple doughnuts hot from the oven.

The handler was a lieutenant commander pilot who had left the Navy for two years, then changed his mind. The only billet available when he came back was this one – two years as the aircraft handler on *Columbia*. He took it, resigning himself to two years of shuffling airplane cutouts around this model, two years of listening to squadron maintenance people complain that their airplanes weren't where they could properly maintain them, two years listening to the air boss grouse that the go birds were spotted wrong, two years checking tie-down chains and weight chits, two years listening to the hopes, dreams and fears of young, homesick sailors while trying to train them to do dangerous, difficult jobs, two years in purgatory with no flying . . . yet the handler seemed to be weathering it okay. True, his fuse was getting almighty short and he wasn't getting enough sleep, but his job performance was first-rate, from everything Jake had seen and heard. And behind the tired face with the bleary eyes was a gentle human being who liked to laugh at a good joke in the dirty-shirt wardroom. Here in Flight Deck Control, however, he was all business.

'Forty-six thousand five hundred pounds? That right, Grafton?' The handler was reading from Jake's weight chit. This would be his weight if he launched.

'Yessir.'

Savoring the hubbub in Flight Deck Control while surreptitiously watching the handler, Jake Grafton felt doubt creep over him. Was getting out a mistake? It had been for the handler. An eight-to-five job somewhere, the same routine day after day . . .

He turned for the hatch that led to the flight deck. The first blast of cool air laden with rain wiped the future from his mind and left only the present, this moment, this wild, windy night, this airplane that awaited him under the dim red island floodlights.

His bird was sitting on Elevator Four. The tail was sticking out over the water, so he checked every step with his flash-light before he moved his feet. If you tripped over the three-inch-high combing, you would go straight into the ocean to join that Russian sailor who went in yesterday. Poor devil – his shipmates didn't even stop to look for him. How would you like to go to sea in that man's navy?

Going around the nose he and Flap passed each other. 'What a night,' Flap muttered.

Both men were wearing their helmets. They had the clear visors down to keep the rain and salt spray out of their eyes. The wind made the raindrops hurt as they splattered against exposed flesh.

Jake took his time preflighting the ejection seat. He was tempted to hurry at this point so he could sit down and the plane captain could close the canopy, but he was too old a dog. He checked everything carefully, methodically while he used his left hand to hang tightly to the airplane. The motion of the ship seemed magnified out here on this elevator. The fact he was eight or nine feet above the deck perched on this boarding ladder and buffeted by the wind and rain didn't help. He pulled the safety pins, inspected, counted and stowed them, then he sat.

The plane captain climbed the ladder to help him hook up the mask, don the leg restraints, and snap the four Koch fittings into place. Then the plane captain went around to help Flap. When both men were completely strapped in, he closed the canopy.

Now Jake checked the gear handle, armament switches, circuit breakers, and arranged the switches for engine start. He had done all these things so many times that he had to concentrate to make sure he was seeing what was there and not just what he expected to see.

When he had the engines started, Flap fired up the

computer while Jake checked the radio and TACAN frequencies.

'Good alignment,' Flap reported, and signaled to the plane captain to pull the cable that connected the plane to the ship's inertial navigation system.

They were ready. Now to sit here warm and reasonably dry and watch the launch.

The E-2 taxied toward Cat Three on the waist. A cloud of water lifted from the deck by the wash of the two turbo-props blasted everything. The plane went onto the cat, the JBD rose, then the engines began to moan. Finally the wing-tip lights came on. The Hawkeye accelerated down the catapult and rose steadily into the night. The lights faded quickly, then the goo swallowed them.

'Uh-oh,' Flap said. 'Look over there at Real's plane.'

A crowd of maintenance people had the left engine access door open. Someone was up on the ladder talking to McCoy. In less than a minute a figure left the group and headed for Jake's plane.

The man on the deck lowered the pilot's boarding ladder while Jake ran the canopy open. Then he climbed up. The squadron's senior troubleshooter. 'Mr McCoy can't get his left generator to come on the line,' he shouted. 'Jake had to hold his helmet away from his left ear to hear. 'You're going in his place.'

'His tough luck, huh?'

'Right.'

'The breaks of Naval Air . . .'

'Be careless.' The sergeant reached for Jake's hand and shook it, then shook Flap's. He went down the boarding ladder and Flap closed the canopy.

'We're going,' Jake said on the ICS. 'In McCoy's place.'

'I figured. By God, when they said all-weather attack, they meant all-weather. Have you ever flown before on a night this bad?'

'No.'

308

'Me either. Just to send a message to the Russians, like the Navy was an FTD florist. Roses are red, violets are blue, you hit our ships and we'll fuck you. The peacetime military ain't what it was advertised to be. No way, man.'

The yellow-shirted taxi director was signaling for the blue-shirts to break down the tie-downs. Jake put his feet on the brakes. 'Here we go.'

It never gets any easier. In the darkness the rain streaming over the windshield blurred what little light there was and the slick deck and wind made taxiing difficult. Just beyond the bow the abyss gaped at him.

He ran through possible emergencies as he eased the plane toward the cat.

Total electrical failure while taking the cat shot was the emergency he feared the most. It wasn't that he didn't know what to do – he did. The doing of it in a cockpit lit only by Flap's flashlight as adrenaline surged through you like a lightning bolt would be the trick. You had just one chance, in an envelope of opportunity that would be open for only a few seconds. You had to do it right regardless or you would be instantly, totally dead.

'Why do we do this shit?' he muttered at Flap as they taxied toward the cat.

'Because we're too lazy for honest work and too stupid to steal.'

The truth of the matter was that he feared and loathed night cat shots. And flying at night, especially night instrument flight. There was nothing fun about it, no beauty, no glamour, no appeal to his sense of adventure, no sense that this was a thing worth doing. The needles and gauges were perverse gadgets that demanded his total concentration to make behave. Then the night flight was topped off with a night carrier landing – he once described a night carrier hop as sort of like eating an old tennis shoe for dinner, then choking down a sock for dessert.

Tonight as he ran through the launch procedures and

ran the engines up to full power, rancid fear occupied a portion of his attention. A small portion, it is true, but it was there.

He tried to fight it back, to wrestle the beast back into its cage deep in his subconscious, but without success.

Wipe out the cockpit with the controls, check the engine instruments . . . all okay.

Jumping Jack Bean was the shooter. When Jake turned on his exterior lights, he saluted the cockpit perfunctorily with his right hand while he kept giving the 'full power' signal with the wand in his left hand. Jake could see he was looking up the deck, waiting for the bow to reach the bottom of its plunge into a trough between the swells.

Now Bean lunged forward and touched the wand to the deck. The bow must be rising.

The plane shot forward.

Jake's eyes settled on the altitude instruments.

The forward edge of the flight deck swept under the nose.

Warning lights out, rotate to eight degrees, airspeed okay, gear up.

'Positive rate of climb,' Flap reported, then keyed the radio and reported to Departure Control.

The climb went quickly because the plane was carrying only a two-thousand-pound belly tank and four empty bomb racks. But they had a long way to climb. They finally cleared the clouds at 21,000 feet and found the night sky filled with stars.

An EA-6B Prowler was already there, waiting for them. It was level at 22,000 feet, on the five-mile arc around the ship. Its exterior lights seemed weak, almost lonely as they flickered in the starry night.

The Prowler was a single-purpose aircraft, designed solely to wage electronic war. Grumman had lengthened the basic A-6 airframe enough to accept two side-by-side cockpits, so in addition to the pilot the plane carried three electronic warfare specialists known as ECMOs, or electronic counter-measures officers. Special antennae high on the tail and at various other places on the plane allowed the specialists to detect enemy radar transmissions, which they then jammed or deceived by the use of countermeasures pods that hung on the wing weapons stations. Tonight, in addition to the pods, this Prowler carried a two-thousand-pound fuel tank on its belly station. Although the EA-6B was capable of carrying a couple missiles to defend itself, Jake had never seen one armed.

As expensive as Boeing 747s, these state-of-the-art aircraft had not been allowed to cross into North Vietnam after they joined the fleet, which degraded their effectiveness but ensured that if one were lost, the Communists would not get a peek at the technology. Here, again, America traded airplanes and lives in a meaningless war rather than risk compromising the technological edge it had to have to win a war with the Soviets, a war for national survival.

Jake thought about that now – about trading lives to keep the secrets – as he flew in formation with the Prowler and looked at the telltale outline of helmeted heads in the cockpits looking back at him. Then the Prowler pilot passed Jake the lead, killed his exterior lights, slid aft and crossed under to take up a position on Jake's right wing.

The Prowler pilot was Commander Reese, the skipper of the squadron. He was about five and a half feet tall, wore a pencil-thin mustache, and delighted in practical jokes. Inevitably, given his stature, he had acquired the nickname of Pee Wee.

Jake retarded the throttles and lowered the nose. In seconds the clouds closed in around the descending planes and blotted out the stars.

'Departure, War Ace Five Oh Two and company headed southeast, descending.'

'Roger, War Ace. Switch to Strike.'

'Switching.'

Flap twirled the radio channelization knob and waited for the Prowler to check in on frequency. Then he called Strike.

Flying in this goo, at night, wasn't really flying at all. It was like a simulator. The world ended at the windshield. Oh, if you turned your head you could see the fuzzy glow of the wing-tip lights, and if you looked back right you could see your right wing-tip light reflecting off the skin of the Prowler that hung there, but there was no sense of speed or movement. Occasional little turbulence jolts were the only reminder that this box decorated with dim red lights, gauges and switches wasn't welded to the earth.

The big plan was for each bomber and its accompanying Prowler to run a mock attack on the Soviet task group as close to simultaneously as possible. Jake would approach from the southwest, Colonel Haldane from the northwest. The E-2 Hawkeye, the Hummer, would monitor their progress and coordinate the attack. However, each A-6 BN had to find the task group on radar before they sank below the radar horizon. Then the bombers would run in at five hundred feet. In an actual attack they would come in lower, perhaps as low as two hundred, but not at night, not in this weather, for drill. The risks of flying that close to the sea were too great.

Flap started the video recorder, a device that the A-6A never had. This device would record everything seen on the radar screen, all the computer and inertial data, as well as the conversation on the radio and in the cockpit.

'Recorder's on,' he told Jake. 'Keep it clean.'

This electronic record of the attack could be used for poststrike analysis, or, as CAG had hinted in the brief, sent to Washington to show to any bigwigs or congressmen who wanted to know what, exactly, the Navy had done in response to the collision at sea.

Had the Soviet skipper intended to bump the carrier?

Did he tell the truth to his superiors? These imponderables had of course been weighed in Washington, and orders had been sent to the other side of the earth.

It was midafternoon in Washington. The city would be humming with the usual mix of tourists, government workers anxious to begin their afternoon trek to the sub-urbs, the latest tunes coming over the radios, soap operas on television . . .

Jake wondered about the weather there. Late November. Was it cold, rainy, overcast?

All those people in America, finishing up another Monday, and he and Flap were here, over the Indian Ocean, passing ten thousand feet with a Prowler on their wing and a Soviet task group somewhere in the night ahead.

'See it yet?'

'No. Stop at eight thousand and hold there.'

As they flew eastward the turbulence increased. Jake had Flap arrange his rearview mirror so he could keep tabs on the Prowler. Pee Wee Reese seemed to be hanging in there pretty well. He had to. If he lost sight of the bomber, he would have to break off. Two planes feeling for each other in this soup would be a fine way to arrange a midair collision.

'The Commies aren't where they're supposed to be,' Flap said finally.

'You sure?'

'All I know is that the radar screen is empty. Rocket scientist that I am, I deduce the Reds aren't where the spies said they would be. Or *Columbia*'s inertial was all screwed up and this is the wrong ocean. Or all the Reds have sunk. Those are the possibilities.'

'Better ask Black Eagle.'

It turned out the E-2 was also looking for the Soviets at the maximum range of its radar. It soon found them, steaming hard to the northeast, directly away from Jake and Flap and directly toward the line of thunderstorms that had just passed over them.

'They know something's up,' Jake said

'Terrific. They're at general quarters expecting us and we'll have to go under thunderstorms to get to them. And to think we almost didn't get a date for this party.'

'Man, we're having fun now.'

Flap didn't reply. He was busy.

After a bit he said, 'Okay, I got 'em. Give me a few moments to get a course and speed and then we'll go down.'

While he was talking the electronic warfare (EW) panel chirped. A Soviet search radar was painting them. In addition to the flashing light on the panel when the beam swept them, Jake heard a baritone chirp in his headset.

So much for surprise.

The turbulence was getting worse. The bouncing was constant now. Rain coursed around the windscreen and across the canopy. 'Radar is getting degraded,' Flap muttered. 'Rain. I got them though, course Zero Five Zero at fifteen. Lots of sea return. Swells are big down there, my man.'

'Can we go down?'

'Yeah.'

Jake glanced over at the reflection of the Prowler in the mirror. Pee Wee was riding fairly steadily, cycling up and down as the planes bounced, but never slipping too far out of position. Jake carefully eased the throttle back and let the nose go down a half a degree. When he was sure the EA-6B pilot was still with him, he lowered the nose some more.

A pale green light caught his eye, and he glanced at the windscreen. Dancing tendrils of green fire were playing across it.

'Look at this,' he told Flap. 'Saint Elmo's fire.'

'This makes my night,' the BN said. 'All we need is for

the Russians to squirt a missile at us and this will be a complete entertainment experience.'

'Will a lightning bolt do?'

'Don't say stuff like that. God's listening. You're passing five thousand.'

'Radar's altimeter's set.'

'Roger. Station one selected, master arm to go.'

They were up to four hundred knots indicated now. The EA-6B was right there, hanging on. Eighty miles to go.

Wasn't Saint Elmo's fire an indicator that lightning might strike? Wasn't that what the old sailors said? Even as he wondered the flickering green fire faded, then disappeared completely.

Black Eagle gave them a turn. Jake banked gently to the new heading. The steering to the target was forty degrees left, but the controller in the E-2 was trying to coordinate the attack. When he had one of the formations four miles farther from the target than the other, he would have them turn inbound and accelerate to five hundred knots. The pilots would call their distance to go on the radio every ten miles. The plan was for the bombers and their EA-6B escorts to pass over the Soviet task group thirty seconds apart. Neither formation would see the other, so this separation was required for safety reasons.

Jake eased his descent passing twenty-five hundred feet. He shallowed it still more passing a thousand and drifted slowly down to five hundred, keeping one eye on the radar altimeter. He adjusted the barometric pressure on the pressure altimeter so it matched the radar altimeter's reading exactly.

The turbulence had not let up, nor had it increased. The rain was heavier, though. The high airspeed kept the windscreen clear but the water ran across the top and sides of the canopy in sheets.

'War Aces, turn inbound.'

Jake came left to center the steering and fed the throttles

forward until they were at ninety-eight percent RPM. Pee Wee stayed right with him.

'Five Oh Two, seventy miles.'

Fifteen seconds later he heard Haldane's voice: 'Five Oh Five, sixty miles.'

Each plane was inbound on a bomb run at eight and a third nautical miles per minute. They were a little over thirty seconds apart, but the extra margin was an added safety cushion.

'I should get them at about thirty miles, I think,' Flap said.

And when we can see them, they can see us.

Jake reached down and flipped the IFF, the transponder, to standby. No use giving the Reds an easy problem.

He glanced at the EW panel. Still quiet. When they rose above the Russians' radar horizon it would light up like a Christmas tree.

'Five Oh Two, sixty miles.'

The turbulence was getting vicious. The radar altimeter beeped once when Jake inadvertently dropped to four hundred feet. He concentrated on the instruments, on the altitude indicator on the VDI, on the needle of the rate-of-climb indicator, cross-checking the radar and pressure altimeters, all the while working to keep his wings level and steering centered. Every moment or two he glanced in the mirror to check on Pee Wee Reese, who was sticking like glue. No question, the guy was good.

'Five Oh Two, fifty miles.'

Rain poured over the plane, so much that a film of water developed on the windscreen even though they were doing five hundred knots.

'Five Oh Two, forty miles.'

A lightning flash ahead distracted him for several seconds from the instruments. When he came back to them he had lost fifty feet. He struggled to get it back as he wondered if Haldane had seen the lightning flash. Should they go under a thunderstorm? It was Haldane's call. Jake wasn't breaking off the run unless the skipper did.

'Five Oh Two, thirty miles.'

Twenty-nine, twenty-eight . . .

'They've turned,' Flap said. 'They're heading southeast. Follow steering.'

Even as Jake eased right to center the bug, the EW panel lit up and the tones assailed him. X-band, Y-band – the Russians had every radar they had turned on and probing, looking for a target.

Now the tones of the radars became a buzz. The bomber was so close to the EA-6B, which was jamming the Russian radar, that the bomber's EW gear was overwhelmed.

'Five Oh Two, twenty miles.'

'Master Arm on, we're in attack,' Flap reported.

The attack symbology came alive on the VDI.

Another lightning flash. Closer. Lots of rain.

'Five Oh Five, ten miles.' That was Haldane.

Fifteen miles . . . fourteen . . . thirteen . . .

'They're jamming me. Keep on this heading.'

Now Flap flipped on frequency agility, trying to change his radar's frequency to an unjammed wavelength long enough to get a look.

'Five Oh Two, ten miles.'

Three lightning flashes in a couple seconds. They were flying right under a boomer. The turbulence was so bad Jake had trouble concentrating on the instruments. Pee Wee was still hanging on, though.

Five miles.

Four.

Three.

Symbols marching down toward weapons release.

Lights. The Russian ships should be lit up. He should pass over them just after weapons' release. *But don't look!* No distractions. *Concentrate!*

Two.

One.

Release marker coming down. Steering centered. Commit trigger pulled.

Click. Flag drop on the ordnance panel and the attack light on the VDI went out.

If there had been a bomb, it would now be falling.

A searchlight split the night. Three or four, weaving.

Instantly he had vertigo. He stared at the VDI, forced himself to keep his wings level as he tugged the stick slightly aft to begin a climb.

And then the lights were behind. That quick.

More lightning ahead. Jake eased into a left turn, toward the north. The skipper went out to the southeast, so this direction should be clear.

He would climb away from this ocean, turn west to head for the carrier, get out of this rain and turbulence and lightning, and to hell with the Ivans!

Message delivered: fuck you very much, stiff letter to follow.

He had the power back to ninety percent and was up to two thousand feet, in a ten-degree angle-of-bank left turn passing north on the HSI when the lightning bolt struck. There was a stupendous flash of light and a sound like a hammer striking, then nothing.

He was blind. Everything was white. Flash blindness. He knew it.

He keyed the ICS and told Flap, 'Flashlight—' but there was no feedback in his headset. A total electrical failure. And he was blind as a bat, two thousand feet over the water, in a turn.

He *had* to see.

He blinked furiously, trying by sheer force of will to see the instrument panel.

But there was no light, no electricity.

He reached behind him with his left hand, found the

handle for the ram-air turbine – the RAT – and pulled hard. Real hard.

The handle came out.

Perhaps four seconds had passed, not more.

The white was fading. He reached for his oxygen mask with both hands and unfastened the right side.

What the plane was doing he had no way of knowing, although he knew whatever it was, it wasn't good. But he couldn't fly blind. His seat-of-the-pants instincts were worthless. Oh, he knew *that*, had had it drummed into him and had experienced it on so many night carrier landings that he wasn't even tempted to try to level the wings.

The white was fading into darkness. He blinked furiously, then remembered his L-shaped flashlight, hanging by a hook on the front of his survival vest. He found it and pushed the switch on.

In the growing darkness he saw the spot the beam made on the instrument panel. Another few seconds . . .

But there was already a spot of light on the needle-ball turn indicator! *Flap!* He must have had his head in the scope when the lightning hit.

He could see. The VDI was blank. The standby gyro showed a thirty-degree left turn. Ten degrees nose-down.

Cross-check with the turn indicator!

Turn needle pegged left. He rolled right to center it, overdid it and came back left some. The standby gyro responded.

The altimeter! Going down.

Back stick. Stop the needle. Gently now. Coming down on eleven hundred feet. Stop it there, center that turn needle. Standby gyro disagrees by five degrees. *Ignore it!*

Flap was shouting and he caught the muffled words: 'Reese is still with us. He has his lights on. I think he wants to take the lead.'

Jake could see now. His vision was back to normal. How many seconds had it been?

He risked a glance in the rearview mirror. There was Reese, with his exterior lights on, bobbing like a cork on Jake's right wing. Reese must be the world's finest formation pilot, to hang on through that gyration.

Should he chance it? Should he pull the power and try to ease back onto Reese's wing without a radio call or signal?

Even as the thought shot through his mind, he was retarding the throttles. Reese's plane began to move forward.

Okay! Flap was flipping his flashlight at Reese in the EA-6B's cockpit.

Pee Wee knows. He wants me to fly on him. It's our only chance if the TACAN and radar are screwed up. We'll never find the ship on our own.

Now Reese was abeam him, the two planes flying wing tip to wing tip and bouncing out of sync in the turbulence.

Be smooth, Jake. Don't lose him. Don't let him slip away into this black shit or you'll be swimming for it.

He stabilized in parade position on Reese's left side, so that he was looking straight up the leading edge of the swept wing into the cockpit. Reese was just a dark shape limned by red light, the glow from his instrument panel.

No comforting red glow in this cockpit. This place was dark as a tomb.

The bouncing was getting worse. He had to cross under, get on Reese's right side so he wouldn't be looking across the cockpit at the other plane.

He tucked the nose down gently and pulled a smidgen of power. Now power back on and a little right bank while he wrestled the stick in the chop.

Right under the tail, crossing, surfacing on Pee Wee's right wing. Okay. Now hang here.

Another flash of lightning. He flinched.

Flap was shouting something. He concentrated, trying to make sense of the words. '. . . must've zapped us with a zillion volts. Every circuit breaker we got is popped. I'm going to try to reset some, so if you smell smoke, let me know.'

'Okay,' he shouted, and found reassurance in the sound of his own voice.

All he had to do was hang on to Reese. Hang on and hang on and hang on, and someday, sometime, Reese would drop him onto the ball. The ball would be out there in the rain and black goo, and the drop lights, and the centerline lights, and the wires, strung across that pitching, heaving deck.

All he had to do was hang on . . .

As Flap pushed in circuit breakers and the cockpit lights glowed, then went out, then glowed again, the planes flew into and out of deluges. The torrents of rain were worse than they had been coming in. Several times the rain coursing over the canopy caused Reese's plane to fade until just the exterior lights could be seen.

Jake concentrated fiercely upon those lights. Each time the rain would eventually slacken and the fuselage of the EA-6B would reappear, a ghostly gray presence in the blacker gloom.

Finally the clouds dissipated and a blacker night spread out before them. Far above tiny, cold stars shown steadily. They were on top, above the clouds. Behind them lightning strobed almost continually.

Jake eased away from Reese and put his mask to his face. The oxygen was flowing, cool and rubbery tasting. He lowered it again, then swabbed the sweat from his eyes and face with the fingers of his left hand.

When he had his mask fixed back in place he glanced at the instruments. The instrument lights were on – well, some of them. It was still dark on Flap's side. The VDI was still blank, but the standby gyro was working. The TACAN needle swung lazily, steadily, around and around the dial.

He pushed the button to check the warning lights on the annunciator panel. The panel stayed dark. Both generators were probably fried. Maybe the battery. He recycled each of the generator switches, but nothing happened. Finally he just turned them off.

Fuel – he checked the gauge. Nine thousand pounds. He pushed the buttons on the fuel panel to check the quantity in each tank. The needle and totalizer never moved. They were frozen.

Flap was still examining the circuit breaker panel with his flashlight.

'Hey, shipmate, you there?' Flap – on the ICS.

'Yeah.'

'A whole bunch of these CBs won't stay in.'

'Forget it.'

'We're gonna need—'

'We'll worry about it later.'

Later. Let's sit up here in the night above the storms and savor this moment. Savor life. For we are alive. Still alive. Let's sit silently and look at the stars and Reese's beautiful Prowler and breathe deeply and listen to our hearts beating.

CHAPTER NINETEEN

The radome on the nose of the aircraft had a hole in it. Jake and Flap examined it with their flashlights. It was about the size of a quarter and had black edges where the Plexiglas or whatever it was had melted. They had shut down on Elevator Two so the plane could be dropped below to the hangar deck.

Now they stood looking at the hole in the radome as the sea wind dried the sweat from their faces and hair and the overcast began to lighten toward the east.

Dawn was coming. Another day at sea.

The hole was there and that was that.

'Grafton, you're jinxed,' Flap Le Beau said.

'What do you mean?' Jake asked, suddenly defensive.

'Man, things happen to you.'

'I was doing fine until I started flying with you,' Jake shot back, then instantly regretted it.

Flap didn't reply. Both men turned off their flashlights and headed for the island.

Lieutenant Colonel Haldane had rendezvoused with Pee Wee Reese and Jake had transferred over to his wing. An approach with a similar aircraft was easier to fly. Fortunately the weather had cleared somewhat around the ship, so when the two A-6s came out of the overcast with their gear, flaps and hooks down they were still a thousand feet above the water. There wasn't much rain. The ship's lights were clear and bright.

Jake boltered his first pass and made a climbing left turn

off the angle. He and Flap had been unable to get the radio working again, so he few a close downwind leg and turned into the groove as if he were flying a day pass. He snagged a one-wire.

The debrief took two hours. After telling the duty officer to take him off the schedule for the rest of the day, Jake went to breakfast, then back to his bunk. The Real McCoy woke him in time for dinner.

Jake and Flap didn't fly again for four days. The skipper must have told the schedules officer to give them some time off, but Jake didn't ask. He did paperwork, visited the maintenance office to hear about the electrical woes of 502, did more paperwork, ate, slept, and watched three movies.

The maintenance troops found another lightning hole in the tail of 502. Jake went to the hangar deck for a look.

'Apparently the bolt went in the front and went clear through the plane, then out the tail,' the sergeant said. 'Or maybe it went in the tail and out the front.'

'Uh-huh.' The hole in the tail was also about quarter size, up high above the rudder.

'Was the noise loud?'

'Not that I recall.'

'Thought it must be like sitting beside a howitzer when it went off.'

'Just a metallic noise,' Jake said, trying to remember. Funny, but he didn't remember a real loud noise.

'You guys were sure lucky.'

'Like hell,' Jake told him. He was thoroughly sick of these philosophical discussions. 'Pee Wee Reese was on my wing and the lightning didn't hit him. It hit me. He didn't get a volt. *He* had the luck.'

'You were lucky you didn't blow up,' the sergeant insisted. 'I've heard of planes hit by lightning that just blew up. You were lucky.'

'Planes full of avgas, maybe, but not jet fuel.'

The sergeant wasn't taking no for an answer. 'Jets too,' he said.

Thanksgiving came and went, then another page was ripped off the ready room calendar and it was December.

Jake had that feeling again that his life was out of control. 'You just got to go with the flow,' the Real McCoy said when Jake tried to talk to him about it.

'It's a reaction to the lightning strike,' Flap said when Jake mentioned it to him. Jake didn't bother telling him he had had it off and on for years.

Yet gradually the feeling faded and he felt better. Once again he laughed in the ready room and tried to remember jokes. But he refused to think about the future. I'm going to take life one day at a time, he decided. If a guy does that there will never be a future to worry about. Just the present. That makes sense, doesn't it?

'What does it feel like to die?' Flap Le Beau asked.

He and Jake were motoring along at 350 knots at five thousand feet just under a layer of cumulus puffballs. Beneath them the empty blue sea spread away to the horizon in every direction. This afternoon they were flying another surface surveillance mission, this time a wedge-shaped pattern to the east of the task group. They were still on the outbound leg. They had not seen a single ship, visually or on radar. The ocean was empty.

All those ships crossing the Indian Ocean, hundreds of them at any one time, yet the ocean was so big . . .

'Did you ever think about it?' Flap prompted.

'I passed out once,' Jake replied. 'Fainted. When I was about fourteen. Nurse was taking blood, jabbing me over and over again trying to get the needle into a vein. One second I was there, then I was waking up on the floor after some nightmare, which I forgot fifteen seconds after I woke up. Dying is like that, I suspect. Not the nightmare part. Just like someone turned out the light.'

'Maybe,' Flap said.

'Like going to sleep,' Jake offered.

'Ummm . . .'

'What got you thinking about that, anyway?'

'Oh, you know . . .'

The conversation dribbled out there. Flap idly checked the radar, as usual saw nothing, then rearranged his fanny in his seat. Grafton yawned and rubbed his face.

The radio squawked to life. The words were partially garbled: the aircraft was a long way from the ship – over two hundred miles – and low.

'This is War Ace Five Oh Eight,' Flap said into his mask. 'Say again.'

'Five Oh Eight, this is Black Eagle. We'll relay. The ship wants you to investigate an SOS signal. Stand by for the coordinates.'

Flap glanced at Jake, shrugged, then got a ballpoint pen from the left-shoulder pocket of his flight suit and inspected the point. He scribbled on the corner of his top kneeboard card to make sure the pen worked, then said, 'War Ace is ready to copy.'

When he had read back the coordinates to the controller in the E-2 Hawkeye to ensure he had copied them correctly, Flap tapped them into the computer and cycled it. 'Uh-oh,' he muttered to Jake. 'It's over four hundred miles from here.'

'Better talk to the controller.'

Flap clicked his oxygen mask into place. 'Black Eagle, Five Oh Eight. That ship looks to be four hundred twenty-nine miles from our present position, which is' – he pushed another button on the computer – 'two hundred forty-two miles from the ship. We don't have the gas and we can't make the recovery.'

Grafton was punching the buttons, checking the wing fuel. They launched with a total of 18,000 pounds, and now had 11,200.

'Roger, War Ace. They know that. We're talking to them on another frequency. They want you to go look anyway. They only got about fifteen seconds of an SOS broadcast, which had the lat-long position as a part of it. The ship thinks you can get there, give it a quick look-over, then rendezvous with a tanker on the inbound leg on this frequency.'

Already Jake had swung the plane fifteen degrees to the right to follow the computer's steering command to the ship in distress. Now he added power and began to climb.

'Set up a no-rad rendezvous, just in case,' Jake told Flap.

He wanted to know where to find the tanker even if the radio failed. The only way to fix positions in this world of sea and sky was electronically, in bearings and distances away from ships that were radiating electronic signals that the plane's nav aids could receive. Unfortunately the A-6s radar could not detect other airplanes. And the tanker had no radar at all. Of course, Flap could find the carrier on radar if he were within 150 miles of it and the radar worked, and they could use the distance and bearing to locate themselves in relation to the tanker. If the radar kept working.

There were a lot of ifs.

The ifs made your stomach feel hollow.

Seventeen days had passed since their night adventure in the thunderstorm and here they were again, letting it all hang out.

Jake Grafton swore softly under his breath. It just isn't fair! *And the ship in distress might not even be there.* A fifteen-second SOS with the position. Sounded like an electronic program, one that could have easily broadcast the wrong position information. The ship could be hundreds of miles from the position they were winging they way to, and they would never find it.

The emergency broadcast might have been an error – a radioman on some civilian freighter might have inadvertently flipped the wrong switch. There might not be any emergency at all.

No doubt the bigwigs on the carrier had considered all that. Then, safe and comfortable, they had sent Jake and Flap to take a look. And to take the risks.

Finding the tanker would be critical. Jake eyed the fuel gauge without optimism. He would go high, to forty thousand feet, stay there until he could make an idle descent to the ship in distress, make a quick pass while Flap snapped photographs, then climb back to forty thousand headed toward the carrier. The tanker would be at 150 miles, on the Zero Nine Five radial, at forty grand. If it were not sweet, or this plane couldn't take fuel, they wouldn't be able to make it to the ship. They would have to eject.

At least it was daytime. Good weather. No night sweats. No need to do that needle-ball shit by flashlight. That was something.

Now Jake turned in his seat to look behind him at the sun. He looked at his watch. There should be at least a half hour of daylight left when they reached the SOS ship, but the sun would be down by the time they got to the tanker. Still, there would probably be some light left in the sky. Perhaps it would be better if the sky were completely dark, then they could spot the tanker's flashing anticollision light from a long distance away. But it would not be dark. A high twilight, that was the card the gods of fate had dealt.

One of these fine Navy days we're gonna use up all our luck. Then we two fools are gonna be sucking the big one. That's what everyone is trying to tell us.

'We won't descend unless you have a target on the radar,' Jake told Flap.

'Uh-huh.'

That was a good decision. No use squandering all that fuel descending to sea level unless there was a ship down there to look at. And if there was a ship, it would show on radar.

What if the ship had gone under and the crew was in lifeboats? Lifeboats wouldn't show on radar, not from a long distance.

'How far can you see a lifeboat on that thing?' he asked Flap, who had his head pressed against the scope hood.

'I dunno. Never looked for one.'

'Guess.'

'You were right the first time. We don't go down unless we see something.'

He leveled at forty thousand feet and retarded the throttles. Twenty-two hundred pounds per hour of fuel to each engine would give him .72 Mach. Only they had used four thousand pounds climbing up here. Seven thousand eight hundred pounds of fuel remaining. It's going to be tight. He retarded the throttles still farther, until he had only eighteen hundred pounds of fuel flowing to each engine. The airspeed indicator finally settled around 220 knots, which would work out to about 460 knots true.

Flap unfolded a chart and studied it. Finally he said, 'That position is in the channel between the islands off the southern coast of Sumatra.'

'At least it isn't on top of a mountain.'

'True.'

'Wonder if the brain trust aboard the boat plotted the position before they sent us on this goose chase.'

'I dunno. Those Navy guys . . . You never can tell.'

After much effort, Flap got the chart folded the way he wanted it. He wedged it between the panel and the Plexiglas so he could easily refer to it, then settled his head against the scope hood. After a bit he muttered, 'I see some islands.'

Land. Jake hadn't seen land in over a month, not since the ship exited the Malay Strait. *Columbia* was scheduled to spend three more weeks in the Indian Ocean, then head for Australia.

Rumors had been circulating for weeks. Yesterday they were confirmed. Australia, the Land Down Under, the Last Frontier, New California, where everyone spoke English – sort of – and everyone was your mate and they drank strong, cold beer and they liked Yanks . . . oooh boy! The crew was buzzing. *This* was what they joined the Navy for.

Those few old salts who claimed they had been to Australia before were surrounded by rapt audiences ready for just about any tale.

'The women,' the young sailors invariably demanded. 'Tell us about the women. Are they really fantastic? Can we really get dates?'

Tall, leggy, gorgeous, and they *like* American men, actually prefer them over the home-grown variety. And their morals, while not exactly loose, are very very *modern*. One story making the rounds had it that during a carrier's visit to Sydney several years ago the captain had to set up a telephone desk ashore to handle all the calls from Australian women wanting a date with an American sailor! Any sailor! *Send me a sailor!* These extraordinary females gave the term 'international relations' a whole new dimension.

That was the scuttlebutt, solemnly confirmed and embellished by Those Who Had Been There, once upon a time Before the Earth Cooled. The kids listening were on their first cruise, their first extended stay away from home and Mom and the girl next door. They fervently prayed that the scuttlebutt prove true.

The Marines in the A-6 outfit were as excited as the swab jockeys. They knew that, given a choice, every sane female on the planet would of course prefer a Marine to a Dixie cup. Australia would be liberty heaven. As someone said in the dirty-shirt wardroom last night, *Columbia* had a rendezvous with destiny.

All this flitted through Jake Grafton's mind as he flew eastward at forty thousand feet. He too wanted to be off the ship, to escape from the eat-sleep-fly cycle, to get a respite from the same old faces and the same old jokes. And Australia, big, exotic, peopled by a hardy race of warriors – Australia would be fun. He hummed a few bars of 'Waltzing Matilda,' then glanced guiltily at Flap. He hadn't heard.

Jake's mind returned to the business at hand. Hitting the tanker on the way back to the ship was the dicey part . . . Why did fate keep dealing him these crummy cards?

The fiercely bright sun shone down from a deep, rich, dark blue sky. At this altitude the horizon made a perfect line, oh so far away. It seemed as if you could see forever. The sea far below was visible in little irregular patches through the low layer of scattered cumulus, which seemed to float upon the water like white cotton balls . . . hundreds of miles of cotton balls. To the northeast were the mountains of Sumatra, quite plain now. Clouds hung around the rocky spine of the huge island, but here and there a deep green jungle-covered ridge could be glimpsed, far away and fuzzy. The late afternoon sun was causing those clouds to cast dark shadows. Soon it would shoot their tops with fire.

'There's something screwy about this,' Flap said.

'What do you mean?'

'Ships don't sink in fifteen seconds. Not unless they explode. How likely is that?'

'Probably a mistake. Radio operator hit the wrong switch or something. I'll bet he thought no one heard the SOS.'

'Wonder if the ship tried to call him back.'

'Probably.'

'Well, I say it's screwy.'

'You'd better hope we find that tanker on the way home. Worry about that if you want to worry about something.

331

Extended immersion in saltwater is bad for your complexion.'

'Think it might lighten me up?'

'Never can tell.'

'Life as a white man . . . I never even considered the possibility. Don't think it would work, though. You white guys have to go without ass for horribly long periods. I need it a lot more regular.'

'Might cure your jungle rot too.'

'You're always looking for the silver lining, Grafton. That's a personality defect. You oughta work on that.'

The minutes ticked by. The mountains seemed closer, but maybe he was just kidding himself. Perspective varies with altitude and speed. He had noticed this phenomenon years ago and never ceased to marvel at it. At just a few thousand feet you see every ravine, every hillock, every twist in the creeks. At the middle altitudes on a clear day you see half of a state. And from up here, well, from up here, at these speeds, you leap mountain ranges and vast deserts in minutes, see whole weather systems . . . In orbit the Earth would be a huge ball that occupied most of the sky. You would circle it in ninety minutes. Continents and oceans would cease to be extraordinarily large things and appear merely as features on the Earth. The concept of geographical location would cease to apply.

At this altitude he and Flap were halfway to heaven. On his kneeboard Jake jotted the phrase.

He was checking the fuel, again, when Flap said, 'We're a hundred twenty miles out. I can see the area.' The area where the ship in distress should be, he meant, if it were really there.

Odd day for an emergency at sea. Most ships got into trouble in bad weather, when heavy seas or low temperatures stressed their systems. On a day like this . . .

'I got something on the radar. A target.'

'The ship?'

'The INS says it's about four or five miles from the position Black Eagle gave us. Of course, the inertial could have drifted that much.'

'Big ship?'

'Well, it ain't a rowboat. Not at this distance. Can't tell much more than that about the size. A blip is a blip.'

'Course and speed?'

'She's DIW.' Dead in the water, drifting.

He would pull the power at eighty miles, descend with the engines at eighty percent RPM initially to ensure the generators stayed on the line.

'It's about fifteen miles from the coast of Sumatra, which runs northwest to southeast. Islands to seaward, west and southeast. Big islands.'

'Any other ships around?'

'No. Nothing.'

'On a coast like that . . .'

'Maybe we'll see some fishing boats or something when we get closer.'

'Yeah.'

'I'll tell Black Eagle.' Flap keyed the radio.

They arrived over the ship at seven thousand feet, the engines at idle. Peering down between cumulus clouds, Jake saw her clearly. She was a small freighter, with her super-structure amidships and cranes fore and aft. Rather like an old Liberty ship. No visible smoke, so she wasn't obviously on fire. No smoke from the funnel either, which was amidships, and no wake. There was a smaller ship, or rather a large boat, alongside, right against the starboard side.

Jake put the plane into a right circle so Flap could get pictures with the hand-held camera and picked a gap in the clouds to descend through. The engines were still at idle.

They dropped under the clouds at 5,500 feet. 'Shoot the whole roll of film,' Jake told Flap. 'From every angle. We'll circle and make one low pass down the rail so you can get a closeup shot of the ship and that boat alongside, then we're out of here.'

'Okay.' He focused and snapped.

'Looks like the crew has been rescued.'

'Swing wide at the stern so I can get a shot of her name.'

Jake was passing three thousand feet now, swinging a wide lazy circle around the ship, which seemed to be floating on an even keel. Wonder what her problem was?

'Can you read the name?'

'You're still too high. It'll be in the photos though.'

'Fuel? Sixty-two hundred pounds, over six hundred miles to *Columbia*. He shivered as he surveyed the drifting freighter and the small ship alongside. That small one looked to be maybe eighty or ninety feet long, a small superstructure just forward of amidships, one stack, splotchy paint, a few people visible on deck.

'There's people on the freighter's bridge.'

'About finished?'

'Yeah.'

'Here we go, down past them both.' Jake dumped the nose. He dropped quickly to about two hundred feet above the water and leveled, pointing his plane so that they would pass the two stationary vessels from bow to stern. Jake adjusted the throttles. If he went by too fast Flap's photos would end up blurred. He steadied at 250 knots.

'They aren't waving or anything.'

Jake Grafton saw the flashes on the bow of the small ship and knew instinctively what they were. He jammed the throttles forward to the stops, rolled forty degrees or so and pulled hard. He felt the thumps, glimpsed the fiery tracers streaming past the canopy, felt more thumps, then they were out of it.

'*Flak!*' Now Flap Le Beau found his voice.

'Fucker's got a twenty-millimeter!'

They were tail on to the ships, twisting and rolling and

climbing. The primary hydraulic pressure needles flickered. So did the secondary needles. The BACK-UP HYD light illuminated on the annunciator panel.

'Oh sweet fucking Jesus!'

Jake leveled the wings, trimmed carefully for a climb.

The plane began to roll right. The stick was sloppy. Jake used a touch of left rudder to bring it back.

Heading almost south. He jockeyed the rudder and stick, trying to swing the plane to a westerly heading. The plane threatened to fall off on the right wing.

It was all he could do to keep the wings level using the stick and rudder. Nose still a degree or so above the horizon, so they were still climbing, slowly, passing two-thousand feet, doing 350 knots.

'Get on the radio,' Jake told Flap. 'Talk to Black Eagle. Those guys must be pirates.'

He retarded the throttles experimentally, instinctively wanting to get down to about 250 knots so the emergency hydraulic pump would not have to work so hard to move the control surfaces. He trimmed a little more nose up. The nose rose a tad. Good.

'Black Eagle, Black Eagle, this is War Ace, over.'

They were in real trouble. The emergency hydraulic pump was designed to allow just enough control to exit a combat situation, just enough to allow the crew to get to a safe place to eject.

'Black Eagle, this is War Ace Five Oh Eight with a red hot emergency, over.'

And the emergency pump was carrying the full load. All four of the hydraulic pressure indicator needles pointed at the floor of the airplane, indicating no pressure at all in any of their systems.

'Black Eagle, War Ace Five Oh Eight in the blind. We cannot hear your answers. We have been shot up by pirates on this SOS contact. May have to eject shortly. We are exiting the area to the south.'

Just fucking terrific! Shot down by a bunch of fucking pirates! On the high fucking seas in *1973!* On a low, slow pass in an unarmed airplane. Of all the shitty luck!

'Squawk seventy-seven hundred,' Jake said.

Flap's hand descended to the IFF box on the consol between them and turned the mode switch to emergency. Just to be sure he dialed 7700 into the windows. Mayday.

'There's an island twenty miles ahead,' Flap said. 'Go for it. We'll jump there.'

The only problem was controlling the plane. It kept wanting to drop one wing or the other. Jake was using full rudder to keep it upright, first right, then left. The stick was almost useless.

He reached out and flipped the spin assist switch on. This would give him more rudder authority, if the loss of hydraulic pressure hadn't already made that switch. It must have. The spin assist didn't help.

When the left wing didn't want to come back with full right rudder, he added power on the left engine. Shoved the power lever forward to the stop. That brought it back, but the roll continued to the right. Full left rudder, left engine back, right engine up . . . and catch it wings level . . .

'Seventeen miles.'

'We aren't gonna make it.'

'Keep trying. I don't want to swim.'

'Those fuckers!'

Three thousand feet now. Now if he could just maintain that altitude when the wings rolled . . .

They were covering about four and a half nautical miles per minute. How many minutes until they got there? The math was too much and he gave up. And could see the island ahead. There it was, green and covered with foliage, right there in the middle of the windscreen.

'Fifteen miles.'

The roll was left. Full right rudder, left engine up. The

336

roll stopped but the nose came down. Full back stick didn't help. He ran the trim nose-up as he pulled the right engine to idle.

The nose was coming up. Yes, coming, so he started the trim nose-down. The wing was slowly rising, oh so slowly, rising . . .

They bottomed out at fifteen hundred but the plane began a very slow roll to the right, the nose still climbing.

He reversed the engines and rudder, played with the trim.

Slowly, agonizingly, the wings responded to the pilot's inputs. Now the nose fell to the horizon and kept going down.

Full nose-up trim! He held the button and glanced at the trim indicator on the bottom of the stick. Still nose-down! Come on!

They bottomed out this time at one thousand feet and the entire cycle began again.

'We won't make it the next time,' Jake told Flap.

'Let's jump at the top, when the wings and nose are level.'

'You first and I'll be right behind you.'

Nose coming down, right wing coming down, soaring up, up, to . . . to twenty-three hundred feet.

'Now,' Jake shouted.

An explosion and Flap was gone. Jake automatically centered the rudder as he pulled the alternate firing handle. Instantly a tremendous force hit him in the ass. The cockpit disappeared. The acceleration lasted for only an instant, then he began to fall.

CHAPTER TWENTY

The parachute opened with a shock. As Jake Grafton turned slowly in the shrouds the airplane caught his eye, diving toward the ocean like a wounded gull. The nose rose and it skimmed the sea, then began to climb. It soared skyward in a climbing turn, its right wing hanging low, then the wing fell and the nose went through and it dove straight into the sea. There was a large splash. When the spray cleared only a swirl of foam marked the spot.

The pirates! Where were they?

He got his oxygen mask off and tossed it away, then craned his head. He saw the other parachute, lower and intact with Flap swinging from it, but he couldn't see the pirate ship or its victim.

Oh, what a fool he'd been. To fly right over a drifting ship with another craft tied to it – and to never once think about the possibility of pirates! These waters were infamous . . . and the possibility never even crossed his mind. Son of a bitch!

The sea coming toward him brought him back to the business at hand. There was enough of a swell that the height was easy to judge – and he didn't have much time. He reached down and pulled the handle on the right side of his seat pan. It opened. The raft fell away and inflated when it reached the end of its lanyard. He felt around for the toggles to the CO_2 cartridges that would inflate his life vest. He found them and pulled. The vest puffed up reassuringly.

Good! Now to ditch this chute when I hit the water.

Amazingly, the thoughts shot through his mind without conscious effort. This was the result of training. Every time the ship left port the squadron held a safety training day, and part of that exercise involved each flight crewman hanging from a harness in the ready room while wearing full flight gear. Blindfolded, each man had to touch and identify every piece of gear he wore, then run through the proper procedure for ejections over land and sea. Consequently Jake didn't have to devote much thought to what he needed to do: the actions were almost automatic.

The wind seemed to be blowing from the west. He was unsure of directions. The way he wanted to go was toward that island – yes, that was south – and the wind was drifting him east. Somehow he also knew this without having to puzzle it out.

The raft touched the water. He felt for the Koch fittings near his collar bones that attached his parachute harness to the shroud lines and waited. Ready, here it comes, and . . . He went under. Closing his mouth and eyes automatically as the surge of cold seawater engulfed him, he toggled the fittings as he bobbed toward the surface. He broke water gasping for air.

The parachute was drifting away downwind. Now, where was that line attached to the raft?

He fumbled for it and finally realized it was wrapped around his legs or something. He began pulling toward the raft with his arms and finally grabbed the line. In seconds he had the raft in front of him.

All he had to do was get in.

The first time he slipped off the raft and went under on his back. Kicking and gasping, he managed to get upright and swing the raft so it was in front of him again.

This time he tried to force the raft under him. And almost made it before it squirted out and his head went under again.

The swells weren't helping. Just when he had the raft figured out, a swell broke over him and he swallowed saltwater.

Finally, after three or four tries, he got into the raft. He gingerly rolled so that he was on his back and lay there exhausted and gasping.

A minute or two passed before he realized he was still wearing his helmet. He removed it and looked for a lanyard to tie it to. He might need it again and everything not tied to him was going to be lost overboard sooner or later. He used a piece of parachute shroud line that he had tucked into his survival vest months ago.

Only then did he remember Flap and start sweeping the horizon for him.

The radio! He got out his survival radio, checked it, then turned it on. 'Flap, this is Jake.'

No answer.

Jake lay in his bobbing, corkscrewing raft looking at clouds and thinking about pirates and cursing himself. In a rather extraordinary display of sheer stupidity he had managed to get himself and Flap Le Beau shot out of the sky by a bunch of pirates. Yo ho ho and a bottle of rum. After the war was over! Not just any Tom, Dick or Harry can put an almost-new, squawk-free A-6E into the god-damn drink! Is that talent or what? The guys at the O Clubs were going to be shaking their heads over this one for a long long time.

Colonel Haldane was going to shit nails when he heard the happy news.

He looked at his watch. The damn thing was full of water. It had stopped. Perfect!

And his ass was six inches deep in water. Occasionally more water slopped in, but since the doughnut hole in which he sat was already full, the overflow merely drained out. Useless to try to bail it.

Luckily the water wasn't too cold. Sort of lukewarm.

340

The tropics. And to think real people pay real money to swim in water like this.

He tried to radio again. This time he got an answer. 'Yo, Jake. You in your raft?'

'Yep. And you?'

'Nope. It's like trying to fuck a greased pig.'

'You hurt?'

'No. You?'

'No.'

'Well, nice talking to you. Now I gotta get into this sonuvabitching raft.'

'Pull the damn thing under you. Don't try to climb into it. Pull it under you.'

'Call you back after a while.'

A cigarette. He could sure use a cigarette. He made sure the radio was firmly tied to his survival vest, then laid it in his lap. The cigarettes and lighter were in his left sleeve pocket. He got them out. The cigarettes were sodden. The lighter still worked though, after he blew repeatedly on the flint wheel and dried it off somewhat. It was one of those butane jobs. He extracted a wet cigarette, put it to his lips and lit the lighter. The cigarette refused to burn.

He put the cigarette back into the pack and stowed the pack away. If he ever managed to get ashore he could dry these things out and smoke them.

Wait! He had an unopened pack in his survival vest. Still wrapped in cellophane, an unopened pack would be water-tight.

He wanted a cigarette now more than anything else he could think of. He got the left chest pocket of the vest open and felt around inside, trying not to let the rest of the contents spill.

He found it. Thirty seconds later he had a cigarette lit and was exhaling smoke. Aaah!

Bobbing up and down, puffing away, he decided he was thirsty. He had two plastic baby bottles full of water in his survival vest. He got one out and opened it, intending to drink only a little. He drained it in two long gulps.

He almost tossed the empty away, but thought better of it and slipped it back into the vest pocket.

Something on top of a swell to his left caught his eye, then it was gone. He waited. Flap, sitting in his raft, visible for a second or two before the out-of-sync swells lowered Jake or Flap.

He checked the radio. He had turned it off. He turned it on again and immediately it squawked to life. 'Jake, Flap.'

'Hey, I saw you.'

'I've seen you twice. How far apart do you think we are?'

'A hundred yards?'

'At least. We've got to do some thinking, Jake. We're going to be out here all night. The ship won't be close enough to launch a chopper until dawn.'

Jake looked longingly at the island, the one he and Flap had been trying to reach when they ejected. He saw flashes of green occasionally, but it was miles away. And the wind was blowing at a ninety-degree angle to it.

'Let's try to paddle toward each other. If we could get together, tie our rafts together, we'd have a better chance.'

A better chance. The words sprang to his lips without conscious thought, and now that he had said them he considered their import. A night at sea in one of these pissy little rafts was risky at best. The sea could get a lot rougher, a raft could spring a leak, the pirates might come looking, sharks . . .

Sharks!

A wave of pure terror washed over him.

'Okay,' Flap said. 'You paddle my way and I'll paddle toward you. I don't think we can make it before dark but we can try. I'm going to turn my radio off now to save the battery.'

Jake inspected himself to see if he was injured, if he was bleeding. Adrenaline was like a local anesthetic; he had been far too pumped to feel small cuts and abrasions. If he were bleeding . . . well, sharks can smell blood in the water for miles and miles.

He felt his face and neck. Tender place on his neck. He held out his gloved right hand and stared at it: red stain. Blood!

For the love of God!

Must be a shroud burn or Plexiglas cut.

He got up on his knees in the raft. This was an inherently unstable position and he took great pains to ensure he didn't capsize. Crouching as low as he could, he began paddling with his hands, making great sweeping motions. Then he realized he didn't know where Flap was, so he forced himself to stop and look. There, just a glimpse, but enough. He turned the raft about sixty degrees and resumed paddling.

It was hard work. Every thread Jake wore was of course soaked, so even though the air was warm and humid, he stayed cool. Stroke for a while, pause to look for Flap, stroke some more, the cycle went on and on.

Finally he became aware that the sun was down and the light was fading. He got out his survival light, triggered the flash, and stuck it onto the Velcro that was glued to a spot on the right rear of his helmet. Then he put the helmet on. Three minutes later he saw that Flap had done the same thing. They were, at this point, maybe fifty yards apart.

Jake paused for a moment to rest.

What a mess! And if he had had a lick of sense, used an ounce of caution, they wouldn't be floating around out here in the middle of the ocean, at the ends of the earth.

He cussed awhile, then went back to work.

It was completely dark when they got the rafts together. Lengths of parachute shroud from their survival vests were quickly tied so the two rafts lay side by side. They arranged themselves so that Jake's feet were adjacent to Flap's head, and vice versa.

The two men lay inert in the rafts for minutes, resting. Then Flap said, 'This is a fine mess you got us into, Grafton. A very fine how-do-you-do.'

'I'm sorry.'

Flap was silent for several seconds. 'You really think this is your fault? I'm sorry I said that. It ain't. It's the fault of that asshole son of a bitch over there that smacked us with that twenty mike-mike. Talk about a cheap shot! I'd like to cut his nuts off and make him eat 'em.'

'Think Black Eagle heard any of our transmissions?'

'I don't know.'

'Boy, I hope so. I'd hate to think that that chicken-shit pirate cocksucker might get a free shot at somebody else tomorrow.'

'Turn off that flashing light on your helmet. Makes my eyes hurt.'

Jake did so. He took off the helmet. Then he got out his second baby bottle of drinking water and took a big slug. He held it out for Flap. 'Here.' Flap had to feel for it. The darkness was total. There were some stars visible, but the moon wouldn't be up for some hours yet.

'Shit. This is water.'

'What did you expect? Jack Daniel's?'

Flap drained the bottle and handed it back. Jake carefully screwed the top back on and stowed it.

'Want to try mine?'

Jake felt in the darkness. Another baby bottle. He sipped it. Brandy. The liquor burned all the way down. He passed it back. 'Thanks.'

'So what's for supper?'

'I got a candy bar in my vest someplace,' Jake told the Marine. 'Stuck it in here while we were in the Philippines, so it's only three months old.'

'I'll wait. I got one from Singapore. Maybe for breakfast, huh?'

'Yeah. You hurt any?'

'Scratched up in a couple places. Nothing bad.'

'I did a little bleeding from a cut on my neck. Maybe the sharks will come.'

Flap had nothing more to say, so Jake sat thinking about sharks. He hated the whole idea. An unseen terror that stalked and *ate* you – it was something from a horror movie, some poorly animated, low-budget monstrosity designed to make kids scream at the Saturday afternoon matinee.

But it was *real*.

Real sharks lived in these waters and they would come – of that he was absolutely certain.

Lying there in the darkness in this rubberized canvas raft with your butt in the water, shivering because the water kept wicking up your flight suit and evaporating, bobbing up and down, up and down, endlessly, up and down and up and down, your mind fixated upon sharks, on the giant predators with row upon row of huge, sharp teeth that even now were following the blood trail, coming closer, coming up from deep deep down towards this flimsy little raft that their teeth could slash through as if it were tissue paper, coming to rip and tear your flesh and *eat you!*

At some point he realized that he had his Colt automatic in his hand. He hadn't thumbed off the safety, thank God, but it was there in his hand and he couldn't remember pulling it from his shoulder holster.

He hefted it.

He had always liked the bulk of it, the thirty-nine ounces of smooth blued steel and oiled wood that promised deadly power if he ever needed it. Tiger Cole had given it to him. It held eight big .45 caliber slugs, any one of which would kill anything from a mouse to a moose. If he shot a shark with this thing, it was going to die quick.

The problem was that the sharks were under water and bullets don't go very far when fired into water. Certainly not these big slow lead slugs. It would be better if he had his .357, but life wasn't like that. If the shark would only stick his head out of the water and hold still . . .

His survival knife! It wasn't all that sharp and, to tell the truth, wasn't really much of a knife, but he could stick a shark with it. And probably get his hand ripped off.

He transferred the automatic to his left hand and got the knife from his survival vest.

The first thing the sharks would do was bump the raft. He would feel that, he hoped. They would bump it and rub it with their sandpaper hide and sniff the blood and finally use their teeth. If they punctured the raft he would go into the water. Then he was doomed. Sooner or later they would get a leg or foot and even if he killed the bastard that did it, the blood would draw more sharks that would finish the job, if he hadn't already bled to death.

He was living a nightmare. If only he could wake up.

He sat in the darkness listening to the slop of the water and waiting for the bump and shivering from the cold. Every sense was alert, straining.

How long he sat like that, half-frozen with fear, listening, he didn't know, but eventually the moon rose and a sliver of light came through a gap in the clouds. Flap saw him then.

'Hey, what's the knife and gun for?'

He was so hoarse that he had trouble with the word and had to clear his throat before he got it out. 'Sharks.'

'You stick that knife into your raft and you'll be swimming.'

Jake just sat shivering.

'Throw out some shark repellent. You got some in your vest, don't ya?'

'It don't work. Ain't worth shit.'

'Won't hurt. Throw it out.'

Now he had the problem of what to do with the gun and knife. 'Hold the gun, will ya?'

'Holster it. The knife too. Believe me, there'll be plenty of time if you need 'em.'

When he had tossed the shark repellent packets into the water, Jake felt better. It was crazy. The repellent – allegedly a mixture of noxious chemicals and ground-up shark gonads – was worthless: someone had done a study and said it had no noticeable effect on sharks and was a waste of government money to acquire. Even though Jake knew all that, throwing the repellent into the water still gave him a sense that he was doing *something*, so he felt better. Less terrorized and more able to cope.

The moonlight helped too. At least if he got a glimpse he could shoot or stab.

'Sorry I got you into this,' he told Flap.

'If this moonlight cruise causes me to miss Australia, Grafton, I'm going to kick your ass up between your shoulder blades. I've been sitting here thinking about Australia and those chocolate aborigine women who will think I'm Sidney fucking Poitier, and believe you me, this buck nigger is really really ready.'

'Those aborigine men may show you how to use a boomerang for a suppository if you mess with their women.'

Flap dismissed that possibility with an airy wave. He was shivering too, Jake noticed.

'Actually I ought to charge you a travel agent's fee,' Jake told the BN. 'You'll cadge free drinks on this tale for years. A silver moon, a tropical lagoon—'

'And you. I wouldn't pay ten cents Hong Kong money to go on a moonlight cruise with you. You got all the romance of a . . .'

They bantered back and forth for a while, then talked seriously about their situation. The US Navy would search until Jake and Flap were rescued or the heavies were convinced they were dead, no matter how long it took. Right this very moment the ships of the task group were

347

making their best speed eastward, eating up the sea miles, their screws thrashing the black water into long foamy ribbons that stretched back under that pale slice of moon to the horizon. At dawn the carrier would pause in her eastward charge only long enough to veer into the wind and launch her planes.

Just in case someone was up there right now, Flap got out his radio and made a few calls. There was no answer, which didn't upset them.

In the morning. The carrier's planes would come in the morning. And if that pirate was anywhere around when the sun came up, he was going to Davy Jones's locker faster than the *Arizona* went to the bottom of Pearl Harbor.

Eventually the conversation petered out and exhaustion caught up with them. Both men dozed as their tiny rafts rocked in the long swells.

Jake woke up to vomit. The equilibrium of the raft was too precarious to stick his head over the side, so he heaved down his chest. He slopped some water over himself to wash the worst of it away.

Seasick. Fuck it all to hell!

He heaved until his stomach was empty, then retched helplessly as his stomach convulsed.

Flap was philosophical. He wasn't sick. 'These things happen in the best of families, even to swab jockeys. It won't kill you. You're tough.'

'Shut up.'

'Wait until I tell the guys in the ready room about this. Sailor Grafton, puking his guts like a kid on the Staten Island ferry.'

'Could you please—'

'It'll get worse. You'll see. You'll think you're gonna die. You're really in for it now.'

The convulsions had subsided somewhat when Jake felt the first nudge, just an irregularity in the motion of the raft. He almost missed it.

His seasickness was forgotten. He was reaching for the automatic when Flap said, 'Uh-oh. I think a shark bumped me.'

Now he scanned the water. His eyes were well adjusted to the moonlight. He glimpsed a fin break water, for maybe two seconds. Then it was gone.

'Shark,' he told Flap. 'I saw one!'

'See what you caused! All that moaning about sharks and you attracted the sons of bitches.'

Another bump, more aggressive this time. Jake thought he could feel the grinding from the rough hide rubbing against the fabric of the raft. They didn't have to bite it – if they rubbed it enough they would rub a hole through it.

Fear coursed through him, fear as cold as ice water in his veins. Automatically he had drawn his feet into the raft and tucked his elbows in, which drove his butt deeper into the water. And there was nothing between his butt and those teeth but a very thin layer of rubberized canvas.

He tried to see downward, into the depths where the predators were. Not enough light. It was like looking into a pot of ink.

'See anything?'

'If I scream,' Flap said, 'you'll know they got me.'

'You asshole! You stupid perverted Marine asshole!'

'They're just curious.'

Another nudge. Jake thought he saw something pass out to his right that was darker than the surrounding blackness, but he wasn't sure.

'You hope,' Jake muttered. 'Maybe they're hungry too.'

A fin broke water fifty feet or so away, slightly to the right of the way Jake was facing. He thumbed off the pistol's safety, leveled it and couldn't see the sights clearly! He squeezed off the shot anyway. The muzzle flash temporarily blinded him.

The report was strangely flat. There was nothing to echo

or concentrate the noise. The recoil of the weapon in his hand felt reassuring though.

He blinked his eyes clear and looked at Flap. He had some kind of knife in his right hand and was watching the water intently. It wasn't a government-issue survival knife.

'What kind of knife is that?'

'Throwing knife. For stabbing.'

'What if you want to cut something?'

'Got another knife for that.'

'What are you, a walking cutlery shop?'

'Just look for sharks, will ya? Try not to shoot me or either of the rafts. If they get you I may need your boat.'

'Maybe they like dark meat. Can I have your stereo?'

'My roommate has first dibs.'

They sat staring intently at the water near them. Occasionally a shark nudged them, but the level of aggression didn't seem to increase.

Maybe they would get out of this with whole hides. Then again . . .

A fin broke water just ten feet to Jake's immediate right. He swung the pistol and squeezed the trigger in almost the same motion. The water seemed to explode.

Dimly he saw a tail slashing furiously and spray cascaded over them. The rafts rocked dangerously.

In seconds it was over. The shark sounded.

'Think that was the only one?' Flap asked, his voice betraying his tension for the first time.

'We'll see.'

For some reason the terror that had gripped Jake earlier was gone. He still had enough adrenaline coursing through his veins to fuel a marathon and his heart was thudding like a drum, but for the first time he felt ready to face whatever came.

Nothing came.

If there were any more sharks out there, they stayed away from the raft. After a while Flap tried his radio again.

This time he got an answer. One of the E-2 Hawkeyes from *Columbia* was up there somewhere far above, the crew warm, dry and comfortable.

Flap told them of the pirates, of being shot down, of flying south trying to keep the A-6 airborne on the backup hydraulic system and finally ejecting into the sea.

'We're all right. Both of us are in our rafts, uninjured, and the rafts are lashed together.'

Jake had his radio out by this time and heard a calm voice say, 'We'll get planes off at dawn to look for you. You guys check in after sunrise about every fifteen minutes, okay?'

'Roger that. Keep the coffee hot.'

Jake Grafton spoke up. 'Black Eagle, tell the Ops guys that they need to arm the planes. If anybody shoots at them, they need to defend themselves vigorously.'

'I'll pass that along. Wait one while I talk to the ship on the other radio.'

They sat in the darkness with their radios in their hands. Finally the radio came back to life. 'Five Zero Eight Alpha, just how sure are you that you were actually shot at? Is there any way the hydraulic failure could have been a coincidence?'

The question infuriated Grafton. 'I've been shot at before,' he roared into the radio. 'I've been shot at and missed and shot at and hit. You tell those stupid bastards on the ship that we were *shot down*.'

'Roger. You guys hang tough. Talk to you again fifteen minutes after sunrise.'

His anger kept Jake warm for about five minutes. Then he was just cold and tired. With every stitch they wore sopping wet, Jake and Flap huddled in their rafts and shivered. After a time their thirst got the better of them and Flap broke out his two baby bottles full of water. He passed one to Jake, who drank it quickly, afraid he might spill it.

The moon rose higher and gave more light, when it wasn't obscured by clouds.

Eventually, despite the conditions, exhaustion claimed them and they dozed. Jake's mind wandered feverishly. Faces from the past talked to him – Callie, his parents, Tiger Cole, Morgan McPherson – yet he couldn't understand what they were saying. Just when he thought he was getting the message, the faces faded and he was half-asleep in a bobbing raft, wet and cold and very miserable.

Occasionally they talked. Once Jake asked Flap, 'If that attack last month against the Russians had been real, do you think we would have made it?'

'I dunno.'

'Think we would have hit the cruiser?'

'Maybe.'

'They said it was eighty percent probable.'

'I say maybe. I don't do numbers.'

'I think we would be dead.'

'Maybe,' Flap said.

Time passed too slowly, every minute seemed like an hour. The temptation to call Black Eagle to see if he was still up there was very strong and hard to resist. Jake got his radio out twice. Each time he stowed it without turning it on. He might need all the juice in those batteries tomorrow. Wasting battery power now would be stupid.

The worsening sea state brought them fully and completely awake. The swells were bigger and the wind was stronger.

At the top of each swell the rafts pitched dangerously, forcing each man to hang on tightly to keep from being thrown out. They made sure they still had a lanyard attached to each raft.

They had been hanging on to their seats in their frail craft for an eternity when Flap said, 'You shouldn't have called the heavies stupid bastards.'

'I know.'

'Someone will ream you out when we get back.'

'Give me something to look forward to.'

Gradually they became aware that the sky was lightening up. Dawn. It was coming.

Incredibly, the wind strengthened and began to rip spindrift from the swells. Jake reeled in his helmet – it had fallen overboard at some point during the night – dumped out the water and put it on. He ran the clear visor down to keep the salt spray out of his eyes.

It worked. Incredibly, his head was also warmer. He should have been wearing this thing all night!

'Put on your helmet,' he shouted at Flap, who had his tucked under his thighs.

The clouds were just beginning to show pink when they saw the ship. It was almost bows on and coming this way. A little ship, one stack, coming with a bone in its teeth.

Jake pointed.

'Of all the fucking luck!' Flap Le Beau swore.

It was the pirate ship.

CHAPTER TWENTY-ONE

'They've seen us,' Flap shouted over the wind. 'They're coming this way.'

'Better ditch the guns and radios,' Jake told him. He drew the Colt .45 from its holster under his life jacket and survival vest and slipped it over the side. In a holster sewn inside a pocket of his survival vest he had a five-shot Smith & Wesson .38 with a two-inch barrel that he kept loaded with flares. He ditched that too.

The radio – he held on to the radio for a moment as he watched the bow wave of the oncoming small ship subside. They were stopping.

Son of a . . .

He used his survival knife to cut the parachute shroud line that tied him to the radio and lowered it to the water, then released it. Out of the corner of his eye he saw Flap slip his .45 over the side.

'The knife,' Flap told him. 'Dump it too. They'll just take them away from us.' Jake opened his hand and the knife made a tiny splash.

The small ship drifted to a stop on the windward side of the two rafts, about fifteen feet away. Her bulk created a sheltered lee. It was a nice display of seamanship, but Jake and Flap were in no mood to appreciate it.

Staring down from the rail were eight brown faces. Malays, from the look of them. They held assault rifles in their hands.

The sides of this little ship had once been blue, but now

the blue was heavily spotted with rust. Where some of the paint had peeled glimpses of gray were visible. Apparently she had once been a patrol boat. Forward of the bow was a gun mount, now empty. That was where they had had the twenty millimeter. It must be stowed below.

The men on deck lowered a net and made gestures with their rifles. Jake and Flap slowly paddled over. Flap went up the net first. Jake followed him. The ship was rocking heavily in the swells. The net was wet, hard to grasp firmly. His foot slipped on the wet cordage and he almost went into the sea. When he was clear of the raft the people on deck began shooting bursts of fully automatic fire. He looked down. Holes popped everywhere on the inflated portions of the rafts and spray flew.

By the time he pulled himself up enough to grasp the rail, the rafts were completely deflated and sinking.

Hands grabbed him and pulled. He scrambled on up the net. As he was coming over the rail, someone hit him in the helmet with a rifle butt and he sprawled onto the deck. Flap was already lying there on his back looking upward.

Most of the crew were barefoot. A couple of them looked like teenagers. Their clothes were ragged and dirty. There was nothing half-assed about their weapons however, worn AK-47s without a fleck of rust. Several of them had pistols stuck into their belts or the tops of their pants.

One of them gestured toward a ladder with the barrel of his weapon. Up. Jake glanced at Flap. His face was expressionless. Grafton prayed that he looked at least half that calm.

At the top of the ladder was the bridge.

The man working the helm and engine was a bit larger than medium height, apparently fit, and had a wicked scar on his chin. The ship was already gathering speed and heeling in a turn. The captain, if captain he was, glanced at them, then concentrated on putting the ship on the course he wanted. When he had the helm amidships and had

355

checked the compass, he said, 'Gentlemen, welcome aboard.'

Jake looked around. Two of the crew were behind them and the rifles were leveled at his and Flap's backs. He turned back to the captain.

'Take off all that . . .' He gestured toward their life jackets and survival vests. 'And the helmets. You look very silly in those helmets.'

Jake and Flap unsnapped their torso harnesses and let them fall into the puddle that was spreading away from each man. They got rid of the G-suits and helmets. Jake took off his empty shoulder holster and dropped it into the pile.

'Where's the pistol?'

Jake shrugged.

The captain took one step and slapped him, quickly and lightly. He stood with his hands on his hips in front of Jake, looking up at him. 'I think you will answer my questions. Where is the pistol?'

'In the ocean.'

The captain went back to the wheel and checked the compass. 'And your survival radios? Where are they?'

'Same place.'

'Where did you fly from?'

'USS *Columbia*.'

'Where is she?'

'West of here.' He toyed with the idea of lying for less than a heartbeat. 'Maybe two or three hundred miles now.'

'When will the planes come looking for you?'

'Shortly.'

'When?'

'I don't know. Sometime soon. After the sun comes up.'

'My men must learn to shoot better. Now we have this complication.'

'Must be a tough way to make a living.'

The captain continued as if he hadn't heard. 'The question is, do we need you alive? You disposed of your radios so you cannot talk to the airplanes on UHF. You could have warned them that you would die if they attacked us. Alas, we have only a marine band radio. It's a pity.'

'You speak English pretty well.'

The captain was scanning the ocean and glancing occasionally at the sky. He didn't bother looking at the two Americans. 'But I do not think they will attack. They will look us over and take many pictures. That is all.' His eyes flicked to their faces. 'What do you think?'

Unfortunately Jake thought he was right. He tried to keep his face deadpan but his turmoil probably showed. The captain apparently thought so. He said something to the guards and waved his hands. They prodded the aviators in the back and turned them around. As they left the bridge, Jake saw one of the crewmen opening the pockets of the survival vest and dumping the contents on the deck.

They were shoved into a tiny compartment below the main deck. There was a large hasp on the door.

'Can we have some water?' Jake asked the three men who pushed him inside right behind Flap. They ignored him.

The door swung shut and they heard the padlock snapping closed. The compartment was only slightly larger than a bedroom closet and had apparently been used for storage. There was no light and no electrical sockets, although there was one small, filthy porthole that admitted subdued light.

Flap leaned against the door and listened. After a bit he shrugged. 'They've gone, I think.'

'Maybe there's a bug.'

'Go ahead and look for it, James Bond.'

Jake sat against a wall and began taking off his boots. He took off his socks and wrung the water out, then put them back on. 'They'll probably shoot us after a while,' he said.

'Probably,' Flap agreed. He also sat. 'The captain ain't

sure if he'll need us or not. The bastard has it figured pretty good. I'll bet he can get this thing to port before the US Navy can get a surface ship here to board him. He thinks so too. But he's saving us just in case.'

'What do you think they did with the freighter?'

'Sank her would be my bet. They were probably off-loading high-value items when we showed up.'

'And the crew?'

Flap shrugged.

'Then why in hell did these guys shoot at us?'

'Perhaps someone panicked. Or they didn't want their picture taken. The airplane overhead was a problem they hadn't figured on.'

'So you think this is some kind of local industry?'

'Don't you?'

'I don't know.'

'Well, look at it. Here we are on the southern coast of Sumatra, about the most out-of-the-way corner of the earth it's possible to imagine. In among these islands we're well off the shipping lanes, which go through the Sunda Strait or the Strait of Malacca. So these dudes from a local village sail out into the shipping lanes, board a ship – probably at night when only one or two people are on watch on the bridge – then bring it here and loot it. They probably kill everyone aboard and scuttle the ship. The high-value items from the cargo that can't be traced eventually end up in the bazaars in Singapore or Rangoon or even Mombassa. The ship never shows up at its destination and no one knows what happened to it. Say they knock off one ship a year, or one every two years. Be a nice little racket if they don't pull it too often and get the insurance companies in a tizzy.'

'But someone got off fifteen seconds of an SOS and we came to look.'

'To look and take pictures. They probably thought they had killed everyone on that ship, then the SOS burned their eardrums. They should have disabled the radio but they didn't. One mistake led to another. So instead of waiting to loot the ship after dark, they decided to try it in daylight. Then we showed up. You know as well as I do that a good photo interpreter could identify this ship sooner or later. The captain knows that too. So he fired when we gave him a golden opportunity. I'll bet he was the bastard at the trigger.'

'He's going to get photographed again today.'

'But the victim isn't tied up alongside. Now this is just a little ship going about its business in a great big ocean.'

Jake merely grunted. After a bit he said, 'It doesn't figure.'

'What doesn't?'

'That ship they stopped is an old freighter. Looked to me like a Liberty ship. Eight to ten thousand tons, no more than that. Why didn't these guys stop a big container ship? All the valuable electronic stuff gets shipped in sealed containers these days.'

'Beats me.' Flap sat and removed his boots and socks. After a while he said, 'The bastards could at least have given us water. I'm really thirsty.'

He had his boots back on when he said, 'Did you notice the captain's hands? The calluses on the edges of his palms? He's a karate expert. If you had even flinched when he slapped you he might have broken your neck.'

'Now you tell me.'

'You did fine. Handled it well. Be submissive and don't give them the slightest reason to think you might fight back.'

'I'm certainly not going to strap on a karate expert.'

Flap snorted. 'They're the easiest to beat. They're too self-confident.'

Jake didn't think that comment worth a reply. He retrieved his cigarettes from his flight suit shoulder pocket and carefully removed each one from the pack, trying not to tear the wet paper. He laid them out to dry. Then he rolled onto his side and tried to stretch out. The compartment was too small. At least his ass wasn't submerged.

A bullet in the head or chest wasn't a cheery prospect. All these months of planning for the future and now it looked as if there would be no future. Strange how life works, how precarious it is. Right now he wanted water, food and a cigarette. If he got those, then he would want a hot bath and dry clothes. Then a bunk. The wants would keep multiplying, and sooner or later he would be staring at a bulkhead and fretting about insubstantial things, like what the next ready room movie was going to be, his brush with death shoved back into some dark corner in the attic of his mind.

He had faced death before in the air and on the ground, so he knew how it worked. If you survived you had to keep on living – that was a law, like gravity. If you died – well, that was that. Those left behind had to keep on living.

Maybe in the great scheme of things it really didn't matter very much whether these two blobs of living tissue called Jake Grafton and Flap Le Beau died here or someplace else, died today or next week or in thirty or fifty years. The world would keep on turning, life for everyone else would go on, human history would run exactly the same course either way.

It mattered to Jake, of course. He didn't want to die. Now or any other time. Presumably Flap felt the same way.

Fuck these pirates! Fuck these assholes! Murdering and stealing without a thought or care for anyone else. If they get theirs, life is good.

As he thought about the pirates Jake Grafton was swept by a cold fury that drove the lethargy from him.

He sat up and looked at Flap, who had also curled up on the deck. He wasn't asleep either. 'We gotta figure out a way to screw these guys good.'

Flap didn't smile. 'Any suggestions?'

'Well, if they shoot us, we sure as hell ought to take a

couple of them with us. I don't think they'll shoot us in here. Blood and bullet holes would be hard to explain if this ship were ever searched. I figure they'll take us topside, tie a chain around us and put us over the side. Maybe shoot us first.'

'And . . . ?'

'If we could kill a couple of the bastards we ought to give it a try.'

'Why?'

'Don't give me that shit!'

'What's a couple more or less?'

'You'd let them shoot you without a struggle?'

'Not if I have a choice. I'm going to take a lot of killing. But if they want us dead we're going to end up dead, sooner or later.'

'That's my point. When I go to meet the devil I want to go in a crowd.'

Flap chuckled. It was a chuckle without mirth. 'What I can't figure out, Grafton, is why the hell you joined the Navy instead of the Marines.'

'The Navy is more high-toned.'

They sat talking for most of an hour, trying to plan a course of action that would kill at least one and hopefully two pirates.

Flap could kill two men in two seconds with his bare hands, Jake assumed, so it seemed that the only real chance they had was for him to cause enough commotion to give Flap those two seconds. He didn't state this premise, however Flap let it go unchallenged. They hadn't a chance of surviving, not against assault weapons. But if their captors relaxed, if only for an instant . . .

When they finally ceased talking, both men were so tired they were almost instantly asleep, curled around each other on the deck because there was no room to stretch out and rocked by the motion of the ship.

About an hour later a jet going over woke them. The

thunder of the engines faded, then increased in volume. Then it faded completely and they were left with just the sounds of the ship. The plane did not come back.

The pirates came for Flap and Jake after the sun set. Both men stood when they heard the padlock rattle and assumed positions on opposite sides of the door. When the door opened two men were there with their weapons leveled, ready to fire.

One man motioned with the barrel of his rifle.

Jake went first, with Flap behind. They had discussed it and concluded a fight in the confined interior passageways was too risky. They shuffled along with their heads down, going willingly in the direction indicated.

When they came out on deck they saw land close aboard, just visible in the twilight. The shore was rocky, but the dark jungle began just inland from the rocks. Maybe three hundred yards. The water was flat, without swells. The ship was inside the mouth of a river headed upstream.

The two pirates wanted them to go aft. The deck here was probably only six feet wide. Flap was looking scared and had his hands up about head high. Two men stood on the dark fantail watching them come, their rifles cradled in their arms.

'Four,' Jake muttered. 'Jesus . . .'

They had just reached the fantail when they heard a jet running high. They looked up.

'Point,' Flap said, and Jake did, enthusiastically, as Flap shot a quick glance back over his shoulder.

What happened next happened so quickly Jake almost didn't react. Flap half-turned and his right arm swept down. The blade of a knife buried itself in the solar plexus of the gunman just behind him. This man staggered and looked down in stupefied amazement at the knife handle sticking out of his chest.

The man behind him had been looking up, trying to see

the jet. He dropped his gaze in time to see Flap Le Beau hurtling across the ten feet of space that separated them. He swung the rifle, but too late.

With one vicious, backhand swipe, Flap cut his throat from ear to ear. Blood spouted from severed arteries as the man collapsed. In a continuation of his motion, Flap spun and rammed the knife into the left kidney of the first man, who was somehow still on his feet and trying to turn to bring his rifle to bear.

Meanwhile Jake Grafton had launched himself at the two spectators standing with their rifles cradled in their arms. They too had been looking up, which gave him just the break he needed. He took them both down in a flying tackle.

He got his hands on one of the rifles and used it as a club. He smashed the butt into one man's Adam's apple.

The other man had retained his rifle and now it fired, the muzzle just inches from Jake's ear. Deafened, with the strength born of terror, Jake dropped the weapon in his hands and seized the barrel of the other man's AK-47 as he drove a punch at his face. The blow glanced off his forehead, but the man struggled to hold on to the rifle, so Jake let fly again. This time his fist connected solidly and the man went to the deck, still holding on to the rifle. Jake ripped it from his hands and slammed the butt down on his throat with all his strength.

With the rifle coming up, he turned in time to see Flap inserting his throwing knife back into the sheath that hung down his back, inside his flight suit. The fighting knife had a triangular blade about four inches long – it went into the sheath worn on his left forearm, under the sleeve of his flight suit.

Le Beau picked up an AK-47, glanced at the action, then fired one round into each of the four men lying on the deck. Then he flashed a grin at Jake. 'Still alive, by God!'

Jake grabbed the rifle on the deck at his feet and

removed the magazine. He stuck it into a chest pocket of his flight suit. 'I thought you ditched your knives.'

'I haven't been without a knife since I was thirteen.'

'Let's see if we can get to the bridge.'

'If it gets too hot we'll go over the side and swim for shore.'

'Okay.'

With his rifle at the ready, Flap went forward on the starboard side. Jake took the port.

The bridge stuck out over the deck. Someone appeared in the window and Jake snapped off a shot. The window shattered and the head disappeared. A miss.

An open hatch revealed a ladder that probably gave access to the engine room. Jake pulled the hatch shut and rotated the lever that dogged it shut. He looked around for something to block the lever so it couldn't be opened. Nothing.

He came to another open hatchway, a short passage-way across the superstructure to the starboard side of the ship.

He paused, trying to decide what to do. Sweat was running into his eyes. And he was thirsty as holy hell. What he wouldn't give for one drink of water!

Flap's head popped around the corner on the starboard side. He saw Jake and came his way. 'What did ya shoot at?'

'Someone on the bridge.'

'There's at least five more guys on this tub, probably more.'

'How come they aren't coming after us?'

'We're probably pretty near their base. When they pull in, someone on the pier will take care of us.'

'We gotta get off this bucket.'

'They'll gun us in the water.'

Jake wiped the sweat from his eyes and tried to think. 'Somebody is probably in the engine room,' he said. 'The ladder down is here on the port side. What say you go up to the bridge and keep them occupied. I'll go to the engine room and try to disable this tub. Then we go over the side.'

'Which way?'

'Port side. In five minutes.'

'My watch isn't working.'

'*About* five minutes. Or if the engines stop.'

'Okay.'

Jake checked to make sure no one was in sight, then he moved back to the engine room hatch, opened it and latched it open. The ladder down was actually a steep stair.

Uh-oh. He wished he hadn't volunteered to do this.

What the hell! They were dead this morning when this pirate ship came over the horizon.

With the rifle at the ready and the safety off, he eased down the ladder, waiting for the inevitable bullet.

This is like committing suicide slowly.

The area at the bottom of the ladder was shielded by a large condenser. Jake paused behind it, wiped the sweat from his hands and gripped the rifle carefully. He eased his head out, so that he could look with one eye. He was looking aft along a narrow passageway between the ship's two diesel engines. He saw a leg, the back of a leg. He pulled his head back and turned so he could see forward. Ease the head out and peek. No one.

Okay. Someone aft, no one visible forward. He would step out, shoot the guy aft, then swing so he could shoot forward.

That was a good plan.

He was going to get shot. Sure as shit.

He took a deep breath, and exhaled slowly. His heart was pounding a mile a minute.

Now!

He leaped out and squeezed the trigger.

The man was using a pipe wrench on a valve. The bullets slammed him down. Jake spun. A man coming through the door shooting as Jake's bullets caught him, hammered him.

Something slammed into Jake's side, turning him half around.

He staggered, leaned back against the starboard engine and looked aft.

The man there wasn't moving. The man forward had taken at least three in the chest.

Jake dug the extra magazine out of his chest pocket and substituted it for the magazine in his weapon. His left side was numb. Shock. He staggered aft. The magazine of the AK-47 on the floor looked like it still held ten shells or so. He pocketed it.

Now he heard a racket from topside that he knew were shots. Flap. He peered through the open hatch that led forward.

Fuel valves. This guy had been opening or closing these valves. The main tank must be on the other side of this bulkhead.

Which ones were the feed lines? He picked two that looked like they went up over the engines to the fuel injectors. Holding the rifle in his left hand, he began screwing the starboard engine valve shut. Then he closed the one to the port engine.

The engines would take a minute or so to die. If he had picked the right valves.

Unwilling to wait, he spied a large red valve at the bottom of the bulkhead with a pipe that wasn't connected to anything. The valve had a rusty padlock on it. Must be the tank drain valve. He put one bullet into the lock. The lock broke, and diesel fuel began running out of the bullet hole.

Jake twisted the valve. It was rusty.

Desperate to be out of here, he laid down the rifle and used both hands. It opened. Fuel began running out, at first a trickle, then a steady stream. He kept twisting.

The steady throb of the diesels took on a new note. Several cylinders missed. The starboard engine died. By the time the port engine stopped he had the drain valve full open. He was getting splashed with diesel fuel.

The lights died to a dim glow when the port engine quit. With the generators off, the lights were using battery juice.

He grabbed the rifle and started aft through the engine room for the ladder. He heard more shots, quite clearly now that the engines were silent.

His left side was pretty bloody and the pain was fierce.

Well, if he was going to fuck these guys, he should do the job right. He went back to the second man he shot and ripped his shirt off. It was cotton. He went back to the drain valve and let some diesel fuel run onto the shirt. He squeezed the shirt to get rid of the excess and dug his lighter out of his pocket.

The plastic butane piece of shit refused to light. He blew several times on the flint wheel. Come on, goddamnit!

There. He held the flame under a corner of the shirt. It took. He waited until the shirt was going pretty well, then dropped it into the gap between the catwalk and one engine. The diesel fuel was running into the bilges there.

The fire lit with a whoof.

Jake eased his head around the corner of the ladder, and jerked it back just in time. Bullets spanged into the condenser.

The fire was spreading in the bilges. Already the smoke was dense, the lights barely visible.

This couldn't be the only ladder topside. The other ladder must be on the starboard side. Trying not to breathe the smoke, he hurried that way.

Coughing and gagging, he found the ladder.

Was there someone up here waiting for him?

'Come on, Jake.' Flap's voice.

He was having trouble breathing and his feet were getting damned hot. Somehow he lost the rifle. He scrambled up the ladder on all fours, slipped and slammed his head against a step and slid a couple steps before he caught himself.

Hands grabbed him and pulled. He kept scrambling and somehow they made the deck.

'I've been shot.'

'Let's get over the side or you'll get shot again. There's at least four of them forward.'

'Where?'

'We go off the fantail. Ship's sideways in the river.'

They went that way, Jake barely able to walk. He took deep breaths, trying to get enough oxygen. Spots swam before his eyes. 'They'll shoot us in the water.'

'It's our only chance. Come on.'

Flap tossed his AK-47 into the water, then jumped after it. Jake followed.

The darkness was almost total now. Jake was only able to swim with his right arm. His left side felt like it was on fire. Several times he got mouthfuls of water, so he swallowed them. It tasted good.

He was struggling. More water in his mouth and nose. He gagged.

'Just float. I've got you.' And Flap did have him, by the collar of his flight suit.

Jake concentrated on staying afloat and breathing against the pain in his side.

Flap was pulling him backward, so he could see the fore-shortened outline of the ship, and smoke black as coal oozing out amidships. He could also see the glow of fire coming from a ladder well, apparently the one on the port side, since he could now see the top of the bow. All this registered without his thinking about it, which was good, since he needed desperately to concentrate on breathing and keeping his head above water.

They were maybe fifty yards from the ship when he saw muzzle flashes from the bow.

368

'They're shooting,' he tried to say, but he swallowed more water.

'Relax,' Flap whispered. 'Quit trying to help. Let me do this.'

Somehow they must have swum out of the main channel, Jake realized, because the ship was pulling away from them. The current must be taking her downstream.

The current and the darkness saved them. When the twenty-millimeter cannon on the bow opened up, the bullets hit downstream, abeam the ship. Bursts split the night for almost a minute, but none of the shells even came close.

CHAPTER TWENTY-TWO

'I never saw a knife like that before.'

'Designed it myself,' Flap said. 'Call it a slasher.'

Of course Jake couldn't see the knife now, since they were sitting in absolute total darkness under a tree in the jungle, but Flap had borrowed his lighter and gone looking for tree moss. Now he was back and was cutting up his and Jake's T-shirts to use as a bandage. He had inspected the wound in the glow of the lighter when they first got ashore. 'It's nasty but not deep. You are one lucky white boy. I think maybe one rib broke, and it ain't too bad.'

'Feels like one of your knives is stuck in there.'

Jake sat now holding the moss in place while Flap cut up the shirts. The moss was slowing the bleeding, apparently. He heard a motorboat coming down the river. They sat silently while it passed. When the sound had faded, Jake asked, 'So what are we going to do?'

'Not much we can do tonight. There's an overcast so there wouldn't be much light when the moon comes up. The jungle canopy will keep it dark down here. We're going to have to just sit tight until morning.'

'Think they'll come looking for us tonight?'

'In the morning maybe. Maybe not. I hope they come. We need some weapons. All we have are my knives. Be easier to ambush them here than around their village, wherever that is.'

'The stabber and the slasher.'

'Yep.'

'Where did you learn to throw a knife like that?'

'Taught myself,' Flap told him. 'It's a skill that comes in handy occasionally.'

Jake moved experimentally. He tried to stretch out and relax to ease the pain. After a bit he said, 'I don't think their village is far upriver. It was narrowing when we left that ship.'

'We'll work our way upriver in the morning. We need a boat to get out to sea.'

'Tell you what, Tarzan, is there any way you could rustle us up some grub? My stomach thinks my throat is cut.'

'Tomorrow. You like snake?'

'No.'

'Tastes like—'

'Chicken. I've heard that crap before. I ate my share at survival school.'

'Naw. Tastes like lizard.'

'I don't like them either.'

'Sit up and hold up your arms and let me wrap this thing around you.'

Jake obeyed. When Flap finished he eased his arms back into his flight suit and zipped it up. 'What about bugs?'

'They're okay as an appetizer, but you expend about as many calories gathering them as—'

'How are we gonna keep 'em from bleeding us dry tonight?'

'Smear your skin with mud.'

Jake was already encased in mud almost to his waist from wading through the goo to get ashore. He scraped some from his legs and ankles and applied it to his face and neck.

After a bit, Flap asked, 'How many guys were in the engine room?'

'Two. What happened topside?'

'They pinned me down. I needed a couple grenades and didn't have them. Got one of them, though.'

371

'We're lucky to be alive.'

'Grafton, you are the luckiest SOB I know. If that bullet had been an inch farther right you'd be lying dead in that engine room. It's scary – we're using up oodles of luck and we're still young men. We're gonna be high and dry and clean out of the good stuff before we're very much older.'

They lay down on the jungle floor and tried to relax. Lying in the darkness in the muck, swatting at mosquitoes as the creepy-crawlies examined them – Kee-rist! Well, at least they weren't sitting in seawater to their waist or huddled in a steel compartment waiting for an executioner to come for them.

After a while Jake said, 'Are you ever going to get married?'

'You read my mind. I was lying here hungry and thirsty and miserable as hell contemplating that very subject. And you?'

'Smart ass!'

'No, seriously – why don't you tell the Great Le Beau all about it. After all, before a man commits holy matrimony he should have the benefit of unbiased, expert counsel. Even if he plans on ignoring the pithy wisdom he will undoubtedly receive, as you most certainly will.'

'I *might* get married. If she'll say yes.'

'Ahh – you haven't queried your intended victim. Or you have and she refused in a rare fit of eminent good sense. Which is it?'

'Haven't asked.'

'Uh-huh.'

'Met her last year in Hong Kong.'

'I met a girl in Hong Kong once upon a time,' Flap replied. 'Her name was . . . damn! It was right on the tip of my tongue. Anyway, she worked at the Susy Wong whorehouse, a couple of blocks from the China Fleet Club. You know it? She was maybe sixteen and had long black hair that hung almost to her waist and exquisite little breasts that—'

'I met an American girl.'

'Umph.'

'I knew you'd be interested, seeing how we fly together and all, so I'll tell you. Since you aren't sleepy and we got nothing else to do.' And he did. He told about meeting Callie, what she looked like, sounded like, how he felt when he was with her. He told Flap about her parents and about Chicago, about getting out of the Navy and what she said. He had been talking for at least half an hour when he finally realized that Le Beau was asleep.

His side throbbed badly. He changed positions in the detritus of the jungle floor, trying to find one that would cause the least stress on his wound. The sharpness of the pain drove his mind back to the pirate ship, to the prospect of death in a few moments by execution.

Flap threw that knife into that one guy and sliced the other's throat in what – three seconds? Jake had never seen a man move so fast, nor had he ever seen a man butchered with a knife. Shot, yes. But not slashed to death with one swipe of the arm, his throat ripped from ear to ear, blood spurting as horror seared the victim's face.

Life is so fragile, so tenuous.

Luckily he had gotten into motion before the surprise wore off the other two.

And the engine room, the horror as that man came around the engine shooting and the bullet struck him. Now the scene ran through his mind over and over, every emotion pungent and powerful, again and again and again.

Finally he let it go.

He felt like he had that sticker of Flap's stuck in his side right now.

So those other guys died and he and Flap lived. For a few more hours.

It was crazy. Those men, he and Flap – they were like

fish in the sea, eating other fish to sustain life before they too were eaten in their turn. Kill, kill, kill.

Man's plight is a terribly bad joke.

He was dozing when the sound of a motorboat going upriver brought him fully awake. Flap woke up too. They lay listening until the noise dissipated completely.

'Wonder what happened to the pirate ship?'

'Maybe it sank.'

'Maybe.'

After the sun came up the foliage was so thick that Jake had to keep his hand on Flap's shoulder so that he wouldn't lose him. Flap moved slowly, confidently and almost without noise. Without him Jake would have been hopelessly lost in five minutes.

Flap caught a snake an hour or so after dawn and they skinned it and ate it raw. They drank water trapped in fallen leaves if there weren't too many insects in it. Once they came to a tiny stream and both men lay on their stomachs and drank their fill.

Other than the noises they made, the jungle was silent. If anyone was looking for them, they were being remarkably quiet.

Jake and Flap heard the noises of small engines and voices for a half hour before they reached the village, which as luck would have it, turned out to be on their side of the river. It was about noon as near as they could tell when they hit the village about a hundred yards inland. Thatched huts and kids, a few rusty jeep-type vehicles. They could smell food cooking. The aroma made Jake's stomach growl. A dog barked somewhere.

They stayed well back and worked their way slowly down to the riverbank to see what boats there might be.

There were several. Two or three boats with outboard engines and one elderly cabin cruiser lay moored to a short pier just a couple of dozen yards from where Jake and Flap crouched in the jungle. Beyond the boats was a much larger pier that jutted almost to midstream. Resting against the T-shaped end of it was the hijacked ship. Above the ship numerous ropes made a latticework from bank to bank. Leafy branches of trees dangled from the ropes – camouflage. The freighter seemed to be held in place against the current mainly by taut hawsers from the bow and stern that stretched across the dark water to the river's edge, where they were wrapped numerous times around large trees.

From where they lay they could just see the ship's name and home port: *Che Guevara, Habana.*

Flap began to laugh.

'What's so funny?' Jake whispered.

'A Cuban freighter. We got shot down and almost killed over a Commie freighter. If that doesn't take the cake!'

'My heart bleeds for Fidel.'

'Ain't it a shame.'

The ship's cranes were in motion and at least a dozen men were visible. A large crate was lowered to the pier and six or eight men with axes began chopping it open. Apparently they didn't have a forklift.

Inside the box were other, smaller boxes. Pairs of men hoisted these and carried them off the pier toward the village.

'Weapons,' Flap said. 'They hijacked a ship full of weapons.'

'What do you think was in those little boxes just now?'

'Machine guns, I think. Look, aren't those ammo boxes?'

'Could be.'

'They are. I've seen boxes like that before. One time up on the Cambodian border.'

'Maybe this ship wasn't hijacked. Maybe those guys met it in midocean to put aboard a pilot.'

'Then why the SOS?'

Jake shrugged, or tried to. The pain in his side was down

to a dull throb, as long as he held his shoulder still and didn't take any deep breaths.

'These dudes are ripping off a Commie weapons shipment,' Flap said slowly. 'Maybe one bound for Haiphong. Guns and ammo are worth their weight in gold.'

'That little cabin cruiser is our ticket out of here, if it isn't a trap.'

'Maybe,' Flap said shortly. 'We can't do anything until tonight anyhow, so let's make ourselves comfortable and see what we can see. I don't see any floodlights anywhere; these people won't be working at night. But that little boat is just too good to be true. The captain we met yesterday didn't impress me as the type of careless soul who would leave a boat where we could swipe it at our convenience.'

After a few minutes Jake muttered, 'I haven't seen the captain yet on the dock.'

'He's around someplace. You can bet your ass on that.'

'That ship we set fire to isn't here either.'

'Maybe they abandoned it. But remember that boat that went down the river last night, then came back hours later? It was probably that cruiser there, and it probably rescued everyone left alive. The captain is here. I can feel him.'

'Okay.'

'See that shack just up there on the left? From there a fellow would have a good view of the boat and the dock. Keep your eyes on that. I'm going to slip around and see what they're doing with all these weapons they're taking off that ship.'

'Leave me one of your knives.'

'Which one?'

'The sticker.'

Flap drew it from the sheath hanging down his back and handed it to Jake butt-first. Then he took two steps and disappeared into the jungle.

A throwing knife with a needle-sharp point and a slick

376

handle, the weapon was perhaps ten inches long. Jake slipped it into his boot top, leaving just enough of the hilt exposed so that he could get it out quickly. He hadn't the foggiest idea how to throw it, but he had no qualms about jabbing it into somebody to defend himself. His throbbing side was a constant reminder that these people wanted him dead.

Lying under a tangle of vegetation, he rolled on his good side and gingerly unzipped his flight suit. The bandage was encrusted with old blood. Nothing fresh. He zipped the flight suit back up and rolled on his belly. He wormed his way forward until he could just see the shack and the pier beyond, then checked to ensure that he was completely hidden. He decided he was.

At least two hours had passed when Flap returned. It was hard to judge. Time passed slowly when you were lying in a jungle with bugs crawling around and flying critters gnawing at your hide. If you were short of sleep, so hungry that your stomach seemed knotted, suffering from a raging thirst and had diarrhea, every minute was agony. Jake dared not leave his post, so he shit where he lay.

Once he heard a jet. It was far away, the sound of its engines just a low hum.

'Jesus H. Christ!' Flap whispered when he crawled up beside Jake, startling him half out of his skin. 'What died?'

'That's shit, you bastard. Never smelled it before, huh?'

'For crying out loud, you could at least have dropped your flight suit.'

'There's someone over there in that shack. He stuck his head out twice and looked around. Seen smoke a couple times too, just a whiff, like he's standing right inside the door smoking a cigarette.'

'There's two of them in there. I looked in the back window.'

Jake had kept his eyes glued on that shack and hadn't once glimpsed Flap. For the first time he realized just how terrifically good Le Beau was in the jungle.

'Here, this is for you.'

Flap passed over an AK-47. 'It's loaded with a full clip. Safety is on.'

'Found this lying around, did you?'

'Relax. They won't find the guy who had it for quite a while. Maybe never. Gimme my sticker back. I feel kinda naked without it.'

Jake got the knife from his boot and handed it over.

'Lotta good that would have done you in your boot. You should have stabbed it into the dirt right by your hand, so you could grab it quick.'

'Next time. Until then I'll just stick to ol' Betsy here. Appreciate the gift. So what's the setup?'

The bad guys were stacking the weapons back in the jungle, out of sight from the air. Most of the stuff was still in crates. 'They got a hell of a pile out there but I don't think they got it all. Certainly not a shipload. There's no way of telling what's left on the ship.'

'I've been figuring,' Jake said. 'Seems to me that the first thing we have to do after dark is take out those two guys in the shack and check out that cabin cruiser.'

'It may be booby trapped.'

'I don't think so. That was the boat we heard last night. The guys in the shack are supposed to kill us if we try for it.'

'Can't start the engine here.'

'I know. We'll have to cast off and drift downriver. We can use one of your knives to cut us some poles to keep it off the banks. Then when we're a couple miles downriver, we'll start the engine and motor out to sea.'

'What if the engine won't start?'

'We just drift on out.'

'They'll follow.'

'Not if we blow up the ammo dump and sink all these little boats.'

Flap gave a soft whistle of amazement. 'You don't want much, do you?'

'So what's your plan?' Jake asked.

'Kill the guys in the shack and steal the boat. The Navy can come back any old time and bomb these dudes to hell.'

Jake snorted. 'Your faith in the system is truly amazing. Here we are in a foreign country – Indonesia, I think. Whatever. Assuming we manage to get rescued and tell our tale, the only thing the US Navy can do is send a polite note to the State Department. State is going to pass this hot tip to the National Security Council, which will probably staff the shit out of it. The fact that these weapons are going to be sold to revolutionary zealots in Asia, the Mideast or Africa who will use them to cause as much hell as humanly possible and murder everyone who disagrees with them won't cause one of those comfortable bureaucrats to miss a minute's sleep. When the nincompoops who brought you Vietnam get through scratching their butts, they'll give the US ambassador to Indonesia a note to give to whoever is running this country this week. That whoever may or may not do anything. After all, he's probably getting a cut of this operation. There's a whale of a lot of money to be made here: your karate expert captain friend is probably smart enough to spread it around a little.'

'A lot of the weapons are still on Fidel's freighter,' Flap pointed out.

'We'll have to blow it up too.'

'Just out of curiosity, what little army is going to do all this blowing up you envision?'

'You and me.'

Le Beau rolled over on his back and threw an arm across his face. In a moment he said, 'You got gall, Grafton, I'll give you that. You lay there with a bullet hole in your side, wearing your own shit and tell me that 'you and me' are

379

going to blow up a weapons cache and a ship! My ass. They'll smell you fifty feet away. *You* want *me* to go do the hero bit and probably get myself killed.'

'We'll both go. But this is a volunteer deal. You're senior to me and we aren't in the airplane anymore. It's your call.'

'Thank you from the bottom of my teensy little heart. Ah me . . . My second command – I used to lead a whole platoon, you know. Now it's just me and one wounded flyboy with the shits. My military career is going up like a rocket.'

'Oh, cork it. What do you want to do?'

'You think you're up for this?'

'Yeah.'

'Well, you asked for it. Here's the plan.'

As Jake Grafton listened the thought occurred to him that Flap Le Beau had been thinking about screwing these pirates all afternoon. He got a warm feeling. Flap had let him suggest it. Flap Le Beau was one hell of a good guy.

'Not right after dark,' Flap said. 'They'll expect us then. After midnight, in the wee hours.'

'The moon will be up sometime after midnight,' Jake pointed out. 'The clouds will probably obscure it though.'

'It would be good if the clouds let the moonlight through. They'll relax and maybe sleep.'

They pulled back into the jungle to a small stream. Jake undressed and sat in it. The diarrhea was drying up, a little anyway, leaving him very thirsty. He drank and drank from the stream. Then he washed out his flight suit and underwear and put them back on.

Finally he and Flap stretched out in the damp, rotting leaves. The bugs were bad, but they were very tired and the muffled noise from the village and the pier lulled them to sleep. They were both emotionally wrung out from their experiences of the last two days and nights, so their sleep was dreamless. When they awoke the light was fading rapidly and the noise from the ship had ceased. They drank again from the stream, Jake relieved himself, then they crawled back to the vantage point where they could see the shack and the small boats.

The waiting was hard.

When you have finally crossed the threshold, left behind good meals, a comfortable bed, clean clothes and the relaxed company of friends, life becomes a mere battle for survival. The nonessential sinks out of sight.

They lay in the foliage, one man on his stomach watching, the other on his side or back napping. Fortunately there was a small electric light mounted on a pole near the boat dock.

The hours dragged. With nothing to look forward to but battle, and perhaps death, delay was painful. Yet they waited.

The guards in the shack were changed several hours into the night. Two new men came, the two inside left. All of them carried rifles.

No one approached the boats. Even when the rain came. At first it was gentle, then it increased in intensity. Still no one came to cover the boats or check their moorings.

All activity on the dark freighter ceased. From their vantage point the watchers caught occasional glimpses of cigarettes flaring, but the ship was just a blacker spot in the black night.

Finally activity in the village ceased.

The rain continued to fall.

Jake slept again.

When Flap shook him awake, the rain had slowed to a drizzle.

'Look,' he whispered so softly that at first Jake didn't understand. He had to inch around to see what Flap was pointing at. After several seconds he realized he was looking at the two men standing by the boat dock smoking. They were away from the light, but there they were, quite plain.

'They came out of the shack. I'm going now.'

'Okay.' Jake fumbled with the AK-47, made sure the action was clear of leaves, then eased it through the foliage in front of him and spread his feet. Only then did he realize Flap had disappeared.

Minutes passed as he watched the figures by the boat dock. He could hear the murmur of voices. They stood smoking and talking.

Jake waited. If Flap were discovered now, they had no choice but to try for the cabin cruiser.

Finally the men turned and ambled uphill for the shack. One of them paused while the other went on ahead. He was facing in this direction. Only when he turned toward the shack did Jake realize that he was zipping up his pants. He had relieved himself.

The first man was already inside. The second man paused in the doorway. Flap was inside. Jake stopped breathing and blinked rapidly, trying to see in the almost nonexistent light. If the man shouted or fired his weapon . . .

Then he turned for the door and merged with another shadow coming out. Now he disappeared within.

In less than a minute Flap Le Beau came across the open ground toward Jake's position. He was walking calmly, with a rifle in each hand. When he approached Jake's position he said softly, 'Come on. Let's look at the boat.'

Jake wormed his way straight ahead out of the brush, then struggled to his feet. Flap was already at the boat dock. Jake followed along, trying to look as nonchalant as the two guards had.

Flap got into the cabin cruiser. 'The battery works,' he reported.

'Any fuel?'

'There's a can here. Let me see.' A half minute passed. 'Well, it's gasoline. A couple of gallons. I'm going to pour it into the tank.'

382

This cabin cruiser – what if it were sabotaged? Maybe they should take one of the little boats. Jake looked in them for oars. Each of them had a set. They had outboard engines too, but the presence of oars seemed to indicate that the owners of the boats weren't brimming with confidence over the reliability of those engines. Or maybe they were just careful.

It was going to be a big gamble.

Jake turned his back on the cabin cruiser and stood looking at the village. A faint glow from three or four lights showed through the foliage.

Flap joined him on the dock. 'Decision time, shipmate. We can untie this scow and get out of here right now with a chance and maybe a future. They won't know this tub's gone until morning.'

'You're senior,' Jake told him. 'You make the decision and you live with it.'

'I'm giving you a choice.'

'This is ridiculous.' They couldn't stand here in plain sight arguing like two New York bankers waiting for a taxi. 'Lead the way, Le Beau. I'll be right behind you.'

Flap took one of the AKs and lowered it into the water, then released it. With the other rifle in his left hand, he turned and walked off the dock. Jake followed him.

They circled the village through the jungle. The weapons cache was on the side away from the sea, a hundred yards from the long pier. At least two guards were on duty.

Flap picked a vantage point and watched for a while with Jake beside him. The guards walked the perimeter alertly. After the second one passed, Flap told Jake, 'They're too alert. They know something's up.'

'Maybe they missed that guy you killed this afternoon.'

'Maybe.'

'What if there's someone inside the pile?'

'There is. Believe it.'

'Let's go around to the other side and get a look before we go in.'

Flap led the way with Jake behind him. Jake concentrated on following Flap, afraid that he might lose him, and let Flap worry about avoiding the opposition.

Flap halted on a little hill halfway between the ship and the cache. The village was directly opposite them. To get to the boat landing, however, they would have to either pass the village or retrace the route they had just traveled, circling both the weapons cache and the village.

'Has to be here,' Flap said. 'It's shitty, I know. But we'll need a side shot at the ship. From the boat landing we're looking at the stern.' After a bit he asked, 'Think you can get here on your own if you have to?'

'Yeah. Unless they turn off that streetlight across the way.'

'They won't. Let's go.'

They went back toward the cache and settled in fifty feet away, hidden in waist-high foliage. Flap waited until a guard went by and turned the corner, then he flitted across the gap like a shadow and disappeared into an aisle between stacks of boxes. He left his rifle with Jake.

One minute passed, then another.

The second guard came around the corner and walked by.

Flap had to find the man inside amid the aisles, if there was one, kill him, then come back to dispose of the guards outside. It was a tall order, yet these men had to be down before Jake and Flap could rip into the boxes, which could not be done noiselessly.

Several more minutes ticked by. Jake fingered his flooded, useless watch. Perhaps he should have thrown it away.

Okay, Flap. Where are you, shipmate?

Come on! Come on, Flap!

Oh, Jesus, don't let anything happen to Le Beau.

384

Little late to think about that, isn't it, Jake? You two could be on a boat going down the river right this very moment if you hadn't insisted on going through with this.

Well, something had gone wrong. Flap was in trouble.

Jake was torn by indecision. If he went inside looking he could blow this whole deal. Yet if Le Beau were injured he might die without assistance.

Here comes one of the guards. Walking and looking, his rifle held carelessly in the crook of his arm.

As the guard went by the aisle where Flap had disappeared, he hesitated. Jake stared at him across the sights of the AK. Now the guard took a step back and peered into the gloom as Jake's finger tightened on the trigger. *If he points his weapon he's dead.*

Hands reached for the guard and jerked him forward off his feet, into the aisle.

What were you worried about, Jake? Flap's the best, the absolute best, a fucking super-Marine.

More time passed.

Waiting was the hard part. If you didn't know what was happening.

Jake lifted his head and took a long, careful scan of the area. No one moving.

The other guard came around the corner. He was more alert than the first one. He held his rifle in both hands, the muzzle up. He looked puzzled.

Uh-oh, he didn't pass the other guy and now he's wondering where he is.

He stopped and looked about carefully, then turned and went back the way he had come. When he reached the corner an arm shot forward. The guard jerked away.

Even from this distance Jake could see the hilt of the knife protruding just below his chin. The rifle fell harmlessly as the man staggered, grabbing at his throat. Le Beau was right there, an arm coiling around the man's mouth to ensure he didn't scream. When he went down Jake hobbled forward.

Le Beau was bent over holding his side. Blood splotched his flight suit everywhere. The Marine jerked the knife from the man's throat and wiped it on his leg, leaving yet another streak on his filthy flight suit, then slipped it into his sleeve sheath.

'What happened?'

'Guy inside had a knife. He got me good.'

'Let's saddle up and get the fuck outta here.'

'No. They bought us tickets and we're taking the ride. Quick, let's drag this guy out of sight. Grab hold.'

They each took an arm.

'How bad is it?' Jake wanted to know.

'I don't know. Burns like fire.'

'Can you keep going?'

'We'll see.' As they dropped the body in a dark aisle, Flap muttered, 'Always knew I'd get it with a knife.'

He led the way down a gloomy aisle, almost feeling his way along. 'The stuff we want is down here. Fuses and wire. Found it this afternoon.'

They attacked the side of a box with Flap's throwing knife. The nails ripping loose sounded loud as gunshots.

'How do you know what's in each box?'

'Seen crates like these before, in Cambodia. This is all Russian stuff. The crates got symbols on them for the comrades who can't read Russian. Like me.'

The side of the crate came loose. Flap dug into it. He came out with a handful of primers and wire. After a little more digging they extracted a timer.

'Now all we gotta do is find the plastique.'

Jake was horrified. 'You don't know where it is?'

'Couldn't find it this afternoon.'

'Maybe it's still on the ship.'

'Maybe. Get out your lighter and look.'

They found a crate with the lid already open. Grenades. Each man stuffed four or five into his chest pocket, then they went on.

Time was dragging. The lighter got hot and flickered. It was about out of butane. Someone was going to come check on the guards any minute now.

Jake was about to give in to despair when they found the plastique. There were at least five crates of it, piled one on top of the other.

'Boost me up,' Flap said.

Lying on top of the crates, Flap pried at the lid of the topmost one with his knife. More groaning noises, as loud as fire sirens. Finally he said, 'Okay, pass up the primers and stuff.'

'How long do you want on the timer?'

'Thirty minutes.'

The timer was mechanical. Jake began winding it up as fast as he could. When the spring would go no tighter, he used the lighter. The clock face would take up to a twelve-hour delay. He set thirty minutes, then passed it up to Flap.

Two minutes passed before Flap asked for help to get down. His side was wet with warm blood.

'Those anti-tank rockets are down this way,' he murmured. He took four steps and fell.

Jake helped him up. 'Let's try to get a bandage on that.'

'With what?'

'Shirt off one of the corpses.'

'We don't have time. Come on!

They took four of the rockets, two for each man. Flap was visibly weaker now, but in the spluttering light of the butane lighter he took the time to explain how to arm, aim and shoot. The lighter died for the last time before they were through and couldn't be relit. Jake dropped it and slung his rifle over his back. Then he hoisted two of the rockets.

He had to help Flap to his feet. Flap hoisted his two and let the rifle lay. He turned and led the way.

Two steps out of the aisle Flap froze. A figure stood in front of him with a rifle leveled.

The captain!

'You two! I knew you weren't dead.'

He took a step closer. 'You have caused me a great deal of trouble. Now I'm going to cause you a great deal of pain.'

Quick as thought he moved forward and smashed Flap in the head with the butt of his rifle. Flap collapsed.

The captain drove a kick at Jake Grafton that caught him right where his rib was broken. He almost passed out from the pain.

When he came to his senses he was lying almost across Flap. The captain was talking. 'Been into the weapons, I see. What else have you done?' He kicked Jake again, but he took the blow mostly on his shoulder.

Jake felt for Flap's left arm. He found it. The sleeve was loose. The knife came free in his hand.

Another kick. 'What have you done in there? Answer me!'

As the foot flashed out again Jake grabbed it and pulled. Off balance, the captain fell. Jake scrambled to his knees and went for him but the man was too quick. He was coming off the ground so Jake slashed with the knife, a vicious, desperate backhand.

The captain staggered back. Through all the kicks he had kept his rifle in his left hand. Now he dropped it and grabbed his stomach with both hands as a shriek of agony escaped him.

His guts spilled out.

The captain fell to the ground. Jake crawled toward him and stabbed, again and again and again.

When the captain went limp Jake slashed at this throat for good measure, then rolled over moaning. He couldn't breathe. His side!

The captain quivered. In a haze of pain, Jake stabbed the knife into his chest and left it there.

Somehow he got to his feet.

Le Beau seemed only partially conscious. Jake grabbed

him by the back of the neck of his flight suit and heaved. The Marine slid about two feet.

Jake needed both hands.

The boat dock. He had to get Flap to the boat.

No way but to drag him.

In a haze of pain, struggling to breathe, he pulled. He paused occasionally to glance over his shoulder, because he was dragging him backward. Right by the lights of the village.

Someone would see him and shoot him.

He didn't care.

How he made the journey he didn't know. Flap stirred several times but he didn't come to.

Finally he had the Marine on the boards of the dock. In a supreme effort he got him over the side of the cabin cruiser onto its deck.

He paused, breathing raggedly, not getting enough air but sucking hard anyway.

Cast off. He had to cast off.

Somehow he remembered the other boats. He got out on the dock and fumbled with their ropes.

The knife! Damn, he had left it sticking in the captain.

He managed to untie all of the ropes except one, which was knotted too tight for his fingers. In his pain and anxiety he forgot all about the second knife that Flap carried.

The ropes for the cabin cruiser came loose easily.

Jake got aboard just as the current began to ease it away from the dock. Those other boats that were free from their moorings were already drifting.

The grenades.

He fumbled in his chest pocket for one. He pulled the pin and held it as the distance increased.

Now.

He let the spoon fly, gritted his teeth and heaved. It hit on the dock, bounced once, then rolled into the moored boat.

Jake sagged down just as it went off.

The noise would bring the pirates. Maybe this would be a good time to see if the engine in this boat can be started.

Fumbling with the switches by the helm, he found the one for the battery. A little light came on. There was a button just beside it. Here goes nothing!

Please, God.

The engine turned over.

He jabbed the button in and held it. Grind, grind, grind as he played with the throttle.

A choke. Maybe there was a choke. Desperately he felt around the panel.

He found it and pulled it out. The engine ground several more times, then caught. He inched the throttle forward from idle and spun the helm.

He had the boat headed downriver when the first bullets thudded in.

One man shooting. No, two.

He hunkered by the wheel and fed in full throttle.

The boat accelerated nicely. He slewed it and craned his head to see. The banks of the river were even darker than the water.

Stay in the middle.

More bullets whapping in. The windshield in front of Jake shattered. Then something hit him in the shoulder, drove him forward into the panel. Somehow he kept his feet under him.

The shooting stopped. He was rounding a bend. He got himself into the seat behind the wheel.

How far to the sea? Would the pirates follow?

He was worrying about that when he heard the explosion, a roar that grew and grew and grew, then died abruptly.

His head swam and he worked desperately hard to breathe. Somehow he stayed conscious and kept the boat in the channel.

Eventually the darkness of the trees on the riversides merged with the night and the boat began to pitch and roll. The ocean. They were out of the river.

There was a bungee cord dangling from the wheel. With the last of his strength Jake managed to hook the free end to the bottom of the chair where he had been sitting.

He rolled Flap over to check on him. He had a terrible knot on his forehead and the pupil of one eye was completely dilated. Concussion.'

'Hey, Flap. It's me, Jake.'

The Marine moved. His lips worked. Jake put his head down to hear. 'Horowitz had a brother. Tell him . . . Tell him . . .'

Just what Jake was to tell him Flap didn't say.

Jake was so tired. He lay down beside Flap.

The boat ran out of fuel an hour later. It was rolling amid the swells of a sun-flecked blue sea when a pilot of an A-7 from *Columbia* spotted it. The crewman of the helicopter lowered found Jake Grafton and Flap Le Beau lying side by side in the cockpit.

CHAPTER TWENTY-THREE

Jake woke up in a room with cream-colored walls and ceiling, in a bed with crisp white sheets. A sunbeam shown like a spotlight through a window. An IV was dripping into a vein in his left arm.

Hospital.

His curiosity satisfied, he drifted off to sleep again. When he next awoke a nurse was there taking his pulse. 'Welcome back to the land of the living,' she said, and lowered his wrist back to the bed. She annotated a clipboard, then gave him a grin.

'Where am I?'

'Honolulu. Trippler Army Hospital.'

'Hawaii?'

'Yes. You've been here almost a day now. You're just coming out of the recovery room.'

'Le Beau? Marine captain. He here too?'

'Yes. He's still in recovery.'

'How is he?'

'Still asleep. He's had an operation. You've had one too, but yours didn't take quite as long.'

'When he wakes up, I want to talk to him. Okay?'

'We'll see. You take that up with the doctor when he comes around. He should be here in about thirty minutes. Is there anything I can do for you?'

'No.'

She busied herself arranging the sheets and checking

that he had fresh water in a glass by the bed. He lay taking it in, enjoying the brightness and the cleanliness.

After a bit curiosity stirred him. 'What day is it?'

'This is Wednesday.'

'We got shot down . . . December nine. What day . . . is it now?'

'The sixteenth of December.'

'We missed Australia.'

'What was that?'

'Nothing,' he murmured, and closed his eyes again. He was very tired.

He was still pretty foggy when he talked to the doctor, either later that morning or that afternoon. The sunbeam had moved. He noticed that.

'We operated on your left side. Your lung collapsed. Lucky you didn't bleed to death. And of course you were shot in the shoulder. By some miracle the bullet missed your collarbone. Went clean through.'

'Uh-huh.'

'You're also fighting a raging infection. You aren't out of the woods yet, sailor.'

'Le Beau, how's he doing?'

'He's critical. He lost a lot of blood.'

'He gonna make it?'

'We think so.'

'When he wakes up, I want to see him.'

'We'll see.'

'Bring him in here. This room's big enough. Or take me into his room.'

'We'll see.'

'How'd we get here, anyway?'

'The ship medevaced you two to Clark and the Air Force flew you here.'

'I may not be out of the woods, but I'm out of the jungle.'

The next day Flap was wheeled into the room. His bed was placed beside Jake's. A bandage covered half his head.

But he grinned when he saw Jake out of his one unobstructed eye.

'Hey, shipmate.'

'As I live and breathe,' said Flap Le Beau as the nurses hovered around hooking up everything. 'The neighborhood is integrating. Better put the house up for sale while you still can.'

'If you don't stop that racist stuff I'm gonna start calling you Chocolate.'

'Chocolate Le Beau,' he said, savoring it. 'I like it. They hung that Flap tag on me because I talk a lot. My real name is Clarence.'

'I know. Middle initial O. What's that stand for?'

'Odysseus. I picked it out in college after I read the *Odyssey*. Clarence O. Le Beau. Got a ring to it, don't it?' He directed the question to one of the nurses, who looked sort of sweet.

'It *is* very nice,' she said, and smiled.

'So how you feeling?' Jake asked.

'Like a week-old dog turd that's been run over by a truck. And you?'

'Not quite that chipper.'

When the nurses were leaving Flap told the sweet one, 'Come back and see us anytime, dearest.'

'I will, Clarence O.'

When they were gone, Flap told Jake, 'Don't worry. I'll get you one too. Trust me.'

'So what's wrong with your head?'

'Concussion and blood clot. They had to drill a hole to relieve the pressure. Another hole in my head – just what I needed, eh?'

'The captain laid you out with a butt stroke. I killed him.'

'I figured that or we wouldn't be here. But some other time, huh? I don't want to even think about that shit.'

'Yeah.'

'What's for lunch? Have they told you?'

'No.'

'I am really ready for some good grits.'

'Guess we missed Australia.'

'These things happen. Don't sweat it. You can make it up to me somehow.'

The following day they were visited by a Navy commander, an officer on the staff of Commander In Chief Pacific – CINCPAC. He interviewed both men, recorded their stories, then when they tired, left while they napped. He came back for another hour just before dinner and asked questions.'

'If I can do anything for you gentlemen, give me a call.'

He left a card with his name and telephone number on the stands beside each of their beds.

They had lost a lot of weight. When the nurses first sat Jake up he was amazed at how skinny his legs and arms were.

Improvement was slow at first, then quicker. By the fifth day Jake was walking to the bathroom. He bragged, so Flap got himself out of bed and went when the nurses weren't there. He had trouble with his balance but he made it to the john and back by holding on to things.

On the eighth day they went for a hike, holding on to each other, to see what they could see. A nurse caught them and made them retrace their steps.

The hospital was half-empty. 'Not like it used to be. You were the first gunshot victim we saw in two months,' one nurse told Jake.

'Not like the good old days,' he replied.

'They weren't good days,' he was told. 'Thank God the war is over.'

On the day after Christmas they demanded clothes. That afternoon an orderly brought them cardboard boxes containing some of their clothes that the guys on the ship had packed and sent. The orderly helped Jake open his. Inside he found underwear, uniforms, shoes, insignia.

As he was inspecting a set of khakis, the thought went through his head that he should discard this shirt and buy another.

Where had that thought come from? He was getting out – *out* of the Navy!

He sat on the edge of the bed holding the shirt, looking at it but not seeing it. *Out.* To do what? What could he conceivably do as a civilian that would mean as much to him as what he had spent the last six years of his life doing?

He was a naval officer. Lieutenant, United States Navy. That meant something.

He was digging in the box when he found a letter. It was from the Real McCoy.

Hey Shipmate,

When you read this you will probably be getting spruced up to go to the club or chase women. Some guys will do about anything to get out of a little work.

This boat was like a damn funeral parlor the night you and Flap didn't come back. The mood improved a thousand percent when they announced that the chopper was inbound with both of you aboard. The captain and CAG and Skipper Haldane were there on the flight deck with the medicos when the chopper landed, along with a couple hundred other guys.

After the docs got you guys stabilized and you left in the COD, the captain got on the 1-MC and said some real nice things about you. It was pretty maudlin. I forgot most of it so I won't try to repeat it here, but suffice it to say that every swinging dick on this boat is glad you two clowns made it.

Australia is on. TS for you. We'll party on without you, but you'll be missed.

Your friend,
Real

Two days later Jake decked himself out in a white uniform and Flap selected a set of khakis. They strolled the grounds. The days were Hawaii balmy with clouds every afternoon. One day they took a taxi to the golf course and rented a golf cart.

Out on the fairways they went over the whole adventure again, little by little, a scene here, a scene there. Gradually they dropped it and went on to other subjects, like women and politics and flying.

One day Flap brought the subject up again, for what proved to be the last time. 'So *where* is my slasher?'

'I think I left it sticking in the captain. But I might have just dropped it somewhere. It's a little hazy.'

'That was my best knife.'

'Tough.'

'I designed it. It was custom-made for me. Cost me *two hundred* bucks.'

'Order another.'

Flap laughed. 'I can see you are oozing remorse over my loss.'

'To be frank, I don't give a shit about your knife.'

'You're as full of tact as ever. That's one of the qualities that will take you far, Grafton. Ol' Mister Smooth.'

'And the horse you rode in on, Clarence O.'

'It's my turn to drive this friggin' cart. You're always hoggin' the drivin'.'

'That's because *I'm* the pilot. Why don't you tell me about some of the ugly women you've run across in your adventures?'

'Well, by God, I just will.' And he did.

In the evenings there was little to do, so Jake wrote letters. His first was to his former roommate, Sammy Lundeen. He hit the highlights of this last cruise and devoted a whole page to crossing the line. In the finest traditions of naval aviation, he seriously downplayed his and Flap's role in the pirate adventure. Luck, luck, luck – he and Flap had survived due to the grotesque ineptitude of the villains and despite their own extraordinarily stupid mistakes, mistakes that would have wrung tears from the eyes of any competent aviator. All in all, the letter was quite a literary effort, first-class fiction. That thought didn't occur to Jake, of course, when he reread it before stuffing it into an envelope. His buddy Lundeen would chuckle, Jake knew, and shake his head sadly. Good ol' Sammy.

Instinctively he adopted a completely different tone when he wrote to Tiger Cole, his last BN during the Vietnam War. There was no bullshit in Tiger Cole, and no one who knew him would try to lay the smelly stuff on him. You gave it to that grim warrior straight and un-adorned.

He ended the letter this way:

I have never thought of myself as professional. Never. I've been a guy who went into the service because there was a war and I've merely tried to do my best until the time came for me to go back to the real world. Still I have watched so many pros since I have been in the Navy – you included – that I think I'm beginning to see how the thing is done. And why. I hope so, anyway. So I've decided to stay in.

The decision hasn't been easy. I guess no important commitment is.

Whenever I get back to the mainland, I'll give you a call. I'll probably take some leave. Maybe swing by Pensacola if you're still there and we can swill a beer at the club.

Hang tough, shipmate.

Your friend,
Jake

One day Jake penned a letter to Callie. Then he put it in

the drawer beside his bed. Each day he got it out, read it through and debated whether or not he should mail it.

She probably had another boyfriend. There was always that possibility. Jake Grafton had no intention of playing the fool, with this or any other woman. So he kept the letter formal, as if he were writing to a great-aunt. He omitted any reference to his adventure with the pirates or the fact that he was just now residing in a hospital room. But on the second page he said this:

I've decided to stay in the Navy. It has been a tough decision and I've had to really wrestle with it. The arguments for getting out are many and you know most of them. The Navy is a large bureaucracy; anyone who thinks the bureaucracy will miss them when they are gone is kidding himself.

Still, this is where I belong. I like the people, I can do the work, I believe the work is important. Of course the Navy is not for everyone, but it is, I believe, the best place for me. I know full well that there is nothing that I can do here that others cannot do better, but here I *can* make a contribution.

He closed with a few pleasantries and the hope that all was fine with her.

On New Year's Eve he got it out again to read it through carefully.

The tone was wrong, all wrong.

He added a PS.

As I reread this letter it occurs to me that I've made a very stupid mistake. The last few months I've been so busy worrying that you might not love me as much as I love you that I lost sight of what love is. Love by its very nature opens you up to getting burned.

I love you, Callie. You were a rock to hang on to the

last year of the war, the one sane person in an insane world. And you've been a rock to hang on to these last six months. You've been in my thoughts and in my dreams.

If I love you more than you love me, so be it. I'm tough enough to love and lose. But I just wanted you to know how much I care.

As ever,
Jake

In the third week of January he and Flap moved to the BOQ. They continued to visit the hospital on an out-patient basis. Flap took daily physical therapy to overcome the effects of his head injury. The knife wound in his side drained slowly and healed stubbornly. Eventually it did heal, leaving a bad scar.

Jake merely needed a checkup occasionally. His collapsed lung and the resultant infection had been more serious than the bullet hole in his shoulder, which healed quickly, yet by now he was well on his way to a complete recovery. He went with Flap every morning anyway and kibitzed as the Marine went through his exercises. Then they went to the golf course and rode around in a golf cart.

One day they rented clubs. They merely slapped at the balls, since neither man could swing a club with any vigor. Slap the ball a hundred feet, using mostly arms and wrists, get in the cart and drive over to it, slap the thing again. It was crazy, but it felt fine.

After that they played daily. Gradually the shoulders and ribs loosened up and they swung more freely, but neither man had ever played much golf and neither was very good.

They were standing on the carrier pier at Pearl Harbor when *Columbia* arrived in early February.

'Look who has returned!' the Real McCoy shouted when they walked into the ready room. 'The prodigal sons are *back!*'

'We only came aboard for a change of underwear. It's been hell, golf every day, hot women every night . . .'

They were surrounded by people shaking their hands and welcoming them back. When the mob scene had subsided to a low roar, the Real asked Jake, 'By any chance did you bring a copy of the *Wall Street Journal?*'

'I hate to give you the bad news, roomie, but the market is down a thousand points this morning. They're talking about a depression.'

'Aah . . . ,' said the Real, searching Jake's face.

'Millionaires are leaping out of windows even as we speak.'

'You're kidding, right?'

After lunch Jake went to his stateroom with McCoy. He crawled into the top bunk and let out a long sigh. 'Feels so good.'

'Got something to show you,' the Real said. From his desk he brought forth a series of aerial photos. 'We took these before we smacked that hijacked Cuban freighter. See that big blast area – that's where the pile was that you and Flap blew up.'

'You guys bombed the Cuban ship?'

'Oh yes. The government of Indonesia thought those weapons might go to some of their own indigenous revolutionaries, so they asked for our help before we even offered it.'

'I never saw anything about it in the papers.'

'They never told the press.'

'I'll be darned.'

That night the entire squadron went to the O Club en masse. It was an epic party, complete with a letter the next day from the CO of the base to the captain of *Columbia* complaining about rowdy behavior and demanding

401

damages. That night Jake and Flap slept in their bunks aboard ship.

Before the ship sailed, Jake spent a quiet moment with Lieutenant Colonel Haldane. 'I'd like to stay in the Navy, Skipper. I want to withdraw my resignation.'

Haldane smiled and offered his hand. Jake shook it.

'There's one other thing,' Jake said slowly. 'I hear that some of the guys are going to get some traps the first day out of port just in case they need to fly during the transit to the States. I'd need too many to get current, but I'd take it as a personal favor if you'd let me and Flap get one.'

'I need up chits from the flight surgeon.'

'That's the rub. I think I can get one but I don't think they'll give Flap an up. The doctors at Trippler want him to do more physical therapy. He still has some balance problems.'

'According to that report we received from CINCPAC, he took a rifle butt in the head.'

'Yessir. One hell of a butt stroke. He had lost a lot of blood by the that time and didn't have the reflexes to minimize the impact.'

'Well, you and Flap take your medical files to the flight surgeon and have him look you over. Then have him call me.'

'Aye aye, sir.'

Somehow it worked out. Jake and Flap rode the catapult two hours after *Columbia* cleared Pearl. By some miracle he didn't question he got a plane full of gas, so he had to burn down or dump before he could come back into the pattern.

They yanked and banked and shouted over the ICS as they did tight turns around the tops of cumulus clouds. Jake managed a loop and a Cuban eight before Flap begged for mercy. He was dizzy.

Jake smoked into the break at five hundred knots. The air boss never peeped. Better yet, Jake snagged a three-wire.

On the morning of the fly-off Jake took the Pri-Fly duty. All the planes of the air wing were to be launched: the crews were selected strictly on the basis of seniority. Tonight they would be home with wives and children and sweethearts. Jake and Flap were, of course, not flying off. They were riding the ship into port. Flap had an appointment at the Oakland Naval Hospital and Jake was catching a commercial flight to Oak Harbor via Seattle to pick up his car, then he was taking a month's leave. He thought he would head for Virginia by way of Chicago. Maybe look Callie up, see what she was up to. At the end of the month he would report again to Tiny Dick Donovan at VA-128.

The fly-off went well. One by one every plane on the ship taxied to the catapults and was shot aloft. They rendezvoused in divisions over the ship and headed east.

When the last plane was gone and the angel helicopter had settled onto the angle and shut down, the ship secured from flight quarters. Jake went down to the strangely empty flight deck and walked around one last time.

Not really. He would be back. If not this ship, then another. Once again he savored the oily aroma of steam seeping up from the catapults, felt the heat as it mixed with the salty sea breeze.

He was wandering the deck when Bosun Muldowski approached. He stunned Jake with a salute. Jake returned it.

'Hear you're staying in, Mr Grafton.'

'Yep. Your example shamed me into it.'

Muldowski laughed. 'It's a good life,' he said 'Beats eight to five anywhere. Maybe if I had found the right woman and had some kids ... But you can't live on maybes. Didn't work out that way. You gotta live your life one day at a time. That's the way God fixed it up. Today do what you do best and let tomorrow take care of tomorrow.'

Jake was packing in his stateroom when the ship docked at the Alameda carrier pier. The Real McCoy had flown off with the Marines – he had earned it. McCoy's steel footlockers sporting new padlocks sat one atop the other by the door. His desk was clean and nothing hung in his closet. His bunk was stripped and the sheets turned in.

Jake had also turned in his sheets and blankets. Last night he had packed the suitcase he was taking on leave – now he was stuffing everything else into the parachute bags. The suitcase he had purchased in Hawaii. The padlocks for the bags lay on the desk. Net gain after one eight-month cruise: one suitcase and some new scars.

The engagement ring he had purchased for Callie oh those many months ago was the last item left in his desk safe. He held it in his hand and wondered what to do with it. The suitcase might get stolen or lost by the airline, shuffled off to Buffalo or Pago Pago or Timbuktu. For lack of a better option, he put the ring in his shirt pocket and buttoned the pocket.

The telephone rang. 'Lieutenant Grafton, sir.'

'Mr Grafton, this is the duty officer at the officers' brow. You have a visitor.'

'Me?'

'Yes, sir. You need to come sign her in and escort her.'

'Okay, but who is this pers—?' He stopped because he was talking to a dead phone. The duty officer had hung up.

There was obviously some mistake. He didn't know a soul in the San Francisco Bay area. He glanced at his new watch, guaranteed to be waterproof to a depth of three hundred feet or his money back. He had four hours to catch the plane from the Oakland airport. Plenty of time.

He grabbed his ball cap and headed for the ceremonial quarterdeck at the head of the officers' brow. It was on the hangar deck, which was the scene of hundreds of sailors coming and going on a variety of errands, most of them frivolous. Crowds of sailors stood on the aircraft elevators shouting to people on the pier below. Near the enlisted brow a band was tooting merrily.

He saw her standing, looking curiously around when he was still a hundred feet away.

Callie McKenzie!

As he walked toward her she spotted him. She beamed. 'Hello, Jake.'

He couldn't think of anything to say.

'You've lost some weight,' she said.

'Been sick.'

'Oh. Well, aren't you glad to see me?'

'Thunderstruck. I'm speechless.'

She looked even better than he remembered. As he stared her eyes danced with amusement and a smile grew on her face.

'I *never* expected to see you here,' he told her. 'Not in a million years.'

'Life is full of surprises.'

'Isn't it, though?'

He was rooted where he stood, unable to take his eyes off her and unsure what to do next. Why was she here? Why hadn't she written in five months? Then a thought struck him: 'Did you come with someone?' he asked, and glanced around, half expecting to see her mother, or even some man.

'No.' She reached out and touched his arm. 'All these sailors are staring at us. Can you sign me in so we can go somewhere and talk?'

Jake flushed. 'Oh, yes, sure.'

The officer of the deck and quartermaster of the watch grinned shamelessly, enjoying Jake's obvious discomfort. Jake scribbled his name beside Callie's in the visitors' log, then steered her away with two fingers on her elbow.

'Let's go up to the flight deck. Fine view of the bay area from up there.'

Indeed, the view from the flight deck was spectacular. The San Francisco skyline, Treasure Island, airliners coming and going at San Francisco International and Oakland – the panorama would have frozen most people who had spent the largest part of the last eight months looking at empty ocean dead in their tracks. However Jake Grafton was too acutely aware of the presence of Callie McKenzie to give the scene more than a glance.

'How are your folks?' he asked finally, breaking the silence.

'They're fine. And yours?'

'Okay. Almost called you a time or two.'

'And I almost wrote you. I should have. And you should have called.'

'Why didn't you write?'

'I didn't want to influence your decision. To stay in or get out, what to do with your life. This was your decision, Jake, not mine.'

'Well, I made it. I'm staying in.'

'Why?'

Jake Grafton ran his fingers through his hair. 'I was looking for something. Turns out I had it all along and just didn't realize it.'

'What were you looking for?'

'Something worth doing. Something that made a difference. The war was such a mess . . . I guess that I lost sight of what we're all about here. It's more than ships and planes and cats and traps. I realized that finally.'

'I always thought that what you did was important.'

'Your dad didn't.'

'Dad? I love him dearly but this is my life, not his.'

'So what are you going to do with your life?'

She didn't answer. She lowered her head and began walking slowly. Jake stayed with her. When she got to the bow of the ship she stood looking across the water at San Francisco with the wind playing in her hair.

'I guess I'm like most modern women. I want a family and a career. Languages have always fascinated me, and I have found I love to teach. That's the big plan, but some of it is contingent.'

'On what?'

'On you.'

'Well, I don't think that's very fair. After all, lady, you shoved me out into the cold to make up my own mind.'

'You were never out in the cold, Jake. There hasn't been an hour in the last eight months that I wasn't thinking about you. I've read and reread your letters until I almost wore out the paper. Especially that last letter. I think I was wondering too, wondering if you loved me as much as I loved you.'

'You were always with me too,' he confessed, and grinned. 'Maybe an hour or two now and then you slipped away, but most of the time you were there.'

Her hand found his. They began strolling along the deck. The breeze was fresh and crisp.

'So why did you come here?' he asked.

'I came to get married.'

He gaped. It was like a kick in the stomach. He had thought . . . He jerked his hand from her grasp.

'Who's the lucky guy?' he managed.

'You,' she said, her head cocked slightly to one side, her lips twisting into a grin.

'*Me?*'

'Who else could it be? I love you more than words can tell, Jacob Lee Grafton.'

'You want to marry *me?*'

She laughed. He had always liked her laugh. 'Do you want me to get down on one knee and propose?'

'I accept,' he told her, and seized both her hands. 'Where and when?'

'This afternoon. Anywhere.'

'My God, woman! This is sudden. Are you sure?'

'I've been thinking about this for a year,' she told him. 'I'm absolutely certain.'

'Well, I'll be . . .' He took off his cap and ran his fingers through his hair. Then he remembered the ring. He pulled it from his shirt pocket, looked at it, then put it on her finger.

Now she was surprised. 'You knew I was coming?'

'No. I bought that for you over a year ago. Been carrying it ever since.'

'Oh, Jake,' she said, and wrapped her arms around his neck. Her lips found his.

He finally broke the embrace and seized her hand. 'Come on. We'll need a best man. My BN is still aboard. He and I were going to have lunch together.'

The quickest way to Flap's stateroom was into the catwalk behind the island, then into the 0-3 level and down. On the catwalk Jake happened to glance at the pier. There was a pink Cadillac convertible parked at the foot of the officers' brow with four women in it.

Muldowski was walking across the brow. Now he turned and saluted the American flag on the fantail.

Jake cupped his hand to his mouth and shouted, '*Muldowski! Hey, Bosun!*'

The warrant officer looked up. He pointed.

'I'm getting *married*,' Jake Grafton roared. 'Will you give the bride away?'

'When?' Muldowski boomed.

'This afternoon. Wait for us. We'll be down in ten minutes.'

'Is that the bride?'

'Yes.'

'I may keep her my—' The rest of the bosun's comment was drowned by music as the band launched into another tune.

The women in the convertible were on their feet applauding. The bosun started clapping too, as did dozens of people on the pier.

Callie was grinning broadly. She looked so happy. What the heck! In full view of the world Jake swept her into his arms.